T0316747

UNDERGROUND

Cecilia Johanna

Adams Media

New York London Toronto Sydney New Delhi

CRIMSON
ROMANCE

Crimson Romance
An Imprint of Simon & Schuster, Inc.
1230 Avenue of the Americas
New York, NY 10020

Copyright © 2016 by Cecilia Sjölund.

All rights reserved, including the right to reproduce this book or portions thereof in any form whatsoever. For information address Crimson Romance Subsidiary Rights Department, 1230 Avenue of the Americas, New York, NY 10020.

CRIMSON ROMANCE and colophon are trademarks of Simon and Schuster.

ISBN 978-1-5072-0183-1
ISBN 978-1-5072-0184-8 (ebook)

This is a work of fiction. Names, characters, corporations, institutions, organizations, events, or locales in this novel are either the product of the author's imagination or, if real, used fictitiously. The resemblance of any character to actual persons (living or dead) is entirely coincidental.

Many of the designations used by manufacturers and sellers to distinguish their products are claimed as trademarks. Where those designations appear in this book and Simon & Schuster, Inc., was aware of a trademark claim, the designations have been printed with initial capital letters.

CHAPTER ONE

The emergency room at Chrystal Valley Hospital was a chaotic, overcrowded mess. Dr. Andrew Alexander sighed as he checked the clock on the wall. It was almost midnight, and his shift had ended several hours ago. Working overtime was a part of the job description for a first-year resident, but at some point, he had to call it a night.

He paused in front of the glass doors separating the waiting room from the rest of the ER, looking over the patients one last time. Coughing elders, a man cradling his wrist, a woman with a rash—nothing out of the ordinary. He was just about to head home when he noticed two red-haired women on a couch in the corner of the room. One of them was crying but looked perfectly healthy. His gaze moved over to the other woman, and then he froze.

Her face was covered in bruises. Some of them were fresh, while others were turning green and yellow. Her eyes were closed, but he could see that her left one was nearly swollen shut. He'd seen injuries like these before, and he knew exactly what caused them.

He caught a nurse as she rushed by and pointed at the woman. "Why is she waiting outside? We need to get her a room."

The nurse glanced at the clock and then back to him. "She's low priority. Fever. Uninsured. She can wait."

Andrew clenched his jaw. "What about her face? Someone has obviously beaten her up."

"The bruises are several days old. Not an emergency. Besides, she's here for the fever. We don't have time to treat a fever right now."

No, they didn't, but Andrew still couldn't let it go. "Where are the attendings?"

She checked the clock again. "They're still working on that cardiac arrest. I'm sorry, but I really have to leave. If the guy with the second-degree burn doesn't get his morphine he's going to start yelling again."

She picked up a tray with a syringe from the medical cart and half walked, half jogged down the corridor. Andrew turned his gaze back to the red-haired woman. Her skin was pale, but her cheeks were flushed. Pearls of sweat trickled down her temples. She had a fever, all right—a bad one.

He entered the waiting room and approached the women on the couch. The healthy-looking one grabbed his white coat in a desperate grip.

"You have to help me," she said, her voice trembling. "Robyn is sick. Really sick. She's my sister—I *know* it's not just a fever. Please, you have to help us."

"I'm fine," Robyn mumbled. "Lucy worries too much. I'm fine."

I'm fine. The words echoed in Andrew's head. He'd heard that lie way too many times.

A discoloration on her wrist caught his eye. He carefully took her hand in his and raised it from her lap. His eyes widened as he rolled up her sleeve. A badly healed cut went from the bend of her arm down to her wrist, stitched together with something that looked like ordinary sewing thread. He'd never seen a wound so inflamed before.

"What the hell happened here?" he asked, staring at the arm. "These stitches... Who did this to her?"

Lucy sobbed. "She did."

Robyn opened her mouth, but before she could say anything, she collapsed against her sister. Andrew didn't think—he just acted. He scooped her up in his arms and carried her through the glass doors.

"I need a gurney over here," he yelled to whoever might be listening. The nurse he'd just spoken to stuck her head out from one of the examination rooms.

"Dr. Alexander?" She stared at him, then at the woman in his arms, and then at him again. "What on earth are you doing?"

"Sepsis," he said, ignoring her question. "Most likely going into shock."

Understanding dawned in the nurse's eyes. "I'll get the gurney."

• • •

Andrew watched as two nurses rolled Robyn's bed away from the ER toward the ICU. He'd saved her life, but something still gnawed at him. According to her medical records, she was only twenty-two. Most of her bruises were fresh, but some of her scars had to be several years old. There was no record of her ever visiting the ER before. Someone was hurting this woman, and she was handling it all by herself.

Robyn Monroe's life was no longer in Andrew's hands, but he still couldn't get the image of her bruised face out of his head.

• • •

When Robyn opened her eyes, all she knew was that something had gone terribly wrong.

She was lying on a hard bed in a room she didn't recognize. The stench of disinfectant stung her nose, and the bright light from the ceiling lamp made her eyes water. Her body felt strangely heavy, and the pain in her arm was gone. *What the hell happened?*

She remembered Lucy dragging her to the ER—which she would never have succeeded with if Robyn hadn't been in too much pain to protest—but after that, everything was a blur.

She turned her head to the side. Lucy was sleeping in a chair next to the bed, her head resting on the mattress. Her mascara had left smudges on her cheeks, and several locks of her long, red hair had come loose from her braid. She looked much older than her eighteen years.

"Lucy?" Robyn croaked.

Lucy jerked back from the bed. "Robyn? Oh, thank God you're awake." Tears welled up in her eyes. "Thank God."

Robyn didn't know how long Lucy had been watching over her, but judging by the bags under her eyes, it had to have been a while. She swallowed hard. Things weren't supposed to be like this. Robyn was the oldest. She was supposed to take care of her sister, not the other way around.

She thought about saying so but was distracted by a strange feeling in her nose. There was something on her face. She wanted it gone. When she tried to lift her arm to remove it, she found that there was a needle and a tube attached to her hand. Dumbfounded, she let her arm fall back onto the mattress.

"What happened?" she finally asked.

"Your stitches got infected. You almost died." Lucy took a deep breath and wiped away her tears. "This is it, you hear me? I can't go through this again. You have to stop fighting."

Robyn looked away. "I will. Soon."

Lucy shook her head. "That's what you always say."

They both fell silent when the door opened. A tall, slender man in a white coat entered the room.

"Oh, she's awake?" He flashed a smile that could only be described as perfect. "That's great. Am I interrupting?"

"Of course not." Lucy smiled back at him. "Robyn, this is Dr. Alexander. He's the man who saved your life."

"Oh."

"He's been checking up on you ever since," Lucy continued. "He's really dedicated."

"Oh." Robyn didn't know what else to say. She had a faint memory of a man picking her up and carrying her in his arms, but she'd thought it was a dream. She'd *hoped* it was a dream. *Oh God.*

Dr. Alexander approached the bed. He had a strong jaw and well-defined cheekbones, and his sky-blue eyes formed an interesting contrast against his black hair. Robyn fixed her eyes on the ceiling, her cheeks heating up. *And he had to be hot, too.*

"How are you feeling?" he asked.

"I'm fine."

He sighed. "Of course you are."

"Just stop it, Robyn," Lucy said. "You're allowed to feel like crap when you've been out for two days."

The words hit her like a punch in the gut. Two days. She'd been at the hospital for two days. Her heart pounded in her chest as she tried to calculate the cost of a two-day hospital stay. All she could come up with was *way too much.* Her breathing quickened. *This can't be happening.*

"Lucy, we need to leave," she said. "Right now."

Dr. Alexander looked at her as if she was crazy. "You're still being treated for your sepsis. You'll have to stay for at least a couple more days."

"We can't afford it!" Robyn sat up. Her head spun, but she forced herself to remain upright.

"I don't think that's a good idea," Dr. Alexander said. "Robyn…"

"Fuck off," she hissed. Before anyone could stop her, she'd pulled the weird plastic thing from her nose and the needle out of her hand. She put her feet on the floor, stood up—and then the world turned sideways. Her knees buckled, but Dr. Alexander caught her before she hit the floor. When he helped her back up on the bed, she was too embarrassed to protest.

7

"Okay. That was a little unexpected." He pressed a compress against her bleeding hand. "People don't usually do that."

Lucy let out a dejected sigh. "No, they don't." She glared at Robyn. "You're staying here until the doctors say you can leave, okay? I don't care about the cost. Your health is more important."

No, it's not. Robyn closed her eyes. She didn't even want to think about what she was going to have to do to pay for this hospital stay. It was going to hurt, that was for sure.

"You've never been to the hospital before, is that right?" Dr. Alexander said.

Robyn nodded.

"Because you can't afford it?"

She sent him a dirty look. "Because I haven't needed it."

"I've seen your scars. You've been badly injured many, many times before, and if I'm not mistaken, it's only a matter of time until you're injured again. Am I wrong?"

Robyn blinked. *Shit.* She hadn't expected a doctor to be that perceptive.

"No," she said. "I'll be fine."

He raised his eyebrows. "How did you get that cut?"

"Accident in the kitchen."

"And the bruises?"

"Fell down the stairs."

They stared at each other. Dr. Alexander's piercing eyes seemed to see right through her. He knew she was lying, and he wasn't going to let it go.

"I want to make a deal," he said. "The next time you get hurt, you call me. I'll help you for free."

Robyn narrowed her eyes. "Why would you do that?"

"Because someone has to make sure your injuries don't kill you." He gave her a strained smile. "It would make me sleep easier at night."

His offer was too good to be true. Way too good. He had to have some ulterior motive. No one was nice to someone like her without expecting something in return.

"I don't need your pity," she said. "I'm—"

"Enough, Robyn." Lucy's eyes were filled with tears again, but her voice was steady and unwavering. "You're not fine. You haven't been fine for a very long time. I'm tired of being worried all the time. The next time you get injured, you're going to call Dr. Alexander. Understand?"

Robyn didn't know what to say, so she just nodded. She might be the older of the two, but she was definitely not the one calling the shots in their little family.

"It's a deal, then." Dr. Alexander flashed another flawless smile, turned around, and left.

Lucy sat by the bed again. Her eyes didn't look quite as weary anymore, and her posture had lost some of its stiffness. Robyn closed her eyes. The deal with the handsome doctor didn't sit right with her, but if it made Lucy happy, she could live with it. And besides, having access to free health care could be of use someday. She was a street fighter, after all. Sooner or later, street fighters always got hurt.

• • •

Andrew had known Robyn got hurt a lot, but he hadn't expected her to be back at the hospital less than two weeks after she left it. He told his colleagues some convenient lies before sneaking away at the end of his shift, taking great care not to run into any attendings.

You're going to lose your job, his inner critic whispered. *This is going to ruin your career.*

Andrew ignored the intruding thoughts. Everything would be fine—as long as he didn't get caught. He had to do this. He would never be able to live with himself if he didn't. The last time he'd seen injuries like that, he'd been too much of a coward to help. He'd regretted it ever since.

He headed down to the floor below the ER. There was an old examination room there that hadn't been used for years. He'd told Lucy he'd meet them there.

When he entered the room, he only found one person in it. Robyn was sitting on a gurney, pressing a bloodstained towel against her forehead. She looked up at him and then fixed her eyes on the wall.

"Lucy has an exam tomorrow morning," she muttered. "Let's just get this over with."

There were new bruises on her face, and her lip was swollen. His gaze fell on the hand holding the towel. There were scrapes all over her knuckles.

Andrew carefully approached her. "What happened?"

"Walked into a door."

He clenched his jaw. She was a terrible liar.

"Let me see your forehead," he said.

"It's nothing. Lucy overreacted." She slowly removed the towel. "It just won't stop bleeding."

A deep cut ran from her eyebrow to her hairline. The moment she stopped pressing the towel against it, blood began to trickle down her face. Andrew grabbed the soaked piece of cloth and pressed it against the wound again.

"Okay. That's going to need some stitches."

Robyn rolled her eyes but didn't say anything.

When he injected her with the local anesthesia, she didn't even flinch. The way Robyn reacted to pain—or the way she *didn't* react to it—was concerning. She sat perfectly still as he stitched up the cut.

"I wish you'd tell me what's happening to you," he said without really expecting an answer.

To his surprise, she glanced up at him. "Why?"

"What do you mean?" he asked.

"Why do you care?"

She was looking at him expectantly, and her curiosity made her face look less intimidating than usual. Sweeter. Auburn locks that tumbled down her back in wavy curls framed her heart-shaped face. Faint scars crisscrossed over her face and body, creating intricate patterns on her pale skin. Her big, brown eyes looked like dark wells.

"I'm a doctor," he finally said. "It's my job to care."

He tore his eyes away from hers, fearing those dark wells would swallow him whole if he looked into them any longer. Her face was bruised and swollen, but it didn't make her any less beautiful.

She fixed her eyes on the wall again. "Right."

"Wrong answer?"

She didn't answer. Her silence saddened him more than it should have.

He finished stitching up her forehead and put a bandage over the wound. When Robyn stood up from the gurney, the movement caused her to flinch.

Andrew raised his eyebrows. "I saw that."

She let out an annoyed groan. "I hit my rib, okay? It's nothing."

"I'll be the judge of that. Let me see."

She glared at him. At first, he thought she'd protest, but then she removed her bulky hoodie and the tank top beneath it. She was thin. Way too thin. As she stood there in her sports bra, Andrew couldn't stop himself from looking at her scars. She was so young, yet there were so many of them.

Robyn crossed her arms, covering up some of the more gruesome marks. "Just get on with it."

He placed the clock of his stethoscope on her chest. Clear, even breathing sounds. He put the stethoscope back in his pocket and placed his hands below her armpits, letting them wander down her sides. When he reached her seventh rib, a sharp gasp escaped her lips.

"That's most likely a fracture," he said. "I'd need an x-ray to know for sure, though."

"No." Robyn shook off his hands and pulled on her clothes again.

"Robyn, please—"

"I said no."

She rushed past him, heading toward the door. Without thinking, Andrew reached out and grabbed her arm. Her reaction was instantaneous. Before he could even blink, she'd spun around, pushed him up against the wall, and pressed her forearm against his throat. He couldn't move. He couldn't breathe. He just stood there, frozen in place, staring at her in shock. This was not the poor, abused woman he'd thought he'd been helping. This was someone completely different.

Robyn's eyes widened. She removed her arm and scrambled away from him, almost tripping over her own feet.

"I'm sorry," she said, looking frailer and more insecure than he'd ever seen her before. "I didn't mean to… I'm so sorry."

Andrew coughed and cleared his throat. "It's okay. I shouldn't have done that. It's okay." His words seemed to calm her, and he found himself wanting to wrap her in a blanket, give her a cup of tea, and tell her everything would be okay. He also realized that she would probably kick his ass if he tried, so instead he took a deep breath and asked her the question he'd wanted to ask her from the moment he first saw her.

"Robyn, is someone hurting you?"

"No." Her lips twitched. "Well, not in the way you think."

"What's that supposed to mean?"

"Interpret it however you like." There was a tone of amusement in her voice, as if the whole thing was part of a joke he didn't quite get. "Thanks for the stitches, Dr. Alexander. I appreciate it."

Andrew didn't know what to say. Instead of trying to find an eloquent response, he went with a simple, "Please, call me Andrew."

Robyn nodded. "Andrew. Sure."

When she walked toward the door again, he was too perplexed to stop her. She cast him a quick glance over her shoulder, and this time, he was certain—the twitch of her lips was the beginning of a smirk.

"You think *my* injuries are bad? You should see the other guy."

With those words, she walked through the door, leaving a speechless Andrew behind her in the examination room.

He ran his fingers through his hair, staring at the closed door. He'd been so sure about his theory on what was happening to Robyn Monroe that he hadn't noticed the things that didn't match up. Some of her injuries didn't fit the abuse-case stereotype. Some of them, like the scrapes on her knuckles, indicated that *she* was the one dealing the blows.

He pulled out his cell phone. A friend of his knew everything there was to know about Chrystal Valley's underworld, and Andrew was going to need his expertise.

"Hey, Jason, it's Andrew Alexander. This is a strange question, but…you don't happen to know anything about street fighting, do you?"

CHAPTER TWO

Never before in his twenty-seven years of living had Andrew been so far out of his comfort zone.

The underground parking garage was filled with people, most of them men in their early thirties. Everyone's eyes were fixed on the two men beating the crap out of each other in the middle of the crowd. The fight was held inside an octagon-shaped cage: a rickety construction consisting of chicken wire wrapped around eight iron poles. The stench of sweat and stale beer, the nonexistent personal space, the grunts and low-pitched groans coming from the cage— Andrew just couldn't fathom why people *paid* to take part in it.

The crowd cheered as one of the fighters received a savage kick to his stomach and crashed into the fence. For a moment, he looked like he was going to pass out, but he somehow kept himself on his feet. He staggered back into the middle of the cage, just to get punched in the face by his opponent. Blood gushed from his nose. Andrew's stomach lurched. The brutality of the fight horrified him, but he still couldn't bring himself to look away.

"This is insane!" he said to Jason. "A kick like that could cause internal bleeding! And what about his spleen? That kick could definitely have damaged his spleen."

"Stop it." Jason scowled at him. "I'm risking a lot by bringing you here, so could you at least *try* to fit in?"

Sometimes, Andrew wondered if Jason really was an undercover cop pretending to be a gang member, or if he was in fact a gang member pretending to be a cop. Jason didn't seem to be completely certain about that either. His nose was crooked from a fracture that had never healed right, and his eyes were gray and hardened. With his leather jacket and steel-toe boots, he looked like the kind of guy no one would like to run into in a dark alley late at night.

A couple of months ago, Andrew had helped Jason after a particularly violent gang fight. By doing so, he'd made an unexpected friend. Jason was living his undercover gang life to the fullest, and Andrew had patched him up more times than he could remember. Andrew wasn't overly fond of daredevils in general, but he did like Jason. He was one of the few policemen in Chrystal Valley who cared about protecting *all* of the city's inhabitants—not just the ones who happened to be sponsoring the police station.

"And he's down! Is it a knockout? I believe it's a knockout!" the commentator yelled into his microphone, bouncing around outside the cage like an overexcited toddler. Fighter number one let out a guttural roar, standing triumphant over fighter number two's motionless body.

"He needs a doctor." Andrew started to move toward the cage.

Jason grabbed his arm. "If you keep this up, I'm never bringing you to a fight again. If you want to find this Robyn chick, you're going to have to let this go. Endgame, Alexander. Focus on the endgame."

Andrew knew Jason was right, but he still had a hard time holding himself back.

"Do you think she'll be here tonight?" he asked, trying to take his mind off the fighter and his most likely severe injuries.

"Maybe. The Valkyrie usually shows up about twice a month, and it's been two weeks since I last saw her. There's definitely a chance she'll be fighting tonight."

The Valkyrie. Andrew had no idea why Robyn had chosen to fight under that name, but somehow, it fit. "Are you sure it's her?"

"Skinny girl with red hair, it does sound like our Valkyrie. Tough little lady, never taps out." Jason grinned. "Pretty damn hot, too. I get why you're interested in her."

Before Andrew could answer, the commentator once again picked up his microphone.

"Next fight will begin in just a moment!" he shouted. "I hope you've placed your bets wisely, ladies and gentlemen, because this is gonna be a tight one."

Another pair of muscular men entered the cage, and soon, the fight was on again. Still no sign of Robyn.

Andrew suffered through almost a dozen more fights that night, but the fighter called the Valkyrie never showed up.

• • •

A couple of blocks away, Robyn finally finished cleaning the last booth at the café. Sandy's was widely known as the café with the latest closing hours in Chrystal Valley, and Robyn often took the night shift. At half past one in the morning, a group of hungry, intoxicated college students had decided they needed some sandwiches, and they'd managed to make a total mess of their booth. Extra work late at night always sucked, but she appreciated the tips. She was falling behind on bills, and she needed all the money she could get.

It was almost half past two when Robyn took off her apron and locked up the café. She took a deep breath before opening the back door. Several days had passed since she last spoke with her manager, and Swanson usually made his visits late at night.

Because of the gambling debts she'd inherited from her mother, she'd ended up owing money to at least half the bookies in Chrystal Valley. Swanson had taken care of that. Now, there was only one bookie left to pay—Swanson himself. The deal they'd made wasn't too bad. She fought for him to repay her debt, and he helped her out every now and then. Most of the money she earned from her fights went straight to him, but she got to keep some of it.

There had been times when she'd wanted nothing more than to stop fighting, but as long as the debt remained, quitting wasn't an option. Swanson had always been civil to her, but she knew what happened to those who crossed him. He was the most powerful bookmaker in Chrystal Valley. Ruining her and Lucy's lives would be simple for a man like him.

She stepped out onto the parking lot outside the café. A thin old man in a pinstriped suit waited for her under a streetlight. He slowly approached her, leaning heavily on his cane.

"Good evening, Ms. Monroe." Swanson smiled. "How is the rib?"

His eyes, gunmetal-gray like his bushy eyebrows and sharply parted hair, were cold and calculating. Robyn had never seen them express any kind of emotion.

"It's fine, thank you," she lied. Her rib still hurt every time she took a deep breath, but she knew Swanson's concern was as false as his smile.

"Good, good. I took care of that medical bill for you. I thought you'd appreciate that."

"I do." A knot of worry grew in her stomach. Swanson's gifts always came with a price.

"I've set up a game for you," he said. "Tomorrow at 6 p.m. in the Circle."

Robyn felt the blood drain from her face. "I thought I was supposed to fight at the Octagon on Thursday."

"That was the original plan, yes," Swanson said, "but plans change. The tournament is coming up, and your odds...well, let's say they're looking a bit *too* good right now. You've had an impressive winning streak lately, and people are starting to notice it. Two-to-one odds don't make any real money, dear."

"I guess not..." *Please don't say it, please don't say it, please don't say it.*

Swanson's lips smiled, but his eyes remained emotionless. "I want you to lose."

•••

The following day went by in a haze. When Robyn sat down on the couch in the lunchroom during her break, she could barely remember anything from the morning. All she could think about was the upcoming fight.

The arena called the Circle could barely be called an arena—it was just a bunch of cars parked in a circle around a patch of grass. In the Circle, it wasn't just the opponent you had to watch out for. Most of the cars had shards of glass and rusty pieces of metal sticking up all over the place, and some fighters liked to use arena perks like that to their advantage. The still healing cut on her forearm was a constant reminder of how dangerous a broken rearview mirror could be.

In the beginning of her fighting career, Robyn had often wondered how the owners of the Circle could run a fighting arena out in the open without getting caught by the police. Then she'd found one of the local police officers in the audience after one of her fights. She'd realized that the police were all very well aware of the many fighting locations in Chrystal Valley. They just didn't care.

She wasn't sure how a small city like Chrystal Valley had become so corrupt. It always had been, and most likely, it always would be. It didn't matter that NYC was only a fifty-minute train ride away—Chrystal Valley played by its own rules and unwritten laws.

"Are you okay?" Her oldest friend and coworker, Suzanna, bounced down on the couch and tilted her head to the side, playing with her curly, rainbow-colored hair. "You shouldn't take the morning shift right after a night shift. Your aura looks sad."

"My aura is fine." Robyn gave Suzanna a halfhearted smile. "I'm just tired."

Suzanna blinked, fluttering her long, feathery false lashes. "No, it definitely looks sad. Sad and worried."

"Turn off your inner eye and eat your sandwich," Robyn scoffed. She didn't believe in auras, but she had to admit that Suzanna's ability to read emotions was freakishly on point. It always had been.

Robyn could still remember the nights when Suzanna had curled up in Lucy's bed, making herself as small as possible as the three of them waited for their mothers' two-man party in the living room to end. Robyn's mother had made crappy life choices when she was drunk. Suzanna's mother had been the violent type.

Suzanna gave Robyn a bright, carefree smile as she picked up a sandwich from her lunch box and divided it in two. "I'll eat it if you agree to share it with me. Your aura looks sad, worried, and hungry."

Robyn rolled her eyes but gratefully accepted the sandwich. She needed all the energy she could get before the fight.

Suzanna looked at her, and for a moment, the cheerful façade faltered a little. "When?"

Robyn didn't have to ask her what she meant. "Tonight."

"Where?"

"The Circle."

Suzanna nodded slowly. "Is there anything I can do?"

"I don't think so." Robyn faked a smile. "Thanks anyway."

Suzanna was right—Robyn was worried. Terrified, even. She'd lost fights on purpose before, but never in the Circle. This time, she would get hurt. Badly.

"Please be careful," Suzanna said.

Robyn swallowed hard. "I'll try."

• • •

Robyn took off her apron and left the café a little after five. She knew she probably should have grabbed something to eat before the fight, but she didn't have the time or the money to spare. Ignoring her growling stomach, she put her hair up in a ponytail and began to jog.

She ran south, passing the community college on the way. The well-lit area around campus soon turned into an industrial district cloaked in darkness. The sound of her steps echoed against the concrete walls, uncomfortably loud on the empty street. She didn't like spending time in this neighborhood, and most people seemed to share her opinion.

When she reached the outdoor arena, Swanson was already waiting for her, wearing the gray wool coat he always wore before fights. The coat made his back look more hunched and thereby made him look older, tricking people into underestimating him.

"You're late, dear." Swanson's faked smile was just a notch colder than the night before.

"I warmed up. I was—"

"You need to last at least two minutes," he interrupted. "Two minutes, then a knockout. No tap-out. Knockout. Do you understand?"

She nodded. "How much do I get?"

"Enough to cover your monthly fee. If you handle this nicely, I'll even add a little extra pocket money. Wouldn't that be nice?"

She nodded again.

"Good girl." Swanson raised a wrinkly hand and patted her on the cheek. "Two minutes, then knockout."

Robyn had already stopped listening. She pointed at a man already standing in the Circle. "Is that him?"

"Yes. His name is Tyler, also known as the Griffin, and he's been a first-class fighter for years. He's surprisingly fast for his size, so if you're going to last two minutes, you'll have to be even faster. Good luck, dear."

Swanson patted her on the shoulder and then went to join the rapidly increasing audience. She pulled the hood of her sweater over her head and followed him into the crowd.

Tyler was huge. He was at least a hundred pounds heavier than her, and he had to be almost a foot taller. His dark skin glistened with sweat, bringing out his oversized muscles. She recognized the distended stomach and disproportionate upper body muscles. *A steroid user.* Fantastic. This was really going to hurt.

Robyn was just about to enter the ring when she bumped into a thin young woman with waist-length white hair. The city's own betting clairvoyant Cassandra was wearing a thick, marine-blue coat even though it was just October, and her crimson-colored lipstick made her skin look even paler than usual.

"Hello, Valkyrie," she said. "Would you like some advice about tonight's fight?"

"Not tonight. I…" Robyn paused, unsure how to put it without giving too much away. "I just won't need it."

"I see." Cassandra nodded slowly. "I wish you luck anyway, Valkyrie. You're competing in the tournament this year, right? First class?"

Robyn shuddered. "Yes."

The tournament was the event of the year in Chrystal Valley's underworld. Out of the three classes, the first class was without a doubt the most violent. Robyn was not looking forward to it.

Cassandra smiled. "Good."

The woman disappeared into the crowd again. Robyn shrugged. Her conversations with Cassandra always tended to be a bit strange.

About a year ago, Cassandra had showed up in Chrystal Valley out of nowhere, and she'd soon become famous for her ability to accurately predict the outcomes of fights. Rumor had it that many of Chrystal Valley's bookies paid Cassandra so they could base their odds on her predictions. As far as Robyn knew, she was the only one who received information for free. It freaked her out a little.

She walked into the circle of parked cars and dropped her backpack on the ground. Ignoring the audience's usual comments about her substandard size, she rummaged through the bag and fished out a roll of gauze. She wound the gauze around her wrists and hands, and then secured the wraps with tape.

"Christ, you're a tiny one," Tyler said. "And you're a girl, aren't you? Jesus. What the hell were they thinking?"

She ignored him. After putting everything back in the bag and throwing it outside the ring, she finally took a closer look at her opponent. He was even bigger up close, but her earlier fear was already dying down. The fight was closing in and her other self was taking over. She smirked and watched as a hint of hesitation flashed in Tyler's eyes. Then, she performed her final magic trick— she pulled off her sweater.

The audience gasped as she threw the sweater out of the ring. She stood tall in her sports bra and sweatpants, proudly showing off all her bruises and scars. In her ordinary life, she was ashamed of her body and its many imperfections. In the ring, those imperfections were merit points—marks showing exactly how dangerous she could be. In her ordinary life, she was Robyn: small, shy, and forgettable. In the ring, she was the Valkyrie: everything Robyn was not.

She'd picked her stage name from one of her favorite books— an encyclopedia of Norse mythology. Valkyries were angels of death who reigned over the battlefields, choosing whether a soldier would live or die. They were merciless and brutal, just like Robyn had to be every time she stepped inside a fighting ring. The name fit her like a glove.

"What the hell is this? He's going to crush her!" someone yelled from the audience.

"She's so tiny! I thought this was supposed to be an even fight," yelled another.

Robyn didn't mind the spectators' comments. It was the reaction she usually got from the audience, even after several wins in a row. When they looked at her, all they could see was a five-foot-seven girl who weighed a lot less than she probably should. They had no idea what she was capable of.

"Are you sure you want to do this?" Tyler asked.

She raised her eyebrows. "Are you?"

He shook his head, grinning. "All right. Show me what you've got."

The referee didn't bother giving any instructions or setting any rules—it was the Circle, after all. Instead, he initiated the fight with a simple, "Go."

A few seconds passed in which Robyn and Tyler just observed each other. Tyler's fists were raised, and the heel of his rear foot was lifted slightly off the ground. Judging by his stance, he seemed to be a boxer of some sort—and hell, he was big. Each of his fists was about the same size as her face. *Two minutes, then knockout,* she thought. *One hundred and twenty seconds.*

After ten of those one hundred and twenty seconds had passed, Tyler made his move. He ran toward her and threw his fist toward her face—only her face was no longer there. He was fast, but she was faster. She quickly found her rhythm, blocking and dodging his increasingly aggressive punches. He was good, but as long as she focused on her defense, he was going to have a hard time getting close enough to harm her. She spun around and gave him a quick kick in the face. The audience gasped in surprise. Tyler flinched and took a step back, looking more confused than hurt. She used his moment of distraction to jab him in the jaw. He flinched again but immediately retaliated by aiming a punch toward her stomach. His fist missed her by less than an inch. She was faster than him, yes, but not by much.

Thirty seconds into the round, Tyler managed to hit her shoulder before she could move out of the way. She lost her balance for a moment and braced herself against the hood of a car. Pain pulsated from her shoulder down her upper arm. Tyler was even stronger than she'd predicted. She tuned out the pain and bounced back up again. Even if she ultimately had to lose, she still had to make the fight look believable. Before he could follow up his punch, she lunged forward and hit him hard in the gut. The spectators had been promised an even fight, and she was going to give it to them.

When the first minute came to an end, both Robyn and Tyler were sweaty and breathing heavily.

"Just punch his fucking face in!" someone yelled from the audience. "End him, Valkyrie!"

She grinned. The hateful comments had turned into cheers of excitement. *Everybody loves the underdog.*

Her heart was pounding in her chest. For a moment, she actually felt excited. She hadn't had the opportunity to fight someone this good in a long time, and a part of her couldn't help but enjoy it.

One hundred seconds in, she made her first real mistake. She blocked a punch she should have dodged, and the power behind Tyler's fist made her lose her balance again. She took a step back to steady herself. Her heels touched the ground. She tried to bounce back into the fight, but her rhythm was broken. Tyler centered his blows, making them impossible to avoid. She blocked the first punch, a right hook that would most likely have broken her nose, but the second punch hit her fractured rib. She heard a loud crunch, followed by an odd, wheezing sound. It hurt like hell, but she could handle the pain. Her sudden shortness of breath was worse.

She did a quick twirl and delivered a hard kick to his face. His nose broke under the sole of her foot. He let out a low-pitched groan and took a step backward before throwing himself at her again. Robyn's inner timer finally reached one hundred and twenty, so when Tyler once again aimed for her face, she only turned away enough for him to hit her cheek instead of her nose. The punch sent her flying through the air, and the world started to fade away the moment she hit the ground. The last thing she saw before the darkness claimed her was Swanson's triumphant grin.

CHAPTER THREE

After the knockout, Robyn drifted in and out of consciousness. She was almost awake when Mark Schmidt, Swanson's right-hand man, carelessly threw her over his shoulder to carry her away from the Circle. Her broken rib slammed into his suit-clad back, causing a surge of pain so intense she passed right out again. The next time she came to, she was in the backseat of Swanson's car. Someone, presumably Mark, had covered the seats in a sheet of tarpaulin before placing her there. *I'm supposed to do his dirty work, but God forbid I bring dirt into his car,* she thought, feeling both amused and somewhat insulted.

She wasn't aware she'd blacked out again until she once again found herself hanging upside down over Mark's shoulder. Her rib bumped into his back over and over as he climbed the stairs to her apartment, sending small explosions of pain through her chest.

He put her down on the floor right outside her front door and rang the doorbell.

"You're excused from Swanson's assignments until the tournament," he said in his usual, monotone voice. He wiped small pearls of sweat off his bald head before dropping her backpack next to her. "The money is in the bag."

She nodded without really listening. Mark hadn't bothered helping her into her hoodie so she should have been freezing, but instead she felt like she was burning up from the inside. Her chest hurt, and the pain only got worse every time she tried to breathe.

"I'm coming!" Lucy finally shouted from inside the apartment. Mark spun around. Now that he'd transferred the responsibility of taking care of Robyn to Lucy, his mission was over. He always did what Swanson told him to do—nothing more, nothing less. Robyn sometimes wondered if he could think for himself at all.

"Get out while you still can, Valkyrie," he said over his shoulder. "You don't have what it takes to survive in a world like this."

When Lucy opened the door in her pale-blue pajamas, Mark had already left the building. Lucy looked around in confusion. She was just about to close the door again when Robyn grabbed her ankle.

"Robyn? Oh my God, Robyn, what happened?" Lucy kneeled next to her. "Did you fight again? How bad is it?"

"Can't breathe."

"Oh God… What do I do, Robyn? What the hell do I do?" Lucy's eyes filled with tears. "Oh God, oh God, oh God—"

"Hand," Robyn said, interrupting the panicked chanting. Lucy took a deep breath, calming herself, and reached out her hand. Robyn grabbed it and slowly pulled herself up. Together, they stumbled inside the apartment. Robyn collapsed on the black leather couch in the combined hallway-living room.

The next time she opened her eyes, someone else was in the room. Someone who wasn't Lucy. Robyn panicked and tried to sit up, but a firm hand on her shoulder held her down.

"Don't move," Lucy said, using her authoritative teaching voice. Robyn glanced up at her. Lucy's eyes were rimmed with red, but she was no longer crying. Her fear seemed to have given way to anger.

Robyn shuddered. Even though Lucy had only just begun her pre-teacher education at the community college, her teaching voice was already powerful enough to strike fear into anyone exposed to it—Robyn included.

The somewhat familiar figure kneeled next to the couch. "Hi, Robyn."

She blinked. Why the hell was Dr. Andrew Alexander in her living room? He was wearing a blue shirt and slacks. For a moment, she hadn't even recognized him without his white coat.

"Lucy called me," he continued. "She said it was an emergency, so I drove here as fast as I could." He turned to Lucy. "When did the breathing problem start?"

"I don't know," Lucy said. "I found her like this. She's been… She…"

"I know about the fighting."

"Oh."

Oh. Robyn cringed. There were only a handful of people in her life who knew about her being a fighter—she wasn't sure how to feel about Andrew being one of them.

Andrew gave Lucy a small smile and then turned back to Robyn. "Did you hurt the fractured rib?" he asked.

She nodded.

"I told you your rib was fractured. Why did you go out fighting again?"

She shrugged and then winced at the pain the movement caused. Andrew placed the clock of his stethoscope on her chest and listened carefully.

"That's definitely a tension pneumothorax." He pulled a smartphone from his pants pocket. "Damn it. I should have called an ambulance before I left the hospital."

The word "ambulance" hit Robyn like an electrical shock.

"No!" she gasped, snatching Andrew's phone from his hand. With a sudden burst of adrenaline, she scrambled off the couch and onto her feet. She grabbed the floor lamp next to the coffee table and raised it like a baseball bat. "No ambulance," she said, waving the makeshift weapon.

"Robyn, please listen to me." There was a hint of panic in his voice. "Your broken rib has pierced your lung, causing it to collapse. You're going into cardiogenic shock, and I can't help you without the proper equipment. You have to let me call an ambulance."

He reached out for the phone but had to take a step back as Robyn swung the lamp through the air.

"No. Ambulance." She was swaying, but her grip on the lamp was firm. Her decision was made, and nothing he said could make her change her mind. She'd finally earned enough money to pay the bills, and she would *not* be spending it on an ambulance ride. If she kept relying on Swanson's favors, she would never be free. *I'll be fine,* she thought. *I'm always fine.*

"Can't you drive her to the hospital?" Lucy asked Andrew.

"It's too far away. An ambulance could probably be here in ten, but getting to the hospital in my car would take at least twenty with all those traffic lights. We're running out of time. Shit…" Andrew ran his fingers through his hair, furrowing his brow in concentration.

Robyn could tell the exact moment the idea hit him. His eyes widened, and his lips formed a triumphant grin. "I've got a chest tube kit at home! I knew it would be of use one day."

"A what?" Lucy stared at him.

"Just a thing that can save your sister's life. I live five minutes from here. I can fix this. I can fix you, Robyn. Please, let me fix you."

"No ambulance?" Robyn's head spun, and the pain in her chest was only getting worse.

"No ambulance."

She didn't know why, but Andrew was actually worried about her. He seemed to genuinely *care*. She just couldn't wrap her head around it. What did he gain from helping her?

Something that almost looked like anger flared in Andrew's eyes. "We don't have time for this."

He tore the floor lamp out of her hands and dropped it on the floor. Before she could object, he'd already scooped her up in his arms. Her body tensed from the unexpected intimacy.

"I'm sorry." He eased his grip around her back and legs before rushing out of the apartment. "Just hold on, and try not to gasp or cough."

Robyn nodded. She burrowed her fingers in Andrew's shirt but then remembered her hands were still wrapped in dirty, bloodstained gauze. She quickly let go of the fabric, but her hands had already left stains.

"It's okay," Andrew said, hurrying down the stairs. Robyn reluctantly held on to the shirt again, realizing that she herself was probably just as dirty, bloodstained, and disgusting as the gauze. She closed her eyes and tried not to think about how horrible she must smell. She was ashamed and embarrassed, just like she always seemed to be around Andrew Alexander. There was something about his altruism and picture-perfection that made everything about her seem so *dirty*.

Lucy opened the door to the backseat of Andrew's car. Robyn didn't know much about cars, but she could tell it was an expensive one. She tried to object when he carefully put her down on the leather seat, knowing she'd ruin the luxurious upholstery, but all she got out was a pitiful whimpering sound.

"Don't worry about it." He turned to Lucy. "Make sure she stays in an upright position."

Lucy nodded, scooting closer to Robyn in the backseat. "You're such an idiot," she said with an exhausted sigh. "Why didn't you tell Swanson you were injured? I'm sure he would have understood."

No, he wouldn't have. Lucy knew about the debt, but there were many details Robyn had never shared with her. The part about Swanson being the most dangerous man in Chrystal Valley was one of them.

Four minutes later, Andrew parked the car on the driveway outside a large two-story house.

"You live here? All by yourself?" Lucy asked.

"Yes." Andrew's answer was short, and he clearly didn't want any follow-up questions. He opened the door to the backseat and picked Robyn up again.

"You need to eat more," he said as he jogged toward the front door.

Robyn gave him the finger.

"Stop it!" Lucy exclaimed. "He's saving your life, so could you for once in your life *try* to behave?"

"At least she's not completely out of it." Andrew looked at Robyn with curious amusement. "Lucy, there's a set of spare keys in the flowerpot over there. Open the door."

Lucy hurried to the flowerpot, found the keys, and opened the front door. *He never asks for things,* Robyn noted. *He's used to ordering people around.*

She had to use all the mental strength she could gather to stop herself from hyperventilating. Her body needed oxygen, and breathing didn't seem to do the trick anymore. She was getting tired, and her body was going numb. All she wanted was to sleep.

Andrew carried her inside. Her vision was getting blurry, but she could tell he had a beautiful home. The hallway was spacious, with a high ceiling and an expensive-looking parquet floor. Every piece of furniture seemed to have been carefully picked out to create the image of a perfect home. But it wasn't perfect. It didn't even look like anyone lived there.

Andrew gently put her down in an armchair in the hallway, which was—of course—white. Robyn felt like she probably would have left stains just looking at it. He disappeared into the kitchen, and she could hear him rummage through some drawers. When he returned, he was carrying a cardboard box. He made her put her arm over the armchair's backrest and tore the box open.

"Normally, the patient's given local anesthesia before a chest tube insertion, but we're running out of time." He wiped the skin on her chest with a damp tissue. The stench of alcohol prickled her nose. "This is a bad idea of epic proportions, you know that, right?"

She nodded.

"All right. All right." Andrew put on a pair of surgical gloves and picked up the scalpel from the box. He took a deep breath, and for a moment, he almost looked nervous.

"This is really going to hurt," he said, and made the first incision.

Robyn had always had a high pain threshold, but when the scalpel cut through her skin and muscle she couldn't help but gasp. The cut itself turned out to be nothing compared to when he had to plunge his finger into her chest to create a passage for the chest tube. The white-hot pain seared through her. She wanted to scream, but she couldn't make a sound. She threw her head back in a silent cry, burrowing her nails deep in the armchair's upholstery.

"I'm sorry. I'm so sorry," Andrew whispered, and then forced the tube into her chest.

She felt the pain for about one tenth of a second before her consciousness decided to give up completely. *Finally,* she thought, welcoming the painless oblivion.

•••

The next time Robyn opened her eyes, she was once again in the arms of Andrew Alexander. He held her close to his chest, and she could feel the heat of his body through the thin fabric of his shirt. Her heart started to race.

"Please don't hit me," he said. "I'm just moving you to the guest room. There hasn't been any air leakage from the chest tube for a while now, so you don't have to be in an upright position anymore. I'll keep the tube in for a couple of more hours, though. I want to make sure the lung re-expands properly."

Robyn nodded. Her chest still hurt, but she could breathe. She took a deep breath, savoring the feeling of being fully oxygenated again. She'd missed breathing.

Someone, presumably Andrew, had wrapped her in a soft fleece blanket. She stared up at him. He'd saved her life. She was a street fighter, an absolute nobody, yet he'd still saved her life.

"Thank you," she whispered hoarsely. Andrew just smiled.

He carried her to the guest room, where Lucy was already sleeping in the double bed.

"Everything will be okay," he said, tucking Robyn in next to her sister. "I promise."

No, it won't, she thought when Andrew had left the room. *The world doesn't work that way.*

She knew all too well that Andrew's words weren't true—she'd seen firsthand how awful the world could be, after all—but she still liked hearing him say it. When Andrew said it, he sounded like he truly believed it. He was special that way. A nice kind of special.

Even though there were things in her life that would never be okay, she still fell asleep with a small smile playing on her lips.

• • •

When the sun rose the next morning, Andrew was still awake. He paced back and forth on the balcony, trying to make sense out of what had just happened.

He had never been an impulsive person. Even as a child, he'd always thought before he acted. He was the kind of person who planned things ahead, calculating every possible outcome before proceeding when faced with a problem. He hated uncertainty and surprises, and he always wanted to be in control. So how the hell had the Monroe sisters ended up in his guest room?

The at-home chest-tube insertion had been a terrible idea. If he'd had more time he would have come up with something better, but he'd panicked. Robyn had been dying, and he'd panicked. He was glad his slightly unhealthy habit of hoarding medical equipment had finally been of use for something, but he still couldn't stop thinking about all the ways he could have messed up.

He took a deep drag from the cigarette in his hand. The soothing warmth of the nicotine spread through his body. It was a nasty habit, especially for a doctor, but in moments like this, smoking was the only thing that could calm him down.

"Pulmonary edema, hemothorax, empyema," he muttered to himself as he wandered back and forth on the balcony. "Hematoma, seroma, subcutaneous emphysema…infection. Infection, infection, infection."

"Is there a point to whatever it is you're doing, or are you just blurting out fancy medical terms for fun?" someone behind his back asked. He quickly dropped the cigarette in the ashtray before turning around. Lucy was leaning against the doorframe, looking at him curiously. His mouth went dry, and he felt the blood drain from his face. There was nothing more hypocritical than a smoking doctor.

"Possible complications after a chest-tube insertion," he finally said. *I need to stop smoking.*

"My sister is the strongest person I know. She'll be fine." Lucy fiddled with her braid. "You saved her life yesterday. I can never thank you enough for that."

"I'm glad I could help." He was already sinking back into his thoughts. Would that shot of prophylactic antibiotics he gave her be enough, or should he prescribe her a weeklong treatment? Was it even possible to convince someone as stubborn as Robyn to go on medication for an entire week?

"I'll be going soon," Lucy continued. "I wish I could stay until she wakes up, but I have to get home and change. I have a mandatory seminar today, and there's a bus I need to catch. You'll take care of her, right?"

"Of course. I'll watch over her."

"Thank you. And, uh…" Lucy looked down at the floor, staying silent for a moment. When she looked up again, she had a new, fiery glow in her eyes. "I'm not a fighter like Robyn, but if you do something to her when she's helpless like this, I *will* come up with a way to ruin your life. That's a promise."

Andrew took an involuntary step back. The petite eighteen-year-old's death glare sent shivers down his spine.

"I would never take advantage of Robyn," he said. "Never."

"Good." Lucy's murderous aura disappeared instantly. She gave him a bright smile, as if nothing had happened.

"Why on earth would you even think that?" He stared at her in shock. "I would never do anything to hurt her. I thought you knew that."

"I'm just making sure we're on the same page." She shrugged. "People tend to be a lot shittier than they appear, especially to people like me and Robyn. I'm just taking precautions. She'll wake up in…" She paused to check her watch. "Four minutes. I have to go now, so I guess I'll see you later."

Andrew raised his eyebrows. *That was oddly specific.*

Lucy gave him a little wave and went back inside the house, the high heels of her pumps clicking against the parquet floor. Andrew cringed at the sound but chose not to say anything. He'd always assumed Robyn was the scarier of the Monroe sisters, but now he wasn't so sure.

He felt an unexpected sting of envy. Lucy would do anything for Robyn, just like Robyn would do anything for her. They had each other, no matter what. Andrew couldn't remember ever having a bond like that with anyone.

There had been Julie, though.

He and Julie had interned at the same ER back in New York. They hadn't been all that close, but he'd considered her a friend— probably the first real friend he'd had for years. With her calm confidence and never-ending optimism, she'd been pretty much his polar opposite, but he'd really enjoyed being around her. Then he'd failed her. He'd failed her hard.

A couple of months into their internship, Julie had started showing up to work with bruises on her face. When he asked her about them, she only gave him bad excuses and endless amounts of "I'm fine." He never pushed her any farther than that, despite his suspicions of what her boyfriend was doing to her. He didn't have the guts.

It went on like that until the night Julie was rolled into the ER on a gurney, half beaten to death. Andrew never saw her again after she went into witness protection, but the image of her bruised, battered face would stay with him forever. Andrew hadn't really seen the point in trying to befriend someone after that. Most of the time, the solitude didn't bother him at all. He enjoyed being on his own. Seeing the Monroe sisters' unconditional love for each other just made him wonder what it was like to have a person you'd do anything for. Most of all, it made him wonder if it was worth the trouble.

He quietly opened the door to the guest room. Robyn was curled up in the fetal position, wrapped in the pale-blue blanket he'd covered her with the night before. Her auburn locks were spread around her head like a fiery halo. Her lips were slightly parted, looking impossibly soft. She was beautiful. And in his guest bed. And not to mention really, really beautiful. He closed his eyes and took a deep breath. *She's a patient. Keep it professional.*

He took a seat on the edge of the bed. "Hey, Robyn?"

She pulled her knees up even closer to her chest but otherwise remained unresponsive.

"Robyn?" After making sure the chest tube and the portable pump were still properly attached to her body, he grabbed her shoulders and shook her lightly. "You need to wake up now, Robyn. You're making me nervous, here."

She continued her calm snoring.

He shook her harder. "Robyn!"

Andrew's brain scanned through all of his medical knowledge regarding post-surgery complications, trying to find a reason she wouldn't wake up. He felt the panic creeping up on him. What had he done wrong? Had the lack of oxygen damaged her brain? Should he have put a cannula in her intercostal space instead of going with the chest tube?

A piercing alarm blasted through the room. Andrew's body jerked in shock, causing him to fall off the bed.

Robyn gracefully rolled out of the bed and crossed the room. She picked up her backpack from the floor and pulled out an alarm clock, the unmistakable source of the horrible noise. When she finally turned it off, Andrew wondered if his ears—or his heart, for that matter—would ever be the same.

Robyn turned around. "You're on the floor," she stated, tilting her head to the side.

"Yeah." He slowly got to his feet, his knees creaking audibly. "I tried to wake you up."

"Oh." Her lips twitched, almost forming a smile. "I'm a heavy sleeper. That alarm clock is basically the only thing in the world that can wake me up."

"'Heavy sleeper' is an understatement." He answered her almost-smile with a grin. "How are you feeling?"

"Fine," she mumbled, distracted by the buzzing apparatus strapped to her side. She raised her arm and looked at it quizzically.

"It's a Thopaz pump. It removes the leaked air from your chest."

Robyn nodded. She looked even paler than usual, and she'd started to sway a little. She blinked a couple of times, as if trying to force her eyes to focus.

"Go back to bed. You need to rest." He hurried to her side and reached out an arm for her to lean on, which she—of course—ignored.

"I'm fine," she muttered. "I should go home." She took a step toward the bedroom door, and her knees immediately buckled. Andrew caught her and helped her back up onto the bed, once again surprised by how light she was.

"See?" he said. "You're exhausted. You need to rest."

"But—"

"No buts. Doctor's orders."

They stared at each other. Robyn seemed to be aiming for a death glare, but not even she could look threatening while wrapped up in a fluffy, pale-blue blanket cocoon.

"Fine," she finally said. "Five minutes. After that, I'm definitely leaving."

There was no possible way she'd be up again in five minutes, but neither of them commented on it.

"So, now that you know about me and my…you know…the fighting…are you going to stop treating me?" she mumbled. "You doctors have to hate fighters like me. We injure people, and we get injured ourselves."

"I still want to help you," Andrew replied without hesitation. "I hate street fights, and I hate how most people in this city seem to think street fighting is an acceptable source of entertainment. I don't hate the fighters, though—and I definitely don't hate you. As long as you and Lucy need me, I'll be there for you. I promise."

A look of relief swept over her face. She nodded and closed her eyes, and a few seconds later, she was asleep. Andrew sat down next to her and gently stroked some wavy red locks from her eyes. He had a lot of paperwork to do, but he couldn't bring himself to stop looking at her.

He'd been too close to losing her this time. *Way* too close. The night he'd treated her inflamed forearm had been a close call too, but not like this. If he hadn't answered that call from Lucy, Robyn would have been dead right now.

Every time she stepped inside one of those disgusting fighting cages, there was a risk of her not walking out of it again. According to Jason, this happened at least twice a month. The thought made him nauseous.

Robyn wasn't being abused by a boyfriend. For every punch she received, she gave one in return. She wasn't Julie—but the image of Julie's battered face still flashed before his eyes every time he looked at her. He had to help her, or he'd never be able to live with himself.

He stared down at Robyn, watching her breathe. She was alive. This time, his skills had been enough. She was still breathing.

When he finally went to get his laptop from his briefcase, Robyn was already snoring again. He thought about setting up the computer on the kitchen table as usual but decided to use the desk in the guest room instead. *Something might happen*, he thought. *She might need me.*

His inner critic laughed. *You're the one who needs her.*

• • •

When Robyn woke up a couple of hours later, she was a lot more alert.

"I have to get going," she said. "I'm working tonight."

"You can't be serious—you're fighting again? Tonight?" Andrew's panic returned in an instant. Her lung could collapse again. If she fought tonight, it might actually kill her. He had to stop her. He had to...

His panic faded again when Robyn shook her head. "No, I...I won't be doing that for a while. Fighting, I mean. I work at Sandy's. It's a café close to the community college. You should go there sometime." She gave him one of her rare almost-smiles. "Could you please remove the tube thing now?"

Removing a chest tube without taking an x-ray first was another bad idea of epic proportions, but Robyn still refused to go to the hospital.

"If you don't take it out I'll just do it myself. Can't be that bad," she said with a shrug.

"You're impossible," Andrew muttered, but in the end he did as she said and removed the tube. The procedure went surprisingly well, and had it not been such a terrible idea to begin with, he would have put it on his résumé.

"You've got sutures from the insertion, so you'll have to visit me sometime next week so I can remove them," he said, watching Robyn get ready to leave.

She nodded. She'd abandoned the borrowed blanket and was now wearing her usual black hoodie. Her skin was covered in bruises, and she favored her right arm. It drove him crazy to think about how someone had purposely inflicted all those injuries on her.

"If I told you to stop fighting, would you listen?" he asked. She turned her back on him, remaining silent. Then she picked up her backpack and walked through the hallway to the door.

"What if I begged you?"

Robyn stopped, her hand already on the doorknob. "Why? Why would you do that?"

"You're my patient. I care about your well-being."

She snorted. "That's such a lame answer."

"What did you want me to say?" Andrew wished he could see her face, but she was still facing the door. Her back didn't give him much to go on.

"Something that wasn't a lie." She finally turned around. He couldn't fully read her expression, but there was definitely disappointment in her eyes. "You don't get it, do you? No one does things for selfless reasons like that. No one. Especially not for people like me." She raised her chin, her eyes unrelenting. "Tell me. Why are you doing all this?"

He hesitated. The emotions she triggered in him were too complicated to be put into words. A feeling of responsibility, a need to protect her, a desperate craving for redemption—and guilt. An endless amount of guilt.

"It would be irresponsible of me to let someone handle a situation like yours on their own," he said. "You're just twenty-two years old. I don't know how you ended up having sole responsibility for your sister, but the way you've handled it… It isn't optimal, to say the least. I'm worried about you—both of you. How are you supposed to take care of Lucy if you can't take care of yourself? If you're doing this for financial reasons, I'm sure I could…"

He stopped talking when he saw the look in her eyes. Her hands curled into fists, and for a moment, he thought she would attack him again.

"I've been taking care of Lucy since I was seventeen," she said in a low voice. "You don't know me. You don't know *us*. I've worked my ass off to support Lucy and me since my mother died, and you know what? I've done one hell of a job. She studies at the community college now. She's becoming a teacher. I don't care what you think about me, but don't you dare look down on how I raised Lucy." The fury in her eyes gradually turned into weary resignation. "Wow. Lucy's upbringing is probably the only thing I've ever been proud of, and you made me feel ashamed of that too."

"I didn't mean it like that," he said, desperately trying to get the conversation back on safe ground. "I really didn't."

"Yeah, you did. If you didn't, it wouldn't hurt like this." She sighed. "It's not just your fault. I'm the one who, for some reason, began to give a damn about your opinion of me. I shouldn't have let that happen." She turned away from him again, but not before Andrew caught sight of the tears in her eyes. He'd never seen her so emotional before, and he despised himself for being the cause of it. Before he could think of anything to say, she'd already opened the door.

"I'll come up with a way to repay you for this. For everything," she said. "If you're going to be one of those people who looks down on me and Lucy, then I don't want your pity." She bounced down the stairs and began to jog, seemingly paying no mind at all to the fact that only a few hours ago, she'd still had a plastic tube in her chest.

"At least let me drive you home!" he shouted after her.

"Fuck off," she yelled back, and then she was gone.

Andrew went back inside and closed the door behind him. *I really messed up this time.* He'd made Robyn—stone-cold, unapproachable street fighter Robyn—*cry.* Oh yes, he'd messed up. He'd messed up badly.

His spacious house seemed to be even quieter than usual, and the rooms were emptier than ever. He sighed. He liked being on his own, but he wasn't particularly fond of being lonely.

CHAPTER FOUR

Running had always been Robyn's main method of getting from point A to point B. It was a cheap and effective way to move around in a small city like Chrystal Valley, and somewhere along the way, it had turned into her main method of handling stress, sadness, and anger, too. Usually, she could run for hours without stopping. Being forced to take a break after just a couple of minutes was not a part of her usual routine. Her lungs didn't seem to work the way they should, and the sharp, throbbing pain in her chest had gone from bothersome to somewhat alarming. She leaned against a wall, trying to catch her breath. She almost regretted turning down Andrew's offer to drive her home. Almost.

Did I overreact? Her chest hurt, but not as much as her pride. Andrew's pity had been more painful than any slap or punch ever could have been. Yes, she might have overreacted, but she'd still meant every word she said. Even if he was...*special,* she knew she could never be around someone who looked down on her and Lucy. She would come up with a way to pay him back for all his help, and then she would get by on her own again—even if it meant going back to doing her own stitches. *And the tournament starts in three weeks,* she thought. *Brilliant timing, Robyn. Brilliant.*

She slowly staggered home. Autumn leaves rustled under the soles of her sneakers. The air was chilly but not uncomfortably cold. If her lungs had been working properly, it would have been a nice afternoon for a run.

She passed the border between Andrew's neighborhood and hers. The big two-story houses turned into worn-out apartment complexes, and the perfectly manicured lawns turned into cracked concrete driveways. The distance between their houses was less than a mile, but the neighborhoods were like two different worlds.

About fifteen minutes later, she stepped through a wide hole in the hedge surrounding the apartment complex. She stopped outside one of the timeworn brick buildings and crouched on the ground.

"Tiny? Are you there?" she called.

Something moved in the bushes, and a small, black cat strolled out of the shrubbery.

"Hi, Tiny." She scratched the cat behind its ear. "Still homeless, I presume?"

The cat purred. Tiny—or Tiny Little Fucker, as she'd originally called him—had only been a kitten when he'd first showed up outside her building. Five months had passed since then, and Robyn still hadn't found Tiny's owner, despite all the notes she'd put up around the city. Robyn's landlord didn't allow pets in the apartments, so Robyn had made Tiny a temporary home in the bushes instead. Tiny's lair was just a rickety construction consisting of an umbrella and a blanket, but he seemed to like it.

"We need to find you a home before winter comes, you know," she said.

Tiny meowed.

"I know. I wish you could live with me too, but you can't. My landlord's a bitch."

Tiny meowed again.

"Yes, you should totally leave dead rats on her doormat. You know where she lives."

Robyn gave the cat a final pat on the head before entering the building. Tiny howled miserably when she closed the door in his face. The guilt nagged at her, but until she found him a proper home, there was nothing more she could do.

When she'd climbed the stairs to the apartment, she found a ridiculously tall man in a threadbare trench coat waiting by the door. She groaned. Lucy's boyfriend, Mike, was a political science student who seemed to spend more time starting brawls than studying. His messy brown hair looked like it hadn't seen a comb in a while, and the stubble on his chin was about a day or two from turning into a beard. Robyn had no idea what Lucy saw in him.

"Hey, Robyn." Mike grinned. "What's up?"

She glared at him. "What do you want?"

"Lucy asked me to pick up some stuff. We're having a street protest against the cops' habit of turning a blind eye to organized crime as soon as certain bookmakers are involved. Wanna come?"

"No. And stop dragging Lucy into this bullshit." She clenched her fists. This was what she hated the most about this guy.

Mike was the leader of a political organization known as FTS, short for "Fuck The System"—a ridiculous name for a ridiculous group. Unsurprisingly, their demonstrations against Chrystal Valley's corruption weren't popular with the either the underground world or the police. Nearly all of their demonstrations ended in total mayhem.

"Don't you get it?" she said. "Lucy's not a fighter. She could get seriously hurt."

"I'm not dragging her into anything," he replied. "She's the one who wants to go."

"Why the hell would she want that?"

He peered down at her with something that almost looked like pity in his eyes. "She has a sister who's stuck right in the middle of the corruption, and she feels that this is the only thing she can do to help."

His words hit her like a slap in the face. She pulled out her keys and opened the door to the apartment.

"Can I come in?" Mike asked.

"No," she snapped before slamming the door in his face.

She leaned against the door, trying hard to ignore the pang of guilt in her stomach. Mike was the one ruining Lucy's life. Not her.

Her skin was still covered in layers of sweat, blood, and dirt from the fight the night before, so the first thing she did was take a shower. The soap made her wounds burn, but she didn't care. She just wanted to be clean. Before she could stop herself, she'd begun to think about the white bed sheets in Andrew's guest room, and how she'd probably ruined them permanently. That white armchair was most likely beyond salvation, too. And his shirt...

She shook her head. *Stop thinking about Andrew.*

When Robyn stepped out of the shower, she glanced at her bandaged chest in the bathroom mirror. She didn't doubt Andrew's suturing skills, but a wound like that would still leave a scar. She frowned at her reflection. She often tried to convince herself that she didn't care about her scars, but it still bothered her every time she got a new one.

She made an attempt to comb out the tangles in her hair, but in the end she just gave up. Her chest hurt every time she raised her arm, and her hair would look like a mess when it dried anyway. At times like this, she questioned her decision to keep it long. It was impractical, both at work and during fights, but she still couldn't bring herself to cut it off. It was like the scars—she didn't know why she cared, she just did.

Her vanity was most likely a remnant of a different life, originating in a childhood dream she should have given up on ages ago. Just thinking about it was a waste of time. She still missed it, though. The spotlights, the stage, the feeling of her body moving in perfect synchronization with the music... She missed it a lot.

When she got out of the bathroom, she found that she was no longer alone in the apartment. A heavily tattooed woman lounged on the living room couch with her feet on the coffee table. Her muscular arms were crossed, and the look she gave Robyn made her feel like *she* was the one intruding. Robyn could never decide whether Ananya Patel was the greatest best friend in the world or the worst.

"Well, well, well," Ana said, raising a perfectly arched eyebrow. "Look who finally decided to show up."

Robyn sighed. "Nice to see you too. How did you get in here?"

"You forgot to lock the balcony door again. It's a bad habit, you know. Anyone could waltz in here." Ana shook her head, running her fingers through her short, black hair. "Enough about that. What have you been up to? Been fighting again, huh?"

She got up from the couch and stood to her full height: an awe-inspiring six feet and then some in her black high-heeled boots. Her face softened when her gaze fell on the big bruise on Robyn's cheek. "I heard about what happened from Lucy. Is it true you almost died yesterday?"

Robyn didn't know what to say, so she remained quiet. Her silence was answer enough.

"You have to stop fighting!" Ana exclaimed. "I don't care about your manager. If you don't stop, this shit is seriously going to kill you. You're lucky you have that doctor guy…"

Robyn flinched. Ana's dark eyes hardened.

"What did he do? Did he do something to you? I'll—"

"It's nothing like that," Robyn said quickly. "He just won't be helping me anymore."

"Do you want me to go kick his ass? Say the word, and I'll beat the shit out of him."

Robyn didn't doubt it for a second. Their classmates in elementary school had been terrified of Ana, and there was a good reason for it.

"It's fine." She gave Ana a small smile. "Don't worry. And if someone in my life needed a beating, I'd beat them up myself, thank you very much."

Ana sighed. "Call me if you need me, all right? You're not alone in this shit, you know. I always have your back."

Before Robyn could tell her to use the front door like a normal person, Ana had already disappeared into Lucy's bedroom to use the balcony door instead. The fact that the apartment was on the third floor didn't seem to bother Ana at all. It never had.

Robyn and Ana had been classmates since they were kids. They'd both been outcasts, but they'd barely known each other until the day in seventh grade when Ana was kicked out of her home. Robyn had found her out on the balcony, cradling a gym bag against her chest. Ana had just come out to her parents, and it had not gone well. Her eyes had been rimmed with red, and her wrists and neck had been covered in bruises. Robyn had let her in without a word. That night, Ana cut off her waist-length hair and started a new life. It was the first and the last time Robyn ever saw her cry.

Ana hid in the Monroe sisters' bedroom for several weeks before Social Services found her. Robyn's mother never even noticed the extra houseguest. By then, she had already stopped caring about anything going on in her daughters' lives.

Images flashed before Robyn's eyes the moment she started thinking about her mother. The silent apartment, the empty wine bottle, the closed bathroom door...

Stop it. She pushed the uninvited memories out of her mind. After gathering her damp, messy hair into a ponytail, she put on her hoodie and went to work.

• • •

Ten days after the fight in the Circle, Robyn decided to remove her stitches with a pair of scissors. She'd managed to give herself stitches once. Pulling them out should be a lot easier. Right?

She stood in front of the bathroom mirror, raising the scissors. *Okay. I can do this.* She cut off the first stitch and carefully pulled out the hardened thread. Ouch. Ouch, ouch, ouch. Her hands shook. Was it supposed to hurt like this? If Andrew had been there to help her, he would have—

Stop it. She scowled at her reflection. Missing him was not acceptable.

She removed all the stitches by herself. The puncture wounds bled a little, but considering her lack of medical knowledge, she thought she'd done a decent job. She didn't need him. She could do just fine without him.

For the rest of the day, Robyn felt pretty good about herself. Even though it was a Saturday and the café would be overcrowded all evening, she was still in a decent mood.

"Your aura looks happy," Suzanna commented. She tilted her head to the side, making the big silver hoops in her ears clink. "Happy and hungry."

"Shut up." Robyn flicked Suzanna on the forehead. "You make it sound like I'm always hungry."

"Your aura is always hungry." Suzanna grabbed an apple from the fruit bowl behind the counter and tossed it to Robyn, who caught it with a sigh.

"Someday, you're gonna get us busted for doing things like this."

Suzanna shrugged. They both knew that if she did get caught one day, she'd only smile her way out of trouble. She'd always been like that, even when she was younger. There were no blood ties between them, but Robyn still thought of Suzanna as family. It was impossible not to, considering the things they'd gone through together.

Ana was a part of their little family too. It was a strange family, considering the fact that Suzanna and Ana were now dating, but a family nonetheless.

Robyn turned to greet her next customer and almost dropped her apple.

"Andrew?"

She hated how seeing him made her heart race.

"I'm sorry for showing up like this. Can we talk?"

Andrew wore a black coat over a white shirt and light-gray slacks, and his jet-black hair looked perfect as usual. His casual flawlessness annoyed her. She felt the urge to run her fingers through that perfect damn hair, just to mess it up a little.

"I'm working," she said.

"When do you get off?"

"Two a.m."

Andrew pulled up his sleeve and checked his watch. Robyn could see the conflict in his eyes when he realized he'd have to wait almost four hours.

"I knew Sandy's had late closing times, but this is just ridiculous," he muttered.

She gave him an expressionless look, hiding the fact that she was actually a bit curious about what his next move would be.

He sighed. "I'll just have to wait, then. One cup of tea, please."

She raised an eyebrow. "Seriously?"

"Yeah. Listen, Robyn, I want to apologize for—"

"Earl Grey?" she interrupted. She wasn't ready for an apology. Frankly, she wasn't ready for any interaction with Andrew at all.

He nodded and smiled. "How did you know?"

"The smell. Your house smells like Earl Grey." She quickly looked away and started typing on the cash register. It wasn't just his house that smelled like Earl Grey—Andrew himself smelled like it too, and the fact that she knew that was weird on so many levels.

After getting his tea, Andrew took a seat in a booth close to the register. To say he looked out of place would be an understatement. Robyn liked the café's wooden floor and flowery wallpaper, and she thought the worn-out, pale-pink seats in the booths gave the place a vintage kind of charm—but she also knew that some people thought Sandy's just looked cheap and old. Andrew, with his air of elegance, didn't fit in at all.

A group of students entered the café then, and Robyn was busy for the next hour or so.

"Who's that?" Suzanna whispered, nodding toward Andrew, when they finally got a customer-free moment.

"He's just my doctor," Robyn said.

"Oh, really? Because Dr. Handsome has been sitting there for a while now, and let's face it, our tea is not that spectacular."

Suzanna tilted her head to the side, observing the man in the booth. Andrew had pulled a laptop from his briefcase and was now squinting at the display, his brow furrowed in concentration.

"Damn." Suzanna giggled. "He's really into you, isn't he?"

Andrew looked up from his computer and gave them a little wave. Robyn immediately looked away, while Suzanna happily waved back.

"You should keep him," Suzanna said with a wink right before a group of new customers arrived at the counter. Robyn gave Suzanna an indiscreet glare and went back to work.

• • •

Andrew couldn't remember if he'd ever been at a café for four hours straight before. Sure, the tea was nice, but it was still a pretty desperate thing to do just to talk to a girl.

He watched Robyn as she worked. She was wearing a white apron over her usual tank top and sweatpants. Her hair was tied up in a ponytail, but some of the unruly red locks refused to stay in the hairdo. She automatically tucked the stray pieces of hair behind her ears every time they fell into her eyes. He wasn't sure why, but the action made him smile.

When it was finally time for Robyn to close the café, Andrew still wasn't sure what he was going to say. He watched as she shooed the last group of intoxicated teenagers out the door and began to clean the tables. Her coworker with the crazy hair had left half an hour earlier, saying something about catching a bus.

"Can we talk outside? I need to lock this place up," Robyn said when she was finished. She took off her apron, put on her oversized hoodie, and then grabbed her backpack from behind the counter. After locking the front door from the inside, she motioned for him to follow her through the door next to the cash register.

He put the laptop back in his briefcase and followed her through a small kitchen and then out the back door. The parking lot was empty, his own car being the exception. Robyn locked the door behind them.

"So." She turned around to face him. "Why are you here?"

"I wanted to apologize."

"For what? Having an opinion?"

"For making it sound like I don't respect you and all the sacrifices you've made to take care of your sister."

Robyn blinked. Whatever she'd expected him to say, that clearly hadn't been it.

Andrew took a deep breath. "I was an inconsiderate jerk. You're right, I don't know you, and I don't know what you and your sister have gone through. All I know is that I want to help you." He hesitated. "I... I knew a person like you once."

She cocked an eyebrow.

"Well, not exactly like you, but she got hurt a lot too." He swallowed hard. "I was too much of a coward to do something back then, and that person almost died because of it. I can't let that happen again. I'm not going to stand idly by and wait for you to get beaten to death. You wanted a selfish reason for why I've been helping you. There it is."

Robyn stared at him. Her face was impossible to read.

"I care about you, Robyn." He gave her a tentative smile. "You may be good at taking care of Lucy, but you're terrible at taking care of yourself. That's why I feel the need to look after you. It doesn't mean I don't respect you. It only means I care." He tilted his head to the side. "Are you going to question that too, or is that selfish enough for you to believe it?"

He tried to meet Robyn's eyes, but she avoided his gaze. Her cheeks had gained a faint tint of pink. A smile tugged at his lips. Apparently, this was how you flustered a person like Robyn Monroe.

"I believe you," she finally said. "I'm sorry too. I overreacted."

Andrew sighed in relief. "Does this mean you'll let me help you again? I need to look at those sutu—"

"Shut it." Robyn held up her hand in a silencing gesture, staring into the darkness on the other side of the parking lot. "Who are you, and what do you want?"

He looked at her in confusion. "Who are you talking—"

"I said shut it!" She bit her lip and took a deep breath. When she spoke again, her voice was softer. "Please, just do as I say, okay?"

A tall man stepped out of the shadows. "Are you the Valkyrie?"

She pulled her hood over her head. "No."

"Oh, really?" the man said, his voice dripping with sarcasm. He came to a stop a couple of steps away, still half concealed in the darkness.

"Really." Robyn stepped forward, covering Andrew with her body. Andrew stood frozen in place, paralyzed by the conflict of two equally strong instincts: one to protect Robyn and the other to get the hell away from there.

Something moved behind the dumpsters beside them. Three men stormed out, one of them significantly larger than the others.

"Sorry about this." The large man grabbed Robyn's shoulders and slammed her back into the wall. He pulled the hood off her head, took a firm hold of her hair, and tugged her head back. The light of a nearby streetlight lit up her face.

"It's her," the giant confirmed. "Am I done here?"

"You're done." The first man frowned. "Mind your tone. You may be new to this organization, but you should still be aware of Mr. Swanson's opinion on disrespect toward your superiors."

The giant rolled his eyes before letting go of Robyn's hair. Andrew ran to her side, steadying her as she slumped against the wall.

"Listen, I'm genuinely sorry about this," the giant said, his voice too low for the others to hear him. "Swanson can force me to identify you, but that's it. I'm not taking part in this." He glanced at the men behind him before turning back to Robyn. "I know our fight was staged. Next time, I want a real fight, all right?"

Her lips twitched as she gave him a short nod.

He smirked. "Give them hell."

Robyn turned to the first man, who was now joined by his two companions. The giant disappeared into the shadows again.

"Was that the guy you fought last week?" Andrew stared at her in shock. He couldn't even imagine her fighting someone of that size. "Robyn, please tell me what's happening."

"It's…complicated. My manager doubles as a bookie. My odds were going in the wrong direction, so he told me to lose my last fight on purpose. These guys… They're his men. I guess losing a fight wasn't enough." She snorted. "'The Valkyrie, beaten up by random strangers in a parking lot.' A rumor like that would definitely work in his favor."

"Are you serious?" He continued to stare at her. "Your own manager would order people to beat you up?"

She nodded. "Andrew, you need to leave. Run to your car and go. They won't follow you—I'm the one they're after."

"I can't just… I can't…"

The fear was overwhelming. He tried to come up with a way out, something that could save them both, but his brain seemed to work in slow motion. He couldn't move. He couldn't think. All he could do was stand there and stare.

"You see, Valkyrie, we're having a bit of a betting problem," the first man said. He stood closer to the streetlight now. It was hard to tell, but he seemed young—probably younger than Robyn. "It was a beautiful performance you did last week, but your odds are still a little bit too good. Nothing personal. We just have to… *incapacitate* you a little."

This can't be happening, Andrew thought. *This can't actually be happening.*

Robyn pulled off her hoodie and raised her fists. "Andrew. If you're not gonna run, then stay the hell out of my way." And with those words, Robyn attacked.

She ran toward them. The first man and one of his companions took a step back while the third man moved forward. He aimed a punch at her face and missed by several inches. Robyn spun around and delivered a merciless roundhouse kick to the man's chin. He went out like a light. The first man and his companion lunged for her, but she dodged them both.

Andrew felt like he should do something, but he still couldn't move. Robyn's movements were hypnotizing. She almost looked like she was dancing. In one of her spins, Andrew could see her face for a moment, and the sight made him drop his briefcase on the ground. She was *smiling.*

It wasn't one of the few almost-smiles she'd given him from time to time, but a real, mischievous grin. It wasn't just her facial expression that was different—her whole body language had changed. This wasn't Robyn. This was the Valkyrie.

Robyn elbowed the companion hard in the nose, making him fall to the ground with a guttural groan. She followed up the attack with a hard kick to his groin, all while grinning triumphantly. Andrew shuddered.

The first man was now the last man standing. They circled each other, both out of breath, waiting for the other to make a move. From the corner of his eye, Andrew saw something move in the shadows again.

"Robyn, watch out!" he yelled, forcing himself to move toward the fight. "He's got backup!"

Robyn turned around just in time to see a fourth man join the fight. The man hit her hard in the stomach, causing her to lose her balance. She rolled on the asphalt and was up again in less than a second, but Andrew could tell by the look on her face that she was in pain.

Using all the mental strength he could gather, Andrew finally made his body obey him. He didn't know how to help Robyn, but he would come up with something. *I can do this,* he thought, forcing his legs to run. *I can do this. I can do this.*

He quickly came to a stop as he ran face-first into man number five. Man number five was bigger than the others—almost as big as the giant who'd identified Robyn.

"Bro, stay out of this," the man said, blocking Andrew from the fight. Andrew tried to move past him, but the man only moved with him. "Seriously, bro. This doesn't concern you."

"Of course it concerns me!" Andrew growled. He tried to duck under the man's arm but was blocked a third time. The man was almost as wide as he was tall and didn't leave any windows at all.

"Ah, she's your girl. Sorry 'bout that, bro." The pity in the man's eyes only made Andrew more furious.

"Could someone just fucking knock her out?" the first man yelled. Andrew could hear a body hit the ground, but he had no idea who the body belonged to since there was still an oversized dudebro blocking his way. He had to see her. He had to know she was okay.

I can do this. He curled his right hand into a fist. *I can do this.* He took a deep breath, raised his fist, and then, for the first time in his entire life, he threw a punch. The world slowed down, and he watched in tense anticipation as his fist connected with man number five's cheek.

Man number five stared at him. "Dude, what the fuck?"

Andrew took a step back. He wasn't sure what reaction he'd expected, but this scenario had *not* been part of the plan. Now what? He stared at his aching fist. No, this wasn't going according to plan at all.

Something hit man number five from behind, making him stumble forward. A pair of legs wrapped themselves around his neck, and he was suddenly being pulled backward. Robyn somehow made him flip over and land on his face, while she landed gracefully on top of him. When she was sure the man wasn't getting up again, she stood and jogged over to Andrew.

"That's the last one. I got them all." Her eyes burned hot with adrenaline. "Are you okay?"

He stared at his fist. "I hit him."

"Yes, you did." She chewed on her lip with a strange look on her face.

"Did you see that? I hit him."

"I saw it." The look on her face only got more intense until she finally burst out laughing. "Hell, that was the worst punch I've ever seen."

"Was it really that bad?" He frowned, feeling a little insulted.

"Yes. It definitely was." Robyn's laugh wasn't pretty, but it was contagious. Andrew's frown soon turned into a grin. As his state of shock died down, he realized he had no idea how the real fight had ended. His eyes widened as he took in the scene. The parking lot could no longer be called "empty." The five men lay scattered all over the lot, and even in the dim light from the streetlight, Andrew could clearly distinguish stains of blood on the asphalt. Two of the men were moaning quietly, and the other three weren't moving at all.

"Wow. You're good at this," he said. *Way too good.*

Robyn shrugged. "They were pretty bad."

She wiped some blood off her lips. She had bruises and abrasions everywhere, and she'd started to sway a little.

"Robyn, are *you* okay? Are you hurt?"

She yawned. "I'm fine. Adrenaline backlash."

She walked over to the first man and turned him onto his back with her foot. "Don't ever come here again," she said in a low, monotone voice, placing her foot on the man's throat. "You'll never touch me again, and you'll never touch him either." She put more pressure on his throat, and the man started to make strangled noises. He tried to move away from her, but she only put more weight on the foot. "If you touch me, him, or anyone I know, I will kill you. That's not a threat—it's a promise."

Andrew shuddered again, staring at Robyn in awe. He didn't doubt her words for a second, and neither did the man on the ground. She yawned again and removed her foot from the man's throat.

"I'm gonna head home," she said, picking up her hoodie from the ground.

"Can I give you a ride?" Andrew asked tentatively.

"I'd just ruin the seats."

"Doesn't matter. Come on." He carefully put his arm around her shoulders and held his breath, waiting for possible death threats, but Robyn seemed too tired to care. She remained silent as he led her to the car, zigzagging between the bodies on the ground.

"Can we really just leave them like that?" he asked, glancing back at the parking lot through the rearview mirror. Leaving injured people unattended bothered him, but not enough to make him stay and take care of them. They'd tried to hurt Robyn, and she'd defended herself. Treating their injuries was not his problem.

Sure, go on, convince yourself that what you just did wasn't a violation of your medical oath, his inner critic mocked.

"Don't worry about them. My manager always cleans up his messes," Robyn said bitterly. "I'm sorry for putting you through all this. You should probably avoid me for a while. I'm not a good person to be around right now."

"I still want to help you."

"And I still want to pay you back for everything you've done for me and Lucy. I don't know how yet, but I will come up with something. Relying on your generosity doesn't sit right with me. I don't have it in me to keep being your little charity case like this. It's just not who I am."

Andrew stayed silent for a few moments. Over the past couple of weeks, it had become all too clear to him that sooner or later, Robyn would get so injured he wouldn't be able to fix her. The only way to stop that from happening was to make sure she didn't get injured in the first place. To do so, he was going to have to get closer to the street fighting world—closer to *her*. He'd had an idea growing in the back of his mind the whole week, but he wasn't sure how Robyn would react to it. He was never sure how Robyn would react to *anything*. He took a deep breath and then decided to at least give it a try.

"You could teach me how to fight."

"What?" She stared at him.

"I give you medical treatment, and you teach me how to fight."

Robyn kept staring.

"It doesn't have to be much. Just a bit of self-defense, and maybe how to throw a punch without spraining my fingers." He raised his right hand from the wheel and showed her his swollen thumb.

"You kept your thumb inside your fist when you hit him, didn't you?" she asked with a sigh. "*Never* keep your thumb inside the fist. You could have broken it."

"Oh." Andrew couldn't remember if his thumb had been inside or outside his fist when he threw the punch, but she was probably right.

"I don't know what I could teach you," she continued. "I never had a teacher myself. But yeah, sure, I guess I could try."

"That's great!" He grinned widely. "So it's a deal, then?"

"I guess it is," she said, giving him her classic almost-smile.

By the time Andrew parked outside Robyn's apartment, they'd spent several minutes in comfortable silence. Andrew usually felt like he had to keep a conversation going at all times, but with Robyn, he could somehow relax.

"I really need to remove those sutures soon," he said as Robyn climbed out of the car.

"I've already removed them."

"Wait, what? How?"

She shrugged. "Scissors and a mirror."

Andrew groaned, pinching the bridge of his nose. "You're impossible."

"A little." A glimmer of mischievousness flashed in her eyes.

He shook his head. "If you need help—"

"I'll call. I promise."

"Really?"

"Really."

He glanced at her. Even if she said she'd call, he knew she still didn't fully trust him. Two times, Robyn had nearly died in his hands, and both of those times could have been avoided if she hadn't been so hell-bent on telling everyone she was fine all the time.

"Just one more thing," he said. "No more lying. No more bad excuses. I get it if you don't trust me, but please...don't lie to me again."

She considered it for a moment, hesitating, and then nodded. "No more lies. It's just that...the truth isn't always pretty, you know. My life isn't always pretty, either. Are you sure you're up for it?"

"I am." If it increased the odds of keeping her alive, he was up for anything.

"Good. We have an agreement, then." She tilted her head to the side. "I guess that makes us partners, or something."

Andrew smiled. "Partners, or something. I can live with that."

CHAPTER FIVE

"So, Andrew…I'm competing in this tournament in a couple of days. I don't know the details yet, because Swanson—you know, my manager—is the one who sets up fights for me. Anyway, my first fight is next Saturday, and I thought you'd probably like to know— Tiny, where the fuck are you going?"

Tiny, who'd just made a weak attempt to escape from Robyn's lap, gave her an angry glare before settling down on her thighs again. She sighed, stroking his black fur. She'd been sitting on the bench outside the apartment building for several minutes, waiting for Andrew to catch up with her. He was a man of many skills, but running wasn't one of them.

"You're not being very helpful," she told the cat. "It isn't really your fault—I mean, you're a cat and all—but you do suck at pretending to be Andrew."

A week had passed since she and Andrew had become partners. This was the second time they jogged together, and she still hadn't figured out a good way to tell him about the tournament. She'd considered "accidentally" forgetting about it, but she couldn't bring herself to do that either. She'd promised him she wouldn't lie to him. Even if this was more of a "leaving out important information" situation than a straight-out lie, it still wasn't the truthfulness Andrew expected of her. He deserved better.

Seconds later, the sound of heavy footsteps and loud, strained breaths came from the other side of the hedge. Tiny jumped down from Robyn's lap and hurried into the bushes, seeking shelter from the slowly approaching stranger.

"How's it going?" Robyn shouted.

When Andrew staggered through the gap in the hedge, he looked like he was about to throw up. His face was flushed, his black tank top was drenched in sweat, and his legs were trembling.

"Time?" he panted, collapsing next to her on the bench.

She checked her watch. "Thirty-five minutes."

"Seriously?" He threw his head back and groaned. "One minute faster than last time. Just one shitty little minute."

"How fast did you think you'd improve?" Robyn cocked an eyebrow, trying hard to hide her amusement.

"I don't know." He sighed. "I don't think I'll ever get it down to twenty-five minutes. Is this really necessary?"

"Three miles in twenty-five minutes. That's the deal. I've always been smaller and weaker than the other fighters around here, but I've learned to compensate for it. I win fights by being faster than my opponents and by tiring them out. Right now, I don't think you're that much stronger than me, so my way of fighting should work for you, too. To use my fighting style, you need good endurance. That's just how it is."

"All right, all right." He scowled at her. "I know I'm weak. You don't have to rub it in."

She snorted. "I just admitted you *might* be physically stronger than me, and that's how you react. Asshole."

"Yeah, but you're a…" He froze, and Robyn could see the exact moment he realized that there was no possible way to end the sentence without fucking up.

"I'm a…?" She concealed her amusement by sounding insulted, which made him look even more flustered.

"Small," he finally finished.

"A small." Robyn could no longer stop the smile from reaching her lips.

"You're teasing me."

"You make it so easy." She shook her head. "How the hell did you ever get through high school?"

He shrugged. "I went to Eden High. People were pretty nice there."

Eden, she thought. *Of course.*

Eden was a private school located right outside the city, with tuition higher than Robyn's yearly income. She had attended Chrystal Valley's public school, where everyone despised the spoilt Eden kids. *I'm hanging out with an Eden kid,* she thought in disbelief. Her fifteen-year-old self would never have forgiven her.

"I have to get going now," Andrew the Eden Kid said, groaning as he forced his body up from the bench. "I'm in desperate need of a shower. See you on Monday?"

Robyn nodded. Andrew smiled and began to walk toward his car.

"Andrew, wait," she yelled after him. "I…"

"Yeah?"

When he turned back and gave her that wide, trusting smile of his, all of her courage disappeared at once. "Don't forget to stretch."

"I won't," he answered, and then he was gone.

"Damn it," she muttered. She'd tried to tell him about the tournament several times now, but the words just wouldn't come out. She wasn't sure why she was having such a hard time telling him, but it probably had something to do with the way he acted around her now.

Ever since the night they became partners, he'd stopped giving her his condescending doctor smiles. The smiles he gave her now were casual and carefree, and he no longer had that infuriating look of pity in his eyes. She wanted things to stay that way. She didn't want to remind him of how messed up her life truly was.

She buried her face in her hands and sighed. "I'm the worst partner ever."

● ● ●

Andrew was sitting in his favorite armchair with a cup of tea when someone rang the doorbell. At first, he remained where he was, waiting for the unexpected visitor to go away. His whole body hurt, and his legs still wobbled a little when he walked. He was not in the mood for company.

A few seconds later, the doorbell rang again. And again. And again. Andrew groaned, his body protesting wildly as he got up from the chair. He had no idea why anyone would visit him at half past eight on a Saturday night, and he wasn't too keen on finding out either.

"What?" he said sourly when he opened the door. He stared at his visitor in confusion. "Jason?"

"'Sup." Jason gave him a short nod.

"Hi?"

Jason grinned. "Wanna go watch a fight? There's a really good one starting in about an hour. It's just outside the city. What do you say?"

"I don't know..." Andrew looked over Jason's shoulder, feeling like something was missing. "Hey, where's your motorcycle?"

"At the mechanic. Something's up with the carburetor, and when I tried to fix it I just fucked it up even more."

"So, the real reason you're here is because you want a ride." Things were finally making sense again.

Jason tried to keep his poker face up for a few moments, but then he gave in. "I really, *really* want to see this fight, okay? The tournament starts tonight. I can't miss it."

"The tournament?" Andrew could have sworn he'd heard about some kind of tournament before, but he couldn't put his finger on where or when.

"Yeah. It's a yearly event for mixed martial arts, and it's bigger than ever this year. They've built a whole new arena for it and everything. It's huge. We've already missed the fights from the lower classes, but we could make it in time for the first-class fight. Trust me, you don't want to miss this. Are you in?"

Andrew didn't hesitate. "I'm in."

He grabbed his thick, black coat from its hanger on the wall and followed Jason outside. If he was going to be Robyn's partner, he needed to know more about Chrystal Valley's underground world. He refused to admit that the sudden thrill in his gut could have anything to do with him longing for action again.

"Is this kind of thing even legal?" he asked Jason as they walked toward his car.

Jason's grin widened. "Not by a long shot."

• • •

The arena was located right outside the city, just like Jason said. On the outside, the place looked like a normal pizzeria. On the inside, the place looked like a pizzeria too. It seemed to be a busy night, and almost all the booths were taken. Waiters and waitresses were half walking, half running between the kitchen and the customers, serving food and beverages left and right.

"Are you sure we're in the right place?" Andrew whispered to Jason.

"Yes." Jason glared at him. "Now shut up."

They were waiting in line to get to the counter, which looked exactly like a normal restaurant counter.

"Two specials," Jason said to the cashier, handing him some wrinkled ten-dollar bills from his back pocket. The cashier accepted the money and pointed at a door right next to them.

"Really? That's the code word?" Andrew asked, raising his eyebrows. He followed Jason through the door and down the stairs hidden behind it.

Jason scowled. "Shut. Up."

Andrew could already hear the music coming from the basement. The deep bass pounded on his eardrums. The farther down the stairs they got, the more the smell of garlic and oregano changed into the smell of sweat and hard liquor. Judging by the length of the stairs, the basement had to be at least two stories high. Jason had been right—the arena was huge.

"Who paid for all this?" Andrew asked.

"This guy named Mr. Quinn." Jason snorted. "Apparently, he's got more money than he can spend. Hands out donations left and right. Honestly, I think he built this building just to mess with the power structure in this city."

"Why?"

Jason shrugged. "Maybe he felt someone has to."

When they reached the bottom of the stairs, there was no longer any doubt that the pizzeria was in fact a gateway to an underground fighting arena. The basement was big—a lot bigger than the parking garage arena. A thick, highly intoxicated crowd had gathered around the octagon-shaped ring in the middle of the room. The size of the audience was mind-boggling. For a moment, Andrew almost felt betrayed by the city he'd grown up in. He'd had no idea Chrystal Valley's underground world was this extensive.

Jason turned to him and grinned. "Welcome to Chrystal Arena."

The fighting ring was placed on an elevated platform in the middle of the room. Above it hung a digital sign with a reset timer, the zeroes glowing bright red in the dimly lit room. Three elevated passages were connected to the platform, leading from the ring to three flights of stairs. Spotlights lighted two of the passages up, but the third was cloaked in darkness. The ring with its padded iron poles and netted walls looked like an actual cage.

"The rounds are five minutes long, then the fighters get a one-minute break, and then it's on again," Jason yelled in Andrew's ear.

"They rarely last that long, though." The noise around them was deafening, even though the fight hadn't started yet. Jason grinned. "This is going to be awesome. Come on, I need a beer."

The bar was located in the corner of the basement. Jason had just received his drink when a petite woman with waist-length white hair stumbled into him. He wrapped an arm around her waist to steady her.

"Jason," she greeted him with a smile.

"Cassandra, hi." Jason smiled back at her. His face had softened the moment he laid eyes on her, and his hand was still resting on her hip.

"If you're going to bet, bet on the Morrigan," Cassandra told him.

"No bets today. I'm here with a friend." Jason nodded at Andrew.

"I see." Cassandra looked at Andrew and reached out her hand. "I'm Cassandra. Nice to meet you."

"I'm Andrew. Likewise." He carefully shook her hand. He couldn't help but notice how dangerously thin her wrists were, and neither could he ignore the needle marks on the back of her right hand. Up close, it was obvious her white hair was a wig. His heart sank. *Cancer.*

"I need to get back to Drake," she said. "Hey, Jason, what are you doing after the fight?"

Jason's eyes lit up. "I don't have anything planned."

"Good. Meet me outside when the fight is over. I want to talk to you."

"Okay," Jason said, smiling like a fool. "I'll see you then."

Cassandra turned around and staggered through the crowd. She stumbled again, but this time a tall man in a suit caught her before Jason could get to her. His black hair hung over his shoulder in a long braid. He had an aquiline nose and sharp cheekbones, and his dark eyes looked hard and unforgiving. He glared at Jason as he led Cassandra to a chair placed next to the bar, keeping a protective arm around her shoulders.

"Fucking Drake," Jason muttered.

"Who are they?" Andrew asked.

"That's Cassandra, our local clairvoyant," Jason said. "Always knows how to bet. That chick's as smart as she's cute. That guy next to her is Drake Locklear. I'm not sure why she's always hanging out with him, but I think he's her guardian or something." He sent a glare in Drake's direction. "He's a pretentious asshole."

Jason was just about to say something else when the music stopped. "It's time," he yelled instead, cheering with the rest of the crowd. A bald, muscular man and an even more muscular black-haired woman were now standing in opposite corners of the ring. Between them stood the referee, a small man in a black-and-white shirt.

While the referee talked to the fighters, the commentator turned on his microphone.

"Ladies and gentlemen, it's finally time for the first-class fight you've all been waiting for!" he yelled, his voice blasting from the speakers on the walls. "We've all gathered here today to witness the battle between the brutal Bonecrusher and the merciless Morrigan. I hope you're ready, because this fight begins…" The commentator paused dramatically. "Now!"

The bell rang, and the referee swiftly jumped out of the way as the fighters lunged for each other. They were a lot more skilled than the fighters Andrew had watched at the Octagon. He was still too inexperienced with fighting to pick out all the details, but he could tell they were faster, more persevering, and a lot better at dodging blows than the Octagon fighters. After two and a half rounds, the woman managed to get a good grip around the man's neck. They both ended up on the mat, the Bonecrusher flailing helplessly as the Morrigan choked him with her thighs. After a while, he stopped moving, and the referee forced the winner away from her unconscious opponent.

"Let's all greet tonight's first-class champion—the Morrigan!" the commentator shouted into his microphone. The audience hollered with him. Andrew felt the adrenaline pulse through him, his heart beating hard and fast in his chest. His thoughts about the fighters' potential injuries were drowned out by the audience's contagious excitement. He now understood why people paid to take part in this. He could feel the excitement too.

"And who will the Morrigan meet in the quarterfinals?" the commentator continued. "Next week's first-class fight is something you *really* don't want to miss: the Bear—stronger, larger, more vicious than his namesake—versus the strong, the fierce, the beautiful…the Valkyrie!"

What?

The audience continued to cheer, but Andrew just stood there, staring into thin air. He knew he hadn't misheard the commentator, but he still couldn't process it. Robyn was in the tournament. She was in the damn tournament, and she hadn't even mentioned it to him.

Technically, it wasn't a lie, his inner critic reminded him. *She never said she'd tell you everything.*

But they'd had an agreement, a partnership, that had helped him sleep at night. He'd convinced himself he'd never have to get a phone call from a hysterical Lucy again—that he'd no longer have to worry about Robyn being beaten half to death without him knowing it. Obviously, he'd been wrong. So very wrong.

"Partners," he muttered, pushing people out of his way as he strode toward the exit. "I can't believe I fell for that one."

With panic and adrenaline pumping through his veins, Andrew made a decision—he was going to pay Robyn a visit, and he was going to get some answers.

CHAPTER SIX

Robyn slammed the door shut behind her as she entered the apartment after her training session with Andrew. She'd once again failed to tell him about the tournament, and it was now only a week until her first fight. *I'm the worst partner ever,* she thought, furious with herself.

She was so busy pondering her failure, she almost missed the note on the kitchen table.

Out on a demonstration with Mike and the FTS gang. Don't wait up.

- Lucy

Robyn groaned, crumpling the piece of paper in her hand. She felt like punching something—preferably Mike's face.

"'Don't wait up,'" she muttered, tossing the wrinkled note in the garbage can. "Like I could possibly sleep when you're hanging out with *them.*"

She spent the rest of the evening cleaning the apartment. She and Lucy had made a deal after their mother died—Lucy cooked, Robyn cleaned. The division worked well, since Lucy had always been the better cook, and Robyn didn't mind cleaning. It was like running—a methodical activity she could do without thinking.

The radio in the living room, tuned to WQXR, kept her company as she cleaned. Every time a piece she recognized came on, she couldn't stop herself from following its rhythm. Step, step, tiptoes, quick spin—the movements were as natural as breathing. This was a part of her she could never get rid of. No matter how hard she tried.

At half past eleven, keys rattled in the lock on the door. Moments later, Lucy rushed into the apartment, dropping her handbag on the floor. Her blue coat had new stains, her hair was disheveled, and her mascara had become dark smudges under her eyes—all signs of another demonstration gone wild. Robyn really, *really* felt like punching Mike in the face.

"Robyn!" Lucy shouted, practically bouncing with excitement. "I have something I need to tell you—something great!"

"Okay...?" Even though she liked seeing her sister happy, she was always skeptical when the happiness had something to do with Mike. *Please don't be pregnant.*

"You should probably sit down first." Lucy fiddled a little with her braid.

"I'm not an old lady. I think my nerves can take it."

Lucy nodded and took a deep breath. "Don't overreact, okay?"

Robyn crossed her arms. "I'm not promising anything. Just tell me already." *Please, please, please don't be pregnant.*

Lucy smiled, lifting her left hand. "Mike just proposed to me. You should have seen it—this guy was just about to shove me or something, and Mike just punched him in the face and carried me out of there. Then he went down on one knee and everything. It was amazing. Can you believe it? I'm getting married!"

Robyn stood frozen in place, staring at the ring on Lucy's finger. "You're...you're what?"

"Getting married. I love him, Robyn. I want to spend the rest of my life with him."

Robyn kept staring at the ring. It was made of silvery material, presumably white gold or platinum, with one larger diamond-like gem surrounded by two smaller ones on the sides. It looked expensive and was definitely not a last-minute purchase.

"You're not pregnant, are you?" she asked anyway. She simply couldn't fathom why her intelligent, ambitious sister would want to spend the rest of her life with someone like Mike.

"No, of course not." Lucy frowned. "Why would I be pregnant?"

"I don't know, I... Lucy, are you sure about this? You've only been dating for six months—"

"He's *the one*. I've never been more sure about anything in my whole life."

"How could you possibly know that?" Robyn exclaimed. "You're eighteen! You've got your whole life ahead of you. Why would you want to waste it on someone like him?"

She regretted the harsh words the moment they left her mouth. Lucy looked like she'd been slapped in the face.

"I'm sorry, Lucy, I didn't mean it like that—"

"Yes, you did. You've never even given him a chance." Lucy's eyes filled with tears. "I know you want to protect me, but I'm an adult now. You have to let me live my own life." With trembling hands, she picked up her handbag from the floor. "And by the way, you have no right to look down on Mike. At least he's trying to take down the people corrupting this city instead of working for them."

Lucy turned around and ran out the door, slamming it shut behind her. Robyn smashed her fist into the wall. The anger and frustration still burned hot within her, but she knew Lucy was right. As long as she kept working for Swanson, she had no right to judge anyone. She stared at the closed door for a few moments, deliberating whether or not to follow her. Lucy's words had hurt her deeply, but the guilt bothered her more. *Fuck it.*

"Lucy, wait!" she shouted, sprinting down the stairs. She'd just reached the ground floor when she almost ran into someone.

"Sorry." She tried to move past the person blocking her way.

"Robyn, I need to talk to you."

She looked up. "Andrew?"

For a moment, she hadn't even recognized him. Instead of his usual calm, professional aura, he was now giving off an almost dangerous vibe. He was clenching his jaw, and his eyes were hard and cold. Even his smell was different—instead of the usual Earl Grey aroma, he now reeked of sweat, smoke, and booze.

"Not now." She pushed past him. Lucy had just disappeared around a corner outside the building. It wasn't too late yet. Robyn could still catch up with her and apologize.

"Yes, now," Andrew growled, grabbing her wrist. Robyn's body moved on instinct, just like it had when he'd tried to grab her in the examination room—but this time, he seemed to see it coming. When she spun around to give him a shove, he dodged her and reversed their positions. Before she could regain her balance, her back had already hit the wall. He kept his manacle-like grip on her wrist and placed his other hand next to her head, caging her in.

"This is not a good time," she said. She tried to push him away with her free hand, but he wouldn't budge.

"The tournament, Robyn. Were you ever going to tell me about it?"

Her eyes widened. "Who told you?"

"'Partners,' huh?" he continued. "I thought we had an agreement. You could have died in this damn tournament, and I wouldn't even have known about it before it was too late. I wouldn't have known a thing, and you would have been…" His grip around her wrist tightened. "I *trusted* you. Were you ever planning on telling me the truth? Or was that yet another lie?"

"Andrew, I…"

He was too close. She couldn't think. His face was mere inches away from hers, and she could feel the warmth of his breath on her skin. His gaze fell to her lips. The intensity in his eyes changed from anger into something different. Something hotter. For a moment, she thought he was going to kiss her—but then they both heard the rumbling of Mike's motorcycle.

"Damn it." She'd lost her only shot of catching up with Lucy. She sagged against the wall and stopped struggling. Lucy was gone, and so was Robyn's chance to apologize. She was now a lousy partner *and* a lousy sister. In that moment, she truly hated herself.

"I wanted to tell you," she said, her body trembling almost as much as her voice. "I just... I just couldn't. I fucked up. That's what I do. I fuck things up. I'm sorry."

"What do you mean, 'couldn't'? How hard could it..." He paused, his expression softening. "Are you crying?"

"No," she lied, although the truth was embarrassingly obvious. She removed her free hand from his chest and covered her eyes. "Don't look at me."

He sighed and let go of her wrist. Robyn tried to move away from him, but Andrew had other plans. Instead of backing off, he wrapped his arms around her and pulled her close.

She stiffened against his chest. "What the hell?"

"You're crying, so I'm holding you," he replied in a matter-of-fact tone.

"I don't do hugs."

"Just humor me."

Robyn nodded, burrowing her face into his coat. She really wasn't the hugging type, but it was better than the alternative. If she stayed in his arms, she could at least hide the tears.

"It's okay," he said, stroking her back. "Everything will be okay."

Robyn snorted. "For someone your age, you're really damn naïve."

The hand on her back abruptly stopped its soothing movement. "Someone my age? How old do you think I am?"

"Thirty-five, maybe?"

"Thirty-five?" He grabbed her shoulders and pushed her away from him. "I'm twenty-seven!"

She wiped away the last traces of her tears and smiled. "I know, you idiot."

"Then why would you… You're teasing me again." He frowned and let go of her.

She shrugged. Though she'd never admit it out loud, the hug had actually helped a little. Her argument with Lucy still felt like a slowly rotating knife in her chest, but she was calmer now. She would talk to Lucy later, when they'd both cooled down. They'd had arguments before, and they always made up sooner or later.

Robyn shuddered. *Mike is going to be my brother-in-law.* The thought still nauseated her.

"Are you all right?" Andrew asked.

She shrugged again. She wasn't too happy with Andrew for stopping her like that, but she couldn't blame him for being mad at her. After all, she was pretty mad at herself, too.

"I'm sorry for not telling you about the tournament," she said, looking down. "I'm not good at trusting people. I'm pretty bad at talking to people I trust, too. I…I push people away. I try not to, but I still end up doing it. I'm sorry." She met his gaze, hoping her eyes would portray her honesty better than her words. *Please believe me.*

Andrew nodded and sighed. "It's okay. I'm sorry too. I don't know what got into me. I didn't hurt you, did I? Give me your wrist." There was a commanding tone in his voice, and Robyn would have objected on principle if she hadn't noticed the panic in his eyes.

"You're not that strong," she muttered.

He rolled up the sleeve of her hoodie and looked at the wrist in his usual meticulous manner, checking it for any sort of injury. When he'd made sure the wrist was fine, he let out a relieved sigh. His fingers lingered on the scar on her forearm that had brought them both together, tracing the still visible pattern of her homemade stitches on her skin.

"I wish I knew why," he said, holding her wrist gently in his hands. "Why you do this to yourself. Why you let them hurt you like this."

Robyn tensed. She'd always known she was going to have to answer those questions one day, but she still wasn't ready for it. She'd probably never be.

"You don't have to answer me," he added quickly. "Not now, at least. Someday."

She bit her lip, making a decision. "I...I could try. Like, right now." *Before I change my mind.*

"Really?"

She nodded. "Would you like some tea?"

• • •

People always assumed Andrew was a naturally calm person. He could see why—he'd gotten really good at faking it over the years.

When he was a kid, his mother had died in a train crash. He'd spent years being mad at his father for not being on the train with them, at himself for surviving the crash instead of his mother, and at the world for simply being shitty. He still carried that anger deep within him, but he'd gotten good at hiding it. At work, he was admired for his way of solving even the trickiest problems with calm rationality, and he was known for never raising his voice. He'd become a master of turning his inner anger into a power of motivation, and he had no idea why all of this seemed to go straight out the window when he was with Robyn.

When he'd left Chrystal Arena, he hadn't really had any plans on how to confront Robyn. His fear of losing her had taken over him completely. Subconsciously, he'd probably expected receiving a punch or two. Holding her while she cried and then ending up on a chair in her kitchen had been an unexpected turn of events.

He watched as she boiled water in a saucepan on the stove, pleasantly surprised that she didn't make tea in the microwave like many of his acquaintances.

"Where's Lucy?" he asked, and immediately regretted the question. He'd almost run into Lucy outside the building. Robyn had probably been trying to catch up with her. *Before I stopped her, that is.* He felt like a total douche bag.

"She's with her boyfriend…no, *fiancé*. Apparently, she's getting married." Robyn's voice was calm and even, but the way she slammed the pantry door spoke louder than words. "She's just eighteen. He's twenty-one, doesn't have a job, and thinks he's some sort of hero for starting fights at demonstrations. I don't know what she sees in him. Milk, no sugar, right?"

Andrew nodded. "Was that what you were fighting about?"

"Yeah. I didn't handle the news very well." She gave him a faint smile. "You know me. I'm good at hurting people."

The sadness in her eyes made him want to get up from the chair and hug her again. Before he could act on the urge, she'd placed the cups on the kitchen table and taken a seat.

She curled up on the chair, pressing her knees to her chest. "So. What do you want to know?"

Everything. He didn't even know where to start.

"Why you fight, maybe?" he finally said. "How it all began?"

"Of course." She didn't seem at all surprised by his choice of questions. Her hands trembled when she raised her cup of tea to her lips.

"It's okay if you don't—"

"No, it's fine. I can do this." She took a deep breath. "How it all began, huh? I guess you could say it all began when my dad left us. Nothing special about it. One day, he just packed a suitcase and left. My mother… She wasn't ready to become a single parent. She tried to take care of Lucy and me, I know she did, but she really struggled. She…"

She bit her lip, trying to get the words out. It was painful to watch, but Andrew knew that if he stopped her now, he would never get to hear her story. He remained silent, watching her take another deep breath before continuing.

"She started drinking. At first, I didn't really think about it, but then it kind of took over everything. I don't know exactly when it happened, but she started gambling. I think one of her friends introduced her to the fighting scene—you know how easy it is to find a bookie in this damn city. She lost control. Her boss fired her, and everything went downhill from there. Five years ago, I found her lying on the floor in the bathroom. She'd mixed something with alcohol, some sleeping pills, and her heart just stopped. I still don't know if it was an accident, or if she just…if she just wanted a way out."

"I'm sorry," Andrew said, trying to take it all in. "I'm so sorry."

"Yeah. It was rough. She left us with a lot of debts—debts I couldn't possibly repay with a minimum-wage job. Since people with alcoholic mothers aren't exactly popular in high school, I've always been good at fighting. Swanson, my mom's bookie, found out about this. He told me he'd get his money back one way or another and gave me a choice—I could either give him everything I owned, including the apartment, or I could start fighting for him. I chose to fight. I did it to make sure Lucy would never have to worry about money like I did when I was her age. I gave her a chance to have a normal life. If I had to do it all again, I would. I have no regrets."

Robyn held her head high, speaking with pride and dignity. She looked at Andrew with fire in her eyes, as if daring him to pity her or question her decision.

"You were just seventeen," he said, truly perplexed. "I was nothing but a spoiled brat at that age. I don't think I could have brought myself to do something like that, especially not on my own."

"There were never any alternatives. It was the only way I could protect her. My best friend, Ana, got stuck in the foster-care system, and I saw what it did to her. I swore I would never let Social Services take Lucy away from me. As a part of our deal,

Swanson convinced them to let me keep custody of her. Life wasn't always easy, no, but it wasn't always bad either. We had each other, Lucy and I."

She took a sip of her tea, her posture still portraying a sense of calm self-confidence. Andrew stared, unable to say a word. The strength hidden in the depths of her dark eyes was breathtakingly beautiful.

As he took her in, he realized he no longer saw Julie's face when he looked at her. For quite some time now, the only face he'd seen was Robyn's.

"So, yeah… I guess that's it," Robyn said. "I fight whenever and wherever Swanson wants me to fight. Once a year, I compete in the tournament. I've worked my way up through the classes, and this year, I'm fighting in the first-class category for the first time. Since there's a pretty big cash prize on the line, those fights tend to be a lot more brutal than the ones in the lower classes. It's not uncommon for first-class fighters to end up in the hospital. But I don't really care about that. I haven't even thought that much about it." She shrugged with unconvincing nonchalance. Andrew shook his head. She was a terrible liar.

"I'll be there," he said. "When you fight. Before, during, and after. I don't like this tournament thing at all, but I know I can't stop you. I'll be your personal physician."

She looked at him skeptically. "Why? What's in it for you?"

"Why do you always have to question everything?" he countered.

Robyn opened her mouth and then closed it again. She furrowed her brow, glaring at him.

"I don't know," she finally admitted.

Andrew grinned. Then he remembered one of the questions he'd planned to ask her. The most important one.

"When will all of this be over?" he asked. "How long do you have to fight for this guy?"

"Until those debts are repaid."

"And when is that?"

She fixed her gaze on the floor, hesitating. "I don't know. I've never asked him."

"You've never asked him?" His anger flared up again. "Do you seriously care that little about your own well-being? Sooner or later, you're going to get so injured I won't be able to fix you. Doesn't that scare you? It scares the hell out of *me*." He ran his fingers through his hair, forcing himself to calm down. "Is this really how you want to spend your life? Fighting for that guy? Wouldn't you prefer to live a normal life instead?"

"Of course I would," she snapped. "Why do you think I'm doing this? I want to finish high school one day. I had dreams of my own, once. I want a normal life, and that's why I need to keep fighting. I'm going to win this tournament and give Swanson my share of the cash prize. If I'm lucky, it might be enough to pay off those debts once and for all."

"Do you even know how much you owe this guy?" he asked. "You've been fighting for him for what, five years? Don't you think the debts would have been repaid by now?"

"If they were, he would have told me," she muttered.

"Would he, really? Are you sure about that? What if—"

A loud *ping* came from his pocket. He pulled out his cell phone and checked the display. *Oh shit.*

U LEFT WITHOUT ME U DICKHEAD

"Damn it," he groaned, knocking back the last of his tea. "I have to go. I was at Chrystal Arena with a friend, and I forgot to drive him home."

She nodded. Her relief was obvious.

"This conversation is not over."

She nodded again.

Before hurrying out the door, Andrew stopped and gave her a smile. "I appreciate you telling me all this, Robyn. It means a lot to me. Thank you."

"That's a weird thing to thank someone for." Her eyes twinkled with amusement. "But you're welcome, I guess."

Andrew nodded, reluctantly leaving the apartment. Somehow, he seemed to feel more at home in the Monroe sisters' small apartment than in his own house. He would have liked to stay a bit longer, but he knew he couldn't just leave Jason like that. He was selfish, but not *that* selfish.

"Good night," he said, turning away from her and heading toward the stairs.

"Good night," she answered before closing the door behind him.

Andrew smiled. He still had a long way to go before Robyn Monroe would truly let him into her life, but their relationship had finally taken a step in the right direction.

• • •

"Where the hell did you go?" Jason asked as he climbed into the car. "I was just about to call a cab. Did you seriously just forget about me?"

"I had to go see a patient," Andrew mumbled. He pulled out of the parking lot and began to drive home.

"A patient? In the middle of the night?" Jason shook his head. "Damn. And here I thought you were one of the good guys."

"It's not like that," Andrew quickly said. "It's that pro bono patient I'm treating off the books. I...I just needed to talk to her."

"You mean the Valkyrie?" Jason grinned. "Shit, I wouldn't mind talking to her in the middle of the night. That chick is really damn hot."

"I thought you were into Cassandra."

"Yeah, but that doesn't make me blind." He raised his eyebrows. "Does that bother you?"

"Of course not," Andrew lied. "She's just a patient."

Jason laughed. "That's bullshit, and you know it. Seriously, just ask her out already."

"I can't. She's a patient. I could lose my license."

"But is she really a patient, though? I mean, everything you do for her is off the books. Technically, she's just a person you've been spending time with who tends to get hurt a lot."

"I guess that's one way of seeing it. I don't think the medical board would agree. Besides, I'm not interested in her. Not in that way."

Jason gave him a skeptical look.

"Okay, so maybe I care about her a bit more than I should, but that doesn't mean I'm going to start hitting on her. She doesn't need a boyfriend right now—she needs a doctor. Someone she can trust. I'm going to be that person for her."

"You think you can do that? Keep your hands off her?"

"Of course I can. I'm not an animal." At least he hoped he could. He'd been dangerously close to losing all control back there in the staircase. He didn't even want to think about what would have happened if that motorcycle hadn't interrupted them.

"What about you, then?" he asked, glancing at Jason. "How did it go with Cassandra?"

"She gave me some new information about the case I've been working on. That woman knows *everything*." He leaned back against the seat and sighed. "I think I'm going to need your help with this."

"With what?"

"My case. I've been working on the corruption in Chrystal Valley for a while, and it runs so much deeper than I first thought. There's a man who runs the whole underworld of this city like a damn mafia boss. He's the one who arranges almost all the independent fights around here, and he's an important name in the tournament. It all just keeps getting uglier. People who mess with his bets get beaten up or disappear. Fighters who try to get out of the fighting world end up severely injured or *dead*.

"The worst thing is that he never does his dirty work himself—he convinces kids to do it for him. He takes them in, gives them shelter, and then manipulates them into doing all sorts of despicable things for him. I need to take him down, and I could really use your help. You have a personal stake in this, now. The Valkyrie...*Robyn* will always be in danger as long as this guy runs free."

Andrew swallowed hard, remembering the night he and Robyn had been ambushed outside the café.

Jason clenched his jaw. "He's already made a move on her, hasn't he? When?"

"She was attacked by a handful of men a while ago. They said her odds were too good or something like that. She took all of them down." Andrew felt strangely proud of his little fighter.

Your little fighter? commented an unwelcome voice in his head. He ignored it.

"I'm not surprised," Jason said. "She's vicious, that woman. She can hold her own. Others don't have that luxury, though, and that's why I need your help. I need you to keep an eye out at the hospital for possible gang-related injuries. This guy is powerful, and I need all the evidence I can get. Are you in?"

"Of course I'm in," Andrew said with a determined nod.

A look of relief swept over Jason's face. "Thanks. I knew I could count on you."

"What's his name?" Andrew asked. "The guy we're bringing down?"

Jason's eyes hardened. "Swanson. His name is Richard Swanson."

CHAPTER SEVEN

One week later, someone rang Andrew's doorbell. He closed his laptop, muttering to himself as he went to open the door.

"Robyn? What's up?" He stared at his unexpected visitor. She was standing on his doorstep with two big plastic bags in her hands.

It was the day of her first tournament fight, and he wasn't supposed to pick her up until later. He had no idea why she was there, but judging by her flushed cheeks and the deep wrinkle between her eyebrows, it had to be important.

"I need a favor," she mumbled, her eyes fixed on the snow-covered ground. The first snowfall of the season had just arrived, turning Chrystal Valley into a picturesque winter wonderland.

"Sure. Anything." He hoped he wouldn't regret his words. He had no idea what could possibly make Robyn so desperate she'd actually ask for help.

"Are you allergic to cats?"

"Not that I know of."

Robyn put the bags down and pulled the hood of her sweater off her head. On her shoulder, pressed snugly against her neck, was a small black cat.

"His name is Tiny. At least that's what I call him. He kind of moved into my backyard a couple of months ago. I can't keep him in the apartment because my landlord's a bitch, and now it's getting way too cold for him to live outside. I can't find his owner, and now it's snowing and I don't know what to do." She bit her lip, scratching the cat's ear. "Could he stay here for a while? It would only be temporary, and I'd take care of everything, I promise. I just don't want him to freeze to death." She swallowed hard and finally met his eyes. "Please?"

"I have no idea how to take care of a cat. I've never had a pet." He tentatively reached out his hand, but the cat ducked into Robyn's red locks.

"You won't even notice he's there. All I need is a warm place for him to stay." She dragged the cat out of its hiding place, pulling out a few strands of her hair in the process.

He thought about it for a few moments. "All right. I rarely use the guest bathroom, so I guess you could set him up in there."

"Thank you." She gave him one of her rare smiles before placing the cat in his arms. Andrew and Tiny stared at each other, the cat looking just as surprised as he felt.

Robyn picked up her bags and pushed past him, kicking off her shoes on the way in. She headed straight to the guest room and into the bathroom, where she began to unpack the bags.

Andrew watched as she redecorated the bathroom, still holding the slightly unwilling cat in his arms. "Did you buy the whole pet store?"

"Just the necessities. I had some money left over from my last fight. No big deal."

Just the necessities my ass. He could see why the cat would need a litter box and bowls for food and water, but he failed to see the absolute necessity of all the cat toys that were now spread out over the bathroom floor. Robyn refused to spend money on an ambulance ride to save her own life, but she didn't seem to have a problem with buying expensive toys for a stray cat. He shook his head. Every time he thought he'd figured her out, she did something even more unexpected.

Robyn took the cat from him and put it on a pillow next to the bathtub. Tiny kneaded the pillow with his claws, purring loudly.

"I told you I'd find you a home." She gave Tiny a warm smile.

Andrew watched the two interact and couldn't help but smile, too. He rarely got to see that expression on her. Compared to the Valkyrie's savage grin, her real smile was much gentler and more serene. He definitely preferred the real one.

"I need to get some work done on my computer, but you can stay if you want," he said.

Robyn glanced at her watch. "Sure. You were supposed to pick me up in an hour anyway. I still have to get some preparations done before the fight, though." She gave Tiny a final pat on the head and got up from the floor. "Thanks again for doing this."

"As long as you're the one taking care of him, it shouldn't be a problem at all."

She gave him a short smile and left the guest room.

The cat jumped up on the bed and began to lick its paws. Andrew carefully sat down next to it.

"So I guess we're roomies, now," he said. The cat only glared at him.

Andrew wasn't sure how he felt about suddenly having a pet, but if it meant Robyn would come over to his house more often, it was definitely worth it.

You really are a manipulative asshole, his inner critic commented. Andrew had nothing to say in his defense.

He left the guest room and found Robyn standing in the other bathroom with a pair of scissors in her hand. She combed through her wavy locks with her fingers and raised the scissors.

"What are you doing?" He hurried to her side. "You're not going to cut it off, are you?"

"I have to do something about it." She stared at her reflection in the mirror over the sink with a sad look in her eyes. "It's too easy to grab like this."

"You don't have to cut it off. Do you have a hair tie?"

She nodded and handed him a hair tie from her wrist. He took it and gently turned her around.

"Remember when you asked me how I got through high school?" he asked, combing through her hair with his fingers before gathering it in a ponytail. He divided it into two sections and twisted them, creating a simple twist braid. "I used to only hang out with girls. I think they all thought I was gay."

"Are you?" She leaned into his touch, humming softly.

"No." He wrapped the braid around the ponytail and secured it with the hair tie. The whole procedure took him less than a minute. His hands still remembered the movements, even though he hadn't done a girl's hair in years.

He let his hands wander from her hair down to her shoulders. His eyes lingered on her slender neck, no longer covered by her messy red locks. What would it feel like to press his lips against that pale skin? He really wanted to know.

Stop it. He tore his hands away from her. *You're not an animal.*

"Wow, thanks." Robyn twirled in front of the mirror, seemingly clueless to his reaction. "Mom used to put my hair up like this. I never learned how to do it myself."

"No problem," he said. *She has no idea what she does to me.*

She pushed past him and returned to the hallway. He watched as she rummaged through her backpack, making sure she had everything she needed for the fight. He swallowed hard. In only a couple of hours, he was going to have to watch her take a beating on stage. Judging by the times he'd had to patch her up before, it didn't matter if she won or lost—somehow, she always got injured anyway. *That's where I come in*, he thought, trying to calm himself. *If she gets hurt, I'll fix her.*

His rational thoughts didn't help him at all. He knew all too well there were things even he couldn't fix.

• • •

They arrived at Chrystal Arena a little after eight. The first-class fight didn't start until nine, but Robyn wanted to be there earlier to warm up. They got past the pizzeria façade, went down the stairs, and joined the people who had already gathered around the ring. If Andrew remembered correctly, the third-class fight was currently taking place in the cage. The fighters in the ring were clearly not as skilled as the first-class fighters he'd seen last week, and the fight wasn't quite as brutal, either. He sighed. Why did Robyn have to be a first-class fighter?

"There's a door next to the bar leading backstage," Robyn yelled in his ear. She grabbed his arm and made her way through the crowd, pulling him with her. Andrew tried not to bump into people, but his larger frame made it hard for him to follow in Robyn's footsteps. He automatically muttered "sorry" every time he walked into someone, but no one seemed to notice it. They were all focused on the fight and whatever alcoholic beverage they were drinking.

Robyn came to a stop next to the bar. The music was quieter there, and Andrew could almost hear his own thoughts again. This was the third time he'd visited a fighting arena, but he still didn't feel comfortable in the environment. He recognized some of the people from the last fight, and he knew Jason had to be somewhere nearby. The thin, white-haired woman was sitting in the same spot as last week, and her guardian was leaning against the wall beside her. Robyn walked over and tapped Cassandra on the shoulder.

"How do the odds look today?" she asked.

Cassandra took a few moments to consider, eyeing Robyn from head to toe. "If he doesn't get a good grip on you, you'll win."

Robyn nodded and turned back to Andrew. "See? I've got this."

Andrew wasn't convinced. He glanced at Cassandra. Something was different about her tonight. He couldn't put his finger on what it was, but she seemed...*colder*.

Cassandra's guardian took a step forward. "Valkyrie."

"Drake?"

Wait, what? Andrew turned to Robyn in confusion. *She knows him?*

Drake tried to grab her arm, but she quickly took a step back.

"What are you doing here?" she demanded. "You've been gone for three years! Why did you..." She hesitated. "What happened to you?"

Drake ignored her questions, a smirk playing on his lips. "You're still looking good, Valkyrie."

He looked at Robyn from head to toe just like Cassandra had, but he had a completely different expression in his eyes—an I-know-what-you-look-like-naked kind of look.

Andrew instinctively took a step closer to Robyn and put his arm around her waist. "We should go."

She nodded. After giving Drake a final glare, she allowed Andrew to lead her away from the bar. They joined the thick crowd again, heading toward the big door on the other side of the bar.

"How do you two know each other? You and that guy?" he asked, his hand still resting on her hip. He had no right to keep it there, he knew that—but he still didn't remove it.

"We used to be together," she replied. "Long ago. *Very* long ago."

"*Together* together?"

"Yeah."

"He has to be a lot older than you." Andrew didn't like this new revelation at all. *He* has *seen her naked.* "Isn't he nearly thirty?"

She cocked an eyebrow. "So are you."

"I'm twenty-seven!" he exclaimed, even though she was right.

When they reached the door leading to the backstage area, a chubby, thin-haired man who seemed to be acting as some sort of doorman stopped them.

"The Valkyrie," Robyn said. "Plus one."

"This ain't a fucking VIP event. You can't just bring a plus one," the man barked.

"Call it whatever you like—he comes too." She gave the doorman one of her trademark death glares.

"It's all right, I can wait outside," Andrew reluctantly said. "It's not like I'm of any help until after the fight anyway. Or is it that you don't want to be alone...?"

He heard his mistake the moment the words left his mouth. This was the absolute worst possible occasion to insult her pride. She spun around, giving *him* the death glare instead.

"I don't need anyone to hold my hand, if that's what you're implying," she snapped and hurried through the door without him.

"That's not what I meant, and you know it!" Andrew yelled after her. The door closed behind her and remained shut.

He dejectedly joined the crowd again. Even though he understood why she acted the way she did, her knee-jerk reaction of shutting people out could still be pretty damn frustrating.

His eyes scanned the audience. Jason was already standing with Cassandra and Drake by the bar. Cassandra looked warmer again with Jason by her side. Andrew considered joining them but decided he wasn't in the mood to be around Robyn's ex-lover. Instead, he leaned against the wall and waited for the clock to strike nine.

Ten minutes before the fight was supposed to begin, a person with red hair hurried past him holding a man's hand. At first he thought it was Robyn, but then he realized the woman in front of him was several inches too short, despite her high heels.

"Lucy?" he called out.

The girl turned around. "Andrew? What are you doing here?"

"The same as you, I presume," he said with a humorless grin.

Lucy tried to smile, but it never reached her eyes. Hand in hand with her was a giant in a beige trench coat. *This has to be Mike, the reckless fiancé.* Andrew had always considered himself relatively tall at six-foot-one, but Lucy's fiancé made him feel small.

"Does she have a chance of winning this?" Lucy asked, fiddling nervously with her braid.

"I don't know," Andrew said. "I hope so."

Together, they moved closer to the ring to get a better view. The reckless fiancé turned out to be pretty handy in a crowd—he had to be almost six and a half feet tall. When he walked, people moved out of the way. They came to a stop near the fence that separated the elevated platform from the rest of the arena.

Lucy took Andrew's hand in hers. "You're just as nervous as I am, aren't you?"

"Yeah."

There was nothing more he could do to help Robyn now, and he hated it. He hated being useless like this.

The doors at the ends of the illuminated passageways opened. The fighters stepped through the doors and began to walk down the stairs toward the ring. Andrew knew he should be focusing on the opponent, but he couldn't tear his eyes away from Robyn. She was wearing a sports bra and sweatpants, and her hands were wrapped in white gauze. Her nervousness seemed to be gone. She walked confidently down the runway, the spotlights lighting up every scar and imperfection marring her skin. Her hair shined brightly in the strong light, looking almost like it was on fire. Andrew swallowed hard. She was stunning.

"Please don't get hurt, please don't get hurt, please don't get hurt," Lucy chanted, squeezing his hand.

"She'll be fine." Andrew faked a smile. "She's good at this, right?"

Lucy nodded. "She's just really good at getting injured, too."

CHAPTER EIGHT

When the door to the backstage area slammed shut behind her, Robyn already regretted her outburst. Why did she always have to do things like this? Andrew had made a comment—a well-intentioned comment—and she'd overreacted. Again. It was just a matter of time before he gave up on her. She was a difficult person to be around, and sooner or later, everyone always gave up on her.

She shuddered. Seeing Drake after all these years had caught her completely off guard. Their relationship hadn't been perfect, but it hadn't been all that bad, either. She still had no idea why he'd left her. One day, he'd just disappeared. He hadn't even had the decency to break up with her first. If he thought she'd take him back after three years of complete silence, he was dead wrong.

The corridor was empty of people, the only exception being a familiar man in a long, gray coat. Swanson slowly approached her, leaning heavily on his cane.

"There you are." He gave her a cold smile that didn't reach his eyes. "Good evening, dear. Lovely night for a game, isn't it?"

Robyn nodded. His emotionless eyes made Andrew's words repeat themselves in the back of her mind. Would Swanson really tell her if she'd repaid her debts? A small seed of doubt had taken root in her mind, and it just wouldn't leave her alone. She'd always thought fighting for him was her only way of getting a normal life one day. What if that wasn't true? There was only one way to find out.

"I need to ask you something," she finally said. "I…"

He gave her a disapproving look, and her courage disappeared in an instant. She couldn't ask him something like that. It was too disrespectful. He'd helped her get custody of Lucy. For that, she owed him more than just money. She owed him everything.

"Is there anything I should know about my opponent?" she asked instead. "Strengths? Weaknesses?"

"The odds are in your favor." He patted her on the shoulder. "You don't have to worry. Just do your thing."

How helpful. She sighed. Swanson rarely gave her any important information when he thought she'd win. To keep her underdog status, he wanted her fights to be as even as possible. She was glad she'd taken the time to talk to Cassandra, who'd at least had something constructive to say.

"I need to get changed so I can warm up," she told him. "Is there a locker room somewhere?"

"Right around the corner. I need to make a few…arrangements, but I believe I can trust you to meet me here five minutes before the game starts. Right, dear?"

"Of course."

Swanson smiled, patted her on the shoulder again, and disappeared through the door. Robyn continued deeper into the backstage area. Compared to the pizzeria front and the actual arena, the backstage area with its cement floor, plywood walls, and total lack of furniture looked only half finished. The locker room was in the same unfinished state.

She dumped her backpack, hoodie, and tank top in one of the lockers and returned to the corridor outside. According to her watch, she had thirty minutes until Swanson returned. She didn't need that much time to warm up, but a long run would help calm her nerves.

She picked a slow pace and began to run through the narrow corridor, following its many twists and turns. When she reached a dead end, she turned around and ran back the way she came. It was a short track, but it would have to do.

Twenty-five minutes and dozens of laps later, Robyn stepped inside the locker room to make her final preparations. She stretched, removed her watch and shoes, wrapped her hands in gauze, and tried not to think about how much nicer everything would have been if Andrew had been there with her.

She put her things back in the locker and slammed the door shut. If Andrew were there, he would probably just have been whining about how dangerous fighting was. Or about her weight. Again. She absentmindedly touched her hair, still firmly pinned to the top of her head. She remembered the way Andrew's gentle hands had worked with it, and the way they'd lingered on her shoulders afterward. The warmth of his fingertips had made her heart pound in a way it definitely shouldn't have.

"I do *not* want him here," she muttered to herself, hoping that saying it out loud would make it sound more convincing. It didn't.

She met up with Swanson outside the locker room right on time. They climbed a flight of stairs and came to a stop in front of one of the many doors in the corridor.

"Good luck, dear," Swanson said. "Do your best, and don't tap out."

Robyn nodded and gave him a polite smile. She could hear pounding music coming from the other side of the door. Her stage fright hit her in the gut like a sledgehammer.

"I have to admit I'm a little disappointed in you, Ms. Monroe."

She turned back to Swanson, her heart sinking. "Why?"

"I thought you were better at following orders."

Shit. The parking lot fight. He'd found out.

"I don't take orders from kids," she said in a low voice.

"But you do take orders from me."

She bit her lip. "So I should have just let them beat me up?"

"Yes."

She glanced up at him. His eyes were colder than ever. She would always respect him because of what he'd done for Lucy, but that didn't make her less terrified of him.

"I only want what's best for you," he continued. "You're an investment. I always have your best interest in mind. You can trust me. You know that, right?"

Like hell I can. She nodded anyway.

The door opened, and Swanson gave her an encouraging shove. By placing one foot in front of the other, she managed to walk down the stairs leading to the ring. People in the audience were probably already making remarks about her size and gender, but she refused to let it get to her. Valkyries didn't care about audiences. Valkyries didn't get stage fright. She was the Valkyrie, and she wasn't afraid of anything.

She stepped inside the octagon-shaped ring and finally got a first look at her opponent. He was about her height but had to be at least twice as heavy. His body was more stocky than athletic, with a lot of muscle hidden beneath the fat. He had short black hair, a black beard, and his naked torso was covered in body hair thick enough to qualify as fur. It was obvious why people called him the Bear.

"You've gotta be kidding me." The Bear looked at her from head to toe, raising his eyebrows. "Don't blame me if I break you in half."

Robyn smirked. She liked when they underestimated her. It only made things easier.

The referee entered the ring. "Okay, let's get this thing started. No eye clawing. No hits below the belt. A clean fight, all right? Obey my commands at all times. Defend yourselves at all times. Let's do this."

The referee backed away from the fighters. Robyn and the Bear stared at each other, waiting for the bell to ring. He was definitely stronger than her, but she had to be faster. No one that heavy could keep up with her. She tried to figure out his main fighting technique from his stance but didn't see any obvious trademarks. According to Cassandra, the Bear had dangerous grips. Wrestler, maybe?

The bell rang. The Bear lunged for her, but she easily dodged his arms. She grinned. Oh yes, she was definitely faster. All she had to do was get him tired and then knock him out. No problem.

For three full minutes, she did nothing offensive whatsoever. She still hadn't figured out what technique her opponent was using, but she wasn't worried. The audience was on her side, cheering with excitement every time she dodged the Bear's attacks. Her rhythm was flawless, and the Bear never even touched her.

It didn't take long before the Bear was gasping for air. The parts of his face that weren't covered by his beard were flushed red, and his movements were getting sloppy. Her plan was working. It was time to make a move.

She waited until the Bear lunged for her again, then dodged the attack and spun around to kick him in the chin. It was a textbook-perfect kick, and it *should* have knocked him off his feet. It didn't. Instead of plummeting to the ground, the Bear stubbornly remained standing. Robyn, on the other hand, felt a sharp, pulsating pain spread through her foot. Her eyes widened. Were his bones made of cement or something?

The Bear grabbed her ankle and dragged her closer. She stumbled toward him. This was bad. Really, really bad. Before she could pull back, he'd wrapped his left arm around her neck, locking her in a chokehold.

She struggled against his arm, trying to free herself. This was exactly what was *not* supposed to happen. She burrowed her nails deep in the Bear's arm. The pain was already taking over her mind and clouding her vision. She couldn't think. Her brain was too focused on getting air.

"Just tap out, you crazy bitch," the Bear grunted.

His words cleared her mind for a moment. *The Valkyrie never taps out.* She jutted her hip out and bent over, pulling the Bear over her shoulder in one final act of strength. He lost his grip on her neck and landed hard on his back. She followed him down and wrapped her legs around his neck in a triangle choke. The Bear flailed wildly with his arms and legs, trying to free himself by hitting her wherever he could reach. His punches hurt like hell, but she refused to let go. She only had to hold out for a few more seconds. Just a few more seconds.

Eight seconds later, the Bear slammed his hand down on the mat twice to admit his defeat. It was over. She'd won. She released him and stood up, clearing her throat. Chokeholds always hurt. She glanced at the referee, who nodded and gave a sign to the commentator.

"The Bear is out," the commentator yelled to the audience. "I repeat, the Bear is out! Let's greet tonight's first-class champion: the Valkyrie!"

Robyn left the ring as the Bear's manager entered with a medical team. Swanson was waiting for her right outside the cage.

"Well done, dear," he said and patted her on the cheek. "I knew you could do it."

She gave him a quick smile and made her way toward one of the passageways. Her stage fright was kicking in again. She quickly hurried up the stairs and back through the backstage area to get to the locker room. The silence was a blessing to her nerves. She put on her hoodie and tried to put on her shoes, but the foot she'd used to kick the Bear was too swollen to fit in her sneaker.

"Great," she muttered, putting the shoes back in her backpack. "Andrew is going to freak out."

• • •

Andrew was on her the moment she left the backstage area.

"Are you having difficulty breathing?" He tilted her chin up to check her throat. "Are you coughing? Are there any changes in your voice? Say something."

"Hi?" Robyn said hesitantly, a little worried about the wild look in his eyes.

"Good. Your voice is fine. That's good. Did you black out?" His hands wandered from her chin to her neck, where he continued to examine her spine.

"No. It was just a simple chokehold. Shit, Andrew, calm down."

"He *strangled* you! Do you know how sensitive the human throat is?"

Robyn flicked him on the forehead. "I'm fine. You have to calm down."

Andrew took a deep breath, and the panic in his eyes faded a little. Then his gaze fell on her shoeless feet. "You're not walking on that foot before I've checked it out." He reached out his arms with the obvious intent to pick her up.

"You're *not* carrying me," she snapped, taking a step back. "My future opponents are somewhere in here. I can't show any signs of weakness. I have to walk out of here on my own."

Before Andrew could protest, she'd already hurried past him into the crowd. She pulled the hood of her sweater over her head again, but considering the highly intoxicated state of the audience, they probably wouldn't have recognized her without it either. Their night had only just begun, and most of them were now focusing on getting as drunk as possible as fast as possible.

She had to stop for a short break once they entered the staircase leading up to the pizzeria. Her rush of adrenaline was coming to an end, and the pain in her foot kept getting worse.

Andrew looked at her with both worry and annoyance in his eyes. "Robyn—"

"I'm fine." She slowly began to walk up the stairs.

"Robyn. As your physician, I am now ordering you not to walk on that foot. No one's here but us. Drop the act, okay? I know you're in pain. You don't have to pretend when you're with me."

She turned around, glaring at him. "I said I'm—"

"No, you're not fine," he interrupted. "You can either jump onto my back, or I'm throwing you over my shoulder. You pick one. Either way, you're not taking another step with that damn foot."

They glared at each other. Robyn got the sudden impulse to take a step just to piss him off, but the look on his face made her reconsider.

"Fine," she finally muttered when he moved toward her. "On the back, you blackmailing piece of shit."

Andrew turned around to let her climb onto his back, but not until she'd caught the triumphant grin playing on his lips.

"Why do we always end up like this?" She reluctantly wrapped her arms around his neck. "I think this is the third, maybe fourth time you've carried me."

"You're the one who keeps getting hurt," he said sourly. "I'm just doing what I can to help you. I can't carry your responsibilities, but I can carry you."

"Really?" She couldn't stop herself from laughing. "You're dropping *Lord of the Rings* quotes in the middle of a serious conversation?"

His earlobes flushed red. "It's a good quote."

"Yes, but you're still a dork."

Robyn leaned down to rest her head in the crook of his neck. Beneath the lingering smell of sweat and booze, she could still sense Andrew's usual scent of Earl Grey. She took a deep breath, feeling calmer already.

He carried her through the pizzeria and the parking lot, refusing to let her down until they'd reached his car.

"Sit. I've got a first-aid kit in the trunk." He opened the door to the backseat. Robyn rolled her eyes but did as he said.

"It's just a little sprain." She said it even though she knew it wouldn't make a difference. Andrew had gone straight into doctor mode and would continue to take care of her until he was sure she was okay. It was kind of sweet and kind of infuriating at the same time. She sighed. The only way to make him stop pestering her was to let him do his thing.

He kneeled on the ground next to the car and gently grabbed her foot. "You're right," he said after carefully examining it. "It's just a sprain. I still need to put a compression on it to stop the swelling, though. I'm a bit worried about post-strangulation injuries… Could you stay over at my place tonight?"

The blood rushed to her face. "What?"

"Just so I can keep an eye on your injuries. You'd stay in the guest room, of course." He scratched the back of his head, looking a bit flustered. "I just want to make sure you're okay."

"I see." Her cheeks grew even hotter. *Get your mind out of the gutter, Robyn.* "I guess that's okay. I don't like to be in the apartment when Lucy isn't there anyway."

Andrew began to wrap her foot and ankle in an elastic bandage. "Is she moving out?"

"I don't know. I haven't spoken with her since our fight last week." She fixed her eyes on the ground. "I get why she's angry with me, and I don't blame her if she hates me right now. I just wish she'd pick up the phone so I'd know she's okay."

"I talked to her today in the arena," he said. "She seemed to be doing all right."

"What? Lucy's here?" Her body tensed up so suddenly she almost kicked him in the face. She tried to get out of the car, but he blocked her way.

"Be still," he grunted.

"I have to see her. Move, damn it!" She pulled her foot out of his grip.

"She's not here anymore! She left with her fiancé right after the fight ended. Sit down and let me do my job!"

She bit her lip, forcing her body to relax. Lucy had been there. Lucy had actually been there. "Did she say something? About the fight we had? About anything?"

"Not really. She didn't seem angry, though, and she definitely didn't seem to hate you. She was worried, just like me."

Robyn nodded. "That's…that's good. Maybe she'll come home soon." She was glad Andrew was concentrating on her foot, because she really didn't want anyone to see the tears of relief in her eyes. Not even him.

"You don't have to pretend when you're with me." Easier said than done. She'd had to be strong for Lucy all her life, and that strength had become a part of her identity. She wasn't sure if she had it in her to show weakness anymore.

But then again, she had let him carry her. That had to count for something.

Andrew was still kneeling on the snow-covered ground, probably ruining his gray slacks permanently. He didn't even seem to notice the snow. Robyn smiled. She wasn't sure if she would ever be able to tear down the impenetrable walls she'd built around herself, but for his sake, she was willing to try. She owed him at least that much.

Please don't give up on me.

CHAPTER NINE

"I'm fine. I really am," Robyn said, yawning widely.

"Of course you are." Andrew focused on the road, fighting to keep his emotions under control.

"Technically, he didn't strangle me. He choked me. There's a difference," she said, as if she could sense his anger.

The image of the Bear's hairy, sweaty arm wrapped around Robyn's neck flashed before Andrew's eyes again. "Not from a medical point of view." He clenched his jaw. He'd given an oath to never harm another person, but for that man, he'd been willing to make an exception.

"Are you mad at me?"

He glanced at her, surprised by the insecurity in her voice. She chewed on her lip, her eyes fixed on her hands in her lap.

"No, of course not," he lied. It wasn't fair, but he *was* mad at her. She kept putting herself in situations like this, where he had to watch her get injured by men twice her size without being able to help her. A part of him was constantly angry with her because of that.

"Does this happen after all your fights?" he asked, changing the topic. "Do you always get this tired?"

"Yeah." She yawned again. "It's embarrassing."

He shook his head. *It's adorable.* She closed her eyes again, and he felt his anger fade away. Robyn had strange ways of showing trust, and her falling asleep right next to him was one of them. He found it oddly flattering.

When they reached his house, Robyn was fast asleep. Andrew gently scooped her up and carried her inside. Once again, he marveled over how light she was. Being able to carry her around like this was convenient and weirdly satisfying, but from a medical point of view, she could definitely use some extra pounds.

"I should shower. I'm sweaty and disgusting," she mumbled when he placed her on the guest-room bed. Tiny jumped up next to her and rubbed his head against her shoulder.

"It's okay. You can shower in the morning." Andrew smiled. "There are clean towels in the bathroom. I'll hang one of my shirts in there, in case you want something clean to wear tomorrow. Go to sleep."

She nodded. When he returned with the shirt, she was already snoring. The cat had curled up next to her, purring contentedly. They looked completely at home.

"Good night." He stroked her messy bangs away from her eyes. She'd let her hair out again, and her red locks were all over the place as usual. She sighed in her sleep, her lips almost forming a smile. Moments like this, he had a hard time understanding how she could be so incredibly dangerous in her waking state.

The relief hit him all at once. She was fine. She was actually fine. He'd watched her go up against a man twice her size, and she was *fine*.

Before he could stop himself, he'd leaned down and pressed a soft kiss to her forehead. His eyes lingered on her face—her long eyelashes, that cute little nose, her lips…

Andrew quickly backed away from the bed.

She's a patient, you unprofessional disgrace of a doctor.

"Shut up," he muttered, but his inner critic was right. Though the relationship between him and Robyn had evolved into something…*different,* it had started out as a relationship between a doctor and a patient. What he was doing—whatever that may be—was wrong on so many levels. He hung the shirt on the bathroom door and left the room without looking back.

• • •

When Robyn opened the door to the apartment, she knew something was wrong. She wasn't sure how she knew it—she just knew.

"Mom?" She dropped her backpack on the floor. "You haven't forgotten about Lucy's parent-teacher conference tonight, right? You promised her you'd go."

The apartment remained silent.

"Mom?"

The living room was empty, and so were both of the bedrooms. An empty glass sat on the coffee table, and next to it was an empty bottle of wine. Nothing out of the ordinary—yet Robyn's heart was pounding in her chest. Something was wrong. Terribly, irrevocably wrong.

With shaking hands, she touched the handle of the bathroom door. "Mom?"

Robyn woke up screaming. She quickly clamped her hands over her mouth, muffling her voice. It wasn't the first time she had that nightmare, and she knew it wouldn't be the last. Every time she slept for longer than six hours straight she seemed to end up in that dream, revisiting the death of her mother. How could she have forgotten to set her alarm? She crossed her arms, trying to make her body stop trembling.

"Robyn? Robyn, what's wrong?"

Fuck. Andrew entered the room with a wild look in his eyes, wearing a long, blue bathrobe and glasses with thick, black frames.

"Nothing." She hid her shaking hands under the blanket. "Just a nightmare."

Andrew's gaze followed the motion, the worry turning into pity. He took a step forward.

"If you try to hug me again, I swear I'll break that perfect face of yours."

He stopped in his tracks, furrowing his brow. Then he grinned. "Perfect face?"

Her eyes widened as she realized her slip. Her cheeks burned. "Shut up. I just woke up. I can't be held accountable for anything I say."

He shrugged, looking annoyingly smug. "Whatever you say. Would you like some Chinese leftovers for breakfast?"

Her stomach growled at the mere thought of food. When was the last time she ate? She couldn't remember. "That sounds great, actually."

Andrew nodded, smiled, and left the room.

She burrowed her face in her hands and groaned. *Perfect face.* She had to get her shit together.

After a quick shower, she put on Andrew's shirt and headed toward the kitchen. The smell of deep-fried whatever-it-was made her mouth water, and the growling in her stomach got even louder.

Robyn knew she should be eating more, especially with the tournament going on. Every time she got stressed out about something, she forgot to eat at regular times. Lucy was still staying at her fiancé's, and Robyn was beginning to worry she'd never come back home. Lucy being away had caused Robyn's already lousy eating habits—she was a horrible cook—to become even worse. She'd survived on sandwiches and scrambled eggs all week.

When she entered the kitchen, Andrew looked up from his cup of tea—and froze. He got a strange look in his eyes as he took her in, especially when his gaze reached her bare legs. She fidgeted with the hem of his shirt. The shirt was way too big for her and reached halfway down her thighs. She'd thought it was covering enough to be worn without pants, but judging by the look in Andrew's eyes, she'd been wrong.

Her cheeks burned, but she refused to give in to the urge to go and put on a pair of sweatpants. A part of her really, *really* enjoyed seeing Andrew react like this.

"Shit." He closed his eyes and took a deep breath. When he opened his eyes again, the weird look was gone. "Sit. I want to check your injuries."

She rolled her eyes but did as he said, taking a seat in one of the kitchen chairs. "I'm fine."

"You say those words so often they're starting to lose their meaning." He tenderly moved her still wet hair away from her neck. His eyes darkened when he looked at the bruises, but his hands remained gentle. After he'd checked her neck, he kneeled on the floor to take a look at her foot. It hurt a little when he removed the bandage, but most of the swelling had already gone down.

He gave her a relieved smile. "You're going to be fine."

"Told you so."

"Well, you're not exactly trustworthy when it comes to this." He scanned her from head to toe. It was nothing like the look he'd given her when she'd entered the kitchen—this time, it was Dr. Alexander who was observing her, not Andrew. Robyn couldn't help but feel a little disappointed.

"You've lost weight."

Oh, crap. "No, I haven't," she lied.

Andrew cocked an eyebrow. She crossed her arms, her cheeks heating up again.

"It's rude to comment on other people's weight," she finally said. "It's none of your business."

He stood up and crossed his arms, matching her pose. "I'm your doctor. That makes it my business."

"Says who?"

"Says me."

They glared at each other for a moment. Robyn tried to make her stare as menacing as possible, but it didn't seem to affect Andrew at all.

"Were you always this annoying?" she said with a sigh.

He grinned. "You bring out the worst in me."

Andrew took the cartons of leftovers from the microwave and placed them on the table. She eyed them curiously. Fried shrimp and spring rolls. Perfect.

Before they could start eating, a loud howl came from the guest room.

"Tiny?" Robyn got up from her chair and ran to the guest room. Tiny was sitting on the windowsill, staring out the window with longing in his eyes. He scratched on the glass and let out another heartrending whine.

"I'm sorry," she said and picked him up in her arms. "You're going to have to be an indoor cat for a while, okay?"

Tiny howled again.

"I know, it sucks, but that's how it is. Calm down, Tiny. Just calm down." She hummed softly to the cat, slowly stroking his fur. She'd always comforted Lucy like this back when they were kids, and somehow, it seemed to work on the cat too. After a while, Tiny stopped struggling and began to purr. She smiled.

"See? That wasn't too bad, was it?" She carefully put the cat down on the bed. When she turned around, she noticed Andrew standing in the doorway. Surprisingly enough, he didn't seem to think she was silly. In fact, he actually looked kind of impressed.

"You weren't supposed to see that," she muttered.

"I'm glad I did." He gave her a warm smile. "You're amazing, you know that?"

She blushed. "I just wanted him to stop howling."

Something beeped in her backpack. When she pulled out her cell, she found a new text from Lucy.

"Lucy's back!" she exclaimed. "I have to go. I have to get home." She put on her sweatpants, grabbed her backpack, and ran to the hallway.

"Hey, be careful," he yelled after her. "You'll make your foot worse."

"It's just a sprain," she yelled back. "I'll wash the shirt. Thanks for letting me stay here."

"Slow down." He followed her into the hallway. "At least let me drive you home."

"Don't be ridiculous. I'll see you later."

Before Andrew could say anything else, she'd already closed the door behind her.

• • •

Andrew found himself all alone in his house again. Had it always been this empty? For a moment, he almost regretted calling Lucy. He wouldn't have minded having Robyn stay a little bit longer.

"Shit," he muttered. He'd told Jason he'd keep his hands off Robyn, but when he'd seen her in his shirt, he'd had a hard time keeping his word. The shirt had been way too big on her, especially over her shoulders. He'd never seen her look so small and delicate before. And then there were her legs. She had the most amazing legs he'd ever seen.

He groaned. She was a patient. He shouldn't want her like this. He couldn't.

A loud howl echoed through the house, reminding Andrew that he was no longer living alone.

"Please don't," he groaned, heading toward the guest room. The cat was sitting on the bed, wailing at the top of his lungs.

"Hi, Tiny," Andrew said, using his best calming doctor voice. "What's the matter this time?"

The cat paused for a moment to give him an angry glare. Then he started howling again.

Andrew sat on the bed next to the cat. "Robyn's not here right now. Let's…let's not do this, okay?"

No reaction. He looked over at Tiny's food and water bowls. They were both half full, so the cat probably wasn't hungry or thirsty. His next attempt was to pat Tiny on the head, but the cat shied away from his hand.

"What do you want?" He sighed as he lay down on the bed. "Robyn isn't here. I wish she was, but she isn't. What the hell do you want from me?" He recalled the way Robyn had calmed him down earlier and groaned. "You're really going to make me do this, aren't you?"

He tried to remember what Robyn had hummed to the cat. He'd recognized the melody, but he hadn't been able to name it.

"This would be a lot easier if you would quiet down a little." He covered his ears with his hands, digging deep into his memories. The song was in there, somewhere.

"Come on," he said, trying to think through the cat's loud wailing. "Come on, come o—"

Then it hit him.

His mom had brought him to the ballet once, and they'd watched Tchaikovsky's *Swan Lake*. Ballet hadn't exactly been his thing, but he still remembered how impressed he'd been of the dancers' graceful movements. Why Robyn had been humming classical, non-vocal music to a cat, he had no idea, but it didn't matter. All he cared about was making the cat calm down.

He began to softly hum the main theme of the ballet. *Please work.*

Tiny's ears twitched. He blinked at Andrew, looking slightly confused. Then, he finally shut up. *Thank you. Thank you, thank you, thank you.*

Tiny stood up on the bed, stretched, and then climbed up onto Andrew's chest.

"Hello, there."

Tiny sent him another glare before settling down, rolling up in a furry little circle.

"Fine, I'll continue," Andrew said with a short laugh. The warm weight on his chest was strangely comforting. Though he'd never really understood the point of pets before, he had to admit that this was pretty nice. He still had to come up with a way to make Robyn stop fighting, but with the cat on his chest, his worry seemed a bit more distant.

"I'm sorry for lashing out like that," he said. "You were just feeling lonely, weren't you?"

Tiny blinked. Andrew carefully reached out his hand. When the cat showed no sign of hostility, he slowly stroked its fur.

"I know that feeling," he mumbled. "She's addictive, isn't she? It's like she fills a craving you didn't even know you had."

He wasn't sure how it had happened, but Robyn was gradually filling the void in his life—and he was getting addicted to it. He was getting addicted to *her*.

"I'll keep her safe," he said, making a promise to both himself and the cat. He'd lost people he cared about before, and he wasn't going to let that happen again. No matter what happened—no matter what he had to do—he wouldn't lose her.

• • •

When Robyn opened the door to her apartment, she was hit by the welcoming smell of pancakes.

"I'm home," she shouted, dumping her backpack on the floor.

"Have you had breakfast yet?" Lucy yelled back from the kitchen.

"Nope." Warmth filled her chest. All she wanted was for things to be normal again, and having breakfast with Lucy was a great start.

She went to the kitchen and sat down at the table. Her sister was standing at the stove, humming a little to herself. Lucy placed the final pancake on a plate and turned around.

"I missed you," she said and put the plate down on the table.

"I missed you, too," Robyn said. "I'm sorry. For everything."

"It's okay." Lucy gave her a genuine smile. "I get it. You don't know Mike, so this is all very sudden for you. But nothing's going to change between us, okay? I'm not moving out yet, and I won't marry him until I'm done studying."

"I don't want to tie you down. If you want to move, I won't stop you." Robyn forced the words out of her mouth. She didn't want to live alone. She wanted to have breakfast with her sister in the morning, and she wanted to fall asleep at night knowing Lucy was only a thin wall away—but not as much as she wanted her sister to be happy.

"Don't be silly. I'm not going anywhere." Lucy's voice took on its authoritative teacher tone, making counterarguments impossible. "Now eat your pancakes. I bet you haven't eaten properly all week."

Robyn rolled her eyes and tried to frown, but her relief wouldn't let her. Everything would go back to normal, after all. *Thank God.*

"What made you decide to come back?" she asked carefully.

"It's your birthday soon. I couldn't miss that, could I?" Lucy smiled. "And besides, Andrew called me this morning. That man can be really convincing when he wants to be."

Robyn smiled back. "Tell me about it."

Turning twenty-three wasn't that big of a deal, but Robyn still looked forward to it. Every year, Lucy gave her the exact same gift, and every year, it was the best gift in the world.

Lucy tilted her head to the side, eyeing her curiously. "I'm not used to seeing you this happy. It's nice." A glimmer of mischievousness flashed in her eyes. "I wonder what caused that change."

"I'm just happy you're home again." It was the truth—or at least a big part of it. She wasn't sure how, but Andrew had managed to bring the person she loved the most back into her life. For the first time in over a week, she could finally relax.

CHAPTER TEN

"Wait, let me get this straight—you have a crush on a damn Eden kid?" Ana asked, raising an eyebrow.

"It's not a crush," Robyn muttered. "It's… Well, I'm not sure what it is, but it's not a crush."

Robyn leaned back on the couch in Ana's tattoo parlor. She'd just filled Ana in on the whole Andrew situation, including the part about him being a former Eden student. The only thing she'd left out was the tournament and her promotion to first class. She knew it wasn't right to hide it from Ana, but she simply didn't want to disappoint her best friend. Or make her angry.

Ana threw her head back and burst out laughing. "Oh, sweetie," she wheezed. "An Eden kid? Your fifteen-year-old self would never have forgiven you for this."

Robyn frowned as Ana lost it again, nearly crying with laughter.

"I didn't plan for this to happen, okay?" She glared at her best friend.

"You and your choice in men. First it's that idiotic fighter guy, and now this." Ana shook her head. "I'm so glad I'm not straight."

"That 'fighter guy' wasn't just a fighter, you know. Drake's actually pretty smart. He used to study law and criminology and stuff." *And then he just disappeared for three years without saying a word.*

Ana rolled her eyes. "Oh, come on. He was a dickhead, and you know it. Otherwise, he wouldn't have taken off like that. Now shut up and let me give you your birthday present."

She grinned widely and grabbed Robyn's wrist. Before Robyn could object, she'd been dragged inside the room with the tattoo equipment.

"You're giving me a tattoo?" Robyn asked, both excited and worried.

"No. Well, yeah, someday I will, but not today. I've got something else for you. Take off your sweater, sit down, and close your eyes."

Robyn did as she was told, even though Ana's mischievous grin freaked her out a little.

"What are you doing?" she asked as Ana rolled up her tank top, baring her stomach. The tattoo chair was tilted back, making her lie flat on her back. She kept her eyes closed, listening carefully to Ana's every move. She could easily keep track of Ana's position in the room thanks to the clicking of her high-heeled boots.

"You'll see," Ana answered. "This is gonna feel a bit cold."

Robyn flinched as Ana wiped her stomach with a damp cloth. "What the hell?" she yelped. She tried to sit up, but Ana pushed her back down again.

"Just trust me, all right? You'll love it, I promise."

"I don't trust anyone," Robyn muttered before closing her eyes again. "Especially not you. You're insane."

Ana laughed. "Fair enough."

Robyn felt her draw something on her stomach, and then something pinched her right above her belly button. *What the hell is she doing?* She forced herself to keep her eyes closed.

"Would you look at that," Ana said a few seconds later. "Damn, I'm good."

Robyn opened her eyes and looked down at her stomach. She blinked, barely believing her eyes. "You can't be serious. Is that real? Is this... Did you just... What the hell, Ana?"

Ana took a step back to admire her work. "I'm expanding the business. I do piercings now, too, and you're my first client. What do you think?"

"You can't just pierce someone without telling them first!" Robyn stared at the silver barbell in her belly button. "What if it gets infected? What if I get stuck in something during a fight?"

"Calm down, would you? It's super easy to take care of, and you can just put some tape over it before the fights." Ana handed Robyn a small brochure from a stack of papers on her desk. "You have the flattest stomach in Chrystal Valley. It would be a crime not to put some bling in it. You have no idea how jealous all the hipsters are gonna be."

Robyn rolled her eyes. She got up from the chair and took a look at herself in the full-length mirror on the wall. The scars were still as ugly as ever, but the silver barbell seemed to move the attention away from them. Well…she didn't hate it. In fact, the piercing made her feel kind of hot.

"Well, look at that—that was definitely a smile." Ana threw her arm around Robyn's shoulders. "I told you you'd like it."

"You were right," Robyn admitted. "You're still insane, though."

"I know." Ana grinned. "And as your only insane friend, I had to make sure you did something insane on your birthday. It would have been easier to give you a bottle of vodka and a night out, but I thought you'd prefer a piercing."

"True." Robyn smiled. "Thanks, Ana."

"You're welcome. Hey, have you opened Lucy's gift yet?"

Robyn nodded.

"Same gift as every year?"

Robyn nodded again, her smile widening.

Ana shook her head. "You're the only person I know who'd get this happy over a pair of shoes. Now get going. I know you want to get home to try them out." She gave Robyn a shove toward the exit. "And hey, maybe you'll get a gift from that Eden kid, too. Maybe he'll even give you a ki—"

"Don't even start." Robyn gave Ana a playful punch in the shoulder. "I'll see you later."

"Hey." Ana grabbed her wrist. She closed her eyes for a moment, and when she opened them again, she looked uncharacteristically serious. "Do you have anything you want to tell me?"

Robyn's eyes widened. *She knows about the tournament. I'm dead.* "No, no, I don't think so, no."

"If you say so." Ana grinned again, but her eyes didn't have their usual glimmer of humor in them. "You know you can talk to me about anything, right?"

"Right." Robyn felt a wave of guilt wash over her, but she still couldn't bring herself to tell Ana about the tournament. She left the tattoo parlor with a bad feeling in her gut. *I'm a horrible friend,* she thought as she jogged home. *I don't deserve a friend like Ana.* Thankfully, her brand-new shoes were waiting for her at home. She would definitely need them to calm down.

• • •

Andrew placed the plastic bag containing Robyn's neatly wrapped birthday gift next to him in the front seat before starting the car. He glanced at it nervously as he drove. Was he crossing a line with this? Maybe. Was he going to give her the damn birthday present anyway? Absolutely.

He'd been at work every time she'd come over to the house to take care of Tiny, and they'd only jogged together once since the tournament fight. The guest room still held her scent, but it wasn't enough. He missed her. Even though he didn't want to admit it to himself, the main reason he'd gotten her a birthday present in the first place had been to have a reason to go and see her.

When he rang the doorbell to the Monroe sisters' apartment, Lucy opened the door.

"Andrew? What are you doing here?" She glanced at the plastic bag in his hand and smiled. "Is that a birthday present for Robyn?"

"Yeah." He scratched the back of his head. "Do you know where she is?"

"She's in the garage." Lucy's smile turned slightly mischievous. "You should go down there. If you're quiet enough, you'll get to see something amazing. She's leaving for work soon, so you have to hurry."

"Yeah, sure." Andrew gave her a quizzical look before heading downstairs. Lucy giggled behind his back.

He hurried down the stairs and carefully opened the door to the underground garage. He could hear music coming from the other side of the room. At first, he didn't recognize the song because of the strange echoes bouncing off the cement walls, but then it hit him. *Swan Lake?* He went around a corner and then stopped, almost dropping his plastic bag on the ground.

The secluded corner of the garage was empty of cars. Instead, there were dumbbells and weights spread out all over the place. An old CD player stood on the ground among the gym equipment, playing one of the pieces from the *Swan Lake* ballet. None of these things caught Andrew's eye for longer than a millisecond. All he could focus on was Robyn.

She was wearing a tank top and sweatpants as usual. On her feet was a pair of pale-pink ballet slippers. She stood on her tiptoes, her body bent in a pose Andrew would have considered impossible if he hadn't seen it with his own eyes. Then, she was off, soaring through the air in a graceful jump. She spun around, landed, and struck another impossible pose on one leg. Every movement was in perfect synchronization with the music, and her messy hair flowed around her head like a fiery halo.

The scene was magical. For a moment, Andrew completely forgot they were in an abandoned garage. It was like he was eleven again, watching a ballet with his mother. He didn't know much about dancing, but to him, Robyn was just as good as those professional dancers he'd seen back then. His eyes followed her every move. It all made sense now. Her dance-like fighting style, her insane cardio, her singing—it was all because of the wonder taking place in front of him. Because she was a ballerina.

Andrew had no idea how long he watched Robyn dance. Time seemed to lose all meaning when her body followed the music so perfectly. He recognized the dance as one of Odette's solo numbers. Robyn's face expressed the emotions portrayed in the music, showing the angst of the heartbroken white swan. She was gorgeous.

The piece's final notes faded into silence, and Robyn came to a stop. She took a deep, shivering breath. Pearls of sweat covered her skin. Her cheeks were flushed red, and she wore a proud smile on her lips. She lowered her heels to the ground. Then she noticed Andrew.

"Shit," she said, wiping the sweat from her forehead. "I didn't know you were there."

"That was amazing," he said. "Absolutely amazing. I… Words can't express how amazing that was, okay?"

"I'm pretty rusty." Her blush deepened in color. "Lucy always gives me a pair of pointe shoes on my birthday. I usually wear them out in less than a year, and pieces like this are impossible without proper shoes. I haven't done *Swan Lake* in almost three months."

Andrew tried to come up with something to say, but he was practically speechless.

"You didn't look rusty to me," he finally blurted out. "You were great. Really, really great."

"Thanks." She gave him a quick smile and crouched on the ground, untying the pink slippers. "What are you even doing here? How did you find me?"

"Lucy told me to come down here," he said. "I came over to give you a birthday present."

Robyn pulled the shoes off her feet and stood up. "You shouldn't have."

"But I did. Happy birthday, Robyn." He smiled and handed her the wrapped box from the bag. She took it in her hands, eyeing it skeptically.

"Fancy," she mumbled, untying the white bow and unwrapping the turquoise paper.

Inside the box was a knife. She picked it up and unfolded the blade from the handle. Andrew eyed her carefully, waiting for her reaction.

"It's beautiful," she said, unfolding and folding the blade again.

"I know it's just a pocketknife, but I would feel a lot better if you brought it to your tournament fights," he said. "There are a lot of dangerous people over there. I know you're a great fighter, but I still think you should have a weapon of some sort."

She gave him a warm, genuine smile. "Thank you. I appreciate it."

"You're welcome." He cleared his throat. His heart still skipped a beat every time she smiled like that. "I don't want to be an enabler, so don't think this means I approve of the fighting, all right? I just want you to take care of yourself."

"I know, I know." She rolled her eyes. "What's your deal about street fighting anyway? I don't want to be a fighter forever, no, but I'm okay with it for now. It's my job, and I'm good at it. What's wrong with that?"

"Isn't it obvious?" He reached out and gently touched her neck, where her skin was still blue and purple from the Bear's chokehold. He felt her swallow hard, but she didn't move away from him. "I care about you. A lot. Every time you step into the ring, I have to watch you get hurt by men twice your size. It doesn't even matter if you win or lose—somehow, you always end up getting hurt anyway. How would you feel if you had to watch someone you care about get injured over and over without being able to protect them?"

She disappeared into her own thoughts, most likely thinking about Lucy. A wrinkle appeared between her eyebrows. "Oh."

"Yeah. Is it really that strange that I hate street fighting?"

"I guess not. I've never looked at it that way before." She fixed her gaze on the ground. "I...I didn't know you cared about me that much. But that's how you treat all your patients, right?"

"No, it's not." He tucked a ringlet of her messy hair behind her ear and smiled. "You're special."

"Oh," she said again. Her blush deepened in color, and she clearly didn't know what to say or do. He grinned. *She's so cute when she's flustered.*

"I have to go to work," she finally said. "Thank you for the birthday present. And for, you know, caring about me and stuff." She stood up on her tiptoes and gave him a quick kiss on the cheek before rushing out of the garage.

For the second time that night, he was speechless. He touched his cheek, barely believing Robyn's lips had been there just moments ago.

Andrew left the garage and walked back to his car. He sank down into the driver's seat with a satisfied sigh. Even if this was as far as he'd ever go with Robyn Monroe, he knew he would always remember how her lips had felt against his skin. *Perfect,* he thought, absentmindedly touching his cheek again. *They felt perfect.*

CHAPTER ELEVEN

I can't believe he saw me dance. Robyn pinched the bridge of her nose. *I can't believe I kissed him.*

It was an early Saturday morning, the day after her birthday. Robyn was sitting on the ground outside her apartment, waiting for Andrew to finish his three-mile lap. She'd finished the lap before him as usual, so she'd already started stretching without him. The asphalt was free from snow, but the ground was still cold enough to give her goose bumps through the thin fabric of her sweatpants. She kept an eye on the opening in the hedge. Andrew hadn't been too far behind her this time, and she suspected this might be the day he reached the twenty-five-minute goal.

When they'd first started training together, she'd dreaded having actual fighting lessons with him. The mere thought of doing something as intimate as sparring with Andrew had made her nervous and uncomfortable. Something had changed since then. She wasn't sure how it had happened, but she'd begun to trust him. Andrew was changing her, and she was pretty sure it was for the better. She was happier and more confident nowadays. *It's still weird, though.* She changed her pose to stretch the back of her left thigh. *I'm going soft.*

The knife Andrew had given her fell out of her pants pocket as she changed position. She picked it up and unfolded the blade from the handle. The knife wasn't big, but the blade was sharp, and she liked how light it was. She folded the blade against the handle again, admiring the smoothness of the mechanism. It was a beautiful and very considerate gift. She folded the blade again and put the knife back in her pocket. It wasn't a toy, but she still couldn't help playing with it from time to time.

Robyn could hear Andrew's panting long before he staggered through the opening in the hedge.

"Time?" he wheezed as he collapsed on the ground next to her.

She checked her watch and smiled. "Twenty-four minutes, forty-five seconds. Congrats."

He lay down flat on his back and let out a relieved sigh. "Finally."

"Ready to begin your real training?"

"Soon," he groaned. "Just…not right now. Soon. When I can breathe again." He rolled demonstratively onto his side, looking as limbless as a rag doll.

Robyn rolled her eyes. "Stop being so overdramatic." She changed position again, leaning her upper body over her right leg to stretch out her other thigh.

"You're one of those flexible people who can pull off a full split, aren't you?" he commented, eyeing her outstretched leg.

"I used to be." Robyn didn't think of herself as flexible, not compared to how flexible she'd been when she'd had a teacher to help her stretch. She'd had to stop taking ballet lessons when her mother died, and even though she'd tried to keep herself in shape, she knew her body wasn't what it used to be.

"You should do something with your dancing," he continued. "You're amazing. I'm sure any dancing group would want you."

She snorted. "I haven't been to a ballet lesson in six years. Trust me, I'm not good enough to join a proper ballet company. Not anymore."

Andrew nodded before disappearing into his thoughts. She shook her head, focusing on her stretching again. She knew he would return to the real world sooner or later.

"Don't you miss it?" he asked after a minute or two of silence. "The ballet, I mean?"

She cast him a quick glance. He was looking at her intently, with genuine curiosity in his eyes. She swallowed hard. His questions were reaching very personal territory. Had it been any other person, she already would have tried to change the subject. She didn't like talking about ballet. Talking about ballet *hurt*. It was a dream that would never come true, and most of the time, she wished she could just forget about it. But she never did. It was always there.

"Yeah…I miss it a lot," she finally answered, fixing her eyes on the ground. "I always thought I'd start taking lessons again when I got my mom's shit sorted out, but then life kind of got in the way. It's okay, though. Becoming a ballerina was just a silly childhood dream. I'm over it."

She tried to sound nonchalant, but she probably wasn't very convincing. The dream was always there in the back of her mind. It was why she kept practicing in the garage, even though she didn't even have a teacher. Holding on to such a juvenile dream was stupid, but she still couldn't bring herself to let go of it. The dancing was a part of her. Letting go of it would be like cutting out a piece of her soul.

"You won't be in debt forever, you know," Andrew said. "When Lucy's done studying and you stop fighting, you could start taking lessons again. I think you'd make a great ballerina."

"Maybe I will." Robyn gave him another small, unconvincing smile. *And maybe hell will freeze over.* "Thank you," she added anyway. Andrew didn't know anything about the elitism of the ballet scene, but his confidence still made her feel a bit better.

Andrew got back up on his feet with a loud groan. "All right. Let's start the real training."

She nodded. "Follow me."

She walked toward the garage with Andrew following right behind her. She wasn't exactly sure what she was going to teach him, but any change in Andrew's fighting style would be an improvement. A smile tugged at her lips again as she thought of the punch he'd given one of Swanson's men. She hadn't exaggerated when she'd said it was the worst punch she'd ever seen.

They went to the corner of the garage Robyn had made her own. Andrew had been there before, but she still felt a bit nervous. The garage was her oasis, her *place*. She'd never thought she'd ever willingly bring another person here. Things really were different now.

She rolled out a mat on the dirty asphalt floor. She'd found the mat in the dumpsters outside the local high school and had brought it home on her back. It had been in a poor state, but after she'd cleaned it and repaired some of the holes in the fabric it almost looked like new—at least if you squinted. It was ugly but fairly functional.

"I think I'm going to teach you to avoid getting punched first," she said. "Go and stand on the mat."

Andrew looked a little disappointed but nodded anyway. He walked over to her on the mat and struck a pose, holding his fists in front of his face like an amateur boxer.

"Don't do that," she said. "That's an invitation to start a fight. Even if the person threatening you never planned to hit you, a pose like that might make him change his mind."

"Or her," Andrew added, lowering his fists. "I know some girls who could probably kick my ass."

She raised her eyebrows. "Probably?"

He grinned. "Definitely, then."

"That's better."

She took off her hoodie and threw it on the ground. Since her black tank top didn't cover her midriff, she had to get some tape from her backpack to put over the piercing. She could feel Andrew's eyes following her every movement.

"That's…new," he said when she'd finished, still staring at her covered belly button. He had a strange look in his eyes, and it reminded her of when she'd entered his kitchen wearing his shirt. Her cheeks heated up, and her heart began to race. She tried to stay calm, but his gaze seemed to set her skin on fire.

"Yeah." She bit her lip. "It was a birthday present from a friend."

"Shit." Andrew ran his fingers through his hair. He took a deep breath and shook his head. The weird look faded away. Robyn tried her hardest not to acknowledge the sudden twist of disappointment in her stomach.

"It looks good on you," he said. "Don't forget to clean it. Piercings like that can cause nasty infections."

"I know. My friend gave me a brochure." She rolled her shoulders and took a deep breath. "Are you ready to begin?"

He nodded. "What do I do?"

"Just stand like you always stand, hands hanging freely. Pay attention to your opponent." She took a quick step toward him and threw a punch, stopping her hand an inch away from his nose. He barely even flinched.

She frowned. "You were supposed to react. Seriously, when a fist comes flying toward your face, most people would at least take a step back."

"I guess I didn't think you'd hurt me," he said with a shrug.

"Really? Think again," she said before flicking him hard on the forehead.

"Ow! What the hell?" He finally took a step back.

"I told you to pay attention. Now try to hit me."

Andrew frowned. "What if I hurt you?"

"You won't."

He took a step toward her and hesitantly raised his fist. She followed his movements, raising her hands as he raised his. When the punch came, she deflected it with the back of her hand and spun around on the outside of his arm. Because of the momentum, Andrew continued forward, almost losing his balance.

"See? It's easy when you pay attention," she said with a smile. "Now it's my turn. If I'm less than three feet away, you have to start moving. Otherwise, you won't have time to stop me. Pay attention and follow my movements."

Andrew turned out to be a quick learner, which didn't surprise Robyn at all. It only took him a few tries to learn how to deflect a punch and move out of the way. After that, it didn't take long before he got cocky, which didn't surprise her either.

"This is pretty easy," he said, grinning proudly as he deflected her punch.

Robyn shook her head. "It's easy when the opponent is predictable. You still have to pay attention, though. You never know if the opponent's gonna do something unpredictable."

When Andrew tried to move past her like she'd taught him, she simply held out her leg. He realized her move way too late and stumbled, and then she only had to give his back a soft shove to send him straight to the mat. He managed to land on his hands and knees, but still let out a grunt of pain.

"Are you okay?" She watched as he turned around and lay down on his back.

"Yeah," he sighed. "I get it. Pay attention. Lesson learned."

"Good." She held out her hand to help him up. When he grabbed it, he suddenly got a mischievous look in his eyes. Before she could pull him up from the floor, he grabbed her forearm with his other hand and began to drag her down. She tried to pull her hand back, but she didn't have much to offer against Andrew's superior weight. She lost her balance and landed right on top of him.

They stared at each other. Andrew looked as surprised as she felt about the fact that his move had actually worked.

"That was pretty smart," she muttered, her cheeks burning. "Using your weight against me, I mean. Rude, but smart." She tried to get up, but Andrew quickly wrapped his arms around her waist. She knew she could probably get away if she wanted to, but a part of her—a frighteningly big part of her—wanted to stay.

She stared down at him. He was gorgeous, as always. Annoyingly, frustratingly gorgeous. The heat between them from before returned in an instant. Her heart began to race, and her impulse control seemed to just fade away. His face was way too close to hers. She reached out her hand and ran her fingers through that perfect hair of his that always annoyed her so much. It was soft and thick, and she loved the way it felt between her fingers. Her gaze fell to his lips, which were just as perfect as his hair. She'd spent way too much time thinking about those perfect damn lips, wondering whether or not they were as soft as they looked. She leaned down, and before she could stop herself, she'd pressed her lips against his.

Her eyes widened when she realized what she had just done. She met his gaze, and the intensity in his eyes made her heart skip a beat. He flipped them over, and she found herself lying on her back with him hovering over her. His hand gently stroked some strands of her hair out of her face before settling on the nape of her neck.

He gave her one of those perfect, toe-curling grins of his and tilted her head back. "You have no idea how long I've wanted to do this."

When he finally kissed her, his lips were hard and demanding. She gasped in surprise, and he took the opportunity to deepen the kiss. His hands wandered down her body, igniting fires within her wherever they went. She moaned quietly into his mouth, which only made him kiss her even harder. Her head was spinning. Why hadn't they done this before?

Andrew pulled back for a moment. "Are you okay with this?"

"I don't know," she answered breathlessly. "Do it again."

He smiled at her and was just about to do as she said when a loud beeping sound echoed through the garage. He sat up and pulled his pager from his pants pocket. His eyes went from the pager back to her, then back to the pager, then back to her.

"Damn it." He sighed. "I really have to go. I'm needed at the hospital."

"Oh." Robyn tried her best to hide her disappointment, but she probably wasn't succeeding. She cleared her throat and got up from the ground. "Come on. You have lives to save, right?"

"Right. I guess I'll see you later?"

She nodded. He gave her hand a final squeeze before turning around, heading toward the exit. He only got a couple of steps before he turned back to her.

"Just one more," he said and pressed his lips to hers again. He gave her a quick smile before hurrying out of the garage, leaving a dumbfounded Robyn behind him.

"What the hell just happened?" she mumbled. Her emotions were all over the place. She'd thought Andrew only saw her as a patient and a friend, but that clearly wasn't true. He'd implied that he'd wanted to kiss her for a long time. What was she supposed to do with a statement like that? Just thinking about it made her feel nauseous in a strangely positive way.

She went back inside to take a shower before heading over to Andrew's house to take care of Tiny. At first, she'd felt weird about entering his home without him being there, but using the spare key to let herself in was starting to feel strangely natural. Even after what had just happened in the garage, the thought of being in his home still made her feel safe. Feeling safe wasn't something she was used to, but she'd found that she really enjoyed it.

She smiled. She was changing, and it was all because of him.

CHAPTER TWELVE

Andrew's heart was still racing when he parked his car outside the hospital. He'd promised himself he wouldn't touch her, but that ship had definitely sailed. *I kissed a patient,* he thought. *I actually kissed a patient.* It was wrong. Horribly, horribly wrong. As a doctor, he was outraged by his behavior. As a man, though? Ecstatic.

He couldn't stop himself from smiling. She'd kissed him first. Even if he'd taken over the situation after that, she'd still kissed him first.

You're using her, commented his inner critic. *She's a patient, and you're using her.*

A wave of guilt washed over him, but it wasn't strong enough to take away his excitement. He should be regretting the kiss, but he wasn't. He couldn't. It was his first kiss with Robyn Monroe. How could he possibly regret something like that?

He checked his pager again. The page hadn't told him much, but it seemed like one of the nurses needed him in the ICU.

People wrinkled their noses as he walked by them in the long hospital corridors. He'd thrown a white coat over his reeking training clothes, but he knew it didn't cover the smell completely. *This better be good,* he thought, entering room 153. The room only had one patient, and next to the patient stood one of the ICU nurses.

"Dr. Alexander!" the nurse said. "I'm so glad you're here."

"You paged me." Andrew approached the bed. "What am I looking at?"

The patient was a white male, but Andrew couldn't even guess his age. The man's face was a swollen, bruised mess, and his body didn't look any better.

"John Doe, early thirties," the nurse said. "He's awake and talking, but he hasn't told us his name yet. Someone found him unconscious in a ditch last night and called an ambulance. He's got several broken bones, bruises, and abrasions. We had to take him to the OR early in the morning for a hemorrhagic stroke. You told us to keep an eye out for possible gang-related injuries, and someone definitely beat this guy up. He's refusing to talk to the police. He says he must have been hit by a car or something—even though his injuries don't match a car crash at all."

"I see," Andrew said. "Thank you for contacting me. Could you give me some time alone with the patient?"

"Of course. Page me if you need me."

When the nurse had closed the door behind her, Andrew turned back to his patient. Most of the man's injuries were located on his head and torso. He'd been beaten to within an inch of his life, and judging by the lack of defense wounds, he hadn't been able to fight back. Andrew swallowed hard. This man hadn't received his injuries in a one-on-one street fight—several opponents had assaulted him at once.

"John Doe, huh?" Andrew asked. "Any chance you'd give me a name?"

"John Doe is fine," the patient answered in a low, raspy voice.

"All right, then. What happened to you, John?"

"I was hit by a car," John Doe deadpanned.

"Of course you were." Andrew picked up the file attached to the bedframe. He felt nauseous as he read about all the times John Doe had flatlined on the operating table. His heart raced. *This could have been Robyn.*

He ran his fingers through his hair, trying to conceal his inner turmoil. This was a wake-up call. How could he have been so blind? By infiltrating Robyn's life, he'd slowly fallen for the delusion that his presence would somehow be enough to keep her safe. It wouldn't be. If Swanson decided to take her out, it wouldn't matter whether he was by her side or not—she still wouldn't stand a chance.

"Just one more question, okay?" Andrew said, making eye contact with the patient. "Do you work for a man named Richard Swanson?"

John Doe's eyes widened in surprise. He opened his mouth and then closed it again, the shock rendering him speechless.

The man's silence was the only answer Andrew needed. "That's what I thought."

When he turned around to leave, a weak hand grabbed the sleeve of his coat.

"Please, don't call the cops," the man whispered. "I have a kid, okay? A little girl. She's staying with her mother right now, but if you call the cops… She's my baby girl. I'm begging you, please don't call the cops on me." Tears fell from his eyes, rolling down his battered face. "I hurt my back a while ago, and I've lost a couple of fights because of it. I'm not as good or as young as I used to be. I knew Swanson wasn't happy with my performance, but I never thought he'd send his thugs after me. I never thought he'd do something like this."

Andrew placed his hand on top of John Doe's. "I won't call the police, but I will bring Swanson down. I swear to you I'll bring him down."

John Doe nodded, retracting his hand from Andrew's sleeve. It was hard to tell, but Andrew thought the man looked relieved.

When Andrew left the hospital, he was still overwhelmed with anger and fear. *It could have been Robyn.* It was all too easy to picture her in the hospital bed instead of this nameless patient. The images flashed before his eyes—Robyn being dumped in a ditch, Robyn's brain bleeding, Robyn flat-lining during surgery,

Robyn being transported in a body bag down to the morgue with a name tag saying "Jane Doe"…

He clenched his fists. He didn't care what he had to do—he was not going to lose her.

He slid into his car and leaned back against the seat. His heart was pounding in his chest. He needed to smoke. All the promises he'd made to himself about quitting went straight out the window. What difference did a single cigarette make anyway? He *needed* it. After rolling down the car window, he pulled out a pack of Marlboros from the glove compartment. He lit a cigarette and took a deep drag. Oh, yes. Much better.

After parking his car in the driveway outside his house, he picked up his cell phone and called Jason.

"You've reached Jason Stevenson's phone," Jason's voice mail answered after a couple of rings. "Please leave a message after the beep."

"Hey, it's Andrew. I've got some new information about your case." He got out of the car and went inside the house while leaving the message. "I have a patient in the ICU who was almost beaten to death by Swanson's men. I've gained Robyn's trust, and I hope I'll be able to convince her to stop fighting soon. We need to bring this guy down. Fast. Please, call me back."

Andrew walked through the hallway, heading toward the shower. His body still ached from the run, and he was getting tired of reeking of sweat. He was just about to enter the bathroom when he caught a familiar glimmer of red out of the corner of his eye.

"Could you repeat that?" Robyn stepped out of the guest room with her arms crossed. "The part about you gaining my trust?"

Andrew blinked in surprise. "I…I didn't know you were here." Had she heard all of that?

"Is that why you've been nice to me?" she asked. "Have you been planning this whole thing? Just to make me stop fighting?"

"Well, yes, but…"

Andrew didn't know how to continue. She was right, yet still so far away from the whole truth. He could deny her claim, but if he lied to her now, he knew she would never forgive him. Looking at her made him question if she'd ever forgive him anyway. It wasn't like the last time he'd accidentally hurt her, when he'd insulted her way of taking care of Lucy. That time, she'd been more angry than sad. This time was different. She didn't have that fiery spark of anger burning in her eyes, and she looked more dejected than mad. The worst part was the way she looked at him—like she'd just been betrayed by a loved one and wasn't even surprised by it.

"I should have seen it coming," she muttered, shaking her head. "I should have known someone like you would never kiss someone like me without an ulterior motive." She pushed past him, hurrying toward the door.

"Robyn, I can explain," he said, following her. "I—"

"You're right—I trusted you, Andrew," she interrupted, her voice trembling. She turned around to look at him, her dark eyes filled with tears. "I barely trust anyone, but I trusted you. I let you in. Congratulations. Your mission succeeded." She opened the door, but Andrew grabbed her arm before she could leave.

"Would you please let me explain?" he said. "You're an adult, Robyn. You can't just run away every time you're having an argument with someone."

Robyn snorted. "Watch me." She pulled free from his grip and started running, just like she'd done the last time they'd been in the same situation. The last time, he'd let her be, letting her work out the misunderstanding on her own. This time was different. She'd taught him how to run, and this time, he would catch her.

• • •

Robyn's chest hurt. She tried to keep her thoughts from racing and just focus on the running, but Andrew's words kept replaying in the back of her mind. *I should have seen it coming.* He'd told her at the start about the person she reminded him of, the one he hadn't been able to save. Now she understood what that meant. He hadn't been nice to her because he'd actually enjoyed being with her. He'd been nice to her to make her stop fighting—to *save* her. It had nothing to do with her as a person. He'd just used her to ease his guilt.

This was why she didn't trust people, why she'd learned to only depend on herself. People were never nice without a reason. Not to someone like her. She'd known this, but she'd still started to take Andrew's kindness for granted.

She'd let him nestle his way into her life—and she'd enjoyed it. After having taken care of others for such a long time, she'd enjoyed having someone taking care of her. How pathetic was that?

He'd changed her. Before she met him, she'd been smarter. Stronger. More independent. *And lonelier,* a voice added from the back of her mind. *So much lonelier.*

She ignored the voice and kept running. Everything hurt, but she knew she could shake it off. She'd done it before, and she'd do it again. So what if it hurt like hell? A girl like her couldn't afford to let a guy affect her like this. She didn't have the time or energy to spare for a broken heart.

"Robyn! Robyn, wait!" someone shouted from behind her. Robyn cast a quick glance over her shoulder. An all too familiar black-haired man was following her, and it looked like he was gaining on her.

"Leave me alone," she yelled back, increasing the pace of her jog. She wasn't a sprinter, but she should be able to outrun Andrew.

"Robyn, please! Just let me explain."

A part of her wanted to stop and listen to his explanation. A part of her—a stupid, naïve part of her—still believed in him. She thought back on everything he'd done for her. Could he really have faked all that worry in his eyes? Was he that good at acting?

She shook her head. This had to stop. It was thoughts like that that had brought her into this situation to begin with.

"Robyn!"

The source of the voice was surprisingly close this time. Before she could glance over her shoulder again, her run came to an abrupt stop as something—or some*one*, more likely—grabbed her forearm. She automatically clenched her fists but managed to stop herself from hitting him.

"Let go of me," she growled.

"Please, listen to me. Look at me." He gently tugged at her arm, turning her around. "Please don't shut me out. I get how it all sounded."

"Do you really?" she snapped. "Because it sounded as if you've been fooling me this whole time. Is it because of that person you lost? Is that why you've been nice to me?"

"No, it's not," he said. "I offered my help at the ER because of that person, but everything after that, I did for *you*. I couldn't live with the thought of losing you, so I knew I had to do something. Do you understand how many times you've been close to dying lately? Do you realize that it's only a matter of time before it happens again? Right now, there's a man at the hospital who was nearly killed by Swanson and his men. The beating they gave him caused bleeding in his brain." Andrew reached out his free hand and tucked some strands of Robyn's hair behind her ear. A part of her wanted to slap the hand away while another part wanted to lean into his touch. In the end, all she did was stand there, her eyes fixed on the ground.

"It could have been you." His thumb caressed her cheek. "It could have been you lying there with a bleeding brain. You have to stop fighting, Robyn."

Robyn flinched, and the grip on her forearm tightened.

"Yes," he continued, "when we first met, I wanted to gain your trust so you'd let me in and start listening to me, but that changed when I got to know you. You're not just one of my patients anymore. I can't lose you. I *won't*."

"So that's why you felt the need to go behind my back?" she sneered. "To try and bring Swanson down and take away my main source of income?"

"What else was I supposed to do?" he exclaimed. "I couldn't convince you to stop fighting, so I had to try a different way. I teamed up with a cop, and we're going to make sure Swanson gets what he deserves. I'll do whatever it takes to make you stop fighting, even if it means going behind your back."

The pain in Robyn's chest returned at full force. "Then how could I possibly trust you again?"

"Maybe you can't." He placed his hand under her chin and tilted her head back, coercing her to look at him. She reluctantly met his gaze. "It's gotten to the point where I care more about your well-being than your opinion of me," he said. The intensity in his eyes sent shivers down her spine. "You can hate me all you like—I'm still going to do whatever I can to protect you. I'm not going to lose you."

Robyn took a step back, shaking off Andrew's hands. "It's my life. What I do with it is my decision. As long as I've got debts to pay off, I will keep fighting."

He looked at her with calm, calculating eyes. "I know. And I'll keep trying to make you stop. That's just how it is."

"That's so selfish!" she yelled, losing her patience. She'd seen glimpses of this side of Andrew before, like that night when he'd found out about the tournament, but she'd never fully understood just how intimidating he could be. She didn't doubt his words for a second—he would do pretty much anything to keep her safe, and not in a Prince Charming kind of way. *He's not as perfect as he pretends to be.*

"I'm not going to deny that," Andrew said. "I'm not a nice person. I'm selfish and manipulative—and even though I'm aware of this, I still want to be a part of your life. I don't deserve it. I don't deserve *you*. I know this, but I'm still going to beg you not to shut me out. Please, Robyn, don't…don't leave me."

There was desperation in his voice, a kind of neediness Robyn didn't think could be faked. Her emotions were going all over the place. He'd said that things had changed when he'd gotten to know her, but when, exactly, had that been? Out of all his acts of kindness, how could she possibly separate the real ones from the ones that had been carefully fabricated to gain her trust?

Had he kissed her because he wanted her, or because it would make her open up to him?

She wanted to hate him—everything would have been so much easier if she'd hated him—but she couldn't. The worst part was that she couldn't forgive him either.

"You can stay in my life as my doctor," she finally said. "You can even stay in my life as my friend. But that's all. Forget about what happened in the garage. I can't…I can't be with someone I can't trust."

Saying the words was painful, but not as painful as seeing the look in Andrew's eyes. He looked about as heartbroken as she felt.

"I understand," he said in a hoarse voice.

"I'm glad we're on the same page." With tears burning in her eyes, she turned around and began to jog home. This time, Andrew didn't follow her.

CHAPTER THIRTEEN

Robyn avoided Andrew for as long as she could. It took her several days to gather the courage to ask him for a ride to Chrystal Arena for her fight. She was a good runner, but running all the way to the arena would take hours. She didn't need Andrew—she *absolutely* didn't need Andrew—but she did need his car.

The silence hung heavily between them as she climbed into his black Volvo on the night of her fight. The awkwardness was close to unbearable.

"It's Christmas soon," Andrew finally said.

"Yeah," she replied. "Time flies."

He glanced at her and then quickly looked away. His jaw clenched as he fixed his eyes on the road. Robyn leaned back in the seat and sighed, wondering if their relationship would ever go back to what it used to be.

The awkward silence hung over them the whole way to the arena. Robyn hated it. A part of her wished she'd never kissed him in the first place. Another part of her wanted nothing more than to climb into his lap and kiss him again.

They left the car and walked across the parking lot toward the arena.

"Do you want me to fix your hair again?" Andrew asked.

They came to a stop outside the pizzeria. Robyn nodded and turned around.

He tied her hair up in a bun again, his hands as gentle as the last time. Before she could stop herself, she'd thought back on the way he'd run his hand through her hair in the garage, how it had settled on the nape of her neck, holding her still as he leaned down and…

Stop it. Her cheeks turned red. Ever since the incident in the garage, she'd been bothered by intruding thoughts like that. She'd told herself she didn't want a relationship like that with Andrew, but there were clearly parts of her that weren't fully convinced.

The moment they stepped into the arena, Robyn knew the upcoming fight would have a much bigger audience than her last one. They'd arrived early so she'd have time to warm up, but the arena was already crowded enough to make it difficult to get to the bar. She glanced at the ring. The third-class fight had just come to an end, and soon, the second-class fight would begin.

Weird. Back when the tournament was held at the Octagon, a second-class fight would never have generated an audience like this. The underground world in Chrystal Valley was changing, turning darker and more violent every passing day. She didn't want to admit it, but it scared her a little.

She glanced at the backstage door. There was something she needed to do in there today—something she'd postponed for way too long. She was not looking forward to it.

Cassandra was sitting on her usual chair, her long, white hair tied up in a ponytail. Next to her stood Drake, leaning casually against the wall while keeping an eye on the crowd. Their eyes met, and he gave her one of his trademark smirks. Robyn rolled her eyes. Ana was right—Drake was a bit of a dickhead.

After pushing through the thick mass of people crowding the bar, Robyn finally reached Cassandra.

"Any comments on tonight's fight?" she asked.

Cassandra studied her calmly. "You'll win tonight. The Morrigan usually relies on speed, but you're faster than her. She's going to have to change her strategy for tonight if she wants to last a single round. She usually waits for the opponent to make the first move, but she has to know that method is not going to work against you. Don't let her provoke you. Your fighting style makes you the worst possible opponent for her."

"I see," Robyn replied, feeling a little bit calmer. Cassandra was rarely wrong in her predictions. "Thank you."

"Make sure you win, Valkyrie," Drake said, joining the conversation. "I want to fight you in the final."

She rolled her eyes again. "Don't get cocky. You still have to get past the quarter- and semifinal."

"I'll be in the final," he said confidently. "The only question is whether you will."

"Whatever." Robyn turned around and left them both, pushing through the crowd again. She stopped outside the backstage door.

"I want to follow you backstage this time," Andrew said.

She hesitated.

"I'm your physician. I need to be able to get to you if something happens during the fight."

Well, he wasn't wrong, she supposed. "I guess I could try and talk to the guard again."

She turned to the man guarding the door. This doorman was younger than the one who'd stopped Andrew the last time, and he didn't look quite as cynical. She wasn't sure if that was a good or a bad thing.

"I'm the Valkyrie," she said, "and this is Dr. Alexander. He's my medic. Is it all right if I bring him backstage?"

"I'm sorry," said the doorman. "Authorized personnel only. We already have a medical team in there."

Robyn nodded before turning back to Andrew. "I'll be fine, I promise. I'll come out as soon as the fight is over."

He frowned but nodded anyway. "Please, be careful out there."

"I will." She gave him a small smile. "Don't do anything stupid while I'm gone."

Robyn couldn't help but feel a bit guilty as she hurried through the door. She could have pushed the guard a lot further, but she'd chosen not to. If Andrew had followed her backstage, she would most likely have postponed her mission once again. She couldn't let herself do that. It was time for her to ask Swanson about her debts, and this time, she wouldn't back down.

Swanson was waiting for her outside the locker room. Mark was leaning against the wall a couple of steps away, glaring at Robyn as she approached them.

"Good evening, dear," Swanson said. "I hope you're well."

She nodded. "I wanted to—"

"I would like you to last two rounds," he interrupted. "And please, try to hold back a little. You are still an underdog in this competition, and I'd prefer if you kept it that way."

She nodded again. "I…I wanted to ask you something."

For a short moment, Robyn could distinguish a look of annoyance in Swanson's eyes. It quickly disappeared, giving way to his usual polite smile. "Go ahead, dear."

She took a deep breath, gathering strength. "I've been fighting for you for five years now. I just… I've been wondering for a while now about my…you know, how much I have left to pay off on the, uh, debts…" She was stuttering, and her cheeks were turning red. Everything she'd planned to say disappeared from her mind.

"You shouldn't worry about that, dear," Swanson said. "I'm taking care of it. All you have to do is keep working for me."

"That's kind of the point. I want to know when all of this, uh, stops." She swallowed hard. "I want to know when I can stop fighting."

Swanson narrowed his eyes. "You will fight until I say you're done fighting."

"Yes, but you can't expect me to just go on with this indefinitely. I—"

A gloved hand grabbed her by the neck and pushed her against the wall.

"You do not tell Mr. Swanson what he can and can't do, you ungrateful little bitch," Mark growled. Robyn grabbed his arm, her short nails clawing at the jacket of his suit. He only tightened his grip on her throat, shoving her higher up on the wall until her toes barely reached the ground. "Where would you be if Mr. Swanson hadn't taken you in? How would you have cared for your precious little sister? He *saved* you, and you come here making demands. You're *nothing*. Everything you have in life is thanks to him. You should be ashamed."

Robyn continued to struggle, growing weaker by the second. Mark was looking at her in total disgust. *I really am nothing.* She already regretted her words. She'd been too disrespectful. Too demanding. Swanson didn't owe her an answer. He didn't owe her anything.

Swanson tapped Mark on the shoulder. "Please, let her down. She has a game tonight."

Mark immediately removed his hand from her throat. Robyn tried to remain standing, but her knees wouldn't carry her. She landed on the floor hard, her whole body trembling. She took a deep, wheezing breath.

"I'm sorry," she croaked. "I shouldn't have said that. I'm really sorry."

"Apology accepted." Swanson gave her an almost fatherly smile. "Go and warm up, dear. I'm expecting a splendid performance from you tonight." He held out his hand, and Robyn allowed him to help her up. She couldn't bring herself to even look at him.

"I'm sorry," she whispered again before heading toward the locker room.

I'm nothing.

• • •

Well, shit, Andrew thought, looking at the door leading to the backstage area. *Now what?* The door was closed, and the guard was beginning to look a bit suspicious. Andrew ran his fingers through his hair. He had to get in there. As her doctor and as her friend, he had to protect her from Swanson.

Like you could possibly see her as just a friend, commented his inner critic.

The voice was right. Andrew's chest still ached every time he thought back on their argument. Robyn seemed to be fine with pretending that they were nothing more than friends, but he didn't have that kind of self-control. He couldn't forget about the kiss. He couldn't forget about the way her body had felt beneath his. His need to touch her flared up every time he looked at her, and it was driving him insane.

A few minutes after Robyn had walked into the backstage area, Jason arrived at the arena. Andrew watched as the young officer pushed through the crowd to get to Cassandra. He waited a little while longer before he approached them, allowing Jason to have some time alone with Cassandra first.

"Alexander!" Jason shouted, grinning widely. "The Valkyrie's going to kick some serious ass tonight. Is this awesome or what?"

"Yeah. Awesome." Andrew couldn't even pretend to share his excitement. "How's everything going? With, you know…?"

"Nothing new." Jason took a step away from Cassandra and her guardian. "I got your voice mail. How's that John Doe doing?"

"Still breathing," he replied. "Barely. Can't you arrest Swanson for this?"

Jason shook his head. "To nail Swanson, we need something more concrete. Right now, it's just your patient's word against Swanson's. It's not enough."

"I understand." Andrew glanced at the backstage door. "Hey, could you distract that doorman for a while? He won't let me in."

"Why do you want to go backstage?"

"Swanson's in there. If I'm lucky, I might find some proof for you in there."

"Wouldn't it be better if I went, then?" Jason raised an eyebrow. "You're just a civilian."

"I'm not just a civilian. I'm a doctor." Andrew faked a smile. "People rarely question doctors. Besides, I could pretend I'm on the medical team if I get caught."

Jason looked skeptical.

Andrew sighed, his façade faltering. "I need to get in there, okay? I can't stand the thought of her being in there alone, especially not when Swanson's around here somewhere. I have to get in there."

Jason considered it for a moment and then nodded. "Go to the door. I'll create a distraction. But be careful, all right? Don't be a hero. If something goes wrong, just get out of there."

"I will. I promise." Andrew sighed with relief. "Thank you."

The doorman looked even more suspicious when Andrew approached him for the second time. "You're still not getting inside."

Andrew smiled politely. "I know. I'm just…waiting for a friend."

The guard scowled, clearly not believing him. Andrew looked back at Jason, who had returned to Cassandra and Drake's little corner by the bar. Jason glanced over his shoulder and gave Andrew an indiscreet wink. Then he punched Drake in the face.

Drake stared at Jason in shock for a moment before raising his fists. When he tried to return the punch, Jason quickly dodged it, making Drake's hand connect with a stranger's shoulder instead. The stranger turned around in surprise, spilling beer on yet another stranger. A few seconds later, the bar had turned into a battlefield.

The guard cursed and pulled a walkie-talkie from his chest pocket. He gave Andrew one last glare before heading toward the brawl, calling into his transceiver for backup. *Thanks, Jason,* Andrew thought as he sneaked through the backstage door.

Entering the backstage area was like stepping into a new world. He could still hear the pounding music and the sound of men screaming from outside the door, but it was all muffled and distant. The air outside had been hot and damp, while the backstage area was close to chilly. Where was everybody? The lack of people would make things easier for him, but it also spooked him a little.

The first door he tried was locked, but the second brought him to an empty locker room. In one of the corners, he found Robyn's hoodie. On a bench on the opposite side of the room, he found a big gym bag he didn't recognize. He looked inside it but didn't find anything out of the ordinary. He'd told Jason he would try to look for evidence against Swanson, but he had no idea what he was looking for.

The door opened, and a big, bearded man dressed in a black suit entered the room.

"What the fuck are you doing with that bag?" the man yelled, his voice echoing against the tile walls.

"Nothing," Andrew said quickly. "I'm just…uh…" He couldn't come up with a single good excuse. The man took a step closer, and Andrew automatically took a step back.

"You're trying to steal from my fighter, is that it?" the man roared. "You think you're gonna get away with that?" He raised his fists. Andrew tried to remember his lessons with Robyn, but his mind had gone completely blank. He watched as the man's hand flew toward his face.

Not until then did he fully realize how far in over his head he was.

CHAPTER FOURTEEN

Andrew closed his eyes, waiting for the man's fist to connect with his face. He wasn't even scared—most of all, he was frustrated with his useless, motionless body.

"Don't touch him!" a female voice yelled, and Andrew was suddenly shoved out of the way. Then he heard a loud thud. He assumed the punch had finally reached its destination, but strangely enough, he didn't feel any pain. He opened his eyes and noticed an all too familiar red-haired woman standing in front of him.

"Robyn?"

She was standing with her back toward him, acting as a human shield between him and the man. His eyes widened when he realized what she had just done. *No.*

Robyn looked over her shoulder. "Are you okay?"

On her left cheek were three parallel red lines, showing exactly where the man's rings had connected with her skin. Small drops of blood were already rolling down her face, but she didn't seem to notice it.

"I'm fine," Andrew said, feeling sick to his stomach. He'd caused that. She was injured because of him.

"What the fuck are you doing?" said the man in the suit. "That guy was trying to steal from my fighter!" He tried to move past Robyn, but she continued to block him.

"I said don't touch him!" she growled, raising her fists.

Snap out of it, Andrew's inner critic hissed. *You're supposed to be good in stressful situations. Time to show it.*

Andrew took a deep breath, forcing himself out of his state of shock. "I'm very sorry, sir," he said, using the calm and confident tone he always used with his patients. "I'm Dr. Andrew Alexander, and I'm with the medical team. I just went into the wrong room, that's all."

The man narrowed his eyes. "And if I talk to the rest of the team, they'll confirm this?"

Andrew faked a polite smile. "Probably not, no. It's my first day. I haven't even met them yet."

"Well, isn't that convenient?" the man said. "I think I'm going to call security now." He reached for something in his chest pocket, but Robyn quickly grabbed his arm.

"I want you to leave," she said in a low voice. "Right now. Or else I'll inform Swanson that his most successful fighter was just punched by the Morrigan's manager."

The man blinked and gave Robyn a closer look. His face turned pale. "You're the Valkyrie?"

"Yes." Robyn's voice was full of unspoken threats. "Leave."

The man glanced at Andrew as he slowly backed away. "If you really are a doctor, please take a look at her cheek."

"I will."

The man closed the door behind him. Robyn immediately turned around.

"You idiot!" she yelled, her eyes shooting daggers. "Are you insane? You said you wouldn't do anything stupid!"

"I'm sorry." Another wave of guilt washed over him. "I'm so, so sorry. I didn't mean for this to happen. I never wanted you to get hurt."

She punched the wall hard enough to leave a dent. "The world doesn't care about what you want! Don't you get it? You seem to think you're living in some fairy-tale world where you can just waltz around and make some kind of difference, but this is the real world. Actions have consequences! You're not a superhero. You're just a damn doctor. You can't keep doing shit like this! I don't have time to worry about you, too." She wiped some blood away from her face and then stared at her stained hand. The anger slowly faded away as a look of sadness swept over her face. She sighed. "Great. More scars."

"He was aiming for me," Andrew said. "You should have let him hit me."

"I didn't want him to ruin your face. I mean, you're still… untouched. My friends refer to you as Dr. Handsome, for fuck's sake." She let out a short, humorless laugh. "You've seen me and all my scars. I'm already disgusting. One more scar won't change anything."

Andrew was speechless. Was that how she saw herself? He could barely comprehend it. *She has no idea how beautiful she is.*

"I should go." She wiped her bloody hand on her sweatpants. "I wasn't done warming up." She turned to leave, but Andrew quickly grabbed her wrist.

"Please, wait," he said. "At least let me clean the wounds. It's the least I can do."

Robyn thought about it for a moment and then nodded. "But after that, I want you to leave. You're not safe in here."

Andrew smiled but chose not to answer. It probably wasn't any safer for him out in the arena, considering the mayhem Jason had caused.

He made her sit down on the locker room bench while he kneeled on the floor in front of her. When he cleaned and bandaged the wounds on her cheek, he found that they weren't as deep as he'd feared.

"I don't think you'll get any scars from this," he said. The overwhelming guilt still reawakened every time he looked at her, but knowing he hadn't caused permanent damage was a great relief.

"Oh." Robyn tried her best to hide it, but Andrew could tell the news relieved her, too.

"Your scars aren't disgusting, you know," he said. "They're like your war paint. They tell a story." He smiled. "They tell the world you're a survivor. In a way, they're actually kind of beautiful."

Robyn blinked, her cheeks flushing red. "Thanks, I guess," she muttered, looking down at the floor. Andrew grinned. *She's so cute when she's flustered.*

He put a final piece of tape on the bandage and leaned back, surveying his work. As long as the cuts didn't get infected, they would heal just fine. He was just about to stand up again when he noticed a weird coloring on her neck.

He gave the marks a closer look. "What's that?"

"It's nothing." She tried to stand up, but Andrew grabbed her shoulders and pushed her down on the bench again.

"Those are bruises." He frowned. "*New* bruises. What happened?"

Robyn continued to stare at the floor. "I don't know. I must have tripped or something."

"Oh, for fuck's sake, Robyn," he groaned. "Are we seriously going back to that? Just tell me what happened."

"I talked to Swanson, okay? I said some stupid things. It was my fault." She pulled her knees up to her chest, making herself look smaller. She still refused to look at him.

Andrew's anger flared up. He'd never hated anyone like he hated Swanson right then.

"Robyn. Robyn, look at me." He cupped her face in his hands, tilting her head back. She reluctantly raised her gaze. "It's never your fault when they hurt you," he said. "*Never.*"

She smiled unconvincingly. "You know I punch people for a living, right?"

"You didn't choose any of this. It's never your fault when they hurt you."

Robyn's lower lip trembled. It was obvious that no one had ever told her that before. He wrapped his arms around her, holding her close. She stiffened a little at first, but then she relaxed.

He wished he could hold her like that forever, shielding her from everything dangerous in the world—but he couldn't. As long as she was fighting for Swanson, he could never keep her safe. He hugged her even harder, breathing in the scent of her hair. He felt helpless again. Useless.

The door to the locker room opened. Andrew quickly let go of Robyn and stood up.

"Excuse me, are you the new guy on the medical team?" asked a pale, freckly young woman in a bright orange jacket. Her long, strawberry-blond ponytail was a little lopsided, and pearls of sweat trickled down her temples. "You're needed out there. They finally managed to stop the fighting. It's a mess."

"Fighting? What fighting?" Robyn asked.

"I asked Jason to create a distraction so I could get past the guard," Andrew said, speaking in a low voice so the newcomer wouldn't hear him. "He punched Drake in the face and started a brawl."

The information made Robyn smile. "I wish I could have seen that."

"It was pretty great." He turned to the woman standing in the doorway, who was looking at them curiously. "I'm finished here. How can I help you?"

The woman tossed him a bundle of orange fabric. "My colleague and I have set up shop in the bar. We could definitely use your expertise."

"I'll be right there." He turned back to Robyn. "Will you be okay?"

"Of course I will," she answered. "Go."

Andrew nodded, reluctantly turning away from her again. He didn't want to leave her on her own, not when Swanson was still around somewhere, but he didn't think he had a choice. Actions had consequences. He'd lied about being on the medical team, and this was the result. He put on the orange jacket, accepting his new job.

"Nice to meet you, by the way." The woman reached out her hand. "I'm Lily. Nurse."

Andrew shook her hand. "I'm Dr. Andrew Alexander. Nice to meet you too."

"Wow, you really are a doctor? We've never had an actual doctor on our team before. This is awesome."

Andrew followed her through the door, giving Robyn one last look. She gave him a little wave and an encouraging smile, probably happy to get him out of the backstage area.

"So, do you work at Chrystal Valley Hospital?" he asked Lily. "I've never seen you before."

"That's probably because I'm not working as a nurse. Yet." Lily fidgeted a little with her ponytail. "I still have two semesters left in school."

Andrew sighed. He'd thought she looked a bit too young to be a fully educated nurse.

They left the backstage area, heading out to the crowd. A long line of injured people led up to the bar. Andrew spotted Jason, Cassandra, and Drake already sitting on chairs behind the bar, being tended to by a tan man with platinum-blond hair. He looked almost as young as Lily.

"Is that your partner?" Andrew asked, trying not to sound too skeptical.

"Yeah, that's Jonas. He's an EMT. Fully educated."

They're just kids. He ran his fingers through his hair. This was going to be a long night.

"Hey, Alexander!" Jason shouted when he noticed him. "Nice outfit."

He was holding some ice against his swollen lip, and the skin beneath his right eye was turning blue. Drake sat on a chair not far away, sending vicious glares at anyone who tried to approach him. He had a cut on his cheek that looked a bit like the ones Robyn had received earlier.

"Please, sir, let me at least tape it up for you," Jonas said. Drake only glared.

"Just let him do his job, Drake." Cassandra sighed. She'd strategically placed herself between Jason and Drake, presumably to stop any further conflicts from happening. "You're supposed to be adults. Adults! Act like it."

Drake muttered something under his breath before turning his head, allowing Jonas to see to his wound. Jason gave Cassandra a smug look. "He started it."

"No, I didn't," Drake immediately countered.

"Stop it," Cassandra said in a surprisingly dangerous tone, making both men shut up.

"Hey, Joe!" Lily yelled. "The doctor's here."

"So he really is a doctor? Awesome," Jonas exclaimed. He looked at Andrew and gave him a smile. "I'm Jonas. It's going to be great to have an actual doctor around."

"I'm Andrew. I'm glad to help."

Jonas nodded and then returned his focus to helping Drake. Andrew headed over to Jason's side.

"Thanks for the distraction," he said. "Are you all right?"

"I'm fine. I've wanted to punch Drake for a long time now." Jason grinned. "How did it go backstage? I thought you said you'd use the medical team as an excuse—I didn't think you'd join it for real."

"Yeah, I didn't see that one coming either. I don't think I'm getting out of this."

Jason shrugged. "Just go with it. You'll have more chances of finding evidence against Swanson this way. You're still in, right?"

"Of course." Now more than ever. The image of Robyn defending Swanson's abuse was forever burnt into his memory.

She'd truly believed she deserved it—she'd even looked guilty. *I will end him,* Andrew thought, his fury still burning hot within him. *He'll never touch her again.*

Andrew wasn't sure how long it took to aid all the people in the line, but eventually, they reached the final victim. By then, Andrew had taken charge of the medical team completely, running the bar like he would have run a smaller emergency room at the hospital. He'd recommended some of the brawlers seek professional help at the hospital later, but most of them would heal just fine on their own.

When he'd put all his medical equipment back in his bag, he tried to join the crowd again, only to be stopped by Lily.

"The medical team has special seats in the gallery," she said. "You've already missed the lower-class fights. You're not skipping the first-class fight too, right?"

"No, of course not." He'd originally planned to watch the fight with Jason, but he'd be closer to Robyn if he sat with the rest of the medical team.

"Good. We couldn't have done this without you, you know." Lily smiled. "Thank you, Dr. Alexander."

"I'm glad I could help." He followed her toward the backstage area. "And please, call me Andrew."

The gallery turned out to be a handful of chairs in a room upstairs, placed close to a large wall-to-wall window facing the arena. Two chairs were placed to the side of the room, close to a narrow door.

"The door leads straight to one of the passageways," Lily said, pulling an extra chair over to the two on the side. "You know, the ones that lead to the ring. Two of them are for the fighters, but the third one is ours. We'll be down there in seconds if something happens."

Andrew nodded. Thanks to the chairs' placement, the medical team could easily observe the arena through the window while still being close to the door. He appreciated the practicality.

They sat down, waiting for the fight to begin. The gallery slowly filled up with people. Andrew observed the newcomers as they took their seats. With their immaculate suits and solemn looks, they would have looked bizarrely out of place in the crowd downstairs. These people were clearly not here for entertainment. They were here to make money.

Andrew's eyes swept over the gallery. Swanson had to be somewhere in the room, and though Andrew had no idea what Swanson looked like, it still made him shudder.

"So how did you get into all this?" Lily asked. "I mean, you're a real doctor. The paycheck must look ridiculous to you."

"I like helping people." He shrugged, hoping she wouldn't push the subject any further. "What about you two?"

"A friend of ours is into this whole underground street-fighting thing," Jonas said. "He said the tournament lacked medically educated staff, so I thought, hell, why not?"

"And I needed the extra cash," Lily added. "Ridiculous paycheck or not, it's still better than nothing. We've been working for Mr. Quinn for quite some time now."

"If that's what we're doing," Jonas muttered under his breath.

She frowned. "And what's that supposed to mean?"

"Oh, come on. We both know Swanson's the one calling the shots now."

She sniffed. "Well, I'm *not* working for that Swanson guy. I'm working for Mr. Quinn. I..." She paused, looking through the window. "Hey, guys, I think it's starting."

The doors at the ends of the elevated pathways opened. Through the door on the left came a tall, muscular woman with black hair pinned to her head in some kind of braid-crown arrangement. Through the other door came Robyn. She was barefoot as usual, and her hands were wrapped in white gauze.

"Ladies and gentlemen, welcome to tonight's event here at Chrystal Arena!" a man yelled into a microphone. There weren't any speakers in the gallery, but the ones in the arena were loud enough to get the sound through the walls. "Tonight, we have something extra special to offer—a first-class fight between two legendary women! Tonight, we'll get to see the clash between the fast and ferocious Valkyrie, and the magnificently aggressive Morrigan! Who's the superior fighter? Who will move on to the semifinals? Let's find out!"

Robyn and her opponent walked toward the ring. The Morrigan wasn't as large as the Bear, but she was still a lot bigger than Robyn.

"This could get ugly," Jonas commented. "She's really small."

"You shouldn't underestimate the Valkyrie," Lily said. "Remember that grip she pulled off in her last fight?"

"Yeah, but the Morrigan does that provoking thing. It makes people do stupid moves."

"I don't think the Valkyrie is that easily provoked," Andrew said. "She's pretty calm in the ring."

The referee backed away from the fighters, and then the bell rang. Robyn and the Morrigan stared at each other, neither of them moving a muscle. The Morrigan opened her mouth, saying something inaudible, and Andrew could have sworn he saw Robyn rolling her eyes.

"She's trying to make the Valkyrie attack first," Jonas said.

Andrew smiled. "I don't think she's going to succeed."

The fighters stood motionless for almost half a minute before the Morrigan finally attacked. She was faster than Robyn's last opponent, but Robyn still dodged her with confident ease.

"Holy shit, she's fast," Lily commented. "She almost looks like she's dancing."

Lily was right. He watched Robyn dodge the Morrigan's kicks and punches in an almost playful manner. Every movement was calculated and full of grace, and it reminded him of when he'd seen her dance in the garage. How had he not seen it before? Now that he knew about her ballerina background, he could easily see how the dancing had influenced her fighting style.

When the bell rang again, the Morrigan was breathing heavily. Robyn had gotten some hits in, but mostly she'd just kept avoiding her opponent. The audience screamed its disappointment.

Two men got up from their seats in the gallery. One of them was the man who'd caught Andrew in the locker room. The other was an old man in a gray coat. Was that Swanson?

Andrew watched carefully as the men went through the door and approached the ring. The man in the black suit headed to the Morrigan's corner, while the man in the gray coat went over to the other. Robyn seemed to shrink as she talked to him, holding her head low. Yes, that was definitely Swanson.

After a while, the two men left the ring, returning to the gallery. Andrew's heart pounded in his chest when Swanson passed him. In his mind, Swanson had become some sort of abstract, nightmarish terror, but up close, he was just an ordinary man. He leaned heavily on his cane as he walked, and his presence wasn't nearly as frightening as Andrew had expected. *But I know what he's capable of,* he thought. *I'm not going to underestimate him.*

The bell rang, signaling the start of the second round.

"Look, the Morrigan is trying to provoke the Valkyrie again," Jonas said. "I've heard she researches her opponents to figure out what will piss them off the most."

"I don't think it's going to work against the Valkyrie," Andrew said confidently. "She's…"

He stopped in the middle of the sentence, mouth ajar. Without warning, Robyn jumped her opponent with more power than should have been physically possible. The Morrigan flew backward with Robyn right on top of her. She hit the mat hard, unable to catch herself since her hands were too busy trying to deflect Robyn's fists. The first punch broke her nose. The second broke her lip. The third, fourth, and fifth crushed her cheekbones.

"How did she even do that?" Lily stared at the ring in awe. "I mean, what does she weigh? One hundred and twenty pounds? The Morrigan has to be a lot heavier."

One hundred and fourteen, Andrew silently corrected, sharing Lily's shock. Robyn punched the Morrigan's face over and over, turning her facial structure into a pulp-like mass. At first, the Morrigan tried to get Robyn off her body and even got in a few punches herself, but her hands soon fell limply to the mat.

"She's not moving." Jonas got up from his chair. "She's out. Someone has to stop the Valkyrie."

The referee made a sign with his hands, causing the bell to ring. Two men wearing orange jackets immediately hurried inside the ring. They each grabbed one of Robyn's arms and pulled her away from the unconscious woman. She squirmed in their grip, her legs kicking wildly. Andrew had never seen her like that before. There was pure fury in her eyes—fury and panic.

"I think that's our cue," Lily said, heading out the door. Andrew and Jonas followed.

When they entered the cage, the Morrigan lay motionless on the floor. Robyn was still fighting to get away from the guards.

"You two need to make sure she's breathing," Andrew said. "Tell someone to call an ambulance. I'll take care of Robyn."

"What? The Valkyrie, you mean?" Lily asked. "Why? She's barely hurt. You're the doctor, you should take care of the Morrigan. She needs you more."

"Do not question me!" he snarled, loud enough to make the young woman flinch. He ran to Robyn's side, putting a hand on her shoulder. "Robyn? You need to calm down. It's over."

She glanced at him, then back at the Morrigan.

"Robyn. You have to stop. She's unconscious. You won."

Her attempts to free herself slowly came to a stop. She dangled helplessly between the two men, the panic fading from her eyes.

"I'll take it from here," Andrew told the guards. "I'm with the medical team."

The men looked at each other before hesitantly backing away. Robyn sank to her knees. Andrew pulled her up and wrapped an arm around her waist, half leading, half carrying her out of the arena.

"Is she... Is she going to be okay?" she asked.

"The medical team is taking care of her," he said, casting a quick glance over his shoulder. "She'll be fine."

It wasn't exactly a lie, but it wasn't the truth either. The Morrigan would most likely live, yes, but her face would never be the same again.

"She said things about Lucy. Things she'd do to her. She knew our address, Andrew." Robyn looked down at her bloodstained hands, her body trembling. "I could have killed her. I *would* have killed her if they hadn't stopped me. Oh my God."

"It's okay." He draped his jacket over her shoulders. "She won't touch Lucy. She was just trying to make you angry. It's okay. Everything will be okay."

He led her to the sink in the locker room. With gentle movements, he removed the gauze and washed the blood off her hands. Most of it was the Morrigan's, but some of it came from abrasions on her knuckles. He cleaned the wounds and bandaged them, all while continuously reassuring Robyn that everything would be okay. He wasn't sure if she was listening, but he still felt the need to say it.

When her hands were clean, he made her sit down on the bench. He quickly examined her, checking out the places where the Morrigan had hit her. "Your chin will be swollen for a while," he said, grazing the bruise with his thumb, "but otherwise you're fine." *Thank God.*

She nodded. "You should go check on her. Her wounds are way worse than mine."

Andrew knew she was right, but he didn't want to leave her alone. She'd pulled her knees up to her chest again, and she was still staring at her hands. She looked small and fragile, so different from the way she'd looked back in the ring. Her eyes were full of fear and guilt. He wanted nothing more than to drive her as far away from the arena as possible, ignoring all other responsibilities. But he'd sworn an oath. The Morrigan needed him more than Robyn did.

"I'll be right back, okay?" he said. "Don't go anywhere."

He reluctantly left her there, hurrying back to the arena. Jonas and Lily had managed to get the Morrigan up on a stretcher, and the men who'd restrained Robyn were now carrying the unconscious woman away. Lily sent Andrew an angry glare before following them, leaving Andrew and Jonas standing alone in the ring.

"How bad was it?" Andrew asked.

"Her face will never be the same again, that's for sure," Jonas answered. "But she'll live."

Andrew nodded. "Good. I'll set her up with a plastic surgeon."

"The board won't like this, you know," Jonas continued. "Especially not Swanson. We're not supposed to send for ambulances unless it's a life-or-death situation."

Andrew shrugged. "I don't care what the board thinks."

"Yeah, I noticed." He paused, remaining silent for a while. "I think I've figured out why you're doing this."

"Oh, really?" Andrew raised his eyebrows.

"Yeah. I think you're the same as me." Jonas sighed. "I fell in love with a street fighter."

Andrew stared at him for a moment and then finally admitted the truth.

"Me too."

CHAPTER FIFTEEN

I could have killed her, Robyn thought. *I could have killed her with my bare hands.*

The Morrigan's words kept ringing in her ears. At first, the fighter had tried to provoke her by insulting her. Robyn had listened to the Morrigan's comments on her body and her scars, but she hadn't really cared. She'd heard it all before. Then, the Morrigan had said things about Lucy and the things she would do to her—and Robyn had snapped. She didn't know how else to explain it. One second, she'd been calm and in control, and the next she'd turned into a mindless murder machine. If the guards hadn't stopped her, that woman would have been dead now.

She shuddered, pulling her knees closer to her chest. She'd always known she was messed up, but she hadn't thought she was messed up enough to end another person's life.

She kept glancing at the door, waiting for Andrew to return. She knew the Morrigan needed his expertise, but a childish, selfish part of her wished he could have stayed with her instead. Things made more sense when he was around. She might not believe in his silly everything-will-be-okay mantra, but she still liked hearing him say it. Most of all, she didn't want to be alone. She didn't want to think about the fight and the crime she'd almost committed.

When the door finally opened, it wasn't Andrew who entered the locker room. Instead, she saw Mark standing in the doorway.

"She's in here," Mark said, holding the door open for Swanson. The old man walked in without using his cane. Panic rushed through her. Swanson was not in a good mood.

"I'm sorry." She lowered her gaze. "I really was planning to hold back. I'm sorry."

"It was quite the performance, but I don't think you altered your underdog status. You did fine, dear." Swanson looked around the room, frowning. "Have you seen that new doctor on the medical team? I need to have a word with him."

Robyn's eyes widened. This was exactly what she'd been trying to avoid.

"I think he followed the ambulance to the hospital," she lied. "Why do you ask?"

"He doesn't seem to share our view on the importance of discretion. Don't worry about it, dear. Focus on the semifinal. We'll take care of this little problem."

She nodded. *That's exactly what I'm worried about.*

Swanson left the room. Mark followed him to the door but then came to a stop, turning around to face her again. His eyes were cold and full of resentment. Swanson may have forgiven her outburst in the ring, but Mark definitely hadn't.

"Swanson might believe your lies about that new doctor, but I don't," he said in a low voice. "I saw how he looked at you. This was not the first time you two met. I don't know why everyone seems to accept that there's a new guy on the medical team no one remembers hiring, but I'm not buying it. If he's up to something, there will be consequences for both of you. Trust me on that. I'll be watching you."

Robyn swallowed hard. "I'm sure he's just an ordinary doctor. He doesn't seem like the kind of guy who'd be up to something— not that I know him or anything. We might have met at the ER once or twice. That's all."

Mark wrinkled his nose. "I have no idea what Mr. Swanson sees in you. He keeps talking about your potential, but you can't even lie properly." He shook his head and left the room, slamming the door shut behind him.

"Shit." Robyn groaned, banging the back of her head against the wall. Andrew was getting tangled up in things he didn't fully understand, and it could only end badly. The incident in the locker room before the fight had been a close call—way too close. If she hadn't arrived in time, that manager would have beaten the shit out of Andrew. What if it happened again? What if she didn't make it in time to protect him next time? She might be stuck in Chrystal Valley's underground world, but he wasn't. She had to get him out before it was too late.

She'd already cut him out of her romantic life. For his own sake, it was time to get him out of her fighting life, too.

• • •

When Andrew returned to the locker room, Robyn's adrenaline rush was long gone. She had to force herself to keep her eyes open. He approached her with easy steps, clearly clueless to the danger he'd put himself in by simply being in there.

"You have to be more careful," she told him. "This is the last time you're coming into the backstage area, okay? Next time, you're watching from the audience."

He shook his head. "That's not going to happen."

"Swanson is looking for you because you called for that ambulance, and his assistant is fully convinced you're up to something." She clenched her fists, trying to remain calm. "Just do as I say, okay?"

"No." Andrew stared her down, his gaze unwavering. "I'm not afraid of them."

"You should be. Aren't you the one who's been trying to convince me that Swanson is dangerous? You're right, he is dangerous. He wouldn't hurt me, not until this tournament is over, but he would definitely hurt you. You've pissed him off, Andrew, and he's not a man you should piss off."

At first, Andrew looked like he wanted to argue with her, but then he hesitated. "And when I endanger myself, I endanger you," he said softly, more to himself than to her. "I'm sorry, I should have listened to you. About many things." His eyes roamed over her face, pausing at her bandaged cheek. "Did my actions put you in danger? Me joining the medical team, I mean?"

Mark's words echoed in her ears. *If he's up to something, there will be consequences for both of you. Trust me on that.* She glanced up at Andrew. He looked worried and ashamed, his eyes full of guilt and regret.

"No," she finally said. "I'll be fine."

Andrew sighed with relief. "Good, because I think I'm going to keep working here. The medical team really needs a doctor."

Robyn felt the urge to smash her face against the wall.

"Are you suicidal?" she groaned. "That's the literal opposite of what I said! Why do you always have to do shit like this? I try to keep you out of danger, and you just keep throwing yourself back in."

He raised his eyebrows. "That's how I feel every time you enter the ring."

"I know what I'm doing in the ring."

"And I, believe it or not, am pretty good at being a doctor."

She glared at him, already regretting her lie. She didn't have any leverage in the conversation, and judging from Andrew's cocky grin, he was well aware of it.

"I guess we'll both have to be careful, then," she muttered. "To protect each other."

"I like the sound of that."

She rolled her eyes. "Let's get out of here."

She opened the locker room door and took a quick look around. The corridor outside was empty, but she didn't doubt that Swanson and Mark were still in the building.

She turned back to Andrew. "Follow me."

They got out of Chrystal Arena without running into anyone who recognized them.

"Do you want me to drop you off at your place, or do you want to use my guest room?" Andrew asked when they reached his car.

She considered it for a moment. "I'd rather stay at your place tonight. Lucy always stays at Mike's place on the weekends nowadays." It was pathetic, but she really didn't want to be alone. She was still too upset about the fight and her encounter with Swanson. Friends slept over at friends' houses, right?

"My place it is, then," Andrew said with a smile. She smiled back. Their relationship wasn't back to what it used to be yet, but it seemed to be going in the right direction.

She leaned back against the passenger's seat, closing her eyes. The sleepiness had returned the moment she sat down, and the warmth from the seat heater was making her tense muscles relax. *I should set my alarm,* she thought, but before she could do anything about it she was fast asleep.

• • •

The next morning, Andrew was awakened by a scream. He jumped out of bed, grabbed his blue bathrobe from a hook on the wall, and ran to the guest room.

"Robyn? Are you okay?" he yelled as he rushed through the door.

Robyn was sitting up in the bed, breathing heavily. Though it was hard to tell in the dim light, he thought he could see traces of tears on her cheeks. Tiny had placed himself on the bedside table, watching her with suspicious curiosity.

Andrew carefully approached the bed. "Another nightmare?"

"Yeah," she panted. "I'm fine."

Her whole body was trembling. He raised his arms and then lowered them again. He wanted nothing more than to hug her, but he wasn't sure she wanted to be touched.

"Hold me," she said.

"What?"

"Hold me," she repeated. "I know you want to."

Andrew was too much of an opportunist to turn down an offer like that. He sat down on the bed and wrapped his arms around her. "I thought you didn't do hugs."

"I don't, but you do." She leaned her forehead against his shoulder, burrowing her fingers in the fabric of his bathrobe. "It calms you down when I let you hold me, and when you calm down, I calm down."

She was right—he did get calmer when he got to hold her. He smiled. He hadn't known his own mood had such an effect on her.

"What was the nightmare about?" he asked, drawing circles on her back with his thumb.

She tensed up, and for a moment, he was certain she would pull herself away from him. Then he felt her relax again.

"I dream about the day my mother died," she said softly. "I'm seventeen again, and I've just gotten home from school. I always know there's something wrong, so I look around the apartment. The dream ends when I find her in the bathroom, and then I scream. I'm sorry for waking you up."

"It's okay." He kissed the top of her head in a way he hoped could qualify as platonic. "I have nightmares about the day my mother died too, sometimes."

"What happened to her?" she asked. "I've never heard you speak about your family."

"I don't have any family left. I lost my mom in a train crash when I was twelve. She got me out of the train, but then she went back inside to help others. She was always like that. Stubborn. Self-sacrificing. Brave." He glanced down at Robyn. "She was a bit like you, actually. I still don't know what happened inside that train, but when she came back out she was pale and feeling dizzy. 'It's nothing,' she said. 'I'm just going to rest for a while.'" He swallowed hard. The memory still hurt to think about, and he hadn't talked about it in a very long time. "She had internal bleeding in her abdomen. She bled out before anyone even understood how serious the injury was."

"That's horrible." Robyn's grip on his bathrobe tightened. "I'm so sorry, Andrew. Your nightmares must be terrifying."

"They are. Thankfully, I don't have them as often nowadays. They weren't all bad, either. Those nightmares gave me the motivation I needed to become a doctor. I hated how helpless I'd been when my mother died, so I swore to myself to never be helpless again." He smiled humorlessly. "I was twenty-five when my father had a heart attack. I did everything I could, but I lost him anyway. That's when I realized doctors are pretty helpless too. It was a while before I could even bring myself to set foot in this place again. I grew up here, but it didn't feel right to move back in here without my parents. I hated the house and everything it reminded me of, but I still couldn't bring myself to sell it. I'd originally planned to stay in New York and do my residency there, but in the end, I chose to move back here anyway. I don't exactly hate the house anymore, but sometimes, it still reminds me of how useless I am."

"You're way too hard on yourself, you know," Robyn said. "You weren't useless when my lung broke. You saved me." She was starting to sound a bit sleepy, and her body was getting heavier against his.

"Your lung didn't break. It just collapsed."

"Whatever." She shrugged. "You still saved me."

He smiled. "I did."

A few minutes later, Robyn started to snore.

Now what? He looked down at the sleeping woman in his arms. She looked calm and peaceful, her hands still holding on to his bathrobe. He knew he should simply pull her away from him and go back to his own room, but he couldn't bring himself to do it. He didn't want to wake her.

You couldn't wake her even if you tried, said his inner critic.

He ignored the voice and lay back on the bed. Robyn made a sound in the back of her throat but remained asleep, burrowing her face in the crook of his neck. Her hair tickled his skin, but he didn't mind it. Her body was soft and warm against his. This was how things were supposed to be. This was where he belonged.

Tiny jumped back up on the bed, curling up next to them. Andrew scratched the cat behind his ear until a soft purr joined the sound of Robyn's snoring. He closed his eyes and smiled. For the first time in many, many years, the house felt like a home.

CHAPTER SIXTEEN

Well, this is new. Robyn slowly opened her eyes. She wasn't exactly sure how she and Andrew had ended up in the position they were in. The last thing she remembered before falling asleep was him telling her about his family, and she was certain they'd still been sitting upright then. Now, her body was pretty much draped over his, and she was still clutching the fabric of his bathrobe in her hands. His right arm was wrapped around her, his hand resting on her hip. Tiny had gone back to sleep right next to them, claiming Andrew's left arm as a pillow. The scene was unexpectedly domestic, and Robyn had no idea how she'd ended up right in the middle of it.

She pushed herself up on her elbow, glancing at her watch. It was already half past eleven. She frowned, trying to calculate how long she'd been sleeping. When the nightmare had woken her up, the sun hadn't risen yet. Weird. She couldn't recall ever before managing to get several hours of sleep after having the nightmare. *He really does calm me down,* she thought, glancing down at Andrew again.

"Hi," said a fully awake Andrew.

She flinched in surprise, scrambled backward, and rolled off the bed. Her body hit the floor with a very ungracious thud.

"I'm sorry, I didn't mean to scare you." Andrew peered down at her from the edge of the bed. He bit his lip, as if trying to force back a smile. "Are you okay?"

She sat up, her cheeks turning red. "I'm fine." She glared up at him. "No thanks to you."

"I'm sorry." He looked like he was about to start laughing at her any second. "Hey, this reminds me of the first time you slept here. I was the one on the floor back then, though. I guess this is karma."

She didn't know what to say, so she continued to glare.

This time, Andrew couldn't hold back the laughter. "I know you're trying to look menacing, but it's really not working. Not with that hair."

Robyn's hands immediately went up to her hair. She'd forgotten to let it down before falling asleep. The bun had turned into a tangled mess during the night, located right above her ear. With an annoyed grunt she pulled at the hair tie.

"You're never going to get it out like that," Andrew said, grinning. "Come on, let me help you."

She gave the hair tie a final tug before giving up, turning her head so he could help her.

"I should cut it off," she muttered. "Things like this would never happen if I had short hair."

"Why don't you?" he asked as he worked with her hair. "You don't seem to like having long hair. Why don't you cut it off?"

"It's a ballerina thing." She chewed on her lip. "I know it's silly, but if I ever take up dancing again I want to have long hair. I want to be able to put it up in a bun like the soloists always did in my old ballet company." She sighed. "It's not very likely I'll ever dance on stage again, but I still can't bring myself to cut off my hair."

"I don't think it's silly," Andrew said, "and I'm not just saying that because I like your hair. No one knows how the future will turn out. You're still young. I'm sure you'll be up on a stage again one day. You've got a talent, and that talent is too extraordinary to be hidden away in a garage."

"I'm not that good," she mumbled, blushing.

"In my eyes, you are. I don't know much about ballet so my opinion doesn't really count, but I enjoyed watching you dance." He gently pulled the last strand of hair free from the elastic and combed through her locks with his fingers. "I would love to see you dance on stage one day."

She smiled. "I'll keep that in mind."

Andrew obviously had no idea what he was talking about, but his words still made her chest feel warm and tingly. The conviction in his voice almost made her believe there was a chance she would go back to dancing one day.

She got up from the floor and stretched. "I should get going. Lucy will be home soon."

"Let me check your injuries first."

She rolled her eyes but sat down next to him on the bed. "The Morrigan barely touched me."

"No, but her manager did."

He carefully removed the bandage on her cheek. His eyes narrowed as he went from being Andrew to being Dr. Alexander. "It's a bit swollen, but I can't tell if it's because of the cuts or the punch itself. I'm going to give you an antibiotic ointment to make sure the cuts don't get infected. You need to keep the wounds covered for about a week, and you have to change the dressing at least once a day. A normal Band-Aid should be fine."

She nodded, zoning out a little. She'd had cuts before, and the only time she'd gotten an infection was when she'd tried to do her own stitches. The cuts on her cheek were nothing. She'd definitely had worse.

"Hey." Andrew flicked her on the forehead, pulling her out of her thoughts. "Pay attention."

"I am." She frowned. "And that's my move."

"I know. Annoying, isn't it?" He grinned smugly and flicked her again in the same spot.

"Stop it," she snapped, grabbing his wrist. When he raised his left hand she tried to grab that one too, but he dodged her and managed to get a hold of her wrist instead.

They stared at each other. She suddenly noticed how close they were, and Andrew seemed to have had the same realization. Her heart began to race. She forced herself to look anywhere but at his lips. One part of her brain told her to remember the way he'd tricked her and all the other reasons why she should stay away, while another part told her to forget what she'd said and just give in to the need burning within her. Her reasons for shutting him out were strong, but as she sat there with her face close to his, she came to realize that her stupid, irrational need for him might actually be even stronger.

He let go of her wrist and instead took her hand in his. "It's important that you take care of the cuts," he said. "We're trying to avoid scarring, remember?"

She lowered her eyes. "Right."

He squeezed her hand. "I know you hate your scars, and I don't think I could ever forgive myself if my actions left permanent marks on you. Please, Robyn, you have to take better care of yourself."

"Wait, let me get this straight—if I get more scars, you'll be upset?"

"That's one way of seeing it, yes."

She sighed. "Just give me the damn ointment."

He smiled. "That's the spirit." He let go of her hand, and Robyn quickly let go of his wrist. The moment ended. "I'll prepare a bag for you with everything you might need. Why don't you put on a pot of coffee?"

She nodded. "But after that, I really have to leave."

• • •

Robyn ended up staying for several hours, simply hanging out with Andrew. The concept of *hanging out* wasn't exactly new to her, but she wasn't used to it either. Andrew was surprisingly easy to talk to, even though they'd had such different pasts. She wasn't sure why, but she liked spending time with him. It felt normal. She liked normal.

They ordered pizza for lunch, confirming Robyn's suspicion that Andrew was about as good at cooking as she was.

"Do you ever eat homemade food?" she asked.

"Not really, no. I know all this junk food is bad for me, but it's better than starving." He shrugged. "I do order salads sometimes."

"You should come over to our place sometime," she said. "Lucy always cooks for us. She's really good at it, too."

He gave her a surprised smile. "I might take you up on that offer."

Robyn chewed on her lip, making a decision. "Maybe…uh…" She flushed. Andrew tilted his head to the side, waiting patiently for her to continue. She took a deep breath. "I just thought… maybe you would like to celebrate Christmas with us? I'd have to ask Lucy first, but since she's probably already invited Mike, she should be fine with me inviting an extra person, too."

Andrew's eyes lit up, but his excitement faded as quickly as it had appeared. "I'd love to. I don't know if I can, though. I'm supposed to be working on Christmas Day."

"I see." She tried to conceal her disappointment but wasn't sure if she succeeded. "It's okay. I should have asked you earlier."

"I'll try my best to get out of it. I can't promise anything, but I'll really try." He smiled. "Thank you for the invitation. It means a lot to me."

"I still need to talk to Lucy," she reminded him. "I hope you can make it. If you don't, I'll probably end up punching Mike before the day is over."

He grinned. "And wouldn't that be tragic."

• • •

When Robyn finally returned to the apartment, Lucy was already home.

"Where have you been?" Lucy asked, stepping out from the kitchen. She was wearing her white, frilly apron, and something was cooking in the oven.

"I slept at Andrew's place last night," Robyn said. "I was planning on leaving right after I woke up, but then...I changed my mind. Sorry, I should have texted you."

"You were with Andrew?" Lucy made no attempt whatsoever to hide her excitement. "That's great! You should have invited him over for dinner."

"I did, actually. He's not coming over tonight, though." Robyn dumped her backpack and Andrew's bag with medical supplies on the floor before heading to the kitchen. "Hey... It's Christmas soon."

"I know. Time flies."

"Yeah..." Robyn leaned against doorframe, trying to find the words. "I know you've always wanted to celebrate Christmas with more people. Other people than just you and me."

Lucy turned around, her skirt twirling around her. "That's not true. I'm perfectly fine with just you and me. I—"

"I know you've always wanted it, and I know you've never said anything because you know how I feel about other people," Robyn interrupted. "But I...I've changed this past year. I think I'm ready for the Christmas gathering you've always wanted. Mike should be here, and Ana and Suzanna, and...and Andrew." She smiled nervously. "What do you say?"

Lucy stared at her sister in shock. "Are you sure? Do you really want to do this?"

"Yes."

Lucy's eyes filled with tears. "Thank you." She threw her arms around Robyn's neck. "Thank you, thank you, thank you."

• • •

Andrew yawned as he parked the car outside Chrystal Arena. He hadn't slept much before Robyn's scream woke him up, and after she'd fallen asleep in his arms, he'd forced himself to stay awake for as long as possible. The moment had been too perfect to waste on sleep. He'd ended up sleeping for an hour or two anyway, but most of the time he'd just lain there, savoring it all. Her body had fit perfectly against his, and her hands had held on to his bathrobe the whole time. How the hell was he supposed to sleep alone after this?

When he'd visited Chrystal Arena before, he'd always felt uncomfortable. Now, wearing the orange medical team jacket, he felt more at ease. He was acting as a doctor, and that was something he knew he was good at. The jacket seemed to make people believe he was part of the staff, and he received several polite nods and waves from other jacket-wearing personnel as he walked through the long corridors in the backstage area.

He found Jonas and Lily in the gallery, sitting on the same chairs as the previous night.

"You're right on time," Jonas said when Andrew took a seat next to them. "The first-class fight starts soon."

"How did the other fights go? Any serious injuries?"

When Jonas had told him they'd only need him for the first-class fights, he'd been skeptical. Now, he was grateful for it. Fitting the first-class fights into his already busy schedule was tricky enough—attending the other fights too would have been impossible.

"Just some scratches and bruises," Jonas said. "The fights in the lower classes tend to be pretty chill."

"The Morrigan is still in the ICU, though." Lily sent Andrew a chilly glare. She clearly hadn't forgiven him for making Robyn his main priority the night before.

"I'm sorry about last night," he said. "I was unprofessional. Robyn…the Valkyrie, she's special to me. I let my feelings rule my actions. I'm sorry."

Lily's eyes softened a little. "I get why you did it, but if you're going to continue working here, you have to get those feelings under control. People get hurt in here. If you're going to be the arena's only doctor, you have to stay rational."

"I know. I can't promise it won't happen again, but I'll definitely do my best."

"Don't be so hard on him, Lil," Jonas said. "We would never have managed to take care of all those brawlers last night if it wasn't for him. He freaked out a little. Shit happens."

Andrew turned to the young man and gave him an appreciative smile, but Jonas didn't seem to notice it. His eyes were fixed on one of the doors leading to the ring, and there was a deep wrinkle between his eyebrows.

"Hey, are you all right?" Andrew asked.

"I'm fine," Jonas answered, still staring at the door.

"Don't mind him," Lily said. "He always gets like that when Tyler fights."

"Oh." Andrew finally realized what was going on. "He's your…?"

"My *friend*," Jonas filled in, a sad expression sweeping over his face. "My very heterosexual friend."

"Oh," Andrew said again, unsure how to react.

Jonas didn't say anything more, but the sadness remained in his eyes. Andrew felt like he should say something, but he had no idea what. He had never been in a situation even remotely similar to Jonas's, but he could imagine how painful it must be to love someone who could never see you as anything more than a friend.

Before the heavy silence could turn even more awkward, the doors opened. Through the left door came a pale, slender blond wearing a pair of black swimming trunks. He was young—a teenager, most likely. Andrew really hoped he was over eighteen.

He glanced at Lily, who shook her head. Not Tyler, then.

A dark-skinned man with fiery red hair entered the arena through the door to the right. After staring at him for a while, Andrew recognized him. The last time he'd seen that man, he had confirmed Robyn's identity in the parking lot outside Sandy's. Andrew shuddered. The thought of her going up against that giant again didn't appeal to him at all.

"So," he said, "the winner of this fight gets to fight the Valkyrie in the semifinals, right?"

"That's right," Lily confirmed. "We're pretty certain Tyler will win this. That kid relies on speed and agility, and Tyler's technique works really well against opponents like that."

Lily's answer didn't calm Andrew at all. Robyn's technique relied on speed and agility, too.

"Ladies and gentlemen, welcome to yet another first-class fight here at Chrystal Arena!" the commentator yelled into his microphone. "In tonight's fight, we'll get to see the quick and vicious Weasel take on the powerful Griffin!"

Andrew didn't have to ask which moniker belonged to which fighter. Standing next to Tyler, the Weasel looked even skinnier than before.

"Tyler will be fine," Lily said, squeezing Jonas's hand. "That rodent doesn't stand a chance."

Andrew swallowed hard. For Robyn's safety, he hoped she was wrong.

• • •

Lily's words turned out to be true. After less than a round, the Weasel lay unconscious on the mat. Jonas sighed in relief, and Lily jumped up from her chair with a happy cheer.

Andrew grabbed his medical bag and opened the door leading to the arena. He turned around in the doorway, facing his teammates. "Lily, you and I will check on the kid first. Jonas, you can check on Tyler. Are you guys fine with that?"

Jonas nodded, and Lily smiled. "That's more like it, Dr. Alexander," she said with a wink. "Let's go and do our job."

Together, they jogged toward the ring. The Weasel had already woken up from his unconsciousness, and Tyler was pulling him back up to his feet.

"You did well, kiddo." Tyler grinned widely. "You almost had me a couple of times. Better luck next time."

The blond nodded, still looking a little dizzy. Tyler gave him a hard pat on the back, almost making him fall over again.

"Hey." Andrew hurried to the Weasel's side. "I'm a doctor. I'm here to help you."

He did a quick examination to estimate the Weasel's injuries. The young man was a little disoriented from the knockout, but other than that, he seemed to be more or less unharmed.

"You'll have a black eye for a while," Andrew told his patient, "but you'll be fine."

The Weasel grinned. "That's all right. I'll probably have two black eyes after my manager's done with me."

Andrew frowned. "Does he hit you? That's abuse, you know. You don't have to put up with that kind of treatment."

"Jeez, calm down." The Weasel lowered his eyes. "It was a joke."

Andrew was not convinced, so he opened his bag and grabbed his notebook and a pencil. "Here, take my number. Call me if you need a doctor but can't go to the hospital."

The Weasel quickly looked around before taking the note, hiding it in one of the pockets in his shorts. "Thank you."

The boy walked away from the ring, presumably to meet with his manager. Andrew sighed. Were all the managers abusive douche bags?

He cast a quick glance at Tyler, who was still being cared for by Jonas. *He'll be fine,* Andrew decided and escaped the scene. He went back up to the gallery and was just about to head out into the backstage corridor when someone tapped him on the shoulder.

"You must be the new doctor," a voice said from behind his back. "I don't think we've met."

Andrew slowly turned around, finally coming face to face with Swanson.

"I am," he said, faking a polite smile. "My name is Andrew Alexander. Nice to meet you." He reached out his hand, and Swanson shook it. Swanson's handshake was surprisingly firm for his age, and the way he leaned on his cane seemed a bit off. If Swanson thought he could make Andrew underestimate him, he was definitely wrong.

"My name is Richard Swanson, and this is my assistant Mark Schmidt." Swanson nodded at the bald man standing right behind him. "We've heard a lot about you, young man."

"Mostly good things, I hope," Andrew said, knowing Swanson's opinion of him was without a doubt negative.

"Absolutely." Swanson smiled. "You seem to be an extraordinarily caring person, Dr. Alexander. It's fairly unusual for the medical team to call an ambulance just because a contestant obtained some injuries."

"I was only doing my job." Andrew tried to remain calm, but he felt the panic creeping up on him. Swanson was incredibly difficult to read. His words said one thing, his tone another—and his cold, gray eyes said absolutely nothing at all.

"Meticulous, too," Swanson continued. "Our dear Ms. Monroe was barely touched, yet you still went to great lengths to make sure she was unharmed. Impressive work, Dr. Alexander." He patted Andrew on the shoulder again before leaving the gallery. Mark followed him out the door without a word.

Andrew waited in the gallery for several minutes to make sure he wouldn't run into the two again. He was sweating, and his pulse was still racing. He understood why Robyn was so afraid of Swanson now.

When he finally reached the back door, he had to fight the urge to sprint to his car. He quickly crossed the parking lot, forcing himself not to run. Not until he closed the car door behind him did his heart rate slow down to a normal pace.

He'd passed the point of no return. Swanson knew who he was now. If Jason didn't succeed in bringing Swanson down, it wasn't just Robyn's life that would be in danger—Andrew's life would be in danger, too.

CHAPTER SEVENTEEN

Robyn was awakened by a loud ringing noise. She ran her hand over the bedside table in search of her alarm clock, but for some reason, she couldn't find it. She opened her eyes and found Lucy standing in her room with the alarm clock in her hand.

"Merry Christmas!" she said, her voice uncomfortably loud. She had already changed out of her pajamas and was wearing her favorite cocktail dress.

"What time is it?" Robyn groaned, rubbing her eyes.

"It's already eight." Lucy was practically vibrating with excitement. "We're gonna have to do things a bit earlier than usual if we're gonna be ready for our guests in time. I know how you feel about cooking, but I could really use some help in the kitchen today."

"Yeah, sure." Robyn sat up in her bed, forcing herself to stay awake.

Lucy smiled and left the room. Robyn opened her closet and got dressed, putting on a brown tank top and her usual black sweatpants. When she joined Lucy in the kitchen, her sister had already begun to prepare the food. She glanced at Robyn and sighed.

"No. You're not wearing sweatpants at my Christmas party."

"Isn't it *our* Christmas party?"

Lucy shrugged. "Call it whatever you like. You're still wearing a dress."

Robyn frowned. "I don't even have a dress."

"Yes, you do."

"No, I don't." Robyn furrowed her brow, mentally going through her closet. "I can't wear *that* dress at a Christmas party. It's my...you know..."

"It used to be your funeral dress," Lucy filled in. "It doesn't look like a funeral dress anymore, that's for sure." She winked and continued to prepare the food.

What the hell did she do? Robyn returned to her room, opened the door to her closet, and pulled out the only dress she owned. The last time she'd worn it had been at her mother's funeral. Back then, it had been a plain, full-length gown. Now, it was a lot shorter, and the neckline looked different, too. She undressed again and put it on. The hemline now stopped halfway down her thighs, and Lucy had turned the modest boatneck into a plunging V-neck. Lucy had also given the dress sleeves made of intricate black lace, long enough to cover the ugly scar on Robyn's forearm.

She looked at herself in the full-length mirror on the closet door and tentatively did a pirouette, watching the skirt flare out around her legs. *This isn't too bad,* she thought, smiling a little to herself. She actually felt kind of pretty.

"Are you done yet?" Lucy yelled from the kitchen. "I could use some help in here."

"I'm coming." Robyn made a final twirl in front of the mirror before closing the closet door. It felt weird to be wearing a dress for the first time in six years—especially *that* dress—but she supposed she could endure it for a couple of hours for Lucy's sake.

"When did you do all this?" she asked as she entered the kitchen. Lucy was standing with her back toward her, stirring a pot on the stove.

Lucy shrugged. "I pulled a couple of all-nighters. I thought that if I was going to force you into a dress, it should at least be a nice-looking one." She turned around to face Robyn, smiling. "What do you think?"

"It's…it's okay, I guess. It looks a lot better than before."

Lucy snorted. "Which means you like it, but you think you're too cool to admit you actually like a dress."

"Something like that."

Lucy shook her head. "You're ridiculous."

"*You're* ridiculous." The comeback came automatically, and they both snickered. It had been a long time since they were both relaxed enough to act like sisters with each other.

"Come on," Lucy said. "Put on an apron and help me cook. Our guests will be here in four hours, and we have a lot to do."

• • •

Andrew took a final look in the rearview mirror, straightening his pale-blue tie. He smiled. It was the first time he was celebrating Christmas in years, and he was really looking forward to it.

He opened the glove compartment and picked up a small, wrapped box. There was definitely a risk that Robyn would freak out about his gift, but he hoped she would accept it.

After getting the bouquet of flowers from the backseat, he locked the car and hurried toward the Monroe sisters' apartment. A quick glance at his watch told him he was almost thirty minutes late. Though he'd tried to get out of his Christmas shift completely, he'd only managed to split it up. He'd still had to work all morning and would have to work all night, but at least he had five free hours between the shifts.

He climbed the stairs to the apartment and rang the doorbell. Music and the sound of people talking and laughing came from the other side of the door.

The door opened. "Hi, Andrew," Lucy said, smiling widely. "Perfect timing. Dinner's almost ready."

"Hi, Lucy. Merry Christmas." He smiled back and handed her the bouquet. "Thanks for the invitation."

"Wow, thanks!" she said, giving the flowers a quick sniff. "I need to put these in water. Please, come in."

He stepped inside the apartment and took off his coat, leaving it on a coatrack next to the door.

"I'll be damned," said a deep female voice with a faint Indian accent. "You were right."

"I know, right?" said a different, somewhat familiar voice. Andrew turned around and noticed two women staring at him. The first voice belonged to a tall, black-haired woman with shoulders broader and way more muscular than his, and the other belonged to the girl with rainbow-colored hair who worked with Robyn at Sandy's.

"Hi. I'm Ananya, Robyn's better half," the tall woman said, holding out her hand. "Nice to finally meet you."

"I'm Andrew." He shook her hand. "Likewise."

"And I'm Suzanna," said Robyn's coworker. "We've met before."

Andrew tried to shake Suzanna's hand, but she went in for a hug instead. He awkwardly hugged her back.

"Andrew! You made it!"

Robyn entered the living room from the kitchen. She hurried to his side, smiling shyly. "Merry Christmas."

"Merry Christmas," he answered, barely believing his own eyes. *Merry Christmas indeed.* Robyn was wearing a dress, and she looked gorgeous in it. It was strange to see her in something other than her usual sweatpants, but it was definitely a good kind of strange. The black dress accentuated her thin waist and delicate curves, and her legs looked absolutely magnificent.

"You look great," he said, which had to be the greatest understatement of the century.

Her cheeks turned pink. "Thank you."

His eyes roamed over her face, pausing at her bandaged cheek. "Have you taken care of your wounds like I told you to?"

She nodded. "They itch a little, but I think they're healing."

"Good." He was relieved. He hadn't been sure if Robyn would take his words seriously or not.

"Dinner's ready!" Lucy yelled from the kitchen. "Robyn, help me get the food to the table."

Robyn sighed. "She's been doing that all day. I've even had to help her *cook*." She shuddered. "I'd almost forgotten how much I hate cooking."

She returned to the kitchen, and the rest of the gang sat down at the table. Even though the dining table had been moved from the kitchen to the living room, it was still a tight fit.

When they had gotten all the food to the table, Robyn took a seat next to Andrew, and Lucy sat down next to Mike.

"I'm so glad you're all here," Lucy said, smiling warmly at her guests. "I hope this is the beginning of a new tradition."

"Christmas with the Monroes," Suzanna said. "I wouldn't mind making this a yearly thing."

"Me neither," Ananya added. "We misfits have to stick together."

Andrew wasn't sure if he qualified as a misfit, but he didn't say anything. He didn't want to ruin the feeling of actually belonging somewhere.

The meal Lucy and Robyn had prepared for their guests was fantastic. Andrew wasn't sure if it was because every course was home-cooked or because of the great company, but it turned out to be the best dinner he'd had in ages. Together, they made a strange group of people, but somehow they all managed to get along anyway. Andrew guessed that this was how families worked. *I have a family again,* he realized. He wasn't sure how it had happened, but he wasn't all alone anymore.

The hours went by way faster than Andrew would have preferred. When the clock struck eight, he stood up and reluctantly left the table. Robyn followed him to the door.

"Do you really have to leave already?" she asked, frowning a little.

"Yeah," he replied. "I'm sorry."

He was just about to open the front door when he remembered the small box in his pocket. "I can't believe I almost forgot to give you this," he said, handing the box to Robyn.

She blinked. "Is this for me?"

"It's your Christmas present. Open it."

Robyn untied the bow and ripped off the paper, revealing a small jewelry box. She tilted her head to the side, looking at it curiously.

"Open it," he repeated. *Please don't freak out.*

She wrinkled her forehead in confusion as she opened the box. "A key?"

Andrew nodded. "It's a key to my house. I had one copied." He swallowed hard. "You're there about as often as I am. You shouldn't have to use the spare key all the time."

She continued to stare at the key. "It's mine? My own key?"

He smiled. "Yes. My home is your home."

Robyn closed her hand around the key and held it against her chest. "Thank you."

"So you like it?"

"I love it," she said, smiling warmly. Then, her eyes widened. "Shit. I didn't get you anything. I didn't think... Damn it. I'm sorry."

"It's okay. Just being invited to this dinner is good enough for me. This is the best Christmas I've had in years."

She didn't look fully convinced, but she nodded anyway. "Thank you for being here today. And thank you for the gift."

They stood in the doorway in silence, looking at each other. Andrew knew he had to leave if he wanted to get back to work on time, but he couldn't bring himself to walk through the door. Not yet.

She tilted her head to the side. "You want to hug me again, don't you?"

"Yeah," he admitted. He always wanted to hug her.

Robyn rolled her eyes before wrapping her arms around his neck. Andrew's arms instantly went around her waist.

She leaned her head against the crook of his neck. "I wish you didn't have to leave."

"Me too." He held her tighter, cursing himself for not trying harder to push his shift onto someone else. In that moment, he wouldn't have minded ruining someone else's Christmas plans if it meant he could stay like that with Robyn for a little while longer.

Someone at the table loudly cleared their throat. Andrew suddenly remembered that the Monroe sisters' hallway was also their living room and that the rest of the guests were still watching them. He reluctantly let go of her, feeling his earlobes turn red.

"I guess I'll see you later," he said to Robyn, who'd backed away several steps.

"Yeah," she said, clearly embarrassed. "I'll come over to your place soon to make sure the key works."

After exchanging goodbyes and thank-yous with Lucy and the rest of the gang, Andrew left. He went down the stairs with heavy steps, already wishing he was back in the Monroe sisters' warm, friendly home. He left the building and was about to head to his car when someone shouted at him.

"Hey, Dr. Handsome!" Andrew followed the sound and found Robyn's friend Ananya on one of the balconies. "Wait up!"

She climbed over the balcony railing and hanged from it for a moment. Then, she simply let go. Before Andrew could react, she'd grabbed the drainpipe and stopped her fall. She climbed down the drainpipe with ease and was standing safely on the ground a few seconds later. Andrew was speechless.

Ananya pulled a lighter and pack of cigarettes from her bra. "Want one?" she asked, holding out the packet.

"No, of course not," he lied. "I'm a doctor."

Ananya rolled her eyes, the expression eerily similar to Robyn's. "Your loss." She lit one for herself and took a deep drag.

"How did you do that?" he asked when he'd fully regained his ability to speak.

"What?"

"How did you get down from the balcony like that?"

Ananya snorted. "I've been doing that since I was thirteen. Getting down is easy. Getting back up is the hard part." She took another drag of her cigarette. "Anyway, I wanted to talk to you about Robyn."

"Okay...?" Andrew had no idea what to expect. Though he didn't want to admit it, the woman scared him a little. She was about as tall as him, and almost every inch of her skin was covered in tattoos. Her eyes were hard and merciless.

"Yeah," she continued. "I guess you could say it's a warning. It's simple: do not hurt that girl. Robyn is special. She has no idea how to handle emotions, and she's bad at letting people into her life. You've somehow managed to make her trust you, which is something I wouldn't have believed if I hadn't seen it with my own two eyes. If you hurt her now, you'll destroy her." She sighed. "What I'm trying to say is, if you're just looking for a fling, choose someone else. Robyn thinks everyone she loves will leave her sooner or later. If you wanna be with her, you have to be in it for the long run."

"I am," Andrew said. "I really am. I know how hard it is for her to trust people, and it only makes me more grateful for how much she actually trusts me. I...I love her. She doesn't feel the same way about me, but that's okay. I'll stay in her life for as long as she'll have me, even if it's just as a friend."

Ananya considered his words for a moment, and then she smirked. "Good answer. I suppose I'll see you around, Andrew."

After putting out her cigarette with her boot, she turned around and walked toward the drainpipe. She stopped after a couple of steps, glancing at him over her shoulder. "You better make sure she doesn't get hurt in that damn tournament. At this point, you're the only one who can protect her in that corrupted mess. I'm putting my trust in you, so you better keep her safe."

"I will," he answered. "I promise."

Ananya gave him a short nod and continued back toward the apartment. Andrew stared as she climbed back up to the balcony, performing acrobatics insane enough to make his jaw drop. When she was finally standing safely on the balcony, she gave him a final wave before going back inside.

Andrew smiled. This was the second time he'd admitted out loud that he was in love with Robyn. He liked saying it.

He was definitely in it for the long run. Even if Robyn would never look at him the way he looked at her, he'd still be there for her. Meeting her had changed his entire existence—and even though his life was now more dangerous than before, he still thought it was a change for the better. He had a family now. Going back to his old, lonely life was unimaginable.

Falling in love with her is the best thing that's ever happened to me.

CHAPTER EIGHTEEN

"Promise me you won't go inside until the fight starts," Robyn said. "I don't want you to be in there any longer than you have to."

"I'll do what I always do," Andrew replied. "I usually go inside ten minutes before the fight starts. I've been doing this a lot lately, you know."

Robyn knew he was right. As the medical team's doctor, he'd attended all the first-class quarterfinals—including the three fights Robyn hadn't been involved in—and he'd watched the first semifinal as well. Andrew had been spending a lot of time at the arena lately, and that meant he'd also been spending a lot of time around Swanson and his men. Robyn didn't like that at all.

The plan was for Andrew to drop her off at Chrystal Arena one and a half hours before the fight started, and then he'd stay away until later. That way, Swanson hopefully wouldn't find out about their friendship. If Swanson found out they knew each other, he would definitely get more suspicious about Andrew's sudden involvement in the medical team, which was something Robyn wanted to avoid for as long as possible. She didn't even want to think about what would happen if Swanson found out about Andrew and his police friend's ridiculous plans.

Swanson finding out about her and Andrew's relationship wasn't the only reason Robyn was worried that night. She was going to fight Tyler, and she honestly wasn't sure if she could beat him. She'd had to hold back in their staged fight at the Circle, but she'd still gotten a taste of what it would be like to have a proper fight with him. He was incredibly strong, but his muscular body didn't slow him down. He was also freakishly good at reading body language and predicting his opponent's actions. Robyn's speed and agility meant nothing if Tyler already knew her future moves.

The thought of losing didn't bother her as much as she'd thought it would, though. The tournament prize could probably buy her the normal life she'd always dreamed about, but she was no longer sure if it was worth it. It wasn't just her life at stake anymore. As long as she was in the tournament, Andrew was in danger too. She'd managed to convince him not to spend more time than necessary in the arena, but he was still adamant about staying on the medical team. She hated it. Risking her own life, she was used to. Risking others? Not so much. She didn't like the feeling of it at all.

"Do you think you can take him?" Andrew asked, parking the car outside Chrystal Arena.

"I don't know."

He clenched his jaw. "You're going to get hurt tonight, aren't you?"

"Probably." She gave him a sad smile. "Maybe it's for the best. If I lose tonight, I'll finally be free from this tournament mess."

"Even if that's true, I still don't want you to get hurt." He sighed. "I can't wait for this thing to be over."

"Me too." She removed the seat belt and opened the door. "I'll see you later."

"Please, be careful."

"I will." She closed the door behind her and began to walk toward the arena's pizzeria front. It was a cold winter night, and it had just started to snow. When she reached the door, she was already shivering.

The line to the register was surprisingly long. It was December 28, only three days after Christmas. Robyn had thought the audience would be smaller than usual because of that, but people seemed to think watching the tournament's semifinal was more important than spending time with their loved ones.

She made her way down the stairs and to the bar. Cassandra was sitting in the corner as usual, with Drake leaning against the wall right next to her.

"Hey," Robyn said. "Do you have any advice for me about tonight's fight?"

Cassandra tilted her head to the side, looking at her from head to toe. "This will be a tough fight for you, but you will be the one who moves on to the final."

Robyn waited for her to continue, but Cassandra didn't seem to want to add anything else to her statement. Robyn turned to leave but then changed her mind, turning back to Cassandra. "Why do you always help me like this?" she asked. "I've never paid you or anything. Why are you so nice to me?"

"Because this city is corrupt and chaotic," Cassandra answered calmly. "The violence is reaching its final crescendo. A change is coming—and you will be the cause of it. You, Jason, and Dr. Alexander will change the underground world of Chrystal Valley forever." She gave Robyn a cryptic smile. "I'm only making sure everything plays out the way it's supposed to."

Robyn frowned. "How do you know all this? You can't really see the future, can you?"

"I'm good at what I do." Cassandra turned away from her and fixed her gaze on the ring, ending the conversation.

Robyn shuddered. It wouldn't surprise her if Cassandra did have some sort of supernatural ability. Cassandra had given her a lot of tips over the past months, and she had never been wrong before—but Robyn still had a hard time seeing how a simple fighter like her could change an entire city.

She gave Drake one last glance. He'd won his semifinal, just like he'd told her he would. It surprised her a little. Back when they'd been together, she'd always been the better fighter. Now, she wasn't so sure.

She pushed through the crowd again, heading toward the backstage area. The doorman glared at her but didn't say anything. She entered the locker room and dumped her hoodie, tank top, and shoes in one of the lockers. The most difficult thing to leave behind turned out to be the key to Andrew's house. She'd attached it to an old shoelace and had been wearing it around her neck like a necklace every day since Christmas. Warmth still filled her chest every time she thought about it. The gift represented Andrew's trust in her, and she really cherished it.

In the end she decided to leave it on, hiding the key in her sports bra. The shoelace was old and would snap if Tyler tried to pull on it, and he didn't seem like the type who would try to strangle her. She locked the door to her locker and went back to the backstage corridor to warm up.

She jogged back and forth until her breathing was completely under her control and she felt like her legs could carry her anywhere. Fifteen minutes before the fight, she ran into Swanson and Mark.

"Good evening, dear," Swanson said. "I hope you're ready for tonight's game."

She nodded.

"Good. You don't have to drag it out tonight. Aim for a simple first-round knockout."

She tilted her head slightly to the side. Swanson never encouraged quick finishes. As far as she knew, he only showed this kind of disinterest when he thought a fight was already lost. She glanced at Mark, searching for more clues. Mark was back to his usual state, keeping a neutral face while pretending she didn't exist. If he had any opinions about the upcoming fight's possible outcomes, he didn't show it.

Swanson patted her on the shoulder. "Just be a good girl and do your best."

Robyn frowned as she watched them leave. If Swanson thought she would lose the fight, he was acting surprisingly calm. Was she supposed to lose? She knew Swanson was Tyler's manager too, but she'd thought she was his primary fighter. After all, she'd been fighting for Swanson for years while Tyler had only done it for a couple of months. Was Tyler her successor? Was she about to get fired?

She finished her warm-up and stopped in front of the door leading to the arena.

"Ten minutes left, everybody!" a man in an orange jacket yelled. "The audience is bigger than ever, so no screw-ups tonight, all right?"

"Man, this tournament is getting way too big," a male voice said from behind her back. She turned around and found Tyler leaning against the wall.

"Yeah," she said. "I kind of miss the fights in the Octagon."

"Me too. Things have gotten so damn serious ever since I let that old man hire me. At least one of us will be free from all of this after tonight. You're not gonna hold back, right?"

"No holding back this time," Robyn said with a small smile. "I promise."

Tyler grinned. "Let's give that audience a show they'll never forget. See you soon, Valkyrie."

When Tyler left to go to his own door, Robyn felt a little better than before. Even if he did end up kicking her ass, he would do it in a fair fight. She smirked. She would not make this an easy win for him.

The door to the arena opened. After taking a deep, strengthening breath, she stepped out on the catwalk-like aisle leading to the ring. She walked down the stairs with her head held high, emitting an aura of faked confidence. *I'm the Valkyrie,* she thought, pushing away her nervousness. *Valkyries don't fear anything.*

She glanced through the gallery's wide window on her way down. She didn't see Andrew, but she knew he was in there somewhere. It calmed her to know he was looking out for her.

She reached the ring at the same time as Tyler. He flexed his muscles, already glistening with sweat.

"Are you ready?" he asked with an unconcerned grin.

"Absolutely."

The referee entered the ring. He gave the two fighters strange looks, most likely wondering what they were smiling about. "I know it's the semifinal and the stakes are high, but please, give us a clean fight. We don't want a repetition of the incident two weeks ago." He gave Robyn an indiscreet glare. "You've been given your instructions. Obey my commands at all times. Defend yourselves at all times. Let's get this over with."

The referee backed away from them, and the bell rang. Robyn and Tyler circled each other, analyzing each other's movements. They'd fought each other before, and they both knew the other's strengths and weaknesses. Even if Robyn preferred to let her opponent make the first move, she was going to have to change her strategy if she wanted to surprise him.

She approached him with three quick steps and threw a punch, aiming for his face. Tyler dodged it, but her movement had been unexpected enough for him to take a step back. Robyn continued with a kick to his side and an elbow to his temple. The hits weren't perfect, but she could tell they hurt. She was close to him now—dangerously close. She quickly backed away, but not before Tyler's fist connected with her cheek. Stars danced before her eyes for a moment. She shook her head. Her vision returned to normal.

"Not bad," Tyler said, still grinning. "I didn't see that one coming." Robyn's elbow had caused a small cut in his eyebrow, and drops of blood were already trickling down his cheek.

"I know." She smirked. "Your turn."

The fight continued for several rounds. Tyler was stronger but Robyn was faster. Even though Tyler was good at reading her movements, she still managed to get in some good hits. It was a fair and even fight, and the audience loved it. It wasn't long before Robyn stopped caring about the tournament completely. She hadn't been pushed to the limit like this for a long time. The adrenaline pumped through her veins as she gave and received hit after hit. Power surged through her, washing away all her fears. This was the one thing in the world she was truly good at.

In the final seconds of the third round, Tyler threw a punch Robyn just couldn't block. His fist connected with her chin. Black spots clouded her vision, and her ears rang. She lost her balance and took a step back. Tyler followed up with a kick to her stomach, sending her flying through the air. She tried to hold on to her consciousness, but it was hopeless. *Cassandra was wrong,* was the last thing she thought before her body hit the floor.

• • •

When Robyn opened her eyes, the fight was over. She looked up and found Tyler looming over her, holding a white towel against his bleeding eyebrow.

"You all right?" he asked, holding out his free hand.

"I'll be fine." She let him pull her up from the floor. "My chin hurts a little, though. That was one hell of a punch."

"You got in some good ones too," he admitted with a grin. "We have to do this again sometime."

Robyn smiled. "Rematch one day?"

"Hell yeah." Tyler punched her playfully in the shoulder.

Before Robyn could say anything else, someone wrapped an arm around her shoulders and pulled her away from Tyler.

"Don't touch her," Andrew said, his voice uncharacteristically cold.

Tyler blinked in surprise. "I only helped her up."

"Don't you think you've done enough?" Andrew turned to Robyn and quickly scanned her from head to toe, estimating her injuries. "Are you all right?" he asked in a softer voice.

"I'm fine." She frowned at him. "Don't be rude. He didn't do anything wrong."

"He knocked you unconscious!"

"It was a fight! If I'd had the opportunity, I would have done the same to him." She put her hand on Andrew's arm, squeezing it gently. "Please, calm down. I lost. It's finally over."

Andrew looked conflicted for a moment, but then he nodded. "You're right." He wrapped his other arm around her waist, pulling her closer. "I just hate watching you get hurt."

Robyn smiled. "I know. I really am fine, though."

He buried his face in her hair. "I'm so damn glad this is all over."

She felt his lips against her ear. His body was hot and firm against hers. In that moment, she didn't give a damn about the promises she'd made to herself. She was high on adrenaline, and she wanted him. She pulled back a little so she could look at his face. Her gaze fell to his lips.

"Ms. Monroe. Dr. Alexander," a voice said, ruining the moment. "I don't think this is the appropriate time or place to show affection like that."

Robyn's eyes widened when she recognized the voice. Swanson had arrived at the scene. She immediately stepped away from Andrew.

"I'm sorry," she said. "Just adrenaline and hormones and stuff. I'm sorry."

Swanson clearly didn't buy her weak excuse. He eyed them both with calm disapproval, his expression showing no surprise at all. "What you do in your spare time is none of my concern, dear, as long as you remain professional at events like this."

"Of course," she said quickly. "It won't happen again. I promise." She looked down at the ground, chewing on her lip. "I'm sorry for losing the fight."

"You gave it your best," Swanson said. "You did well. There will be more games in the future. I'm sure things will turn out for the best."

Robyn blinked. Swanson didn't seem to be upset at all about the loss, and for some reason, he was talking to her instead of Tyler. What the hell was going on?

"We should leave," Andrew said. Robyn nodded, sending Tyler a final glance. He was still being checked out by one of Andrew's coworkers, looking about as confused as Robyn felt. She gave him a wave before following Andrew through the gallery and the backstage corridor.

They walked the rest of the way to the locker room in silence. Robyn fetched her backpack and clothes from her locker and let down her hair. After unwinding the gauze from her hands and removing the piece of tape covering her piercing, she reached out for her hoodie.

Andrew stopped her by placing his hand on her shoulder. "I would like to check your stomach before you get dressed. He gave you a really nasty kick."

She nodded. The kick hadn't felt that bad, but she'd learned to trust Andrew's instincts when it came to injuries.

He made her lie down on the bench. "You don't have any bruising, and nothing seems swollen," he said, slowly moving his hands over her stomach. "I don't think you have any bleeding, but I'd prefer if you slept at my place tonight. You could still have a concussion."

She couldn't tell if he meant the part about the concussion, or if he was just pulling something out of his ass to make her stay over at his place as usual. After some consideration, she found that it didn't actually matter.

"Sure. Lucy won't be home tonight any—"

A gasp escaped her lips when his hand grazed her piercing. Their eyes met, and Robyn felt a surge of electricity pass through her body. Andrew had that look in his eyes again, and his hands were still moving lower and lower down her stomach, igniting fires under her skin. When they reached the hem of her pants, a big and surprisingly convincing part of her wanted him to continue even lower. She couldn't move or even think—her mind was fully concentrated on his hands and those beautiful sky-blue eyes.

Andrew abruptly removed his hands, turning away from her. "I'm sorry," he said in a strained voice. "That was unprofessional. I'll wait outside."

Robyn watched him leave the room, her cheeks burning. *Shit.* She clearly had no self-control today. What would have happened if he hadn't stopped himself? She shook her head, pushing away the intruding thoughts. She was the one who'd said they couldn't be together. Why was she the one who couldn't keep herself in check around him?

She picked up her backpack and left the locker room. Andrew was waiting right outside.

"I'm sorry," he said again. He couldn't even look her in the eye.

"It's okay," she said. "Let's just… Let's just forget about it."

They walked through the backstage corridor in silence. No matter how much she tried, she couldn't stop thinking about Andrew's hands. And his lips. She wanted to kiss him again so badly, but she couldn't.

The fight they'd had should have been long forgotten by then, but it wasn't. They were friends—good friends, even—but Robyn still refused to let things go any further than that. He'd betrayed her trust. How could she possibly let him in again after something like that?

According to her rebellious emotions, the answer was simple. All she had to do was kiss him again.

She pushed away the intruding thoughts. No, she would not kiss him. No, she would not let herself become even more attached to him than she already was. Sooner or later, his fascination with her would end, and then he would leave. That's what people like him did. If she allowed herself to like him any more than she already did, the inevitable separation would be too painful to handle.

They made their way back up to the parking lot. Their original plan had been to let Andrew leave first and then for him to come back and pick Robyn up later, but since Swanson now knew about their friendship there wasn't really any point to it. They had just reached Andrew's car when Robyn noticed someone lying on the ground in the corner of the parking lot.

"Excuse me, are you okay?" she shouted, approaching the motionless body. "Hello?"

When she got closer, she recognized the fiery red hair. She ran the final yards and knelt down next to him. "Tyler?"

Tyler wasn't moving. His eyes were open, but he didn't seem to see anything. A thin layer of snow covered his dark skin. She grabbed his shoulder and shook him. His skin was cold—colder than any human's skin should ever be.

"Andrew!" she yelled, glancing over her shoulder. "He's not waking up. You have to do something. Fix him!"

"Call an ambulance," Andrew said, running to her side. He grabbed Tyler's forearm and placed two fingers against his wrist.

Robyn nodded and pulled her cell phone from her backpack. The display of her old Nokia showed an out-of-service message. She moved closer to the arena until a single bar popped up on the screen. She called 911, and the operator promised he'd send an ambulance. When she'd ended the call, she hurried back to Andrew's side. To her surprise, Andrew was standing up again.

"Aren't you supposed to give him CPR?" she asked, her heart pounding in her chest. "He doesn't have a pulse, so you have to do that compressing shit. I don't know how to do it, so you have to help him."

Andrew remained silent. He looked at her with sadness in his eyes. He still wasn't moving.

"Why aren't you doing anything?" she yelled before giving him a hard shove. "You have to fix him! You always fix me. Why aren't you fixing him?" She shoved him again. "Help him!"

Before she could shove him again, Andrew pulled her into his arms, holding her tightly. "He's gone, Robyn," he said softly. "There's nothing I can do."

"What the hell are you talking about?" She struggled against him. "That can't be true. He's supposed to be in the final. He promised me a rematch. He's not… He can't be…" She tried to finish the sentence, but the words wouldn't come out. She was hyperventilating, but her lungs didn't seem to be getting enough air. Everything seemed unreal. *Maybe it's all just a nightmare,* she thought, but deep inside, she knew it wasn't. This was the reality, and Tyler was dead.

"I'm sorry, Robyn," Andrew mumbled as he held her. "I'm so sorry."

"Tyler?" a male voice yelled from the other side of the parking lot. Andrew's platinum-blond teammate ran toward them. He rushed to Tyler's side and began to shake him.

"Tyler? You have to wake up. You have to wake up!" He stared at Andrew, his eyes open wide. "Why aren't you giving him CPR? He's not breathing!"

"It won't help, Jonas," Andrew said. "He's gone."

Jonas didn't listen. He straddled Tyler's body and pushed on his chest.

"When you elbowed him in the head, did you feel something give in?" Jonas yelled to Robyn before pressing his lips against Tyler's, forcing air into his lungs.

"No. Maybe. I…I don't know. I can't remember."

"How the hell can you not remember whether or not you crushed his fucking skull?" Jonas screamed, pushing harder and harder on Tyler's chest.

"I don't know!" Robyn tried to think back on the fight, but it was all a blur. She looked up at Andrew, her body trembling. "Did I kill him? Did I kill Tyler?"

Andrew hesitated for a moment, closing his eyes. "I honestly don't know."

"Please don't leave me, please don't leave me, please don't leave me," Jonas whispered as he continued to give the dead man CPR. The way he gently cradled Tyler's face in his hands before blowing air into his lungs made her heart ache.

She stared at Tyler's dead body in shock. Had she caused this?

The ambulance arrived a few minutes later. The EMTs had to tear Jonas away from Tyler's body before they could examine it, and he didn't stop struggling until a paramedic declared Tyler dead after a quick consultation with Andrew. Jonas sank to his knees with a loud sob. Robyn tried to put her hand on his shoulder, but he slapped it away.

"I don't even want to look at you," he said, tears falling freely from his eyes. She backed away. She didn't blame him in the slightest for hating her.

Andrew stayed close to her, as if he was waiting for a breakdown to happen. Robyn knew a breakdown would probably be a more normal reaction, but she couldn't even cry. She felt nothing. Her entire being had gone numb.

"You're an MD, right?" a paramedic asked Andrew. "Do you have any comments on possible COD?"

"Blunt force trauma to the skull, most likely," he replied, glancing nervously at Robyn. "That's all I could figure out. A coroner needs to take a look."

I may have just killed a man. Her eyes widened. *Not just a man—a friend.*

She ran over to the bushes surrounding the parking lot and threw up. Her knees buckled, and she crashed to the ground. When gentle hands held her hair back, she knew Andrew had followed her. She emptied her stomach, heaving until she had nothing left to throw up.

"It's okay," Andrew murmured, stroking her hair. "I don't think you caused it. The swelling was in the back of his head, and you never hit him there. Something else must have happened after the fight."

Robyn wiped her mouth with the back of her hand and unsteadily got back to her feet. "But you can't be sure."

"I can't. Not yet. They will have to do an autopsy to confirm cause of death." He ran his fingers through his hair. "We should leave. The police will arrive any minute now. They'll turn this whole parking lot into a crime scene, and then we'll be stuck here for hours."

She nodded. She was tired, and her body wouldn't stop trembling.

"Cassandra was right," she whispered. "I am going to the final."

He wrapped an arm around her and led her toward the car. "We'll figure it out later. Everything will be okay."

Robyn leaned her head against his shoulder. She felt empty inside. Numb. Tyler was dead, gone forever. She would never get the rematch he'd promised her.

"No," she said, her eyes finally filling up with tears. "Some things will never be okay."

Neither of them said a word as they walked to the car. She knew she was right, and judging by his silence, Andrew knew it too.

CHAPTER NINETEEN

"I know you don't want to hear this, but I think Swanson did this," Andrew said. "He seemed way too calm after the fight."

Robyn continued to silently stare out the window. She had already come to that conclusion herself, even if she didn't want to admit it. Swanson had been acting strangely both before and after the fight, and if he still wanted her to fight in the final, he definitely had motive—which meant Tyler's death was still her fault, even if she hadn't dealt the fatal blow. Another tear rolled down her cheek. She hadn't known Tyler for long, but she'd already come to like him. He'd probably been a much better person than she'd ever be.

"I guess the police will have us come in and give a statement later," Andrew continued. "Hopefully, Jason can cover for us if they start asking questions about the tournament."

Robyn didn't answer. She didn't really care.

She was still awake when they reached Andrew's house. The adrenaline had left her system long ago, but every time she closed her eyes, all she could see was Tyler's dead body.

Tiny met them in the hallway when they got inside. She picked him up, cradling the somewhat unwilling cat against her chest.

"I'm going to bed," she said to Andrew. "I really need to get some sleep."

"It's okay. I need to get some sleep, too."

They stared at each other for a moment. Somehow, Robyn knew Andrew was thinking about the last time she'd slept in the guest room too. She didn't know how he'd felt about them falling asleep next to each other like that, but she'd slept unexpectedly well in his arms.

"Good night, then," she finally said. She couldn't bring herself to ask him to share a bed with her. The request was just too weird.

Andrew looked like he was going to say something, but then he just sighed.

"Good night," he said before disappearing into his own bedroom. Robyn wasn't sure, but she thought he'd almost looked disappointed.

"At least I've got you, Tiny," she whispered to the cat in her arms. Tiny answered by licking her chin.

After setting the alarm on her clock, she collapsed on the guest-room bed. Andrew had left a neatly folded button-down shirt on the pillow, but she was too tired to even undress. She put the shirt on the other side of the bed and crawled under the covers. Tiny demonstratively curled up on top of the shirt, purring contentedly.

Robyn closed her eyes. She was exhausted, both from the fight and the shock afterward. *He's dead because of me.* The image of Tyler's dead body flashed before her eyes again. She could still feel the coldness of his skin in her fingertips. *He's dead because of me.*

When the sun rose and the birds began to sing, Robyn was forced to accept that she wouldn't get any sleep that night. She got out of the bed and went to the bathroom to splash some water on her face. When she looked at herself in the mirror, she barely recognized the woman staring back at her. Her face was puffy, her eyes were bloodshot, and the dark circles under her eyes looked like bruises. She needed to take a run. She always felt better after a run.

She left a note for Andrew on the kitchen table before heading out. It was a cold December morning, and her breaths turned to steam as soon as they left her mouth. She knew she should take a few minutes to warm up before running in that kind of weather, but she wasn't in the mood for a slow jog. If she didn't run fast enough, she wouldn't get the distraction she so badly needed.

She ran for hours. When she finally came to a stop outside her apartment, her whole body hurt. She had run until she simply couldn't run anymore, and it still wasn't distracting enough.

After taking a quick shower, she decided to try out her second method of distraction: cleaning. She vacuumed and dusted every single nook of the apartment, including the small space behind the oven and under the bathtub. The cleaning was somewhat distracting, but the guilt was still there, a constant ache in the pit of her stomach. *He's dead because of me.*

When there was nothing left to clean, she sat down on the floor in the living room. Now what? Her home was clean, but her guilt was still there. Tyler's blood would always be on her hands. She tried to motivate herself into going down to the garage and dance for a while, but it didn't feel right. Tyler was dead. She couldn't just dance that pain away.

Robyn sighed and pulled her cell phone out of her backpack. There was one more option she could try, something she'd promised herself she'd never even go near. She punched in the numbers to Ana's tattoo parlor, knowing she'd just hit rock bottom.

"Ananya's Ink," Ana said. "If you wanna disappoint your parents, you've come to the right place."

"Hey, Ana, it's me. I need you to get me really, really drunk."

• • •

Andrew paced back and forth on the balcony. The last time he'd seen Robyn, she had not been in a good place. Her being gone in the morning had not made him any less worried, even though she'd left a note. "*Went for a run—R*" didn't exactly say anything about what state she was in.

He took a deep drag from his cigarette. What if she was injured? What if he'd missed an internal bleeding? What if she had a concussion?

The doorbell rang. Andrew put the cigarette in the ashtray and rushed to the door. For one blissful moment, he thought Robyn had returned to him—but then he found an exhausted cop on his doorstep.

"'Sup," Jason said as he entered the house. "I need you to give me a statement about last night."

"Sure." Andrew tried his best to hide his disappointment. Robyn was fine. She had to be. "Does this mean I don't have to give a statement at the police station?"

"Well, you might have to give a more official statement when this is all over, but right now we're trying to keep a low profile on all of this." Jason took a seat in one of the chairs in the kitchen. "Please, tell me what you saw."

Andrew described everything he'd seen that night, from Swanson's strangely calm behavior to Tyler's dead body in the parking lot. Jason recorded it all on his Dictaphone, listening carefully to every word.

"I couldn't tell the exact cause of death from my quick examination, but I know it was some sort of trauma to the skull," Andrew finished. "When will the autopsy be done?"

"It's already finished. Someone hit him in the head, just like you said. The culprit used some kind of object, and the coroner thinks it was a baton or a really thin baseball bat."

"Or a cane," Andrew filled in.

"Or a cane." Jason sighed. "This is the first time I've seen Swanson doing his dirty work himself. He's getting overconfident, and it's making him sloppy. We're so close to nailing him now, but no one at the station dares to even mention his name. If I only had one final piece of evidence, I'm sure I could put out an arrest warrant." Jason paused for a moment and yawned. He closed his eyes, leaning back on the chair. "Just one more, tiny little thing…"

Andrew could only stare as Jason began to fall asleep in the middle of their conversation. He put his hand on Jason's shoulder, shaking him gently.

"Hey, why don't you crash on my couch? It's a lot more comfortable than the chair, I promise."

Jason nodded and got up from the chair, barely opening his eyes. Andrew had to lead him to the living room to make sure he didn't walk into any furniture. Jason collapsed on the couch, falling asleep in seconds. Andrew sighed. No one in this city seemed to know how to take care of themselves.

Hours passed. Jason continued to sleep on the couch, Robyn continued to be missing, and Andrew continued to pace back and forth on the balcony. *She probably just went home,* he thought. *She doesn't live here, after all.* His weak attempt to calm himself had no effect whatsoever.

A little after six, Andrew's phone rang. He checked the display before answering. The name of the caller sent him straight into panic mode.

"Andrew Alexander," he answered, his heart racing.

"Hi, it's Lucy," she said. "Andrew, I need your help. It's Robyn."

No. No, no, no. "Is she hurt? What happened? Where is she?" He rushed to the hallway to put on his coat.

"No," Lucy said quickly, "she's not hurt. I just got a call from Ana, asking me to pick Robyn up from that bar next to Ananya's Ink. Apparently, they decided it was perfectly normal to get shit-faced on a Sunday afternoon, and now Ana's asking for backup." Lucy paused. "Someone has to pick her up, and I…I really don't want to be around drunk people. Even if it's my sister. I hate myself for putting this on you, but I…I can't. I just can't."

Andrew could hear the disappointment in Lucy's voice. Considering their background, it didn't surprise him. "I understand. I'll go get her."

"Really?" Lucy asked, her voice thick with unshed tears. "Thank you. I'm sorry for bothering you about something like this."

"It's all right. No problem at all."

After leaving a note on the coffee table for Jason, he went to his car to go get Robyn. He was relieved she wasn't hurt, but her behavior still worried him. As far as he knew, Robyn didn't drink. At all. Ever. Tyler's death must have hit her even harder than he'd thought.

The bar next to Ananya's Ink was not a place Andrew would ever have visited of his own accord. The floor was dirty, the light was dim, and a strange smell permeated the air. The pounding music drowned out all his thoughts, and he had never been a fan of R & B to begin with.

He scanned the room, but before he could locate Robyn, he saw Ananya waving at him from the bar.

"Looks like the cavalry finally arrived," she said as Andrew approached her.

"Hi." He took a seat next to her. "What's going on?"

"Robyn's drinking me under the table, that's what's going on," she replied bitterly. "She asked me to get her drunk, and I thought, 'Hey, let's get the missy drunk, it could be fun.' You know what? This is *not* fun. You know what she said when we got here? 'Give me one of everything,' she said. That was three hours ago. I don't know why she hasn't crashed yet. She's small! She should be puking her guts out right now, but no, she's still going at it. Just look at this!" Ananya gesticulated wildly at the glass in front of her. "I don't even know who's paying for these anymore. They just keep coming!" She tried to lean her head against her hand but missed, ending up with her forehead leaning against the counter. "Please, make her stop."

"Where is she?"

Ananya pointed to the corner of the room. "She's dancing on the table."

Robyn was indeed dancing on a table. A crowd had gathered around her, staring at her as she danced. Her hips swayed from side to side in perfect synchronization with the music. She was smiling to herself with her eyes closed, her cheeks flushed. She was probably even drunker than Ananya.

Andrew approached her carefully. He had never seen her move like that before. There was a raw sensuality in her movements, like she knew exactly how to control every single part of her body. Her cropped tank top left her whole midriff visible, and Andrew had to force his eyes away from her gyrating hips and the glimmering piercing in her belly button. He'd wanted to put his lips on that damn thing from the moment he first saw it, and her dancing only made it harder for him to look away.

"Hey," he said, trying to catch her attention. "Lucy called me."

"Uh-huh," she said, keeping her eyes closed as she continued to dance.

"Don't you think it's time to get down from the table?"

"Nah."

He sighed. "Robyn. This isn't you. I get that you don't want to think about Tyler, but this is not—"

"Don't say his name." She opened her eyes to give him a glare. "Not now. Not in here. This is a happy place. A happy, drunk place."

"I can see that. Please get down from the table."

She raised her eyebrows. "Why?"

"You're drunk. You could get hurt."

She laughed humorlessly, almost losing her balance in the process. "I really don't care."

"Well, I care," he said, his frustration turning into anger. "Get down."

She rolled her eyes but finally did as he said. She jumped from the table, almost falling over when her feet hit the ground.

"A lot of people get hurt in this city," she mumbled, more to herself than to him. "At least I'd deserve it."

Andrew frowned. "That's bullshit. Why would you say something like that?"

"Because someone died because of me!" she exclaimed. The crowd that had been watching her took a step back, surprised by her sudden outburst. "You don't get it. I'm nothing—*nothing*—and Tyler still died because of me. I keep dreaming about a normal life, but who am I kidding? All I'm good for is hurting others. It should have been me in that parking lot, not him. I'm not needed. Lucy has Mike now. She doesn't need me anymore. No one does." She clenched her fists, looking at the floor. "It should have been me. I'd rather die myself than see someone else get hurt because of me."

Andrew tried to hold it all back. He really did. For about half a second, he just stood there, staring at her as he tried to contain his anger. Then he exploded.

"How can you be so blind?" He grabbed her shoulders, pulling her closer. "You think you're not needed? *I* need you! I need you more than anything. I…"

He didn't know what to say to make her understand exactly how wrong she was, so instead he kissed her, hard, on the lips. He pulled away before she could even react, looking her deep in the eye. "I won't let you die. I won't accept it."

Robyn's lower lip trembled. "Why?"

"Because I love you."

Her reaction was instantaneous. She closed the distance between them and then her lips were on his. Andrew's heart nearly stopped, and every reason they shouldn't be doing this left his mind in an instant. He wrapped his arms around her, holding her tight as he kissed her back. The details he'd tried so hard to forget returned to him all at once. Her smell, her touch, her taste—everything was as addictive as he remembered it from their moment in the garage. Ever since that day, he'd dreamt about kissing her again, and now that it was finally happening he couldn't get enough of her.

Her lips parted, and Andrew could have sworn he felt a surge of electricity pass between them when their tongues met. He made a sound in the back of his throat, holding her even tighter. The circumstances weren't optimal, but he didn't care. He never wanted to let her go. Ever.

Too bad she's drunk, his inner critic commented. *She's in a vulnerable state, and you're taking advantage of her.*

Using all the mental strength he could gather, he tore himself away from her lips. He grabbed her shoulders again, keeping her at arm's length.

"Don't stop," Robyn ordered. She was breathing heavily, and her already flushed cheeks had turned even redder.

Andrew closed his eyes. She was drunk. Really, really drunk. He was a better person than this.

"Let's get you home." He bent down, grabbed her, and threw her over his shoulder.

"What the hell do you think you're doing?" she yelled. "Let me down! We're not done here!"

"Yes, we are." He went over to the bar and paid the surprisingly cheap bill. He glared at the men who had watched Robyn dance, who were most likely the source of the free alcohol. The men confirmed his suspicion by taking great care not to look at him.

He turned away from them and walked up to the main culprit behind Robyn's intoxication. Ananya was still sitting at the bar with her face pressed against the counter.

"Why did you let it go this far?" he asked her. "You must have known something was up. Why the hell did you take her out drinking?"

"Because she asked me to," Ananya said. "You know how rarely she asks for stuff. I promised myself long ago that if she ever asked me for anything, I would make it happen. Even if she asked me for something incredibly stupid."

"Don't blame her," Robyn said, still trying to wriggle herself free from his grip. "I'm an adult. Getting drunk was my decision. Kissing you was my decision. I'm an adult! Let me down!"

"Yeah, you're really acting like an adult right now." Andrew rolled his eyes. He turned to Ananya again, unable to stay angry with her after a confession like that. Even though her love for Robyn was very different from his, he knew she loved her just as much. "Do you need a ride?"

"Suzie's picking me up any minute," Ananya replied. "I'm gonna have to sleep on the couch for weeks, but I'll be fine. Just get her home. And hey, congrats on the kiss and everything. I gagged for a moment."

"I'll take her home." Andrew's lips twitched, almost forming a smile. "Thanks."

Robyn gave Andrew the silent treatment the whole ride back. He didn't even ask her whether or not to drop her off at her apartment—he couldn't possibly leave her alone when she was like this. He hadn't realized how much she blamed herself for Tyler's death, and at the bar she'd almost seemed suicidal. If she didn't care about her life, he was going to have to do it for her. He would protect her from anyone who might try to harm her—even if that person was Robyn herself.

When they reached Andrew's house, Robyn had sobered up enough to walk on her own. He kept a wary eye on her as she staggered up the stairs to the front door. Her metabolism was impressive.

Jason met them in the doorway, looking at them curiously. "What the hell happened to her?"

Robyn shrugged. "I got drunk."

"No shit." He shook his head. "I guess that's my cue. Thanks for letting me crash here." He looked at Robyn and grinned. "Big fan, by the way."

He patted Andrew on the shoulder before heading out, leaving Robyn and Andrew alone in the house.

Their eyes met. The tension between them was thick enough to cut with a knife.

"What does this all mean?" she asked. "You know, what happened in the bar. We're not just friends anymore, are we?"

Andrew sighed. "We'll talk about this when you're sober. Go and sleep it off."

For a moment, she looked like she was going to protest, but then she nodded. "We'll talk about this later." She lowered her eyes, chewing on her lip. "Thanks for coming to get me. I...I just wanted to think about something else for a while."

"Tyler's death wasn't your fault," he said, fighting the urge to give her a hug. If he held her now, he wouldn't be able to let go. "All of this is because of Swanson, okay? Jason already has the autopsy report. Someone hit Tyler in the head with a cane, and that's what killed him. Swanson killed him, not you. You're not responsible for Swanson's actions."

Robyn smiled dejectedly. "I work for him. As long as he's my manager, I will always feel responsible for his actions."

"Well, you know what I think," he said.

"Yeah... Maybe you're right. I'm not sure if I want to be a part of that world anymore. Not after what happened to Tyler." She paused. "I think it might be time for me to stop fighting."

She gave him another tired smile before entering the guest room. Andrew blinked. Was his wishful thinking now giving him hallucinations, or was she actually considering quitting fighting?

He stared at the closed guest-room door. If she stopped fighting, he wouldn't have to go behind her back to protect her ever again.

He could finally regain her trust. She would be safe. She would finally be safe.

If she stopped getting injured all the time, she wouldn't be his patient anymore either. There would no longer be an ethical dilemma keeping them apart. He smiled as the realization fully sank in. If she stopped fighting, they could finally be together.

• • •

A little after midnight, Robyn woke up from her sleep-it-off nap. Her head was pounding, and she was painfully sober. At first, she wondered how the hell she'd ended up in Andrew's guest room again, but then it all came back to her.

"Shit." She'd kissed Andrew. After all her "we're just friends" and "I can't be with someone I don't trust" statements, she'd still kissed Andrew.

Despite what she'd told him, there was a part of her that had never stopped trusting him—that trusted him more than anyone else on the planet. He was special. To her, he would always be special.

She made a decision and got out of the bed. Andrew had put a stop to the kiss back then because of her drunkenness, but she wasn't drunk now. She wasn't sure if she believed a man like him could *love* someone like her, but he had definitely wanted her. Life was short and volatile. She refused to hold herself back anymore.

Dressed in nothing but panties and Andrew's white button-down shirt, she silently left the guest room. When she reached Andrew's bedroom door, she almost wished she was drunk again. When she had been drunk, things had been a lot less scary. *But this is something I have to do sober,* she thought and opened the bedroom door.

"Andrew?" she whispered.

He sat up in his bed and turned on the lamp on the bedside table. He stared at her in confusion. "Yeah?"

She took a deep breath. "I don't want to sleep in the guest room anymore."

She let Andrew's shirt slide off her shoulders and down to the floor.

Andrew was out of the bed and up on his feet in less than a second. He was wearing a pair of black boxers and nothing else, and his hair didn't look quite as perfect as it usually did. Robyn hadn't thought it was possible, but he somehow looked even hotter like this than in his white coat.

"You don't have to do this," he said in a low voice, looking anywhere but at her naked torso.

"I know." She took a step closer. "I want you, Andrew. I want—"

Andrew's lips crashing into hers cut her off. He entangled his fingers in her hair, tilting her head back to give the kiss a better angle. Robyn answered it with desperate, burning need. Her hands roamed freely over his naked skin. She couldn't get enough of him. She needed more.

Andrew turned them around and began to slowly move them toward the bed, his lips never leaving hers. When Robyn lay down on the mattress, he paused for a moment.

"Are you sure?" he asked in a strained voice.

"Yes."

Andrew stared at her, finally taking in her half-naked body. If all her scars and imperfections revolted him, he didn't show it.

"You're so beautiful," he breathed.

"You don't have to say that." She fought the urge to cross her arms to cover herself. "I'm way too thin, and then there's all the scars. You don't... You don't have to pretend I'm something I'm not."

Andrew finally got up on the bed with her. "You're perfect. Everything about you is perfect." He hovered over her, drinking her in. He had that look in his eyes again, now more intense than ever. Robyn finally realized the meaning of that look—it was need. Pure, unadulterated need. In that moment, she no longer doubted that he needed her just as much as she needed him.

After giving her lips another hungry kiss, Andrew began to move downward. "Since I love your scars," he murmured, kissing her neck, "I've decided to kiss all of them." His lips traced a pale scar on her collarbone. "Every"—he kissed her chest—"single"— he kissed her stomach—"one." His teeth grazed her skin when he kissed her hipbone, sending an involuntary shudder through her body.

"That would take all night," she gasped, stifling a moan as he tugged on her piercing with his teeth.

She could feel him grin as his lips traveled lower and lower down her body. "I know."

CHAPTER TWENTY

Robyn woke up the following morning when a soft paw slapped her nose.

"Tiny, what the hell?" she groaned. When she opened her eyes, she found the cat standing on the bed right beside her head. He lifted his paw again, preparing another slap.

"I am awake, you little shit," she muttered. "Why can't you bother Andrew instead?"

Tiny continued to stare at her expectantly. Robyn sighed. She knew she had to get up and prepare the cat's breakfast sooner or later—preferably sooner, according to Tiny—but she didn't like the thought of leaving the bed. Andrew's arms were still wrapped around her, and she could feel his calm breaths against her neck. She felt safe in his arms. Protected.

Andrew muttered something incoherent in his sleep and pulled her closer. Robyn smiled, entwining her fingers with his. Maybe he wouldn't leave her, after all. Maybe he would be the one who actually stayed.

Tiny meowed and slapped her nose again. Robyn grunted, fighting the urge to push the cat off the bed.

"I'm coming," she muttered. "You don't have to act like you haven't been fed in days."

She lifted Andrew's arm and got out of the bed. When she glanced at the alarm clock on the bedside table, she could barely believe her eyes. It was already after noon, and though she wasn't sure when exactly she'd fallen asleep last night, she had definitely slept for more than six hours—without the nightmare. She glanced at Andrew, who was still snoring peacefully. Thanks to him, she'd felt safe when she'd fallen asleep. Apparently, that was all it took to scare the nightmare away.

"I guess that explains why you're so hungry," she said to the cat as she picked up Andrew's white shirt from the floor and put it on. "I'm sorry, sweetie. I didn't exactly plan this."

She walked toward the guest room with Tiny trotting after her, meowing happily.

"Could you at least try to be quiet?" She scratched the cat on the head before getting his pellets from the guest bathroom. "I have errands I need to run before Andrew wakes up."

She'd made a decision the previous night, a promise to herself to stop letting fear rule her life. Step one had been to accept her feelings for Andrew. Step two would be to get out of the fighting world for good. She'd been afraid of what Swanson would do if she quit, but right now, fighting for him seemed to be more dangerous than not doing it. For Lucy's safety—and Andrew's—she had to get out.

She'd let Swanson control her life for way too long. If she wanted a normal life, she was going to have to get it herself.

Tyler's death had showed her exactly how volatile life could be, and in a way, she felt like she had to live her life for the both of them. The guilt wasn't as overpowering now as it had been the day before, but she still felt nauseous every time she thought about Tyler's dead body. Swanson had killed Tyler to get her to the final. Nothing could ever erase that guilt.

If Andrew found out about her plans, he would insist on coming along with her, no matter what she said. In some situations, she appreciated that confident, determined side of him, but in Swanson's headquarters he would be a liability. She had to do this before he woke up.

After filling Tiny's food bowl, she left the room, heading toward the kitchen. She had a long run ahead of her and would need some food before taking off. She searched the fridge and pantry for breakfast, but both turned out to be as good as empty. *How does he even survive in here?* she wondered as she picked up an apple from the fruit bowl on the kitchen table. It wasn't much, but it would have to do. One of them was going to have to learn how to cook, or they'd both starve to death.

She left the house and began to jog, eating the apple as she ran. Swanson's mansion was about five miles away from Andrew's house. She'd only been there once before, but she still remembered the way.

The last time she'd been at the headquarters, she'd been seventeen years old. Signing a contract to become Swanson's employee hadn't seemed like a big deal back then. He'd promised to help her get emancipated so she could become Lucy's legal guardian, and that promise had been enough for her to sign up for pretty much anything. She'd had so many nightmares back then, dreams where social workers took Lucy from her and placed her in foster care. Robyn would have done anything to keep her small family together, and Swanson had been well aware of it. But Lucy was eighteen, now. The only thing he had on her now was the debt.

The closer she got to the headquarters, the more nervous she got. She was already beginning to regret her decision. In Andrew's arms, she'd felt like a person again. When she was with him, she felt like someone who mattered, but the feeling was already being washed away by overwhelming waves of powerlessness. Swanson had a way of making her feel small, even when he wasn't near her.

I can do this, she thought as she entered Swanson's mansion through the main entrance. The guards at the door glanced at her but let her pass. Most people in Swanson's organization recognized the Valkyrie.

The hallway was furnished in a Victorian fashion, and Robyn suspected the room was bigger than her whole apartment. A gigantic crystal chandelier hung from the ceiling, illuminating the room. Everything looked exactly like she remembered it.

She carefully walked up to the reception desk in the middle of the room, her sneakers leaving dirty footprints on the red carpet.

The receptionist looked at her curiously. "How can I help you?"

Her blond hair was tied up in a strict-looking bun, and she was wearing glasses with thick, black frames. She was obviously trying to look older than she really was, but Robyn could easily see through it. The receptionist couldn't be older than twenty or twenty-one.

"I need to talk to Swanson," Robyn said.

The receptionist blinked. "Do you have an appointment?"

"No, but I need to see him."

"I'm sorry, I can't let you in without an appointment."

"Oh, for fuck's sake," Robyn muttered. "Listen, Blondie, I'm going to talk to Swanson today whether you like it or not. You should probably call him and tell him Robyn Monroe is here to see him. I'm going to his office now. Have a nice day."

She gave the receptionist a chilly smile before heading farther into the mansion. The last time she'd been to the headquarters, Swanson's office had been in the west wing on the ground floor. If his office had been moved since then, she was going to have a problem.

Behind her, she heard the receptionist call out to the guards. Robyn quickened her steps as she entered the corridor that would hopefully lead her to Swanson's office.

She had no idea how Swanson would react to the ultimatum she'd prepared for him. Even though she knew he was behind Tyler's death, she still didn't think he would physically hurt her. At least not this close to the final.

She came to a stop outside the office door. The sign on the door still said "*Richard Swanson*," which solved her first problem. There were men speaking inside the room, and she thought she recognized Swanson's voice.

I can do this. She'd never get her normal life if she backed out now. She had to do this—for herself and for Tyler.

She opened the door without knocking, stepping inside with her head held high. The office looked just like she remembered it, with the same kind of Victorian furniture as the hallway. Swanson was seated behind a big wooden desk in the middle of the room, holding a phone to his ear. The ever-present Mark leaned against the wall right behind him, his arms crossed. They both glared at her as she entered, neither of them looking even remotely surprised.

"Yes, she's here now," Swanson told the person on the phone. "It's fine, dear. There was nothing you could have done. Goodbye, then." He hung up the phone with a sigh. "Ms. Monroe, was it really necessary to scare our dear Victoria?"

"She wasn't going to let me in," Robyn said, trying her best to hold on to the little bit of confidence that still remained within her. "I needed to talk to you."

"I see." Swanson tilted his head to the side in an eerily bird-like way. "What's on your mind, dear?"

He stared at her with his cold, gray eyes, and for a moment she felt like he could see right through her. She clenched her fists. *I'm not nothing.*

"I want to make a deal," she said. "A deal about the tournament final."

"Oh?" Swanson raised his eyebrows, looking genuinely curious. "So you heard about the Griffin's disqualification?"

His death, you mean. She forced herself to remain calm, even though she wanted nothing more than to punch Swanson in the face to wipe that cold smile off his lips. That, or maybe run away and never look back. Both alternatives were just as alluring.

"If I win the fight, I don't want my share of the cash prize," she said. "Instead, I want it to be cut from whatever I still owe you. I want to have the sum on paper, so I know exactly how big my debt is. The fight against Drake will be my final fight. After that, I'm quitting. I'll come up with another way to pay you back. I'm not going to fight for you anymore."

She crossed her arms and took a deep breath before continuing. This was the difficult part. This was the part where things could go really, really wrong.

"You've bet a lot of money on me winning the whole tournament, right? That's why you got rid of Tyler? Well, if you don't agree to rip up the old contract between us and release me from your services, I'll lose on purpose on Saturday."

"Who the hell do you think you are?" Mark growled. He took a step toward her, but Swanson stopped him by holding out his hand.

"Please, Mark, leave us," Swanson said. "Ms. Monroe and I need to have a private chat."

A look of betrayal swept over Mark's face. "I'll wait outside." He pushed past Robyn, slamming the door shut behind him.

Swanson continued to calmly stare at Robyn. He didn't seem angry at all.

"So? Do you accept my terms?" she asked. Strangely enough, she was even more nervous now that Mark had left the room. Swanson may be an old man, but being alone with him still scared her.

Swanson smiled. "Actually, I have a counteroffer for you. Robyn—can I call you Robyn?"

She found herself nodding. Swanson's smile seemed to reach his eyes this time, and the expression scared her more than any of his frowns ever had.

"Robyn," he continued, "you have so much potential. The fighting, the tournament, it's just the beginning of what I've got planned for you. I thought you would need more time to mature, but this little scheme of yours has convinced me of your abilities. I want you to be my new right-hand man."

She blinked. "What?"

"Well, I suppose you would be my right-hand woman." Swanson smiled again. "You're smart and independent, and up until now, you've been very loyal. I considered giving the position to the Griffin, but he turned out to be far from as resourceful as you. Such a disappointment. It doesn't matter now, though. I believe you would suit the position perfectly."

"Isn't Mark your right-hand man?" she asked. The situation was not going according to plan at all.

"Mark is faithful, but he doesn't have an ounce of independence in him. He would never do anything on his own initiative. I took him in when he was just eleven years old, you see, and I'm afraid he never learned to think on his own. He's nothing like you." Swanson stood up, slowly approaching her. "You would have to participate in the occasional game, of course, but most of the time you'd simply be accompanying me wherever I go. What do you say, Robyn? Are you ready to take the next step?"

For a moment, Robyn wanted to accept his offer. No one had ever called her smart before. She was a high-school dropout, a waitress without education. She was nothing, a misfit only good for fighting. She should've felt proud of getting an offer like that.

No. She shook her head to interrupt the poisonous chain of self-degradation. She wasn't that person anymore. She wasn't nothing.

"I'm sorry, but I have to decline your offer," she finally replied. "Please contact me when you're ready to sign a contract that releases me from your service."

She turned around and left the room, walking with calm steps even though her instincts screamed at her to run. She was sweating, and her heart was pounding in her chest. *I did it,* she thought. *I confronted Swanson.* A smile graced her lips. She'd been terrified the whole time, but she'd gone through with it. Even if the meeting had taken an unexpected turn, she was still proud of herself.

Mark was waiting right outside the office, refusing to look at her.

"Well?" he said, crossing his arms. "Am I unemployed now?"

She shook her head. "I turned him down. I won't take your position."

His expression softened. He looked a lot younger when he wasn't scowling, and she realized that she'd been overestimating his age all along. He wasn't that much older than her—probably younger than Andrew.

"You wouldn't have lasted a day as his right-hand man," Mark commented halfheartedly. There was no longer any burning hatred in his voice, and his eyes looked friendlier, too. This explained his weak attempts to scare Robyn away from the fighting world. He'd been afraid she'd steal his job from him.

She smiled. "I guess we'll never know."

After giving the receptionist a quick apology, Robyn left the mansion and began her jog back to Andrew's house. Though the meeting hadn't turned out the way she'd planned it, she'd still given Swanson her ultimatum. She would get out of the fighting world. It was her life, and she was taking it back.

• • •

When Andrew woke up, he was alone in the bed. He placed his hand on the sheet where Robyn had been lying when they'd fallen asleep. The sheet was already cold. His heart sank. *She changed her mind.* He knew Robyn was afraid of letting people into her life, but after the night they'd shared, he'd gotten the impression she was on the same page as him. He must have been wrong.

The night they'd spent together had probably been the best night of his life, and the thought of Robyn regretting it all hurt like hell. It shouldn't have come as a surprise to him that she would leave before he woke up, but it still did. It still hurt.

He got out of the bed and got dressed before heading toward the kitchen. After carefully searching the kitchen table and the counters, he had to accept that Robyn had left without even leaving a note.

He sat in a kitchen chair and buried his face in his hands. Had he ruined their friendship forever? Would she ever want to see him again?

Suddenly, he heard someone unlock the front door. He rushed into the hallway and found Robyn standing in the doorway.

"What's up?" A worried wrinkle appeared between her eyebrows. "You look upset."

He approached her in three quick steps and wrapped his arms around her. "You were gone when I woke up. I thought... I thought you changed your mind." He held her tightly, inhaling her scent. She was there. She was actually there.

"Shit, I forgot to leave a note. I'm sorry." Her hands tentatively stroked his back. "It's the opposite, actually. I want to be with you, and I knew I could never offer you anything long-term as long as I was stuck in the fighting world. I've come to realize that there are a lot of things I want to do in life, things I could never do if I kept fighting. So, I went over to Swanson's place and told him I'm quitting. The fight against Drake will be my final fight."

"Really?" He pulled back a little so he could see her face. "What did he say? Is he really going to let you quit just like that?"

"I think so. I told him I'd lose on purpose on Saturday if he doesn't provide me with a written contract that frees me from his services. I think I'm really getting out this time." She smiled shyly. "I'm getting my life back."

He took a deep breath as a knot of worry settled in his stomach. The thought of her getting out of the fighting world should have been an enormous relief, but he couldn't shake the feeling that

Robyn's plan was not as bulletproof as she thought. Swanson was not a man to piss off.

"You should have told me," he said. "I could have been your backup."

"I knew you'd say that. That's why I left before you woke up." She stood on her tiptoes and pressed a soft kiss to his lips. "This was something I had to do on my own."

He cupped her face in his hand. "You're too brave for your own good sometimes, you know that?"

She shrugged. "You're the one who gave me the courage to do it. I used to be so scared all the time, but I'm not that person anymore. You made me braver." The calm confidence in her eyes shined brighter than ever. "I take back what I said before. I trust you, Andrew."

Andrew didn't know what to say, so instead he tilted her head back and kissed her. He could feel her trust in him with every fiber of his being. It was intoxicating. He'd been hers for a very long time, and now, for the first time ever, he felt like she was *his*.

He pushed her up against the wall, kissing her harder. *Mine.* She wrapped her arms around his neck. Her body fit perfectly against his. Everything about her was perfect. *Mine.* He placed his hands on the back of her thighs, hoisting her up. Her lightness amazed him. She always amazed him. *Mine.* He trailed kisses down her slender neck and nearly lost all control when she threw her head back and moaned. *Mine, mine, mine.*

"Don't leave me," she gasped, burying her nails in his back. "Promise me you won't leave me."

He looked her straight in the eye. "I won't leave you. Not now. Not ever. I love you, Robyn. I'm not leaving you."

She wrapped her legs around his waist and ran her fingers through his hair in a way that always drove him crazy. In her eyes, he could see a possessiveness matching his. When she kissed him hard on the lips, Andrew knew she'd believed him.

...

"I should call Lucy," Robyn said. "She's probably wondering where I am."

"Do you really have to?" Andrew asked. "Do you really, *really* have to?"

She was lying in his arms, her head resting on his shoulder. It reminded him of that time she'd fallen asleep in his arms in the guest room. He'd thought that night was perfect, but he had to admit that the current situation was even better. He loved feeling her naked skin against his.

"Yeah, I really have to. I don't want her to worry about me." She sighed, making no effort whatsoever to move away from him.

He grinned. "You have to leave the bed to reach the phone, you know."

"I'm working on it, okay?" she groaned. "I'm just really, really comfortable here."

"Me, too." He kissed the top of her head. "What do you think Lucy will say about us?"

He asked the question in a light tone, but on the inside, he was pretty worried. He knew how protective the Monroe sisters were of each other, and he wasn't sure what Lucy would think about their relationship.

"She'll be ecstatic," Robyn said. "She's been trying to pair us up for months."

He blinked. "Really?"

"She's discreet. Remember my birthday? She was the one who sent you down to the garage, right?"

"She wanted me to see you dance," he concluded. "Wow. She's sneaky."

"I know." Robyn stretched before getting out of bed. She sent him a glare as she put on her underwear. "Stop staring."

"I have no idea what you're talking about," he said innocently as he continued to stare.

She shook her head, smiling. She left the bedroom and returned a few seconds later with her backpack in her hands. After rummaging through it for a while, she pulled out her old Nokia.

"Five missed calls." She frowned. "And a voice mail, too." She dialed a number and put the phone on speaker.

"Hey, Robyn, it's me," Lucy's voice said. "I'm guessing you're with Andrew, but please, call me back as soon as you hear this. Swanson just entered the building, and that bald guy is with him. I don't know why, but I'm getting a really bad feeling about this. Please, call me back."

Robyn stared at Andrew in shock. "No, he wouldn't… Would he?"

Andrew got out of the bed and reached for his clothes. "Try to call her back. We'll take the car."

"I fucked up, didn't I?" she whispered. "I really fucked up this time."

They rushed to the car as soon as they'd gotten dressed. Robyn tried to call Lucy over and over, reaching her voice mail every time.

"I fucked up," she said again, her hands trembling. "I didn't think he'd go after her. I thought he'd only go after me. Oh my God, I fucked up."

She jumped out of the car as soon as they reached the parking lot outside the building, not even bothering to wait for Andrew to stop the car. She rolled onto the asphalt and was back up on her feet in less than a second.

"Dammit," Andrew hissed. He parked the car diagonally over two spots and rushed after her.

"Robyn, wait!" he yelled. "They could still be in there!"

Robyn didn't listen. He could only watch as she entered the building and climbed the stairs. When he entered the staircase several seconds later, all he could hear was Robyn's panicked breaths. He ran up the stairs, taking two steps at a time.

He found her sitting on the floor outside her apartment, holding a shoebox in her hands. The door to the apartment was open, and he only had to glance inside to see that someone had completely wrecked the place.

"I'll kill him for this," Robyn said in a low voice, tears rolling down her cheeks. "I'll kill him, and Mark, and every single person in that fucking mansion."

He kneeled next to her, finally looking inside the box.

"Oh my God."

Inside was a copper red braid, the thick bundle of hair still tied together by a bejeweled hair tie. Someone had placed a note on top of it, leaving Robyn a short message.

I hope you change your mind.

CHAPTER TWENTY-ONE

He will pay for this, Robyn thought as she put the lid back on the box. She stood, forcing her trembling legs to carry her. Judging from the state of the apartment, Lucy had fought back with all her might. Had they knocked her unconscious? Had they hurt her? The thoughts made her nauseous, so she quickly pushed them away. She took a step toward the stairs, but Andrew stopped her by grabbing her wrist.

"You're planning to confront Swanson again, aren't you?" he said. "Just head straight back to his place and try to get Lucy back with brute force?"

Robyn saw no point in denying it, so she nodded.

"It won't work. You'll never get Lucy back that way."

"There aren't that many people in his headquarters. I could take them. Let go of me." She tried to pull her arm free, but he only tightened his grip.

"Robyn, listen to me. If you go there, you would only be doing exactly what he expects you to do. Don't you think he's planned for this? Called in extra backup?"

"What else am I supposed to do?" she yelled. "He has my sister! I have to do *something.*" Tears rolled down her cheeks. Her whole body trembled. How could she have let this happen?

Andrew pulled her into his arms, holding her tightly. "I'll call Jason. He said he only needed one final piece of evidence to nail Swanson once and for all. Your apartment should be evidence enough. The police can save Lucy and make sure Swanson gets arrested. You don't have to handle this on your own."

It took a few seconds for her to process what he was saying, but when the message finally sank in, some of the blind rage seemed to fade away. He was right—Swanson was definitely expecting her to confront him on her own again. The old Robyn would have been too scared to ask anyone for help—but she wasn't that person anymore. She didn't like the thought of handing the responsibility over to someone else, but she could see that involving the police was the only way she could save Lucy.

She leaned against Andrew, closing her eyes. "I'm so stupid. I should have realized he'd hurt her instead of hurting me. I'm so fucking stupid."

"You're not stupid," he murmured. "You're just too kind to understand someone like Swanson."

She frowned, unsure whether to take his comment as a compliment or an insult. "What's that supposed to mean? I'm a fighter. I'm not kind."

"Yes, you are," he said. "You're honest and straightforward. You would never manipulate someone. You're a genuinely good person, and men like Swanson know how to use that against you. That's why he took Lucy. He knew you would react like this—that you would try to storm his place on your own. By threatening Lucy, he could force you back into the fighting world. I don't even think he'd release her afterwards. I think he'd keep her somewhere close to him, allowing you to see her when it suited him. She would be the perfect tool to make sure you don't rebel against him ever again."

Andrew was right. That sounded exactly like something Swanson would do.

"How do you know all that?" she asked him. "You barely know him—how come you can see through his plans, but I can't?"

"You can't see through his plans because you're a good person. Doing what he did is completely unthinkable for someone like you. I'm…not as good as you. I should have acted before he could do something like this." He took a step back, releasing her from his embrace. "I'm going to call Jason now."

Leaning against the wall, Robyn slid to the floor. It didn't matter what he said. This was still her fault.

Andrew sat next to her as soon as he'd ended the call. "Jason will be here in ten. The apartment and the box should be evidence enough to put Swanson in jail. They're taking down his whole organization tonight."

"And Lucy?"

"They'll get her out before they storm the place. Jason said he had a plan. I'm sure he's prioritizing her safety."

Robyn nodded, leaning her head against his shoulder. "Could you… Could you say it? You know, your 'everything will be okay' thing?"

He kissed the top of her head and took her hand in his. "Everything will be okay."

She smiled faintly. "You're being too hard on yourself again. You really are a good person."

"Am I, really? I keep failing people."

"You never failed me. My life changed that night in the ER. I wouldn't have survived without you. You may have had your own reasons for helping me all this time, but that doesn't make the action any less *good*. You're a good person, Andrew. I have no doubt whatsoever that the people you think you failed would've said the exact same thing."

Andrew remained silent for a while and then squeezed her hand. "Thank you."

His voice was hoarse, and even though Robyn couldn't see his face, she was pretty certain there were tears in his eyes. *No one's ever told him that before,* she realized. *No one's ever told him how good he is.* She made a mental note to remind him of it as often as possible.

Jason arrived ten minutes later, just like he'd promised. Robyn blinked as she took him in, uniform and all. She would never have guessed the guy she'd met in Andrew's hallway was a cop.

"Wow, what a mess," Jason said after taking a quick look inside the apartment. "She really fought back, huh?"

"I tried to teach her some self-defense once," Robyn said. "I guess it wasn't enough."

She hugged her knees to her chest, overwhelmed by guilt. She should have been here. She should have protected Lucy.

Jason kneeled next to her. "We'll get her back, I promise. Don't worry." He smiled confidently. "Most of the guys from the station will be there, and we've requested help from all the other stations in the district. We're not as many as I hoped we'd be, but it doesn't matter. Swanson's going down tonight. Are you sure he's keeping her in the mansion?"

"I'm pretty sure, yeah. You'll get her out before you invade the place, right? You have to get her out."

Jason nodded. "I don't like using civilians like this, but we kind of need your help for that."

"Of course," she immediately replied. "I'll do anything."

"We want to get your sister out of the building before we go in at full strength. We need to find out where Swanson's keeping her, and you're the only one who can talk to him without raising suspicion. If you go inside his headquarters and accept his terms, you could probably get him to tell you where he's keeping her. You would have a microphone hidden on you, of course, and you would get out as soon as you got the information. It's dangerous, and no one will blame you if you don't want to do it. We think this plan has the highest probability of success, but we'll come up with something different if you're not okay with it."

"Are you insane?" Andrew exclaimed. "You want to send her straight into the lion's den all on her own? Anything could happen in there!"

Robyn squeezed his hand. "It will be fine. Swanson would never expect me to turn against him. I'll do it."

"Andrew is right," Jason said. "Anything could happen in there. We'll be ready to storm the place if something happens, but I can't promise we'll reach you in time if Swanson figures out that you're setting him up. Are you sure you want to do this?"

She nodded. "I'm sure."

"All right, then." Jason got up from the floor. "Let's go."

• • •

"I don't like this," Andrew said as he watched a short teenager with spiky brown hair hide a wireless microphone in Robyn's hoodie. "Jason said they could come up with another plan. Please don't do this."

They were standing on the sidewalk one block away from Swanson's mansion. The policemen were making their final preparations, waiting for the mission to start. There were only about a dozen of them, but their eyes shone with determination.

"He also said this was the plan most likely to succeed," Robyn said. "I have to do this."

Her voice was calm and steady, but Andrew could tell she was nervous. Her hands were trembling a little, and she refused to look him in the eye.

"But what if he figures out you're working against him? What if he makes you take off your sweater, and he finds the microphone? What if—"

"Please, stop," she interrupted, her eyes fixed on the ground. "You know I won't change my mind. All you're doing is making me more terrified."

You're freaking out, and you're taking it out on her, his inner critic commented. *Keep it together.*

"I'm sorry." He forced himself to at least pretend to be calm. "I just wish you didn't have to do this alone."

"I'm not alone. This place is crawling with cops."

He rolled his eyes. "You know what I mean."

"Yeah, I know. But I'll be in there for like five minutes, tops. I'll be fine."

"Excuse me, miss?" Jason's technician said. "You need to wear this earbud so we can stay in contact with you. Your hair covers your ears at almost every angle, and the bud is pretty small. I don't think anyone will notice it."

Robyn accepted the small device and put it in her ear. Her messy red locks covered it perfectly.

"All right," the boy said, grinning proudly. "The microphone is in place, and the transmitter is in your pocket. It has a sensitivity range of minus thirty to plus forty decibel, so you don't have to think about speaking louder than usual. It will pick up everything anyway. The alkaline manganese battery lasts for at least five and a half hours, and—"

"Calm down, Luke," Jason said, joining the conversation. "I don't think she's interested in the specs. All that matters is that it works."

Jason was now wearing a bulletproof vest over his uniform. He seemed to be tenser than before, but the look he gave the kid was still warm and brotherly.

"If you wanted something that just *works*, you wouldn't have called me," Luke said, pouting a little. "You wanted me to make it extraordinary, and I did. You could at least give me some cred for it."

Jason ruffled his hair. "You did great, you cocky little brat. Don't let it go to your head."

"Are you sure the transmitter has enough power to reach us all the way over here?" Andrew asked. "We have to be nearly a hundred yards away from the mansion."

"I'm absolutely sure," Luke said. "My transmitter can reach at least three hundred meters."

"But what if something goes wrong?" Andrew continued. "Shouldn't Robyn's backup be closer to the mansion?"

"If we go any closer, the surveillance will notice us," Jason said. "This is as close as we can get."

"I still don't like this."

Robyn squeezed his hand. "I'll be fine. If something goes wrong, you know I can defend myself."

"Try to avoid violence if you can," Jason said. "If something seems off, *anything*, just get out. We don't want to end up with two hostages in there."

She nodded. "Get in, get Lucy's location, and get out. I've got this."

"I guess everything's in place, then." Jason patted her on the back. "Good luck."

"I'll be back as soon as I can." Robyn gave Andrew a quick kiss before beginning her jog toward the mansion.

Luke connected the receiver to a pair of speakers. Andrew closed his eyes, listening to the sound of Robyn's calm breaths. For a moment, the sound allowed him to pretend she was still by his side. The thought of her being on her way to infiltrate the headquarters of the most corrupt organization in Chrystal Valley was too terrifying to process.

When he opened his eyes again, Jason was gathering his teammates. "These are the mansion's blueprints," he said, unfolding several large sheets of paper on the ground. "As soon as we get Lucy's location, we'll come up with the fastest way to get there. We have to be flexible, and we have to work fast."

"What if she's not in the mansion?" one of the men asked.

"Then we'll have to rethink our plan. Fast. Like I said, we have to be flexible."

"Guys," Luke butted in. "I think she's inside the building now."

The group fell silent, listening carefully to the speakers. The sound of Robyn's steps was softer now, and her breaths were a little less regular. Andrew wished he could see what was happening instead of just guessing what was going on. His mind was already coming up with horrible mental images of possible catastrophes. He could tell the policemen were worried too—especially Jason.

"Robyn," a male voice said. "What a pleasant surprise. I hope you don't mind the audience."

Andrew clenched his jaw. It seemed Swanson had called for backup, just like he'd suspected.

"Cut the bullshit," Robyn replied bitterly. "You knew I'd come here as soon as I got your message."

"I hope she doesn't punch him," Jason commented.

"She won't," Andrew said. "She knows what's at stake."

"Fair enough," Swanson said. "Have you changed your mind?"

"I don't think I'm ready for that promotion yet, but I'll continue to fight for you. Please, let my sister go. I promise I'll give my all on Saturday."

"I'm glad you're cooperating, but I think Lucy will have to stay here for a little while longer, just to make sure you keep your motivation for the fight. No harm will come to her. She's perfectly safe here. I hope you understand."

"You bastard," Robyn said in a low, dangerous tone, and for a moment, Andrew wasn't sure if she would really be able to keep herself from attacking Swanson.

"Come on, Robyn, keep it together," Jason muttered, staring at the speakers in deep concentration.

After a few moments of silence, Robyn spoke again. "Can I... Can I at least see her? I need to know she's okay."

"Mark, please bring me the laptop," Swanson ordered.

"He probably has a surveillance camera in the room he's keeping Lucy in," Jason said. "He must be showing Robyn a live stream or something on the computer. Shit. Maybe we should have put a camera on her, after all."

"If we'd put a camera on her, the risk of her getting caught would have been much higher," Luke said. "You know that."

"Yeah, I know." Jason paced back and forth on the sidewalk. "We have to come up with a new plan. I—"

He was interrupted when Robyn spoke again. "Those numbers on the screen, they refer to her location, right? B-W-W-R seventeen, that means she's in the west wing basement, room seventeen, right?"

"All right, people, we've got a location!" Jason grinned triumphantly. "Your girl is good at improvising, Alexander."

"Yeah," Andrew said absentmindedly, still listening carefully to the transmission as Jason's team prepared to leave.

"Yes," Swanson answered Robyn. "Why do you ask?"

"I just… She gets cold easily and has a weak immune system," Robyn said. "I don't think the basement is a good place for her."

Andrew cringed. Robyn was a lousy liar. There was no way in hell Swanson would buy that.

"Her room is warm. She'll be fine in there. If she feels sick, I'll send down a doctor. No harm will come to her, dear. You can trust me on that."

"Okay, Robyn," Jason said into his own microphone. "You can get out now. Great job." He turned to his fellow officers, pointing at the map on the ground. "That's where he's keeping her. We can go in through that window, and then we can take the stairs over there to reach the basement. Come on, hurry!"

Jason took off, running toward the mansion with three of his coworkers. Andrew took his eyes off the speakers for a moment to look around. The rest of the officers and Luke were still waiting on the sidewalk, listening to the transmission.

"I hope they get that Swanson guy," Luke said in a low voice. "Tyler was one of my best friends."

"I'm sorry," Andrew said. "I never knew him, but Robyn was very fond of him, too."

"I should leave," Robyn's voice said through the speakers.

"Are you in a hurry?" a different male voice asked. Andrew was pretty sure the voice belonged to Swanson's assistant, Mark.

"I only came here to make sure Lucy's okay," Robyn replied. "If you're not planning to let her go, I have nothing left to do here."

"That's it? You're giving up just like that? Not even a single death threat? Mr. Swanson, something's up. She's acting way too calm."

Andrew's heart began to race. The cops tensed up.

"This is not going to end well, is it?" Luke said, his face turning pale.

Robyn swallowed hard, the sound loud enough to get picked up by the microphone. "Swanson promised me he'd keep her safe. I trust him."

Her voice trembled. If her previous lie had been bad, this one was catastrophic.

"Victoria? How is the scan going?" Mark asked.

"The detector picked up some unknown RF signals," a female voice said. "There's a transmitter in the room."

"That's it, we're going in," one of the cops said. He gave Luke and Andrew a nod before rushing toward the mansion, his crew following in his tracks.

"What do we do?" Andrew asked Luke, fighting the urge to run after them.

"We stay here. We're civilians. We'll only fuck things up if we try to help."

A loud noise blasted from the speakers, and Andrew could hear Robyn gasp.

"Let go of me!" she yelled, her voice almost drowned out by the crackling noise.

"Who sent you?" Mark growled. "I found the microphone. Who are you spying for? The police? Answer me, you lying little bitch!"

Robyn cried out in pain, and Andrew ran.

CHAPTER TWENTY-TWO

Robyn sank to her knees, blood trickling from her lip. Mark had pushed her hard against the wall before he began to search for the microphone. The punch he gave her after he found the device caused her to black out for a few milliseconds. She collapsed on the floor, spitting blood on the red carpet.

"Whom are you spying for?" Mark grabbed the hood of her sweater and pulled her back up to her feet. "Answer me!"

His voice was all anger, but his eyes were full of terror. Robyn swallowed hard and took a leap of faith.

"You don't have to do this," she said. "You don't have to be his slave."

"What?"

"The police are waiting outside. They're here to arrest Swanson. They've got all the proof they need. After tonight, we'll finally be free. All of us."

They stared at each other. The words hung heavy between them, and the world seemed to slow down.

His eyes widened when her words finally sank in. "What have you done?"

Robyn met his eyes and saw something break inside him. Her heart sank. Swanson had manipulated Mark for too long. He would always be on Swanson's side.

"Code black, everybody!" Mark shouted. "Shred all the files and clean all the hard drives. Destroy everything!"

Swanson's backup scattered, running in every direction. They all looked terrified, and Robyn suspected most of them were just teenagers. For a brief moment, she wondered what would happen to them after this. Prison? Foster care?

Mark glanced over his shoulder, meeting Swanson's eyes. "Mr. Swanson, get out of here. I'll stall them."

Swanson nodded. He walked up to a corner of the room and removed a painting from the wall. Behind it were a keypad and a big red button. Swanson punched in a code and pressed the button, making a nearby bookshelf move a couple feet to the left and reveal a narrow door behind it. Mark watched carefully as Swanson made his escape through the secret emergency exit. Robyn slowly backed away from him.

"Where the fuck do you think you're going?" Mark snapped, turning back to her. "If we're all going down, you're going down with us."

She raised her fists. "Do you think you can take me?"

He smirked. "I could if I wanted to. It's too bad I don't have time to fight you." He reached into the inner pocket of his suit jacket. When the hand emerged, it was holding gun. He raised it and aimed at her head. She took a step back, staring at the weapon in shock. She'd never even considered the possibility that he could have a gun. *What do I do?* If they'd battled it out in an ordinary fight, she could have taken him, but the gun changed everything. She couldn't exactly punch a bullet.

"End of the line, Ms. Monroe." He slowly walked toward her. "Did you really think someone like you could bring down someone like Swanson?"

He placed the muzzle of the gun against her forehead. "I never liked you. I knew you would betray us. Swanson never saw that side of you, but I always knew you were a selfish liar."

Robyn stood frozen in place. The sound of her pounding heartbeats drowned out all her thoughts. The gun was cold against her skin. What was he waiting for? Why hadn't he pulled the trigger yet? At first, she thought he was dragging it out to make her suffer, but then her eyes met his. He was still furious with her, but he was also terrified.

"You've never killed anyone before, have you?" she asked, her voice trembling.

"Shut up," he said in a low voice, cocking the gun. "You're nothing. No one would miss you if you disappeared from this world. You're nothing!"

Robyn took a deep, shivering breath. She was walking on thin ice now. A single misstep would most likely lead to her death.

"Whom are you trying to convince?" she asked. "Me or yourself?"

Mark hesitated, and in that very same moment, the cops arrived. The front door was kicked in with enough force to make it come loose from its hinges. Mark took a step back as the armed policemen entered the room. Robyn used his moment of distraction to pull out the knife from her pants pocket. When Mark put the gun against her forehead again, she put the blade of her knife against his throat.

"Do you think you can pull the trigger before I cut your throat?" she asked. "Do you really wanna take that chance?"

Her voice was trembling, but her grip on the knife was steady. Mark swallowed hard. Robyn couldn't see what the cops were doing, but they seemed to have come to a stop behind her back.

"Drop your weapon!" one of them yelled. "You're surrounded. Drop the gun."

Mark's gaze fixed on a single point behind Robyn's back. She could immediately sense that something had changed in their power dynamic.

He smirked. "I see you brought your doctor."

Her eyes widened. He had to be bluffing. Andrew wouldn't do anything that stupid. She cast a quick glance over her shoulder, and her heart nearly stopped when she saw Andrew standing right behind the cops.

Mark moved the gun away from her head and pointed it at Andrew instead. "Do you think you can cut my throat before I pull the trigger?" he asked, returning her question. "Give me the knife."

Robyn was pretty sure she was faster than Mark, but with Andrew's life on the line, she couldn't take the risk. She slowly lowered the knife from his neck. Mark snatched it with his free hand, keeping his gun pointed at Andrew.

"You!" he shouted. "Dr. Alexander, step forward!"

She glanced over her shoulder again. "Don't do it. Get out of here!"

Mark quickly turned her around with the hand holding the knife and pulled her closer before pressing the blade against her throat. She wanted to struggle, but his gun was still pointing at Andrew.

"Dr. Alexander, step forward," Mark repeated, letting the knife's edge pierce her skin. She flinched and tried to get away from it, but her back was already pressed against Mark's body with no room for maneuvers.

"Don't," Andrew exclaimed, pushing past the policemen. "I'm coming, all right? Please, don't hurt her."

"Andrew, no!" she yelled. "Stay away!"

Mark snorted. "You actually like the guy, don't you? Pathetic."

"Please, don't hurt her," Andrew said again. He was now in front of the cops, slowly approaching Mark and Robyn. "I'm here now. Don't hurt her."

"If anyone moves, I'll cut her throat." Mark backed away from the policemen. "Dr. Alexander, follow me."

The knife against Robyn's throat forced her to move with him. Andrew followed them, never further than a few feet away from her. His eyes burned hot with fury as he observed Mark's every move. The expression frightened her—not because of its harshness, but because of the meaning behind it. Andrew would do anything to protect her. *Anything.*

"You should have run, you idiot," she said softly.

"I couldn't. I made a promise, remember?" He looked at her without a single trace of regret in his eyes. "I'm not leaving you, Robyn."

Mark stopped next to the secret exit. The bookshelf had moved back to its original place, covering the door.

"One, three, two, two, then the red button," Mark told Andrew. He let the blade cut Robyn's throat again. The cut was deeper this time, and she could feel blood trickle down her neck.

Andrew hurried to the keypad on the wall and followed Mark's instructions, his face turning pale. As soon as the shelf had moved out of the way, Mark lunged for the door, still pulling Robyn with him. He dropped the knife and aimed the gun at her head again, grabbing the doorknob with his free hand.

The door wouldn't open.

"Mr. Swanson?" Mark yelled. "I think you locked the door from the inside. Mr. Swanson!"

"Did you really think he would wait for you?" she asked. "He left without you to save his own skin. Are you really surprised?"

"Shut up!" he roared. "He needs me. I'm not like you. He needs me!"

"Just accept it," she said, trying her best to keep him focused on her. If she made him angry, there was a chance he might forget about Andrew. "You're nothing, just like me. You—"

Mark wrapped his arm around her neck. "I told you to shut up," he growled, still pressing his gun against her temple. His chokehold was perfectly executed, and Robyn knew she didn't have much time before she would pass out. She struggled against him, burrowing her nails into his suit jacket. Mark didn't even react.

He moved back to the middle of the room, dragging her with him. "Nobody moves!" he yelled, pointing the gun in every direction. He was running out of options, and Robyn could tell the desperation was clogging his mind. She flailed helplessly in his grip as her lungs and brain screamed for oxygen.

Black spots were clouding her vision, but in the corner of her eye she could see Andrew approaching them. *No,* she thought, *please don't do this. Please stay away.*

"Back off!" Mark yelled, pointing the gun at Andrew.

"No."

Robyn shuddered. The hatred in his voice was terrifying.

Andrew charged forward. He grabbed the gun and aimed it upward, and when the shot went off he'd already spun around on the outside of Mark's arm. Her technique.

Andrew's hand moved from the gun to Mark's wrist, giving it a squeeze. Mark's hand opened and the gun fell to the floor. His grip around her neck loosened, allowing her to take a shallow breath. It wasn't much, but in combination with the adrenaline pumping through her veins it gave her enough strength to throw Mark over her shoulder and down to the floor. Andrew grabbed her arm and pulled her close. She leaned against him, her body trembling. Every breath she took made her throat hurt.

When the cops saw that Robyn and Andrew were out of danger, they could finally act. The leader made a gesture with his hand. His team immediately split up, running after the kids Mark had sent to destroy all the evidence. Two of the officers stayed in the hallway, their guns pointed at Mark's head.

"Well, that went unexpectedly well," Andrew said, his eyes wide. "Did you see that? I can't believe I did that."

"You idiot!" Robyn hissed. "He could have shot you! You could have died! What are you even doing in here? You could have died, you idiot!"

He grinned. "I love you too."

She tried to scowl at him, but she was too relieved to stay angry. "Don't ever do anything like that again," she muttered before giving him a quick kiss on the lips.

"Hey, don't move," one of the policemen said. Robyn glanced at Mark. He was reaching for his gun, which was still lying on the floor about a yard away from him.

"Stop moving immediately, or I'll shoot!" the policeman shouted.

"What the hell is he doing?" Andrew asked.

"He's not trying to reach the gun." The realization hit her like a punch in the gut. "Don't do it! He's—"

The policeman pulled the trigger. The bullet hit Mark right in the forehead, killing him instantly. She sank to her knees, feeling strangely empty inside.

"He wasn't trying to reach the gun," she said. "He just wanted you to think he was. He was committing suicide."

"Why the hell did you do that?" Andrew yelled at the policeman.

"He was reaching for his gun."

"A gun he couldn't possibly reach. Don't you value human life at all?"

"He warned him," the shooter's partner butted in. "He didn't do anything wrong."

Andrew took a deep breath, clenching his fists. Robyn could tell he was forcing himself not to go on a total rampage.

She turned her gaze away from Andrew, her eyes drawn to the small red dot on Mark's forehead. Even though he'd been a constant threat to her for several years, his death didn't give her any relief. In the end, he was just another victim.

Andrew returned to her side. "He really thought Swanson would wait for him, didn't he?"

"Yeah. I want to hate him, but I can't. He wasn't a bad guy. Not really. He was loyal to a fault, and Swanson used that against him."

She coughed, her airways still a bit battered from Mark's grip. Blood trickled from the small cuts on her neck. Andrew instantly switched into doctor mode.

"I need to take a look at that." He placed a finger under her chin to tilt her head back. "I need to stop the bleeding. Wait here."

He crossed the room to pick up the dropped knife. After cutting off a piece of his shirt, he returned to Robyn.

"Hold this," he said after pressing the cloth against her cuts. "I'll put on a proper bandage when we get out of here."

She nodded, placing her hand on top of the makeshift compression. "I wonder how Jason's doing."

"I'm sure he and Lucy are already waiting for us outside." Andrew smiled. "Let's get out of here."

She glanced at Mark's dead body again. He hadn't been a good man, but he'd still deserved a better ending than this. She knelt next to him and closed his eyes. *I'm sorry,* she thought. *I wish I could have saved you, too.*

She stood and took Andrew's hand in hers. "Let's go."

• • •

"Remind me to never, *ever* involve you two in police work again." Jason scowled at them both. "The paperwork for this is going to be an absolute mess."

Andrew smiled. He didn't really care. He'd gotten both him and Robyn out of that nightmarish mansion, and for once, he'd been the one who protected *her.* Though he suspected some of his calm came from him being in shock, he was still pretty pleased with the outcome of the situation.

Robyn's eyes scanned the area. "Where's Lucy?"

"She's over there." Jason pointed at one of the cars. "She's unharmed."

Robyn rushed toward the car, Andrew jogging after her. Lucy was sitting on the edge of the trunk, wrapped up in a thick blanket. Her hair was almost a foot shorter than it used to be, but otherwise she seemed okay.

Her face lit up when she saw Robyn. "I'm so happy to see you."

Robyn wrapped her arms around her sister. "I'm sorry," she whispered. "I'm so sorry. Are you okay? I saw the apartment. Did they hurt you?"

"It's okay. They barely touched me. I started throwing stuff when they broke in, but then they injected me with some drug or something. When I woke up, I was already in that room. It was a nice bed, and the food was pretty decent. Really, I'm fine. I promise."

"I'm so glad you're okay. You have no idea how worried I was."

Andrew was watching them from a couple of steps away when Jason touched his shoulder.

"So. What, exactly, were you thinking when you rushed straight into a hostage situation?" Jason's tone was teasing, but Andrew could tell how pissed he was.

"I'm sorry, okay?" he said. "She screamed, and I panicked."

Jason sighed. "I get it. I should have seen it coming and left someone to guard you. I heard you pulled some pretty neat moves in there, by the way. How did you make him drop the gun?"

"Pressure points. There are two pressure points near the radial bone in the wrist. If you press them, the hand opens."

Jason blinked. "Huh. I had no idea."

Out of the corner of his eye, Andrew saw Lucy get up from her seat on the trunk.

"I can't believe no one called Mike!" the younger sister exclaimed. "Seriously, I get kidnapped, and no one thinks about calling my fiancé? Robyn, give me your phone."

Robyn handed it over without question, taking a step back. Andrew grinned. It amused him how petite little Lucy could make Robyn cower in fear just by glaring at her.

As if she could hear his thoughts, Lucy turned her gaze to him, giving him the same angry glare. He immediately stopped smiling.

"Damn," Jason said. "She's scarier than Robyn."

"Definitely. If you and your team hadn't rescued her, she probably would have gotten herself out in a day or two anyway. The Monroe sisters are resourceful."

Jason grinned. "I don't doubt that at all. She almost knocked one of my teammates out with a chair."

Hours later, the raid was finally over. The sun had set, and the air was getting colder by the minute. The policemen had arrested countless teenagers, though they didn't really know what to do with them. Swanson was gone without a trace. Robyn and Lucy were sharing a thick shock blanket, huddled together in the open car trunk. Andrew and Jason stood a couple yards away, watching as the policemen returned from the mansion with the final group of handcuffed adolescents.

"We took down his organization, but this won't be over until we get him, too," Jason said bitterly. "At least it's out in the open now. His kids destroyed a lot of data, but we still have enough to put out an official arrest order."

"Will Robyn be safe?" Andrew glanced at the sisters. "Do you think Swanson will go after her?"

"I think Swanson will keep a low profile for a long, long time." Jason sighed. "Finding him again won't be easy, but I won't give up. Sooner or later, he'll start something new, and when he does, I'll be ready for him."

A policeman walked up to them, holding a stack of papers. "I think I found that file you were looking for."

Jason accepted the papers and quickly looked through them. "Yeah, this is the right one. Thanks."

"What's that?" Andrew asked.

Jason smiled. "Robyn's file."

As they walked toward the Monroe sisters, Andrew's curiosity grew. The debt didn't matter now that Swanson was gone, but he would still like to know whether or not Swanson had been lying to Robyn for all this time.

She stood up as the men approached the car, automatically putting herself between them and Lucy. Andrew didn't take it personally. She probably wasn't even aware of doing it.

"Have you found out anything more about Swanson?" she asked Jason. "Any clues to where he went?"

"No, he's still lost without a trace. They did find this, though." He handed her the papers.

She eyed the file. "I didn't even know he had one of these on me."

"What's that?" Lucy asked.

"It's my file." Robyn knit her brow. "It says... It says all of mom's debts have been paid off. We've been debt free for three years."

"Gimme that." Lucy snatched the stack of papers from Robyn's hands. She narrowed her eyes, reading through it carefully. "I can't believe this. That bastard made you fight for him while making you think he was doing you a favor. For three years! I hate him. I hate him so much."

"Who cares? We're debt free, Lucy. Debt free!" Robyn laughed out loud, radiating happiness and relief. "We're free!"

Andrew's heart filled with joy. He still despised Swanson for using Robyn, but seeing her happy made his anger seem irrelevant. It was like a physical weight had been lifted from her shoulders, making her stand a little bit taller. Her hair was a mess and her face was covered in bruises, but to him, she'd never been more beautiful. He swore to himself that he would do anything to protect that smile. He would protect it for the rest of his life.

Robyn walked up to him and leaned her head against his shoulder. He wrapped his arms around her and felt her body relax.

"I'm still going to fight in the final," she said.

Her words hit him like a punch in the gut. "Why? Swanson's organization is gone. You're free to do whatever you want now."

She nodded. "I know. And I want to fight Drake."

"Why?" Andrew repeated. "You're out. You're finally *out*. Why on earth would you throw yourself back in again?"

"I don't expect you to understand this, but…" She hesitated. "I've been fighting for so many years now, and most of the time, I've enjoyed it. I think I need my final fight. It's my way of saying goodbye to my old life."

Andrew let out a deep sigh. He hated it—absolutely *hated* it— but he could understand it. The thought of going back to Chrystal Arena made his stomach lurch, but he'd do it. He'd do it for her.

He kissed the top of her head, breathing in the scent of her hair. Once, he'd thought of love as a nuisance, but he'd been proven wrong. He'd found a person he'd do anything for, and now, he knew for sure.

It's worth it, he thought. *She's worth it.*

CHAPTER TWENTY-THREE

When the day of Robyn's last fight finally arrived, Andrew almost missed being lonely. He was hiding out on his balcony, holding a cigarette in his hand. Somehow, he'd ended up with three temporary housemates, and the lack of alone time was starting to stress him out.

When the Monroe sisters' apartment had turned out to be too trashed to live in for a while, Andrew had immediately offered for Robyn to sleep at his place. Robyn had, of course, refused to go anywhere without Lucy, so Andrew had offered Lucy the guest room. Then Mike had arrived at the scene. After a big fight with Robyn, he had come to the decision that he wouldn't let Lucy out of his sight until he knew she was safe. Robyn had been absolutely furious, and to stop the conflict from turning into a fistfight, Andrew had invited Mike to stay in the guest room, too.

In theory, his spacious house should have been big enough to fit four people and a cat. Andrew had even felt happy about the arrangement in the beginning, since it meant he'd get to spend more time with Robyn. Though he still enjoyed sharing a bed with her every night, the crowdedness of the house was slowly driving him insane.

"I thought I'd find you here."

He spun around and found Robyn standing in the doorway. He felt the blood drain from his face.

"This… This isn't what it looks like." He quickly dropped the cigarette in the ashtray.

She snorted. "Oh, come on. Did you seriously think I hadn't noticed you're a smoker?"

"You knew? How? For how long?"

"Since I first met you. I've been friends with Ana for like a decade. I'd recognize the smell of Marlboro Lights anywhere." She walked over to his side, placing her hands on the railing. "It's not that big of a deal, you know. We all have our vices."

"Yeah, but I'm a *doctor.*"

"So what? You're still a human being. Stop being so hard on yourself. No one's perfect. Not even you." She crossed her arms, trembling a little in the cold winter air. He wrapped his arms around her, burrowing his nose in her hair. The soothing warmth that spread through his body as he inhaled her scent was even more calming than nicotine. She made him feel like he wasn't the worst person on the planet after all. She made him feel like he was good enough.

You really are addicted to her, commented his inner critic. *Losing her now would destroy you.*

He held her tighter. Jason seemed to think the whole thing with Swanson was over, but Andrew knew he'd never be fully calm again as long as that man was running free. He could tell Robyn was worried about it too, even though she didn't say anything out loud.

And then there was the fight. Drake had to be almost a foot taller than Robyn and twice as heavy, and judging by his body language, his muscularity didn't seem to slow him down. Even if she did win, she'd definitely get hurt. She always got hurt.

"Hey, don't worry about tonight," Robyn said. "I've fought Drake before. It's going to be okay. I promise."

He wished he could believe her, but it was impossible. He knew all too well how her fights usually ended.

"How did you know what I was thinking about?" he asked, changing the subject.

"You're always freaking out about something." She shrugged. "You're not that hard to read."

"Oh." When had she learned to read him so well? Strangely enough, he didn't mind it. "What about you? Are you nervous about tonight?"

"A little. Drake is good, but I'm not that worried about the fight itself. I don't really care if I win or lose. It's the audience that makes me nervous." She shuddered. "There are always so many of them, and they all stare at me. It makes me uncomfortable. I don't belong on a stage."

"I thought you wanted to be a ballerina," he commented. "Don't you have to be on a stage for that?"

She tilted her head slightly to the side. "Yeah, I suppose. I never really thought about that. I just wanted to dance."

"Well, I've seen you dance, and I've seen you fight in the arena. You have this…*thing* going on when you move. It doesn't matter if you're dancing or fighting—no one can look away when you're performing. They're not staring because they're judging you. They're staring because they can't tear their eyes away from you."

Robyn turned around in his arms, hiding her face in his shirt. "You're embarrassing me."

"Am I?" he asked innocently. "So I shouldn't add that they're also staring at you because you're breathtakingly beautiful?"

The visible parts of her face turned even redder. "Shut up."

He grinned but didn't say anything else. If he pushed her any further, she would most likely leave. He loved teasing her, but not as much as he loved having her in his arms.

"I've been thinking," she said. "I really like being here. In your house. With you. Lucy will be done with her pre-teacher program in a year and a half, and after that, she's probably moving out of the apartment. If she moves out, I'll have to sell the apartment, and…you know…"

"You want to move in with me?"

She nodded. "If it's okay with you. Like I said, it's more than a year until then, so you have a lot of time to think about it if—"

Andrew cupped her face in his hands and kissed her. "I don't have to think about it. Of course it's okay with me. Nothing would make me happier."

"Good." A shy smile lit up her face. "I'm sorry for taking this long to say it back, but…I love you, Andrew."

This time, she was the one to initiate the kiss. He ran his fingers through her hair as he answered it, knowing that he was without a doubt the luckiest man in the world.

"I didn't mind the wait," he murmured against her lips. "You're not that hard to read, either."

• • •

A couple hours later, Andrew and Robyn arrived at the arena. There was more than an hour left until the first-class fight would start, but the parking lot was already almost full.

"You'll be okay," Andrew said when her face went pale. "Just pretend everyone in the audience is in their underwear."

She frowned. "How the hell would that help?"

"I don't know. In the movies, they always tell people with stage fright to do that."

"It's stupid," she grumbled. "And I don't have stage fright. I just don't like when people look at me."

Andrew shook his head. He was too nervous to start an argument. Robyn didn't seem to be worried about the fight itself, but he certainly was.

They got out of the car and began to walk toward the main entrance.

"I want to talk to Cassandra before warming up," she said.

"Do you really think she'll give you any advice tonight? Won't she be rooting for Drake?"

"Probably. I still want to talk to her, though. She said some pretty creepy stuff the last time I saw her. In a way, she predicted Tyler's death."

He raised his eyebrows. "That's impossible."

"I thought so too, but then her prediction came true. She said that Jason, you, and I would change the fighting world in Chrystal Valley forever, and I guess we kind of did."

"It's a coincidence. There's no such thing as a psychic."

She shrugged. "She makes predictions about the future, and those predictions always turn out to be true. That makes her a psychic in my eyes."

"There has to be a logical reason behind it. Like, I don't know, math."

She rolled her eyes. "Whatever makes you sleep at night."

They entered the pizzeria and descended the stairs to the arena. It was more crowded than ever, and people seemed to have started drinking even earlier than usual.

The crowd around the bar was almost impossible to push through. When they reached Cassandra's chair, Andrew was already sweating in his orange medical team jacket.

The local clairvoyant was sitting alone this time. The wall behind her looked strangely empty without her guardian leaning against it.

"Hi, Cassandra," Robyn said. "Has Drake gone backstage already?"

Cassandra nodded. "Are you here to ask me how to beat him?"

Robyn shook her head. "I have a different question this time. How did you know about everything that happened with Swanson? How did you know Andrew and I would take part in Jason's plan to take him down?"

Cassandra smiled cryptically. "I have my ways."

"Did you know Tyler was going to die?"

She lowered her eyes. "No. I knew Swanson would make sure you ended up in the final, but I didn't think he'd take it that far. I miscalculated."

"You *miscalculated*?" Robyn exclaimed. "He died! Do you seriously not care about that?"

Cassandra didn't answer.

Robyn glared at her, clenching her jaw. "Forget it."

She turned to leave, but Cassandra grabbed her arm. "Aim for his left knee. He hurt it in the quarterfinals, and it hasn't healed yet."

"What?" Robyn turned back to her, staring at her in surprise. "Why would you tell me that?"

"Because you have to win. It's not over yet."

"She's not a psychic, damn it," Andrew said, unable to stay silent any longer. "She can't predict the future. No one can."

Cassandra narrowed her eyes. "You should watch your back, Dr. Alexander."

"And what's that supposed to mean? Are you threatening me?"

Cassandra didn't answer. She fixed her gaze on the ring again, ending the conversation.

"Let's go," Robyn said, linking her arm with Andrew's. "We won't get anything more from her."

Andrew glanced back at Cassandra as he and Robyn headed toward the backstage door. Cassandra's cold, calculating eyes sent shivers down his spine. Over the past weeks, he'd seen her guide Robyn through the tournament, making sure she ended up in the final. Somehow, he got the feeling Robyn wasn't the only one who'd been manipulated into being in this exact place at this exact time. He shuddered. How much of what had just transpired in Chrystal Valley was this woman's doing?

He didn't think Cassandra was completely carefree about Tyler's death, but she seemed to think that her goal—whatever that was—was worth it. The attitude scared him.

Don't be a hypocrite, said his inner critic. *Where would you draw the line if Robyn's life was in danger? What would you have done if the situation with Mark had taken a different turn?*

Andrew shuddered again, thankful he'd never know the answer to that question.

• • •

Cassandra's words kept ringing in Robyn's ears as she made her preparations in the locker room. *"You have to win. It's not over yet."* Before their chat, Robyn hadn't really cared about the outcome of the fight. Her debts were gone. One way or another, she'd get that normal life she'd always dreamed of. The only reason she hadn't backed out already was because of the fight itself. She really did want an official ending to her fighting years, just like she'd told Andrew.

The words echoed through her head again. She had no idea *why* she had to win, but if Cassandra said so, it had to be important.

"Do you want me to do your hair?" Andrew asked, pulling her out of her thoughts.

"Yes, please." She closed the door to her locker and sat down on the bench with her back against him. He combed through her hair with his fingers a couple of times before twisting the locks up in a bun.

"You're getting good at this," she murmured, enjoying the way his calm, confident hands worked with her hair. "You're a lot faster nowadays."

Robyn felt him fix the bun with a hair tie. She stood up, believing he was finished, but Andrew pulled her back down onto the bench.

"I'm not done yet." He pulled a sky-blue piece of fabric from his pocket.

"A tie?" She eyed it skeptically.

"Yeah. I couldn't find a ribbon, so this will have to do." He wrapped the tie around the bun and finished the hairdo with a bow. "It's the final. I thought I'd add something extra."

"Oh, come on, I can't wear this. I'm a fighter. Fighters don't have bows in their hair."

"Right. You're just a heartless, violent street fighter who punches people for a living."

She frowned at the sarcasm in his voice. "Well, it's true."

"No, it's not. You're a street fighter, yes, but that doesn't define you as a person. You're so much more than that. You're kind and compassionate, and you genuinely care about everyone around you. You're stubborn. Strong. Beautiful. You're one hell of a ballerina, too—and ballerinas have bows in their hair. Do you still want me to remove it?"

Flustered beyond belief, she found herself shaking her head.

He kissed the nape of her neck. "That's what I thought."

When she left the locker room to warm up, her cheeks were still burning. *He's impossible,* she thought, hoping she didn't look as disheveled as she felt. She was beginning to suspect that Andrew enjoyed making her flustered—and he was way too good at it.

At the end of her usual jogging lap, she ran into Drake. He was sitting on a chair close to his stage door, wrapping gauze around his left knee. He was wearing a black tank top and shorts, and he'd tied up his long hair in a braid as usual. He looked a lot more like his old self without his suit.

"Valkyrie," he greeted her with a smirk.

Robyn rolled her eyes. "I have a real name, you know." She glanced at his knee as discreetly as possible, but Drake still noticed.

"Cass told you," he stated, his smirk turning into a frown.

"Yeah. She said I had to win."

"She told me I had to lose." His eyes narrowed. "Don't think I'll hold back because of that, though. Or because you're *you.* I want to win this tournament."

"Good." She smiled. "This is my final fight. It wouldn't feel right if it wasn't an honest one."

Drake raised his eyebrows. "You're quitting?"

She nodded. "I've paid back all my debts. There's nothing keeping me in the underground world anymore."

"Congratulations. I wish you all the best."

"Thanks," she said, slightly taken aback by his friendliness. "I appreciate it."

They both fell silent. This was the first civil conversation they'd had in years. Robyn felt good about being on somewhat good terms with him now that her fighting days were ending. He was a part of her old life—one of the many people she'd leave behind when she left the fighting world.

"What happened to you?" she finally asked. "You just disappear without a word, and then you show up again three years later in a freaking suit. What happened? Why..." She swallowed hard. "Why did you leave me?"

"I got a job offer I couldn't refuse. Everything about it was classified, so I couldn't tell anyone about it." He knit his brow. "I'm sorry, really. I never wanted to hurt you."

"Oh." She felt strangely relieved. Yeah, he'd picked a job over her, but at least she wasn't the one who'd driven him away. He hadn't given up on her, after all. "So, what have you been up to all these years?"

Drake smirked. "It's classified."

"Seriously?"

"Seriously. I can't tell you much, but the people I work for are really, really high up in this country's chain of command. Cass has... *abilities*. She can see patterns others can't see. She's dedicated her life to bringing people like Swanson down, and to do so, she needs someone like me. According to her, my education in combination with my fighting experience makes me uniquely qualified to assist her."

"Wow." Robyn tried to process the new information. "So you're some kind of agent now?"

"Something like that."

"Is that why you're in the tournament? To get inside info?"

"That's one of the reasons, yes, but I'm mostly here for my own entertainment." Drake grinned. "I didn't want to miss the chance to fight the notorious Valkyrie one final time."

She snorted. "You're going to regret that decision when I kick your ass."

His grin widened. "Bring it on."

•••

When Robyn returned to the locker room after her warm-up, Andrew was waiting for her right outside. His face lit up with a smile the moment he saw her. He always seemed genuinely happy to see her, and his happiness never failed to brighten Robyn's mood.

"Are you ready?" he asked as she came to a stop in front of him.

She smiled. "As ready as I'll ever be."

They walked together through the corridor until they reached the gallery.

"Please, be careful tonight," he said. "It's your last fight. It's not worth getting permanent injuries for."

"I'll be careful. I promise." She stood on tiptoe and gave him a quick kiss. "I'll see you after the fight."

They parted ways. Andrew went through the door to the gallery, and Robyn continued forward toward the door that would lead her to the ring. People in orange jackets ran back and forth in the corridor, trying to finish all their tasks in time for the fight. She focused on the door in front of her, shutting out the chaotic environment around her. She was the Valkyrie. Tomorrow, she'd be an ordinary woman again, but tonight, she was the Valkyrie.

The door opened.

Showtime.

CHAPTER TWENTY-FOUR

Andrew went over to his usual seat in the gallery. Lily greeted him with a polite nod. She had dark rings under her eyes, and she looked like she'd aged a decade since the last time he saw her. Tyler's death seemed to have hit her hard.

He glanced at Jonas's empty chair. He didn't blame the guy for not showing up. It was frighteningly easy for Andrew to imagine their roles reversed. If anything were to happen to Robyn, he didn't think he'd be able to go back to Chrystal Arena again either.

After tonight, he'd never have to set foot in this place again—and, more importantly, neither would she.

A man in an orange jacket entered the gallery, holding a walkie-talkie in his hand. "Hey, do any of you guys know what music I'm supposed to play when the Valkyrie enters? I've tried to contact her manager, but he hasn't called me back. Which isn't that surprising, since, you know…" He scratched the back of his head.

"Since when do you play background music when the fighters enter?" Lily asked.

"It's the final." The man shrugged. "Mr. Quinn said it would be cool to have some entrance music."

"The main theme of *Swan Lake*," Andrew said. "You know, the Tchaikovsky piece. That's the music the Valkyrie would want to enter to."

"Seriously?" the man asked. "The other guy has some generic industrial music. Are you sure she wants some classical shit?"

"I'm sure."

"I guess I could try to find it on Spotify," the man said, shaking his head. He left the room, muttering something about hipsters having gone full circle.

"Mr. Quinn and his ideas," Lily sighed. "Entrance music? That's so cliché."

"I've heard a lot about this Mr. Quinn," Andrew said. "What's he like?"

"You've never met Mr. Quinn?"

He shook his head.

"He's about as strange as the rumors say. Very unpredictable. Really, though—you've never met our boss?" She tilted her head to the side, looking at him curiously. "So the rumor's true, then. No one hired you—you just showed up out of nowhere."

Busted.

"I wanted to be closer to Robyn during the fights, but the security guard at the backstage door refused to let me in. I improvised, and everything got out of hand after that." He smiled apologetically. "Are you mad at me?"

Lily considered it for a few moments. "Nah. I can tell you're a real doctor, which means you're more than qualified to be here. I don't like that you lied to me, but I'm not angry." She lowered her eyes. "Life's too short to be mad at people on principle."

He placed a hand on her shoulder. "I'm sorry about Tyler. I wish there was something I could have done."

"Yeah. Me too."

They both fell silent when a drum machine accompanied by an eerie-sounding synthesizer boomed through the arena. One of the doors opened, and Drake stepped out on the passageway. His eyes were fixed on the ring, as if he didn't even notice the massive audience.

"Ladies and gentlemen, the finale of this dramatic tournament is finally here!" the commentator yelled into his microphone.

"First, I bring you...the man with the strength of an unworldly beast—the Leviathan!"

The crowd cheered loudly as Drake walked down the stairs toward the ring. He walked with long, confident strides. His limp was barely visible at all.

The industrial music faded away as Drake reached the ring. As soon as the final dissonant chord rang out, a soft murmuring of strings took its place. When the melodious oboe started playing, Andrew knew the technician had found the right piece.

The second door opened. Robyn strode down the passageway, her Valkyrie persona radiating power and confidence. She looked exactly like the cold, merciless street fighter she always pretended to be—until she heard the music. Her face softened, and he could see her mouth his name. She continued her walk toward the ring with a small smile playing on her lips.

The crowd fell silent for a moment. Everyone was staring at Robyn. She walked with her head held high, but her expression remained soft. Together with the classical music, the scene was almost magical.

"And here we have our second contestant!" the commentator continued. "I give you the fierce, the beautiful, the surprisingly resilient—the Valkyrie!"

The commentator's words broke the spell of enchantment, and the crowd immediately began to cheer.

"How strange," Lily said. "I thought it would be weird to see her enter with a classical piece, but it fits her, somehow. It's in the way she moves, you know?"

"I know." Pride bloomed in his chest. "You should see her dance to it."

The music stopped when Robyn stepped inside the ring. She nodded at Drake, who nodded back at her. The referee spoke with them both for a few seconds before backing away. The bell rang, and the fight began.

Drake threw a punch, immediately going for an offensive approach. Robyn dodged it by taking a quick step back. Before Drake could retract his arm, she spun around and kicked him, aiming for his abdomen. The kick was perfectly executed and would have caused Drake to bend over—if he hadn't been expecting it. He twisted his torso, causing Robyn's foot to only graze his side. When Drake tried to grab her ankle, she danced out of the way, almost making a pirouette to get her leg away from him. They both took a moment to breathe, staring at each other from opposite sides of the ring. Then they were at it again, throwing kicks and punches in perfect synchronization.

Even to Andrew's untrained eye, it was obvious Robyn and Drake had fought each other before. They read each other's movements perfectly and always knew exactly how to respond. Their complete synchronization made the fight look almost choreographed.

Minutes passed. To Andrew's surprise, Robyn didn't aim for Drake's injured knee at all. *What's her plan?* he wondered, flinching every time she received a hit.

When the bell rang and ended the first round, the fighters were both sporting minor injuries. Robyn was holding a towel to a wound in her lip and Drake's right eye was swelling up, but neither of them was seriously harmed.

"Why isn't she aiming for his knee?" Andrew asked Lily. "Is that part of some kind of street-fighting code? Are you supposed to avoid your opponent's injuries?"

"Not really. I guess it depends on what kind of person you are. Tyler never aimed for injuries. He thought it made the fights less fair."

"I see."

When Andrew had heard about Drake's injury, he'd taken for granted that Robyn would use it to her advantage. If he himself had been a fighter, he would have used it. But she wasn't like him. She was a genuinely good person.

He sighed. This was going to be a long night.

The bell rang again, signaling the start of the second round. Drake and Robyn were soon exchanging blows again, neither of them showing any signs of slowing down. Andrew glanced at Lily and noticed she had her eyes fixed on the audience instead of the ring.

"What are you looking at?" he asked.

"There are cops in the crowd." Her eyes narrowed. "Lots of them."

Andrew searched the crowd. He could see Lucy and Mike standing near the ring, and Jason and Cassandra were standing close to the bar. He couldn't find any cops.

"I can't see any," he finally admitted.

"They're dressed as civilians." Lily shrugged, lowering her eyes. "It's kind of my thing. I look out for cops when FTS is out protesting."

"You're an FTS member?"

She nodded. "Luke says hi."

"Oh." It finally made sense how Jonas, Lily, Tyler, and Luke knew each other—they were all members of Mike's group of violent protesters.

"Are the cops here to do a raid?" Lily asked, fidgeting with her ponytail. "Like they did on that Swanson guy's organization? If that's the case, I'm getting out of here. Right now."

"I don't think that's what they're here for," he said. "I think they're here to see if Swanson is going to show up."

Jason obviously hadn't been honest with him. If Jason had truly thought things were over, he wouldn't have brought half the police station to the arena.

Andrew turned back to the ring, just in time to see Robyn execute a beautiful roundhouse kick. Drake took a step to the side to dodge it. He raised his hand to deliver a punch but seemed to put too much weight on his left leg. He stumbled, and the motion took them both by surprise. Robyn's kick hit Drake's neck, and his fist connected with her chin. They both fell to the floor, Drake landing flat on his stomach and Robyn on her side. When they both hit the ground, neither of them was moving.

"Oh my God, was that a double KO?" Lily exclaimed, getting up from her chair. "Who won?"

"I don't know." Andrew didn't really care. He rushed through the door and out to the ring. *Concussion, neuronal injuries, intracranial hemorrhage.* He could go on all day about the endless list of complications after a head trauma like that.

The referee was just about to call the fight off when Robyn began to move. She pushed herself up on one elbow, shaking her head.

"I'm conscious," she said. "I'm not knocked out. I'm still conscious."

The referee nodded and gave the commentator a sign.

"It seems we have our winner!" the commentator shouted into his microphone. "Raise your glasses and cheer for the tournament's champion—the Valkyrie!"

The crowd roared with excitement. Andrew entered the ring and kneeled next to Robyn. He put his arm behind her back, helping her sit upright.

"Are you okay?" he asked.

"I think so." She smiled. "I did it. I beat him."

Andrew pressed a kiss to her forehead. "You did."

"The Leviathan is coming to," Lily said from behind his back. "No signs of anything serious."

Andrew sent her a quick smile over his shoulder. He turned back to Robyn and began to assess her injuries. Her eyes were still a little unfocused, but otherwise she seemed fine.

"Excuse me," a black-haired man in a white suit said, entering the ring. "I'm here to greet the winner."

"That would be me," Robyn said, getting back to her feet with a little help from Andrew.

The newcomer shook her hand. "My name is Simon Quinn, owner of Chrystal Arena. I wanted to personally congratulate you." He pulled an envelope from an inside pocket in his suit jacket and gave it to her. "I was supposed to give this to your manager, but I decided I'd rather give it straight to you."

Robyn carefully opened the envelope and pulled out a pale-blue piece of paper. "Oh my God," she said, her eyes widening. "Are you serious? Is this... Is this mine?"

Mr. Quinn nodded, smiling. "I've heard about your situation. I'm sure you need this a lot more than Mr. Swanson."

"What is it?" Andrew asked, looking over her shoulder. In her hands was a check with a *lot* of zeros on it. "*Oh.*"

"I have to show this to Lucy," she said before taking off. She ran to the fence separating the ring from the crowd and began to climb.

"Excuse me, miss?" one of the security guards said. "Could you like, not do that? Please, get down."

Robyn ignored him and gracefully jumped over the top of the fence. She landed on the other side right next to Lucy and Mike.

"Robyn!" Lucy shouted, hugging her tightly. "You were absolutely amazing in there. I'm so proud of you."

"Lucy, look," Robyn said, holding up the check. "With this kind of money, you could study at any university you want. Hell, you could even study at Columbia if you wanted to. We'd still have to take a loan, but it's possible."

When Robyn tried to hand Lucy the check, Lucy grabbed her hands and gently closed them over the piece of paper.

"No."

Robyn frowned. "What?"

"This is your money," Lucy said determinedly. "I'll find my own way to pay for my education. You put your life on hold when Mom died to make sure I would get the childhood you never had. I'm an adult now, and it's time for you to start living your own life." She smiled. "I want you to use this to take up ballet again. You haven't been yourself since you stopped dancing. I remember how good you were. Your teacher always talked about you with Mom, saying you'd be a professional one day. With that check, you could go to college. You could finally make your dream come true."

Robyn stared at her sister, her eyes tearing up. "I don't know what to say."

"Say that you'll start dancing again."

Tears of happiness rolled down her cheeks. "I will. I promise."

Andrew watched them from the other side of the fence. Though he really wanted to take a closer look at Robyn's injuries, he couldn't bring himself to interrupt the sisters' moment. He left the ring and returned to the backstage area, heading toward the locker room. Since Robyn would probably stay with Lucy for a while, he thought he'd pick up the things she'd left in her locker. He didn't know if he was going to have to drive her to the hospital or not, but if she did turn out to be concussed, he wanted to leave the arena as soon as possible.

When he entered the locker room, he saw something moving out of the corner of his eye. Before he could turn around, he felt something hard hit his head—something suspiciously cane-like. His body went limp, and he fell to the floor. The last thing he saw before passing out was the hem of a long, gray coat.

• • •

After speaking with Lucy for a while, Robyn began to wonder where Andrew had gone. The last time she'd seen him he'd been in the ring, but the ring was now empty.

"I'll be right back," she told Lucy before heading toward the fence. Before she could begin to climb back, she felt a hand on her shoulder. She turned around and found Ana leaning against the fence. She fit in surprisingly well with the crowd, which was probably why Robyn hadn't seen her earlier. Robyn's eyes widened. *I'm screwed. She's going to kill me. I'm screwed.*

Ana snorted. "Stop looking at me like that. I'm not going to punch you, you idiot."

"What are you doing here?" Robyn asked, still in shock. "You knew about the tournament? How did you find out? *When* did you find out?"

Ana rolled her eyes. "I knew about it from the start. This damn tournament is all my clients have been talking about for months."

Shit, Robyn thought. *Shit, shit, shit.*

"Calm down," Ana said. "I'm not going to punch you, okay?"

Robyn glanced up at her. She looked surprisingly calm, and she didn't seem to be angry either.

"Are you mad at me?" Robyn asked anyway. "I'm sorry for not telling you. I just…you know…"

"You're a self-deprecating moron, and you suck at relying on anyone but yourself. I know." Ana put her hand on her hip. "You knew how I felt about your fighting habits, and you didn't want to worry me. I get it. I was pretty pissed when I found out, but now I'm just glad it's over. You did great up there. I'm proud of you."

"Thank you." Robyn smiled. "I'm glad it's over, too." She'd felt guilty about lying to Ana for months, and the relief of finally coming clear almost made her cry again. "This was my final fight. I'm quitting street fighting for good."

Ana blinked in surprise. "Seriously?"

"Seriously."

"Like, for good as in permanently? No more fights? Ever?"

"Yeah."

Ana threw her arms around Robyn's shoulders. "Thank God," she said in a thick voice. "Thank God, thank God, thank God."

Robyn awkwardly hugged her back. She wasn't a hugger, and neither was Ana. She was just about to ask her what the hell she was doing when she felt something wet against her neck. Ana was crying.

She hugged Robyn tighter. "If you ever tell anyone about this, I'll kill you. You know that, right?"

Robyn smiled. "I know."

• • •

A few minutes later, Robyn was climbing back over the fence. It was a lot harder this time since her wrist had started to seriously hurt. She'd landed on it after Drake's punch, and she was beginning to suspect it was sprained or even fractured. She sighed. Andrew was going to freak out about it when she found him.

He wasn't in the gallery or in the corridor outside. Confused and a little worried, she decided to check the locker room.

The first thing she noticed was Andrew lying motionless on the tiled floor. The second thing she noticed was the sound of someone cocking a gun.

"Hello, Robyn," Swanson said calmly. He leaned back on the bench, his gun aimed at Robyn's head.

"What did you do to him?" She stared at Andrew, her heart racing. He wasn't dead. He couldn't be dead. She felt like she was about to throw up. *He wouldn't leave me. He said he wouldn't leave me.*

"Don't worry, dear. He's only unconscious." Swanson didn't have to add "for now." The threat was obvious enough as it was.

He slowly stood up. His movements were stiff, and the way he leaned on his cane didn't look like acting.

"What do you want?" she asked with a trembling voice. "Why are you here?"

Her body was frozen in place, paralyzed by terror. She'd been scared when Mark had pointed a gun at her, but not like this. On some level, she'd known Mark hadn't had it in him to pull the trigger. With Swanson, it was different. If he felt like it, he would kill her—and Andrew—in a heartbeat.

"Did you win?" he asked, ignoring her questions.

She nodded.

Swanson made an expression that was probably supposed to be a smile. "That's my girl. Now, all we have to do is get out of here. Let's go."

Robyn didn't know what to think. For some reason, Swanson didn't seem to be mad at her. How was that even possible?

Swanson pointed at the door with the gun. "What are you waiting for?"

"Please, let me make sure he's okay first," she said. "I need to know he's okay."

Swanson's eyes narrowed as he considered her request. "Make it quick. We don't have much time."

She kneeled next to Andrew. He was still breathing. Thank God. She placed her hand on his shoulder and shook him lightly. "Andrew?"

He didn't open his eyes.

She shook him harder. "Andrew, please wake up." *Don't leave me, don't leave me, don't leave me…*

"We have to go," Swanson said.

She glanced up at him. "I can't just leave him, I…" She silenced herself as Swanson aimed the gun at Andrew's head instead of hers. The threat was crystal clear.

"I'm ready now," she said quickly. "Don't hurt him. Please don't hurt him." She reluctantly got back to her feet. "I'm sorry about what happened at the mansion."

"I accept your apology," Swanson said. "It must have been a frightening situation for you. I'm sure you didn't mean to cause this mishap. Did they threaten you?"

"Y-yeah," she lied. "When I got to the apartment, the police were already there. They said I'd never see Lucy again if I didn't cooperate with them. I didn't know all of this would happen. I'm so sorry."

She glanced up at him to see if he'd bought it. Her eyes were tearing up, and she wasn't sure if she was faking that part. In a way, she was glad she didn't have to fake being terrified. She'd never been a good actor, but her fear was genuine.

"It's fine, dear." He smiled. "You're one of my kids. I know you'd never try to harm me. Get dressed. We have to leave immediately."

After Robyn had put her tank top, hoodie, and shoes back on, Swanson walked toward the door. She quickly went to hold it open for him, just like she'd seen Mark do countless times. She could barely believe he'd bought her story. *It's not me he believes in,* she realized. *It's his ability to manipulate that he truly trusts.*

Swanson thought she was like the other kids he'd taken in over the years, brainwashed to worship him without ever questioning him. One year ago, that would have been true, but she wasn't that person anymore. She wasn't nothing. She was a person, with a family who loved her and a future full of promises. Swanson would never have that kind of power over her ever again.

They walked through the backstage area and left through a back door hidden at the end of the corridor. Swanson led her out to the parking lot and unlocked a rusty Volvo parked in a dimly lit corner. She immediately stopped. If she stepped into the car, there was no going back. No one would ever find her again.

"Well? Let's go," Swanson said. He licked his lips, his eyes darting between her and the arena.

"Did you hear about Mark?" she asked in an attempt to buy more time. "He died for you."

"Yes, yes, very tragic," Swanson said without a trace of sorrow in his voice. "That boy always showed tendencies toward the melodramatic. But that's all in the past, now. Come on. We need to get away from this rotten place."

"Where are we going?" Her voice was trembling, and her eyes kept returning to his gun.

"Anywhere we want. With my intelligence and your skills, we could start a new organization. I'm sure you brought that check you won. It's more than enough to set up shop in another city, somewhere the police are a bit more…approachable. We could take in some new kids—kids with nowhere else to go. We could save them, just like I saved you and your sister. What do you say, Robyn?" He smiled and reached out his hand. "Are you ready to take the next step?"

Robyn was speechless. She stared at his hand, unsure how to react. If she said yes, she would have to get in the car with him, but if she said no… She didn't even want to think about that.

"What will it be, dear? I need your answer." He took a step toward her, and she unwittingly took a step back.

"I don't know, I-I need more time," she stuttered.

"Time is a luxury we cannot afford right now." Swanson slowly raised his gun. "Are you coming with me or not?"

That's when she knew for sure he was going to kill her. She could see it in his eyes. Even if she said yes, he would eventually find someone new to take her place, just like he'd found her to replace Mark. It didn't matter what she said. She was screwed either way.

She clenched her fists. It wasn't fair. She'd been so close to finally getting the normal life she'd always dreamed of, and now, Swanson was going to take that away from her. He never stopped taking things away from her.

The anger that had been building up within her for almost six years finally erupted.

"Fuck you, and fuck your organization!" she yelled. Swanson's eyes widened, and this time, he was the one who took a step back. He clearly hadn't been predicting an outburst like that. She used his moment of distraction to spin around and kick the hand holding the gun.

Swanson swore loudly and pulled back his hand. The gun fell to the ground. She threw herself after it, and before he'd even moved a muscle, she already had the gun in her hands. She slowly stood up, pointing it at him.

Swanson licked his lips. "Don't be stupid, Robyn. Give me the gun."

"No."

"You're being overdramatic. Just give me the gun."

"No."

His gaze darted between her face and the gun. "Come on. You don't want to do this. I took you in, remember? You're one of my kids. I saved you. I saved your sister. You don't want to do this."

Her hands trembled. No, she didn't want to kill him. She didn't want to take a life. But she couldn't let him go, either. If she didn't end him for good, she would live the rest of her life in fear. He'd hurt her sister. He'd hurt Andrew. She was not going to let him hurt anyone she loved ever again.

Blinding lights suddenly lighted up the parking lot.

"Freeze!" a male voice yelled. "You're surrounded!"

Robyn squinted against the lights. There were men and women in bulletproof vests all around her, their guns pointing at Swanson.

"You can drop the gun now, Robyn," Jason said, taking a step forward. "We've got it from here."

She fixed her gaze on Swanson again. She had to end him. She *had* to.

"Robyn? Can you hear me? Shit, she's freaking out. Alexander, I need some help here."

Someone approached her from behind. She recognized the sound of his steps.

"Robyn. You don't have to do this." Two arms encircled her waist, and she was awash with the calming scent of Earl Grey. "Jason's going to arrest him. Everything will be okay."

Tears rolled down her cheeks. The words echoed in her head. *End him, end him, end him...*

Andrew pulled her closer. "Just let go of the gun, okay? You don't have to kill him."

The anger and the fear slowly faded away from her body. She looked at Swanson again. He no longer looked like the nightmarish threat her mind had made him out to be. He looked like a scared old man.

"Just let go of the gun."

The gun clattered against the asphalt as it hit the ground. Andrew turned her around and wrapped his arms around her again, holding her tightly.

"Thank God you're okay," he whispered in her ear. "When I woke up and couldn't find you, I knew he'd taken you. I thought it was too late. I thought... I thought I'd lost you."

"I'm okay." She burrowed her face in the crook of his neck. "We're okay."

They watched as Jason cuffed Swanson's hands behind his back and led him to a police car.

"This isn't necessary." Swanson had a feverish look in his eyes. "I could make you rich. I could give you anything you want. Let's talk. Negotiate. We should negotiate. Please."

Jason closed the car door without a word.

A few minutes later, the police cars began to pull out of the parking lot. Robyn stood with Andrew's arm wrapped around her shoulders, watching Jason and his colleagues leave the arena. Jason had assured them that whatever happened, the police had enough proof to keep Swanson locked up for the rest of his life.

"I think it works both ways," she said. "You know, the thing you said about me being unable to understand someone like Swanson.

I don't think he could understand me, either. If he'd known me at all, he would have realized that I would never have forgiven him for taking Lucy. Or for hurting you."

"You're probably right," Andrew said. "He underestimated you."

They stood in silence. Robyn had a hard time processing that Swanson was finally out of her life for good. She was happy about it, but in a way, she felt a bit empty. Her life had always been a mess, and though she'd dreamed of having a normal life, the thought of that dream coming true scared her a little. A part of her wondered if she would ever be normal enough to pull it off. She smiled a little to herself. *I won't know for sure until I try.* Even though the concept of living a normal life scared her, she was still looking forward to giving it a shot.

"Well done, Robyn," said a female voice. "I knew you could do it."

Robyn turned around and found Cassandra and Drake standing in a corner of the parking lot. Drake was holding a big suitcase in his hands, and he'd put on his suit again.

"We have to leave now," Cassandra continued. "As Dr. Alexander has probably figured out, I'm not going to live much longer. There are more cities in need of my help, and I'm running out of time. Chrystal Valley is clean now, so it's time for me to move on."

"Is this what you do?" Robyn asked. "You travel to a corrupted city, pick out your puppets, and pull on their strings until the bad guy is caught?"

Cassandra smiled. "It's not a very ethical method, but it works. I don't need your approval or respect. I didn't come here to make friends. I came here to save your city, and that's what I did." Her smile faded a little. "I would appreciate if you didn't tell Jason about my mission. If he knew about all of this, he would think I only spent time with him to get information. That's not true.

He's a nice man, and under different circumstances, I would have called him a friend."

"You're seriously asking us for more favors?" Andrew butted in. "You used us. We don't owe you anything."

"You don't owe me anything," Cassandra agreed, "but I'm fairly certain you'll keep quiet about me to protect your friend's emotions. Isn't that right, Dr. Alexander?"

Andrew clenched his jaw. His silence was an obvious answer.

Cassandra nodded. "Thank you for your cooperation."

She turned around and walked back into the shadows. Drake gave Robyn a final nod before following her. Somehow, Robyn knew this was the last time she'd ever see them. The realization saddened her a little, but at the same time she was happy for Drake. His years with Cassandra had definitely changed him, and having a purpose in life seemed to do him good.

"How are you feeling?" Andrew asked, breaking the silence. "Are you dizzy? Nauseous?"

"I'm fine," she said, but then she remembered her wrist. "You should probably take a look at this, though."

She held up her arm and rolled up the sleeve of her hoodie. The wrist had swollen to almost twice its usual size, and the pulsating pain kept getting worse.

He groaned. "That's it, we're going to the hospital. You need an x-ray."

"Only if you do one of those brain-scan thingies for your head," she countered. "You could have a concussion too."

"Oh. Yeah. I'd forgotten all about that." He rubbed the back of his head. "I can't believe you thought of that before I did."

She grinned smugly. "I don't know if you've noticed, but I've been hanging out with a doctor quite a lot lately. I've picked up a thing or two."

"Right." He shook his head, smiling. "Brain-scan thingy it is, then."

Robyn nodded and yawned. The adrenaline backlash was taking over her system, and all she wanted was to get away from the arena. It was probably the last time she'd ever set foot there, and the thought didn't bother her at all.

"So I guess this is it, then," Andrew said as they walked toward his car. "I can't believe everything's finally over."

"Not everything," she said with a smile. "For some things, this is only the beginning."

He put his arm around her waist. "You're right."

She leaned her head against his shoulder, calm and at peace. The Valkyrie's short and violent life had come to an end. It was finally time for Robyn Monroe to live.

EPILOGUE

Robyn walked around in the apartment that had been her home her entire life. Seeing the bare walls and the empty rooms sent a wave of sentimentality through her chest. Everything she owned was already stuffed into boxes. Some of those boxes were still in the living room, but most of them were waiting for her in Andrew's house. *Our house,* she corrected herself. *It's our house now.*

She absentmindedly rubbed her wrist as she returned to the living room, more by habit than to relieve any pain. A year and a half had passed since the night of her final fight, but her wrist still ached from time to time.

"Are you okay?" Lucy asked when she noticed the gesture. "I can move the rest of the boxes if your wrist is hurting."

"I'm fine," Robyn replied earnestly. "It's just a bit stiff."

"Promise me you'll tell me if it starts hurting, okay? You have to think about your career."

Robyn rolled her eyes. "I promise."

"And promise me you and Andrew will come over to our place to eat at least once a week," Lucy continued, using her teacher voice. "I don't know how you two are even alive at this point. At least one of you is going to have to learn how to cook."

Robyn snorted. "It's not like we're starving, you know."

"No, but all that junk food is going to clog up your arteries." Lucy frowned. "Promise me."

Robyn smiled. "I promise."

They carried the last of the boxes down the stairs. The moving truck would be there any minute, so they decided to wait for it outside in the sun. They sat down on the steps leading up to the door, enjoying the spring warmth.

"It's going to be weird not living with you," Lucy said. "I won't miss the apartment, but I will definitely miss you."

A gust of wind played with her shoulder-length hair, making it whirl around the right side of her head. After Swanson had cut off her braid, she'd decided to turn her uneven hairstyle into a sidecut. It looked surprisingly good on her, even though Robyn still found it somewhat strange to have longer hair than her sister.

"We'll be fine. We'll see each other all the time." Robyn wrapped her arm around Lucy's shoulders. "This won't change anything between us."

Lucy smiled. "I know. It's still weird, though."

"Yeah, it's pretty weird."

Even though Robyn was excited about moving in with Andrew, it still scared her a little. She had stayed at his place at least two or three times a week for a long time, but actually moving in was a completely different thing. It wasn't the commitment itself that scared her—what really scared her was how okay she was with the whole thing. She wouldn't mind living with Andrew for the rest of her life, and *that* was scary.

Lucy and Mike were moving into a luxurious house close to Andrew's. Since Lucy had to take the train to Columbia University every morning, an apartment near the train station would have been a more logical choice—but instead, they'd bought a house. That fact made Robyn somewhat nervous. She hoped Lucy would wait until she got her teaching certification before thinking about having kids, but if she wanted to start a family already, there was nothing Robyn could do about it. Lucy was an adult, and Mike had a permanent job now. They seemed to be happy together.

Happy and rich, she thought, smiling a little to herself. Mike's salary was even higher than Andrew's nowadays.

The collapse of Swanson's organization had become the start of a chaotic chain reaction rippling through all of Chrystal Valley. Less than a month after his arrest, nearly half of the city's politicians had been fired. Mike—or Michael, as he now called himself—had maneuvered his way through that war zone and ended up with a surprisingly high position in Chrystal Valley's chain of command. He'd cut his hair and dropped his shaggy image, but his friends from FTS were still loyal to him. Mike had been the first of the new politicians to openly swear that he would never allow corruption to rule Chrystal Valley ever again. One by one, every single Chrystal Valley politician made the very same promise. That promise was later known as "Tyler's pledge."

Some people were fully convinced Mike would one day become the city's mayor. In Robyn's eyes, Mike was still a moron, but it wouldn't surprise her if those people turned out to be right. The citizens of Chrystal Valley seemed to see him as some sort of freedom fighter, and they all adored him. Robyn would never admit it out loud, but Mike and his colorful personality had grown on her over the past year. He was family, after all.

A soft vibration from Robyn's sweatpants pocket alerted her that something was going on with her smartphone. She pulled herself out of her thoughts and picked up the phone, hoping the calendar wasn't spazzing out again. Andrew had given her the phone as a Christmas present, and she still hadn't fully figured out all its functions. It was an e-mail this time—not the calendar sending her triple notifications for some forgotten event. She put her finger on the small envelope symbol to open the inbox.

"Oh my God," she gasped as she looked at the name of the sender.

"What?" Lucy asked.

"The e-mail. It's here."

Lucy's eyes widened. "Open it. You have to open it."

Robyn stared at the display. If she opened the e-mail, she would know if her year of hard work had paid off. She would know if the time she'd spent on distance learning to finish high school and all the money she'd spent on lessons in both ballet and modern dance had been worth it.

Though she wanted to open the e-mail, she couldn't bring herself to do it. Something important was missing—a certain some*one*. Andrew had believed in her the whole time, even when she'd had doubts herself. Without him, she never would have dared to even show up at the audition. It didn't feel right opening the e-mail without him.

"Go," Lucy said. "I know you want to read it with him. Just call me later, okay? I'll finish up here."

"Thank you." Robyn smiled and got to her feet. "I'll call you later, I promise."

She put the phone back in her pocket and began to jog toward Andrew's house. *Our house,* she corrected herself again. *Our home.*

• • •

Andrew was busy filling Tiny's food bowl with pellets when he heard a key enter the lock in the front door. He glanced at the clock on the kitchen wall, noting that Robyn was at least an hour early. *Shit.* He rushed to the bedside table in his bedroom, almost tripping over a bunch of moving boxes on the way, and picked up the small, velvety box he'd left there earlier that day. Not until the box was back in the sock drawer could he relax again.

Hiding his mother's ring from Robyn was getting trickier and trickier, especially since he kept forgetting to put it back in the drawer all the time. He'd been looking at it a lot lately, imagining what it would look like on Robyn's finger. One day, he would give it to her—but today was not that day. He wasn't sure if Robyn was ready for a commitment like that yet, and he still had one year left of his residency. Marriage would have to wait, at least for a little while longer. He wanted the proposal to be absolutely perfect.

He had just shut the drawer when he heard the front door opening.

"Hello?" Robyn shouted before slamming the door shut behind her.

Andrew left the bedroom and entered the hallway just in time to see her put her keys back in her pocket. The movement made him smile. The key she always used to open the door to the house was the second copy Andrew had given her. She still refused to use the first copy as anything other than a necklace.

"Welcome home," he said, loving how natural the words felt as they left his mouth.

"Thank you." Her face lit up with a beautiful smile. "I'm home."

They shared a moment of pure bliss. Andrew knew she'd been a bit hesitant about moving away from Lucy, but if she regretted the decision, it didn't show.

"I know I'm a bit early," she said, her smile turning slightly apologetic. "I got an e-mail."

He raised his eyebrows. "Okay?"

"From Juilliard."

"Oh. *Oh.*" He finally understood the situation. "What did it say?"

"I haven't opened it yet. I didn't want to open it without you."

She pulled out her phone and unlocked it, staring nervously at the display. Andrew placed himself behind her back so he could watch the screen over her shoulder. Her finger hovered over the little envelope symbol, hesitating.

"Wow," she said, swallowing hard. "I didn't realize how much I wanted to get in until I got the e-mail. Shit, Andrew, what if my modern dancing wasn't good enough? I mean, I've only taken classes for a year. I *think* I nailed the ballet part, but the modern part... Oh God."

"I'm sure they thought you were wonderful," he said, wrapping his arms around her waist. "And if they didn't, you could always try again next year, or the year after that. Not getting in on your first attempt is not that big of a deal, all right? Whatever happens, I'm proud of you, and I know Lucy is too."

"You're right." She took a deep, strengthening breath, leaning back against his chest. "It's not the end of the world if I don't get in. As long as we're together, everything will be okay."

He kissed the top of her head. "Exactly."

When she pressed the button, they were both ready for whatever the Juilliard School Dance Division had to say. They were together, and everything would be okay.

Acknowledgments

So this is where things get a little sappy. I apologize in advance. With that said, I want to express my love and endless gratitude to:

Suz, my best friend and beta, who listened to me as I went on and on about this story and then convinced me to actually write it.

My dad, for encouraging me to reach for the sky, and my mom, for catching me every time I fell.

My grandma, who told me she wanted to see my name on the cover of a book one day. (Look, Mormor, that's my name!)

My beta readers and critique partners, who weren't afraid to tell me the things I didn't want to hear.

And last but not least, the editors at Crimson Romance, who welcomed me into their family and made this story shine.

A Sneak Peek from Crimson Romance

Lynked

Bethany-Kris

"Hey, Jordan."

Immediately, Nic's older brother asked, "What's wrong?"

Sighing quietly, she shot a fleeting glance out at the Grand Falls gorge from her apartment's bay window. She should have known better than to call him back before she calmed herself down. There was no hiding anything from Jordan. Or maybe it was just Nic who couldn't hide things from him. After all, because they were only a year apart in age they had grown up stuck to one another and even though he had moved an entire country away, they were still as close as ever.

"Nothing. I just—"

"Liar. You're sniffy again."

"Sniffy?"

A deep laugh filled the receiver. "Yeah, you get the sniffles when you cry and then you act all sniffy for hours after."

"I do not!"

"Whatever you say, sis."

"Did you want something?" Nic asked, trying to draw her brother away from her current emotional state.

"You called me, Veronica."

"You called me first."

"I can't call my little sister for a chat when I'm bored?" When Nic didn't respond, she heard her brother drum his fingers before he said, "Seriously, what's wrong?"

Nic didn't know what to say. Really, it was a lot of things. Between being fired from her job at the clothing store, the sudden emptiness of her bank account, and the crazy ex-boyfriend who just wouldn't get the fucking hint and disappear, she was ready to call it quits.

"Is Don giving you issues again?" Jordan asked, voice turning dark.

"No," she replied. At his disbelieving noise, Nic flinched. "Okay, so he's been around."

"Just around?"

"He showed up at Shreds yesterday going on like he usually does…"

Trailing off, Nic figured she didn't need to say any more. Jordan would get the hint. Her ex-boyfriend was a sore topic, one she didn't like to discuss. Don had a possessive streak, and while it wasn't anything Nic couldn't handle on her own, sometimes he got to be a little bit much. It certainly didn't help that her hometown was so small everyone knew everyone else's business. Or at least they thought they did.

Don happened to be the son of the county mayor, so his behavior was constantly being overlooked and excused. Nic, on the other hand, was the daughter of a less than favorable woman in everyone else's eyes. A woman who had been known to sleep around, dabble in drugs, and neglect the children she'd bore.

People tended to lump Nic and Jordan in the same category as their mother without really giving them a chance. It was just assumed that Nic was a whore and that Jordan would be no better than the father who had up and left when they were only babies. It was a battle they constantly fought against, and a cycle Nic was determined to break. She wouldn't ever be her mother. In fact, she tried so damned hard to be everything her mother wasn't. She never touched drugs, didn't step out of line as a teenager, and rarely took chances that would make her look irresponsible. That wasn't who she wanted to be.

But closed-minded people were still closed-minded.

"And?" Jordan finally asked. Nic didn't miss the tension in his tone.

"My boss wasn't there yesterday."

"Good."

"Today he was," Nic said softly. "And then Don decided to make another appearance."

"Shit."

Yeah, that about summed it right up. Nic had thought, when she'd explained to Don two months earlier that she was done with him and his ridiculousness, that he had finally gotten the point. Apparently, he hadn't.

"I should have kicked his ass when I visited last summer," Jordan muttered angrily. "I knew he was a spoiled little cock—"

"Jordan!"

"Sorry," he mumbled, but he didn't sound a bit apologetic. "Lemme guess, he got you fired?"

Nic exhaled shakily, feeling her shoulders get heavier from the weight. "Yep."

"Screw it. Come to Edmonton. Tomorrow. Why not?"

"What? That's crazy. No way, Jordan."

He grew silent as her panic started to rise. Just the thought of doing something like that screamed crazy and irresponsible. People would talk about her. They'd say things she wouldn't be there to defend or refute. Gossip would spread like wildfire. Don would likely be patted on the back and told he'd dodged a bullet because she'd always been doomed to end up just like her mother.

Oh God, Nic couldn't even breathe when she considered it.

Jordan seemed to pick up on her panic thousands of miles away.

"Nic, take a breath and think about it. The job market in New Brunswick is crap. You were already accepted to the university here in the fall."

"Yeah, but I don't have the money for tuition. That was the point of this job. At least if I didn't save enough for this semester, I'd have enough for the start of the next one."

Not to mention, school actually gave her a responsible, adult reason to get the hell out of her hometown and away from the nonsense and drama.

Again, her brother grew quiet. "What if I could get it?"

"The money?"

"Yes. I could get it like nothing. You know I'm doing well with this company. I don't want to explain it all over the phone, but if I needed a big sum at once, it wouldn't be difficult for me to get my hands on it."

Nic bit her lip, actually considering his offer. It would be a huge change to simply drop everything and move all the way across the country, but she had already been planning to do that anyway. Her roommate wouldn't mind and Nic didn't have a whole hell of a lot of things that she would leave behind. She missed her brother like nothing else, despite him making a serious effort to come and visit at least once a year.

"Veronica?"

"I'm still here. But, honestly, I don't know if I should. You have like what, two roommates? They won't like your little sister bunking with them, too. Not to mention, I won't have a job right away. I still need to do the online courses before my acceptance to the university is approved. That just seems like a mess to me. You know I'm not one to take risks like that, Jordan."

"Just say screw it. We'll figure out the rest when you get here. Take a chance. Do something different, Nic. If you don't, nothing's ever going to change."

Do something different.

"Okay. Buy me a one-way ticket."

...

Nic blinked awake with bleary eyes when her brother shook her shoulder, grinning playfully. The loud laughter ringing outside of the bedroom had her wincing. She was lucky she'd fallen asleep at all. Jordan's friends had absolutely no concept of personal space, privacy, or how to use inside voices.

"Rise and shine, sunshine."

"Go away."

"Nope. Get up, Veronica. You didn't want to stay here alone tonight, right?"

Hell no, she thought.

Rubbing the sleep away, Nic finally sat up in her brother's bed. She had only just arrived in Edmonton that morning, three days after giving her brother permission to buy her a plane ticket. More than once she had second thoughts over the choice, but this was her last ditch effort to try something different and start fresh.

Jordan glanced at the watch on his wrist. "I've got a couple of hours before I need to leave for the venue, so if you're going with me, you need to get yourself done up."

Nic scowled. "Excuse me?"

"Yeah, it's kind of high class, despite the bloodshed."

Great, Nic thought. *A fight club with money and rich people. Awesome.*

"And I need to call Dev, my boss," Jordan added. "If you want, the guys will—"

"No thanks," Nic interrupted.

She didn't want to spend any more time than was necessary with Jordan's roommates while he wasn't around. While they seemed like nice guys, and she was sure they were when they weren't slamming back beers, she'd had more than enough of their rowdy, hands-on approach for one day. God help one of those men if they happened to put their hands on her when Jordan was close enough to see them do it.

"So, hey…I wanted to talk to you for a minute." Jordan seemed to turn nervous under his sister's gaze before Nic waved at him to get on with it. "You know how I was sending money home for you every once in a while and whenever you asked, I wouldn't really talk about it?"

Nic shrugged. "Sure. You didn't need to do that, though."

"I know, but that's not really the point." With a tense sigh, Jordan stood straight up and shoved his hands in the pockets of his dark wash jeans. "Chaine Lynk is kind of infamous around Alberta, okay?"

"Chaine Lynk, that's the name of the company you fight under, right?"

Jordan nodded. "Yeah, but again, not the point. It's not like every other fighting company, Veronica. The people on the guest list aren't regular everyday men and women you could meet wherever. I just…shit, this should be so much easier than it is."

Nic was confused. She didn't understand why her brother seemed unable to explain whatever it was he needed to get out. Surely, it couldn't be that bad—after all, whenever he talked about mixed martial arts, the cage, or fighting professionally, he always seemed to love it.

"Just spit it out, Jordan."

He licked his lips and stared down at the bed avoiding her gaze. "It's a private company. The guests who are allowed inside to view the fights have a lot of money. The men who own Chaine Lynk have a lot of money, too. Sometimes they get bored, so that money gets tossed around between them and the patrons to make it more interesting. Do you understand what I'm saying?"

A lump had formed in Nic's throat. If her brother was involved in something illegal, she wasn't all too sure she wanted to know. "Are you saying they gamble?"

"And if I was?"

Nic tossed her hands in the air, frustrated. "Don't play word games with me. Is that what you're telling me?"

"I'm telling you that when you go in there tonight, you might see stuff like that. If you do, you should turn cheek. It doesn't affect you. You have no hand in it. Ignore it. Say nothing when we leave. That's all."

"Jordan…" He only shrugged again, refusing to acknowledge the warning in her tone. "I know your dreams are wrapped up in fighting professionally, but if it's going to get you locked up, is that really the road you want to travel to achieve them?"

Then she had another thought and had to ask, "Is that where the money for my tuition is coming from?"

If it was, Nic didn't want to touch it at all.

Instead of answering her question, Jordan cleared his throat and reached over to tousle her short hair. The action was teasing and familiar, as he'd done it a million-and-one times to her before. It didn't matter how close they were in age, Jordan never let her forget he was the older one. Sometimes that came in the form of words, and other times it was actions that showed Nic he would always look out for her no matter what.

"Don't worry about it, huh? Just do what I asked and in the morning, you'll be one step closer to getting into the university."

Something akin to worry settled in the pit of Nic's stomach. "Anything else I should know?"

"Well, maybe…"

"What?"

"Stay away from the fighters, okay?" Jordan made a face, feeling wholly uncomfortable. "I know you're twenty-two, and I'm not a fucking idiot, Veronica, but please stay away from the fighters. You're right. This is my career here. It wouldn't look good for my sister to be chumming it with someone involved with Chaine Lynk—it might cause issues."

"I wouldn't—"

Jordan's deep laughter stopped her words up short. "I know you wouldn't, sis. It's not you I'm worried about. God knows you wouldn't do anything that made you look bad. It's *them.* Some of those guys couldn't turn away from a pretty face if their life depended on it. Be careful, that's all."

Nic could do that. "Sure. Just say no, right?"

"Right."

• • •

A chat call rang through on Devon's laptop. His cell phone hadn't stopped ringing all night, and now this?

Why was it that everybody seemed to think he had no life on fight nights? That, suddenly, every second of his time needed to be spent fulfilling those around him with mindless chatter and boring information?

He tapped the key to allow the call without seeing who it was first. "What?" His teeth clenched. "Is it extremely important or could it wait an hour?"

"Well, that depends on what or who you consider important, Dev."

His shoulders relaxed at the sound of his half-brother's voice. "It's been a long day."

"No doubt there." There was a sound of shuffling papers on the other end before Chaine laughed. "Did you see the *Sun* today?"

"You know I don't pay attention to that rag," Devon muttered while he sat down. "There's nothing in it that interests me unless it's a new name to add to the client list for the company."

"Daddy-Dearest and his new wife are sporting three pictures this week."

Devon pulled up the *Sun*'s website, and in an instant the social pages were lining his screen. He rolled his eyes, and disgust fell from his mouth in a half-growl.

"At least she's somewhat pretty," Chaine said.

"She is young enough to be your sister."

"Yours also, bro."

He replied with yet another half-growl. The Albertan oil baron and multibillionaire Jeffery Wolfe had created enough children around Canada that his dick should have been considered a sperm-donating machine. Devon's mother, Mia, was just one of the unfortunate women who'd fallen directly into the trap that was Jeffery.

Chaine, on the other hand, was the only recognized child by their father. Having been married to Chaine's mother when he was conceived and staying with her throughout the vast majority of the pregnancy, it was the longest relationship Jeffery was known to have. The man had been proud of his pretty wife who came from just as good of stock as he in oil country, so he hadn't held back from fawning over the pregnancy like a father would. *Father* being a term Devon used very loosely when it came to Wolfe, as dropping off a weekly deposit of sperm versus actually being a parent when the child was living and breathing were two completely separate things.

"She looks really familiar," Devon noted. He studied the picture for a bit longer before closing the web browser. "But so do the fifty other women who hang off his arms."

"Well…" The brief period of silence caused Devon to freeze. "I've seen her before."

"Please tell me she isn't an old girlfriend of yours because that would be creepy, man," Devon said. Chaine snorted under his breath. "A whole new level of creepy, honestly."

"Not an old girlfriend, Dev. She's, uh… Well, you know that really well-to-do doctor that was kicked out of Chaine Lynk a few months back?"

Devon immediately knew whom his brother was talking about. Very few patrons had been permanently removed from Chaine

Lynk's client list. The doctor in question had liked to drink far too much and then bait their fighters when they were out of the cage. It was unacceptable behavior regardless of the money he was shoving at them.

"Sure. Why?"

"That's his ex-wife."

Devon cussed and slammed the laptop closed. "So she's been to Chaine Lynk?"

"Once, I think, but maybe more," Chaine said. "She certainly knows what's going on behind the scenes, you know? Maybe that's why we've been having these issues with the cops and stuff."

Chaine Lynk was a very lucrative and popular business that had grown to unbelievable heights in the short three-year time span since the brothers founded it and opened the doors to the richest and the best. With his background in mixed martial arts fighting—gaining his first light-heavyweight title at twenty-one—Devon hadn't been ready to say goodbye to the sport when a snowboarding accident had pushed him out of the league.

He'd worked almost every second of his life to gain what he had lost in a simple seven-minute run down a snowy mountain. Devon had made that run more times than he could count and never once had he crashed to that devastating extent before. The impact with the tree shattered his kneecap, nearly splitting his leg in half from the force of the hit. The heavy nerve and muscle damage left the fighter stumbling through the next few months, going in for surgery after surgery to repair the damage.

At only twenty-three and a half, Devon wouldn't fight again, at least not professionally.

There was always opportunity in failure, though. Soon after the accident, Devon's half-brother, who was the definition of hand-me-down riches, had waltzed into Devon's world like he was always meant to be there.

With Chaine's family money and Devon's insurance payout, the brothers founded Chaine Lynk—an exclusive and member's only event where the depth of your pockets determined if you were good enough to pass the threshold. The best mixed-martial art fighters came from all across Canada to be a part of the new up-and-coming fighting company. Devon's experience and titles made the fighters flock. Chaine's connections, money, and last name drew the clients in.

The stats, be them good or bad, of a fighter after each match were added to the pile in the database for Chaine Lynk, which caused a fighter's popularity to grow or plummet within the group of people who were there to watch them battle it out. Unlike most mixed-martial arts companies, Chaine Lynk didn't use rounds to break up the time in a fight; rather the ref who watched and judged the men allowed a single uninterrupted fifteen-minute match—unless injury needed him to step in.

The changes Devon and Chaine made were what made their MMA fighting company so different from the rest. There were no titles to be given or taken away. It was solely based on a fighter's ability against the other opponent, and no one was removed out of the system because of their losses in the cage—though a loss would influence their influx of cash.

The illegal gambling on the fighters had begun as a small thing between Devon and Chaine. Fifty dollars here or there on a particular fighter they liked was nothing to the grand scheme of things. But like everything else with Chaine Lynk, the betting had grown quicker than it should have. Rich people with idle hands and pockets full of cash were a bad combination when they were trying to keep the business on the straight and narrow. The betting between patrons and hosts made the events more profitable, and fighters started gaining cuts from the winnings, adding to their pockets as well. Devon had opened an offshore bank account to hide the illegal cash coming through his business.

The gambling wasn't completely out of control but Devon worried it could be getting there, seeing as how the attention of the police had started looking Chaine Lynk's way in the last year. One raid, six months earlier, had given the police little evidence but enough to know there was something going on.

"Maybe Jeff's money is talking," Devon wondered aloud. "It would certainly explain why they keep hounding the doors like dogs."

Chaine agreed. "Dad has a screwed up way of showing his love."

"That's putting it mildly." Devon gripped at his hair in frustration. "I'm just the bastard from the street corner whore, remember? So, I expect his nonsense to a point. I mean, you're the one he likes, Chaine, and he still can't stop pulling this crap."

"Define *like*." Chaine laughed deeply. "This is getting old."

"That it is."

Behind him, Devon could hear his flat screen lighting up with more information from the automated polls for the fights. "Did Stacey get his draw tonight?"

"Jordan Stacey?" Chaine asked.

"That's the only Stacey we've got, isn't it?"

Turning in his chair, he reached up to the screen behind him and moved the touch-activated cursor upward to find his favorite fighter's name hanging against another popular Chaine Lynk fighter in the heavyweight division. Jordan Stacey's stats were lighting up the screen.

"Yeah, he did. He's against Ron at eight. Pretty much certifies his win, anyway. I'm calling his name for my light-heavyweight choice of the evening."

"You always pick Jordan." The comment sounded suspiciously whiney.

"That's because the kid always wins," Devon shot back. With a couple taps of his fingers, Devon had placed his choice into the system along with the amount of money he was willing to throw in the pile. "It's not my fault you agreed to give me first choice on fighters, Chaine."

"Are you willing to let me take that choice back?"

Devon smirked. "Hell no; then whose money would I take? I like yours the best, Trust Fund."

The topic of Chaine's trust fund was a sore spot and Devon knew it. But he had to give his brother props: since they'd opened the doors to Chaine Lynk, he hadn't touched that part of the bank. Devon knew it had something to do with Chaine's desire to break away from his father and the Wolfe name. There wasn't enough money in the world to push that kid into the oil country life Jeffery wanted to see Chaine living in.

Devon didn't blame him a bit.

"Shut up," Chaine said. "I'm taking on the lightweights tonight, anyway."

Devon noticed that. The screen in front of him started filling with the information other members had recorded in. Their top picks and bet amounts were adding to an already massively growing number.

"I think we might break a record," Devon said, grinning.

There was nothing more satisfying than taking cash off the hands of those who needed their pockets lightened a bit.

"We should probably go back to the old way, though."

Devon knew what his brother was hinting at. The electronic system allowed members who weren't even in Edmonton on fight nights to bet on the divisions or fighters of their choice and be paid out through offshore accounts. While nothing led back to them directly, there was still a chance their systems could be corrupted and then they'd have police stuffing illegal gambling charges down their throats.

"I know. But the guests won't like it and we're going to lose a lot because of it."

"They don't matter." Something in the tone of Chaine's voice stuck Devon as odd but he chose not to press on it. "It's not their company, you know? Besides, we have those contracts to think about, too. We can't have the major companies coming in to plaster their logos across our stuff and the fighters while we keep up the betting on the side. It's not worth that risk, Dev."

"True, but I haven't okay'd that yet, man, so quit bringing it up. I don't like the thought of my boys wearing what someone else wants them to and you know that. They're fighters, not prizes to be put on show while they wear someone else's garbage," Devon said, reiterating an argument the brothers had been having for quite a while. Devon's phone, which was lying on a chair across the room and had been going largely ignored all night, began ringing once more. "I got to go. People are demanding my attention again."

Hanging up on his brother, Devon fumbled to get to his phone before the call went to voicemail again. "Yeah?"

"Mr. Lynk?" Stress echoed in his secretary's voice. "I don't mean to bother you but a fighter would like to speak with you before you leave for the event tonight."

"Was that you calling every five minutes?" Devon asked his secretary.

"Um, yes, I think?"

"I thought their managers understood you weren't the messenger between us?" he asked.

"This request came directly from the fighter, sir," she replied.

They seriously needed to get their fighters better ways to contact their bosses if the guys were still refusing to use the manager to boss system they had in place. "Which fighter?"

"A Jordan Stacey?" Kelly answered.

"Thank you. And Kelly, the next time a fighter calls, be sure to give them their manager's number as a polite reminder for how they're supposed to contact me when I'm away from the offices, venue, and gyms."

"Will do."

Hanging up the phone, Devon was quick to seek out Jordan's contact number. The whole secretary deal was his brother's idea. All the day-to-day tasks of handling the fighters landed on his shoulders and because of his experience, it wasn't all too hard for him to keep up. There was something to be said for a hands-on boss, and that was what Devon preferred to be when it came to Chaine Lynk and the fighters they contracted. However, on fight nights in particular, he couldn't be their go-to guy like he was every other day. Devon had a different mask to wear, and for the most part, the fighters understood and respected that.

"Hello?" Jordan asked when the call picked up.

"Jordan. It's Devon, what's up?" The light laughter of a female followed louder male laughter on the other end of the phone. "Please tell me you're not drinking, Jordan. I just bet on your ass."

"No way, Dev, I'd never do that. The guys were just joking around with my little sister so it's a little loud." Devon said nothing as Jordan continued speaking. "I need a second fight for the night. Can you put it in?"

"We don't do two in a night; you know that. There's a big risk of injury and I don't want you in that position. You've got major scouts looking at you right now, Jordan."

The voices became muted as Devon heard a door shut. "Chaine did it for Sammy a month ago so I know you can." There was a short pause and then a quiet sigh. "Listen, under any other circumstances I wouldn't ask but I finally got Veronica out here from back east and I need the cash."

"That's your sister, right?"

"Yeah," Jordan replied. "She wasn't supposed to come out until the fall but, well it's a mess, okay? So I need a second fight tonight."

A war began battling in Devon's mind. He didn't care much that giving the twenty-three-year-old a second match would possibly cause issues between the fighters because they'd handle that on their own. It was more the dangers of putting Jordan's body through a double round of beatings when the first would certainly take a major toll on his level of endurance and strength.

"If you lose, Jordan..."

Jordan scoffed. "I won't."

"You're too damn arrogant for you own good, you know that?" While it sounded like an insult, Devon meant it as a sort of compliment. The kid had a reason to be a little arrogant, honestly. "Fine, but a medic has to clear you in the back. And don't ask for it again."

"Gotcha, Boss."

With his phone finally silent, Devon sat back in his large chair and stretched. His wrists popped as his neck cracked. The familiar pain in his left knee stung when he extended his leg but it was a sensation Devon had come to ignore out of habit. Despite the medical warnings to not push his old injury, at twenty-seven, Devon still went to the gym three times a week and took a seven-kilometer run every morning. It hurt more than he was willing to admit but there were limits in his life that Devon wasn't willing to put up simply because someone else said he couldn't do it.

At those thoughts, Devon's eyes traveled to the sidewall in his office that was filled with the different awards he'd received for his accomplishments in the fighting world. His time as a professional mixed-martial arts fighter had taught him a simple but harsh lesson: as quickly as you rose, you fell.

A small piece of mesh he'd cut out from the mat where he won his first professional match still hung in a shadow box on his office wall. It solidified everything he'd ever worked for. It was his pride, sweat, and tears on a roughly cut square, stained with a ruddy brown. Only, sometimes the fabric reminded him of what he'd lost, too.

Double edged swords. They were everywhere.

In the mood for more Crimson Romance?
Check out *Nic by J.M. Stewart* at CrimsonRomance.com.

Printed in the United States
By Bookmasters